To Eileen Jenkins, my big-hearted mother-in-law, whose home is a refuge and a place of healing, with all my love. Thanks, Eileen.

ACKNOWLEDGMENTS

Thanks for early feedback from Chris Hill, Paul Storer-Martin, and Bridget McKenna, who also gave me the title. A million thanks to my brother Colm, for combat-shooting lore in general, and for that unforgettable day (a decade ago!) at the gun range in Richmond, Virginia. And if we're going back into history, I guess reading Dr. Strange when I was six had some kind of impact. . . .

For this marvelous U.S. edition, undying (maybe un-dead?) gratitude to Juliet Ulman, editrix extraordinaire, plus Kathy Lord, Josh Pasternak, and all at Bantam.

And respect to the city of New York, without which Tristopolis would not exist.

Donal sketched a fingertip salute to the shadows beyond the stone steps. Stuffing his hands in his overcoat pockets, he looked up at the two hundred stories of police HQ rearing upward, dark and uncompromising. It was late and cold and the sky appeared deep purple, heavily opaque.

Somewhere near the top, Commissioner Vilnar's office waited. And reading between the lines of this morning's phone call, the commissioner had a new job lined up for him—something Donal was not going to enjoy.

"Son of a bitch," he muttered.

From the shadows came a low growl.

"No offense," Donal added.

Donal unbuttoned his coat and moved easily up the steps, two treads at a time, passing between the glowing pillars that lined the stairway. He stopped at the big bronze-and-steel doors.

"Lieutenant Donal Riordan." He spoke clearly. "Badge number two-three-omicron-nine."

A tingling swept down Donal's skin, then huge locks rotated and clunked, and the doors swung inward. Donal passed inside, into the vaultlike reception area.

To the right, the duty sergeant, Eduardo, was a shadowy figure above the imposing granite block of his desk; otherwise, the place was deserted. Donal's footsteps echoed back as he headed for the bank of cylindrical lifts at the rear, his coat swirling capelike in the mixed cool and hot breezes that swept through this place.

He stepped into an empty elevator shaft.

"Hey, Gertie. Floor One Eighty-seven, please."

For a moment, nothing. Then:

Anything for you, hon.

The words felt like a caress.

Donal's stomach tipped as he shot upward.

Ten seconds later, he stepped out into a half-lit corridor.

Later, darlin'.

"See ya."

In the reception offices, Commissioner Vilnar's secretary, known to every cop as Eyes, was sitting with her back to Donal. Slender silver cables hung around her switchboardlike console. Without turning, she waved her pale hand, which Donal took as a signal to go straight in.

"Thank you."

"You're welcome, Lieutenant."

Donal strode past a row of ordinary-looking filing cabinets. Each was marked secure, imprinted with a tiny fist-shaped sigil. He wondered what they contained. Probably the commissioner's expense sheets.

The black doors in front of Donal pulled apart, and he stepped through into Commissioner Vilnar's office. There was a lone visitor's chair made of black iron set before the imposing desk. Behind Donal, the doors closed with a faint screech.

On the other side of the desk, the big chair rotated, revealing the commissioner's bald head, the wide shoulders of his black suit.

"Sit down."

"Thanks."

"Have you ever been to the opera, Riordan?"

"Sir?"

"That"—the commissioner's flat features moved; a sketched-rehearsal for a smile—"is what I thought you'd say. Read this."

A desk drawer slid open, and Commissioner Vilnar pulled out a broadsheet newspaper. It looked like a luxury edition, warm yellow vellum bearing a curlicued violet script: a copy of the *Fortinium Times*. Its layout was similar to the *Tristopolitan Gazette,* though not the flimsy edition that Donal read: the plebeian version shredded apart within hours.

"Um…"

There was a gangland killing featured on the bottom of the first page. A blue-and-white photograph showed an innocent victim, a passing nurse who'd stepped between a slowing car and the real target, Bugs Lander.

"Try the Culture section," said the commissioner. "Under *Theater.*"

"You're kidding." Donal turned the heavy pages. "This? About the opera singer?"

Purple ink shimmered as his gaze moved across the description of Maria daLivnova's performance in *The White Masque.*

"I don't see—oh. She's coming to Tristopolis. The Théâtre du Loup Mort."

The venue was an ornate building off Hoardway that Donal had passed many times.

"That's right. And while the diva is here"—Commissioner Vilnar reached over and retrieved the paper—"absolutely nothing bad is going to happen to her. Am I right?"

Donal closed his eyes, opened them again.

"Are you suggesting protection duty, sir?"

"I don't have to *suggest* anything."

"Um…no, sir."

From another drawer, the commissioner removed

separate vellum sheets. Indigo typeface delineated a series of crime-report summaries, each headed with a location and date, the first crime scene being in the city of
Fortinium. Two other sheets were reprinted newspaper
articles.

"Six months ago," said Donal.

"Read the details."

The report described a famous actor falling dead onstage, accompanied by surprised applause from some of
the audience who failed to realize how premature the
death scene was.

"A fake ambulance crew," added Commissioner
Vilnar before Donal could finish the paragraph, "came
to take the body away. Five minutes before the real
medics arrived."

"Thanatos," muttered Donal.

Commissioner Vilnar frowned: he disapproved of bad
language. Donal continued to read scanning reports
from three other countries in Transifica, plus one from
Zurinam.

"The bodies. That's the common factor." Donal looked
up. "Someone's after the performers' bodies."

"That's right." Commissioner Vilnar pointed at the
third report, of family bodyguards at a heavily fortified
mausoleum, who shot first and asked no questions.
They had killed two of the intruders and driven off the
others. "That was Trelway Boskin the Third, and his
body is still in its sarcophagus."

One of the dead actors, Sir Alyn Conroly, had made it
as far as the city morgue. That was in Lorgonne, on the
dank south coast. There, forensic seers had found microscopic holes left by toxic slivers that had already dis-
solved.

But the morning after their examination, when a
seer's assistant pulled open the lead-lined drawer that
should have contained Conroly, the drawer was empty.

"And it *is* murder," said Donal. "Not just body-snatching."

"In a courtroom, in the other cases, that would be idle speculation."

"Yes. I see."

The reports covered twelve murders in total.

In Zurinam, where a popular foreign singer called Shalaria was visiting—just Shalaria, no last name—the same kind of thing had occurred. But after Shalaria's collapse, according to local custom, city officials had fed her corpse to the glistening albino snakes that lived in the city's largest cathedral.

In the blue-and-white photograph, the snakes were coiled impassively around the stone columns, while a congregation prayed. There were no signs of the digested remains.

The reprinted article, written by a Tristopolitan journalist, commended the city fathers for their speed in committing Shalaria to the snakes *without those bothersome delays incurred by forensic examinations*. Luckily, the authorities were trustworthy, the article continued, otherwise *one might even doubt that it was Shalaria's body at all*.

Donal pushed the papers aside.

"It could be coincidence."

"So. What else could it be?"

"A conspiracy across two continents. With resources and rigorous planning."

"And a burning desire," said Commissioner Vilnar, "to go for lucky thirteen?"

"It could be." Donal tapped the papers. "Even if not, this diva will need a protection detail. It's a question of how thorough the protection is."

What Donal meant was, how much money the department was prepared to spend. For a moment, a flash

of something that might have been humor passed
through the commissioner's eyes.

"She'll be safe in our city."

Donal understood that statement for what it was.

"When do I start, sir?"

"You just did."

In the antechamber, a folder was waiting for Donal on
the desktop. He opened it and drew out a letter.

"You're supposed to read it," Eyes said.

Donal checked the letterhead, which bore the embossed Tree Frog insignia of the City Borough Federation,
as well as the federal Salamander-and-Eagle.

Xoram Borough Council
99 Phosphorus Way
Xoram Precinct
Tristopolis TS 66A-298-omega-2

Tristopolis Police Headquarters
1 Avenue of the Basilisks
Tristopolis TS 777-000

Quatrember 42, 6607

Re: Meeting with Malfax Cortindo, Director, City
Energy Authority

Dear Commissioner Vilnar,

It has been absolutely my pleasure to arrange a
meeting between one of your officers and Director
Cortindo of the City Energy Authority. The latter
body is, of course, a credit to our city, and the
director evinced no hesitation in assuring me that

he will be overjoyed to provide any technical
assistance that is germane.

I have communicated with Director Cortindo that
Lieutenant Donal Riordan will be meeting with
him, as per your indicated request of 40th ult., on
the evening of Quintember 37 at nineteen o'clock,
at the Downtown Core Station. All facilities will
be placed at the lieutenant's disposal.

Kindest regards,
K. Finross
Alderman Kinley Finross

P.S. All best to your honored wife. Sally and I
hope to return the favor at the Styxian Ball.

Donal checked his watch. The appointment was for
tonight in less than an hour.

"Sweet bleeding Death. How am I supposed to get
there on time?"

Eyes shrugged without turning away from her console.

"Sorry. I didn't make the arrangements."

"No, of course not." Donal replaced the letter in the
folder. "You want me to leave this here?"

"Yes, please."

"Then I'll get going."

Gertie quickly took Donal down to the twenty-seventh
floor without a word: Donal's mood was obvious. He
swept through the squad room, ignoring Levison, who
was waving a piece of paper. There was no time.

Inside his office, Donal slammed the door shut with
his heel.

"Death damn it."

Putting his phone's handset to his ear, he spun the first four combination wheels to dial an internal number, then waited.

"Garage."

"Hey, Sam. It's Donal. You got any squad cars down there ready to go?"

"Sorry, Lieutenant. O'Doyle and Zachinov took the last one. The others are still hooked up to the—"

"Shit."

Donal hung up. How—

A dark cable hung outside his office window, and he remembered that the cleaners were working on the exterior this week.

I must be insane.

But he was in a real hurry now, so he reached inside his desk drawer, hooked out a pair of black liquid-metal gloves, and pulled them on. Flipping up the window locks, he took hold and heaved the pane open.

It was a long drop down.

Ah, shit.

He flexed the black metal gloves, thought about it for a moment, then climbed up onto the windowsill and threw himself out.

The gloves took hold of the rope by themselves, and a smell like burning oil rose up. The air was cold as Donal's feet touched the wall every fifty feet or so—an insane rappel—while behind a window, a woman jumped back, her mouth wide in an unheard scream.

Gripping harder now, the gloves slowed Donal's descent—*for Thanatos's sake*—leaving it to the last moment, but his feet touched lightly, and he was down.

A purple taxi slowed, the driver catching sight of Donal, but then began to speed up again.

"Hey!" shouted Donal.

Just then a dark shape shot into the road from beyond the HQ steps. Amber eyes blazed and the taxi screeched to a halt, rocking on its suspension. Donal stared for a moment, then pocketed his gloves and strode to the taxi, his heart still beating fast from the effort and adrenaline.

He pulled open the passenger door and stopped.

"Thanks, FenSeven!"

The huge deathwolf grinned, sitting on its haunches in front of the vehicle. Then it nodded and trotted back to its place in the shadows as Donal climbed inside the taxi and pulled the door shut.

"Police emergency," he said.

"Uh . . . yeah?"

"Thousand Seventh Street. Let's not hang around."

The driver turned, an unlit black cigar hanging from his lips.

"Police?"

"What, you want to see my handcuffs? Or my gun?"

"No, chief." The driver gunned the engine and pulled away from the curb. "No need."

"Good." Donal's voice was soft. "That's a good thing."

From the corner of Avenue of the Basilisks and Hellvue Boulevard, a white-skinned woman in a pale-gray skirt suit watched the taxi depart, admiring the efficiency of the man's exit.

"That's a quality that could be useful."

At her words, a street cleaner paused on the other side of the street, curious. Just then, there was a shimmering movement in the air.

Grabbing a broom from his cart, the cleaner got to work in the gutter, no longer looking up or sideways. Not even from the edge of his vision. Some things are not meant to be stared at directly.

You think he's honest? the air whispered.

The woman in gray pulled a compact out of her handbag and flipped it open. The mirror was one-third silver, the remaining two-thirds black but still reflective: plenty of time remaining.

She snapped the compact shut, replaced it beside her platinum-coated pistol, and slung the bag back over her shoulder.

Well?

"I don't know," she said. "Do you think we could use him if he isn't?"

No.

"Neither do I." The woman looked down the long perspective of the dark avenue, watching as the taxi hooked into a fast left turn and was gone. "If he doesn't survive, it doesn't matter either way."

I thought I was the negative one.

The woman turned and strode toward the nearest black hydrant. Her dark, finned car—a Vixen—was waiting at the curb. As she walked, a half-glimpsed ripple passed through the air alongside her, keeping pace.

Or maybe you're afraid to let yourself admire him. Is that it?

The woman stopped, fingers touching the car's door handle. She looked up at the air.

"Am I that transparent?"

There was another ripple, altering the outline of the art gallery beyond.

Is that meant to be funny?

"Well, I laughed." The woman got inside the car and slammed the door.

After a moment, she opened the passenger door from the inside, waited for approximately thirty seconds, then reached across and pulled it shut.

"Let's go keep watch. If Lieutenant Riordan doesn't reappear, we'll have someone to charge with his murder. There's always a bright side, Xalia. Didn't you know?"

I prefer the darkness, Laura.

"You would."

And you don't?

The car slid away from the curb.

Two great pillars of stone reached up. If a visitor craned his head back, he would see, against a background of purple sky, that each pillar was surmounted by a skull wearing an Ouroboros headband, a flattened Möbius serpent twisting around and swallowing its own tail.

Lowering his gaze just a little, he would register the immense size and weight of the solid black iron gates and the great walls formed of granite stretching off to either side, encircling the Downtown Core Complex.

The taxi stopped, small in the foreshortened black drive that stopped at the gates. Behind the taxi, beyond the street, rose the attenuated blocks of old denuded buildings, empty niches showing where gargoyles once perched.

"Man," murmured the taxi driver. "This place . . ."

Donal said: "Sound your horn."

"Oh, I don't—"

"Sound it."

A long howl rose from under the taxi's purple hood. "There. Are you—"

There was a grinding sound, and the taxi shuddered as the gates began to move, sliding to either side. Donal remained impassive while the driver swallowed twice, three times, then rolled the taxi forward.

As they entered a gargantuan courtyard, the driver almost had his eyes shut, but Donal was scanning the environment, checking the gun slits on the walls, noting the internal stairs that led to watchtowers.

Then the taxi slowed and halted on a brass circular area at the courtyard's center. The brass disk's diameter was perhaps twice the length of a delivery truck.

"PLEASE CUT THE ENGINE." The voice reverberated around the courtyard.

"Oh, man . . ."

"Do it."

As soon as the driver switched off the engine, the taxi shuddered once more. The courtyard wall begin to slide sideways—

"Sweet Hades."

—except that it wasn't the wall that was moving, it was the taxi and the great brass disk it stood on, slowly rotating.

"Is the parking brake on properly?" said Donal.

"Yeah." But the driver yanked up hard on the lever. "Yeah, we're okay."

The wall moved faster now, and Donal could feel the sinking motion as the brass disk screwed itself downward. The driver clutched his face and tried not to look at the hollow threaded wall rising past the windows.

The disk screwed into the earth, carrying the taxi down.

It took seven minutes by Donal's watch to descend through the shaft. Then the walls were gone, replaced by a vast underground space, as the giant screw continued to lower the taxi down to the floor of the cavernous complex.

The place was vast, with great shadowed aisles separating the huge, square-edged stone piles. Even the darkness seemed to flicker, and that might not have been Donal's imagination.

For these were the necrofusion piles, the reactors that kept the city powered and its inhabitants alive.

When the brass disk finally slowed and stopped, the driver was muttering a prayer over and over: "St.-

Magnus-slayer-of-evil-behead-my-enemies-and-keep-me-safe. St.-Magnus-slayer-of . . ."

Donal pulled out his wallet and counted out thirty florins, in accordance with the needle on the dashboard's dial. "I'll need a receipt."

" . . . enemies-and—what? Say what?"

"Receipt. Please."

"Oh. Sure." The driver pulled a receipt book from under the dashboard and looked for a pen.

"Behind your ear," said Donal.

"Huh? Oh." The driver found the pen, pulled the cap. He tried to write while casting glances out the windshield and side windows, but his hands were shaking. "Look . . ."

"What?"

"Take the receipt, man. Write in your own amount, okay?"

Donal handed over the florin notes and took the blank receipt. "All right. If you wait for me on the street up above—out on the street, mind you—you'll get another fifty for the journey back."

The driver stared at Donal in the mirror, then nodded his head, fast. Outside, figures in coveralls were walking their way.

"You won't be there," said Donal.

"Man, I—"

"Better not lie." But Donal had work to do. He opened the door and stepped out onto the brass. "Don't break any speed limits."

He slammed the purple door shut and walked off the brass disk onto solid stone. Behind him the brass cylinder began to screw its way upward once more.

But it was the three men in gray coveralls who dominated Donal's attention. He noted the skull-and-Ouroboros symbol on their chests, the calm look in their eyes—and the protective platinum earplugs, the liquid-amber vests inside their coveralls.

"I'm here to see Malfax Cortindo."

The brass cylinder had reached the cavern ceiling and was now a rotating column, bearing the taxi upward through solid ground.

"Of course, sir. Director Cortindo's office is this way."

"How do you know he'll see me?"

"You're on his schedule," said the largest of the three men. "Lieutenant Riordan."

Donal had presented no ID.

"That's nice," he said.

The large man gestured. "Sir?"

"Lead on."

In fact, the men walked beside and behind Donal, escorting him along a vast black-floored alley that separated two rows of necrofusion piles. Even with the lead-and-carbon cladding, Donal felt a twisting in the air, and his chest labored as he walked.

"You ever had a leak in here?" Donal's voice sounded softer than he had intended.

But none of his escort answered; they walked on in silence. There was only the hum of the reactors (overlaid with gut-liquefying subsonics), plus an ozone tang that hooked at Donal's nostrils, and something else—a feeling that was dry and damp, like poisoned silk drawn softly across his skin.

This was where the dead paid back for the comforts of their life.

And kept repaying.

"Up the staircase, sir. The director's assistant will be waiting at the top."

Repaying forever.

"Thank you."

It was an ordinary iron spiral, and Donal began to climb.

2

At the top of the spiral staircase was a landing, also of black iron. Set in the stone wall was a circular door of polished steel, on which the skull-and-Ouroboros was inlaid in shining brass.

The door swung inward with a faint sucking sound.

"Good evening, Lieutenant." The gray-haired secretary drew her shoulders forward, hollowing her chest, as though afraid to take up too much space. "Director Cortindo will see you right away."

"That's good of him." Donal scanned the outer office. There was a low ceiling and black-flame candles in niches on the walls, though the true illumination was indirect, glowing from channels at the floor's edge.

He pulled off his overcoat and hung it on the black iron coat stand.

"Can I bring you a cup of tea, Lieutenant? Zurinam Black, or we have Axil Red."

"Not for me."

Donal wanted to tell the woman to straighten up and breathe deeply. He wondered if she had always stooped like this or whether the dark, oppressive weight of this place had worn her down over the years.

He smiled, but the woman looked uncertain as she flicked three glass toggles and waited. The big steel door to the inner office swung open.

The man who rose from behind the blue glass desk was perhaps sixty years old, with a gray goatee.

"Lieutenant Riordan. How wonderful to meet you."

This had to be Malfax Cortindo. He wore a silver cravat instead of a tie and a suit cut from some soft, dark fabric. A walking stick leaned against his chair: ebony, with a plain silver handle, instead of the skull-and-worm that Donal had half-expected.

"Thank you. Likewise."

They shook hands. Cortindo's hand was smooth—there was a hint of lilac scent—but strong. Donal decided that there was more to this man than an air of elegance.

"Won't you take a seat?"

"Thanks."

Donal sat down. On the other side of the desk, Malfax Cortindo sat in his more ornate chair, with its curved back and arms. Then Cortindo crossed his legs and steepled his fingers together.

"I'm really happy to help you. Your visit is something out of the ordinary routine, Lieutenant. Thank you for that, at least."

"And the department is grateful for your agreeing to help."

Donal and Cortindo looked at each other. In this insulated office, richly appointed with carvings and other ornaments, the reactors' sound was a background hum. A golden clock, formed of interlocking metal bones wielding a miniature scythe, sliced away the half seconds from a vertical thread of flowing amber liquid, cutting the thread into discrete drops.

They fell into a cup: *snick-snack, snick-snack.*

Malfax Cortindo broke the impasse. "I'm not entirely clear on how I'm supposed to help, mind you."

Donal let out a breath. "You want the truth? Neither am I."

"In that case"—with an elegant chuckle—"can I tempt you with some brandy, while we try to work this out? I have Sintro Mundo, shipped in from Alfrikstan."

"No, thank you." Not in this place. "Now, I have to be careful about giving away specifics about this case."

"Of course. I understand."

"In addition to which, it's more a case of preventing a crime than solving one." Donal never used the word *solve* when talking with fellow detectives; he had never thought of his job as a puzzle or a game. "But in other cities, some notable people have been murdered—"

Something shifted in Cortindo's eyes.

"Murdered? This is serious."

"Yes." Donal held back what he wanted to say: that otherwise he wouldn't be in this place. "And in several cases, the death has been in a public venue, before an audience. The link is that someone took the bodies, sometimes in audacious ways."

Malfax Cortindo uncrossed his legs and leaned on the dark-blue desk. "This sounds like some kind of widespread conspiracy."

"Oh, no," said Donal, lying. "I just mean, there's a particular type of crime that sometimes occurs. A type we've identified and would like to prevent."

"Interesting." Malfax Cortindo's gaze remained fixed on Donal. "Interesting . . . Do I take it you're going to be in charge of Maria daLivnova's security?"

"What?" Donal straightened up in his chair. "Who said anything about her?"

"Ah. You did, Lieutenant. You provided a strong hint, anyway, which you've just confirmed."

"This isn't a game."

"I've always thought a playful spirit allows one to work so much better. But we don't have to agree on that. You want me to explain my thought process?"

"Why not."

"The guesswork was this: when you mentioned deaths in public places, and audiences, and the stealing of bodies, I assumed you meant the...victims...were performers or artists of some kind. Once I'd gotten that far, the subsequent deduction was obvious."

"You mean about the diva."

"I mean Maria daLivnova, of course. Her forthcoming performances will be the highlight of the current season, as I'm sure you're aware."

"Naturally."

"Ah...not an opera fan, Lieutenant?"

"I sometimes sing in the shower."

Malfax Cortindo gestured at his office. "Take a look. You see that statuette? It's Zurinese, maybe four hundred years old. And that painting, the dark one, is by Turinette in the last month before his death. And that embroidery of a poem? If you look closely, you'll see the verses are from Zar Cuchon's epic *Gladius Mortis,* the part where he's in the forest and—"

"Fascinating."

Donal was less interested in statuettes and embroidery than he was in Malfax Cortindo himself. A blizzard of fine-sounding words could not disguise the intuitive leap that made Cortindo identify public performers as the victims of murder and body-stealing.

But the man was too self-possessed to crack easily—and he was supposed to be a resource, not a suspect, for Death's sake.

"The point is, Lieutenant, the people who created these works were very special. Even if they didn't know it themselves, their dreams were priceless, beyond any kind of material worth I know."

"If you say so."

"Perhaps we should take a look at the facility. It'll be a start in explaining what I mean."

This was the part that Donal had not been looking forward to.

"Good idea," he said.

"First, let me show you the overview." Still sitting, Malfax Cortindo made a gesture over the blue glass desk. Something rippled inside the glass. "Here we are."

There was a soft groan, and then the wall to Donal's right began to move. It slid slowly, a vast yard-thick slab of granite, into a recess, revealing the caverns beyond. This room was high up, close to the ceiling. Down below, seven rows of reactor piles were visible; others were out of sight, hidden by supporting columns and walls: this was a whole system of caverns, not a single space.

"See below the ground"—Malfax Cortindo pointed—"where the air appears to shift and waver?"

"Um . . . got it."

"Those are the power-conduction channels. The necroflux itself must remain confined within the reactor piles, or there would be a heterodyning buildup that would become catastrophic."

"You mean an explosion?"

"Exactly." Malfax Cortindo took hold of his elegant cane and stood. "Shall we go down and take a look?"

Down at the floor level, the air seemed thicker, and a buzz floated inside Donal's head. Each reactor was taller and more solid than it had appeared from Malfax Cortindo's office. Workers in gray coveralls moved constantly among the piles, and Donal could see the stress lines clamped on their faces: the price of nonstop vigilance.

They walked, Donal and Malfax Cortindo, for ten minutes along one wide aisle, with minimal conversation. The scale of it was greater than Donal had thought it would or could be. Finally, they came to a reactor whose casing was open.

"Don't worry," said Malfax Cortindo. "It's been scrubbed and decontaminated, ready for recommissioning."

Seven men in heavy protective suits and helmets were working on the casing.

"Could I poke my head inside the cavity?" said Donal. "Just to take a look."

Malfax Cortindo shook his head. "I wouldn't do that if I were you, Lieutenant."

"Didn't you say it's been scrubbed?"

"Cleanliness"—with a quarter-second smile—"is relative, sir. Everything here has a memory, which is part of the problem."

One of the workers stopped and stiffened. Then one of his colleagues snapped open a lead-lined case. "Okay, Karl. I'm ready."

Donal started to step forward, but Malfax Cortindo touched his sleeve. "We need to keep our distance, I believe."

"All right."

The bent-over worker, Karl, was wearing heavy stub-fingered gauntlets as part of his protective gear. It must have made fine work harder, but after a few seconds he straightened up and backed out of the hollow reactor casing, bearing something in one palm. It was a sliver of gray, a bone splinter, no more.

But immediately Donal felt sickness clutch his stomach, and the floor seemed to sway.

"Come along." Malfax Cortindo's grip was strong on his upper arm. "Let's leave these gentlemen to their work."

Screaming, the inchoate mix of faces and touch, softness and the feel of intestines bursting, tears and the stink of . . .

Then they were farther along the aisle, and the air seemed clear, though still heavy.

"What the Hades was that?"

"Sorry, Lieutenant. The splinter was bigger than I thought, or I'd have gotten us out of there right away."

"A bone splinter? Just a splinter?"

"Yes. A fragment that's spent considerable time as part of the reactor fuel. You understand what goes on inside these things?"

"We touched on it in school"—Donal wiped his face with the back of his hand—"which was a damned long time ago."

"Best days of your life. Isn't that what we tell our grandchildren?"

Donal doubted whether he and Cortindo had attended the same kinds of schools. There were places where you needed fists as well as brains in order to graduate.

Malfax Cortindo gestured up at the nearest reactor with his cane.

"It takes the bones of two thousand corpses," he said, "to form the critical mass for a single pile. What we're talking about is a resonant cavity, where standing waves of necroflux vibrate and strengthen, giving off a plethora of harmonics."

Two thousand people's remains, just in that one reactor.

"Okay." Donal blinked, forcing down his natural dread and sadness. "Two thousand. Large number."

"There's no shortage of raw components, Lieutenant."

After a moment, Donal said, "I don't suppose there is."

As they walked back to the staircase together, Malfax Cortindo spoke more of the underlying process. Donal tried to follow, not knowing whether any of this had a bearing on his job.

Cortindo explained how the microstructures of living

bones are altered by the perceptions and actions of the body they're encased in. But after death, when those same bones are part of a reactor pile, the necroflux moans and howls, diffracted by the bones' internal structure as it replays the memories of the dead.

"But not in a coherent whole," said Malfax Cortindo. "They're just mixed-up memory fragments from two thousand individuals. The conglomeration does not truly think or feel anything."

Donal stopped and looked back at the long straight rows of reactors.

"Not even pain?"

"No." Malfax Cortindo looked at him for a long moment, then tapped the stone floor with his cane. "At least, that's what I'll tell anyone who asks me officially. You understand me, Lieutenant?"

Biting his lip, Donal considered how the city would react if there were suddenly no power, no transport, and therefore no food in the stores.

"I understand."

On the wall beside the staircase was a row of brass-encircled, glass-covered dials. Malfax Cortindo stopped to check the leftmost dial, labeled $MN\ f^{-2}$. Beside it, a dial labeled GW showed the total power output, Donal assumed, in gigawatts.

"What's the first dial?" he asked.

"It's the mean flux rating across all piles," said Malfax Cortindo, "in meganecrons per square foot."

"Oh. Of course."

"Hmm. Shall we go back up"—with an elegant smile—"and have a cup of tea?"

In Malfax Cortindo's office once more, Donal accepted the offer of tea. The gray-haired secretary brought it on a tray, served in the best bone china.

Hoping to Hades that there were no real bones involved in the cup's manufacture, Donal took hold of the fragile handle and sipped. It was the best tea he had ever tasted.

"That's good." Carefully, he replaced the cup on the saucer. "That's very good."

"I'm glad you approve, Lieutenant. Now, once you've finished your tea, I've one more thing to show you. Don't worry, there's no more walking involved."

I wasn't worried, Donal was tempted to say. Instead, he took another sip of tea.

Wonderful.

"Let's do it now," he said. "Whatever it is."

"Since you insist...Bear with me a moment." Cortindo went to the bookcase that covered the rear wall. He stared at the books' spines for a moment, then tapped the shelves with his cane in a pattern of strikes that Donal could not follow.

Malfax Cortindo turned around, just as a circular section of the carpeted floor rotated and a yard-wide cylinder of metal rose up to chest height and stopped.

"Here we are." Cortindo laid his cane against the desk and inserted his fingertips into brass-colored depressions in the metal cylinder. After a moment, a steel door popped open on the cylinder's side. "All right, this is what you need to see."

It was a platinum case sealed with a golden catch. Perhaps the size of a gun case for an antique pistol, it looked heavy, and Donal wondered what it could contain.

There was a kind of reverence in the way Malfax Cortindo held the case, snapped back the catch, and pulled open the lid. Then he turned the case around so that Donal could see inside.

On scarlet velvet lay a desiccated bone.

"You can touch it," said Malfax Cortindo, "but—"

Too late.

Something had already drawn Donal's fingertips forward, as though he had relinquished control of his own neuromuscular system, and then he touched the bone and he was lost.

It was a form of drowning.

There was a silver sea, its gentle breakers spreading on a pink beach, while transparent birds flew overhead, singing arias of such magnificence that Donal began to weep. There were flowers inland, on fantastical green-glass structures that might have been plants or might have been art, and the minutest detail of their texture was fascinating. Here a drop of water glistening like a—

Something snatched at him.

No!

—crystalline world in its own right, and all around, the fabric of existence was threaded deep with color, strange nude figures moving in the distance, and landscape filled with—

Another tug, which he tried to fight.

—bands of heavy yellow and red and indigo, and the trees, which—

Were gone.

Everything was gone.

"*No!*" Donal hurled himself at Malfax Cortindo, who backed away in a deceptive circular motion, bypassing Donal's momentum. "Give it—"

"Sorry." Cortindo's footwork became a spiral, then a twisting reversal, avoiding Donal's charge once more.

"Give..."

Donal bent over from the waist, wheezing, more out of breath than after a ten-mile run. He squinted, salt sweat half-blinding him, and he wiped his face with his hand.

What the Death was going on?

"You were lost," said Malfax Cortindo, "in an artist's dreams."

"But you—"

Heavy gauntlets on Cortindo's hands must be shielding him from the bone's influence. Moving with apparent slowness—he was deceptive in his fluid motion—Cortindo replaced the bone inside the platinum case and pushed the lid shut. Immediately, the air inside the office seemed to clear.

Donal staggered back to the visitor's chair and sat.

"Ah, Hades." He picked up the cup and took a slug of tea. "Ugh!"

It was cold.

"Sorry, Lieutenant. But you had to see." Malfax Cortindo was inserting the case back inside the cylinder's opening. "If you didn't experience it for yourself, everything I told you would have been fragile words, immediately forgotten."

"I've got a good memory." Donal made a sour face as he put the teacup down. "How did that grow so—"

"Do you remember how much time passed in your dream?"

"Excuse me?" Donal twisted his wrist and checked his watch. "No. That's . . ."

The time was 22:63.

". . . impossible."

As soon as Malfax Cortindo pushed the metal door shut, the cylinder began to sink back down into the floor. He still wore the heavy protective gauntlets that Donal had not seen him put on.

"Is it, Lieutenant? Surely not."

Malfax Cortindo was right, because there was no reason for Donal to think that his watch had been ensorcelled or that some eldritch process had been used to suck the heat from his teacup. Instead, there was only one conclusion to be drawn.

Donal had been lost in the bone's dreams for nearly three hours.

Sitting down behind his desk once more, Malfax Cortindo stripped off the gauntlets.

"I could have snatched the bone back," said Donal. "What would have happened to me then?"

"My dear Lieutenant, I have trained since childhood in pa-kua, a soft art that enabled me to avoid your somewhat, uh, unsteady lunges."

"I'd just been ripped out of..." Donal let his voice trail off.

Out of paradise.

"I know, and that was in my favor. If there'd been more risk, I'd have had Security in here with me, you understand."

It sounded as if Cortindo expected Donal to thank him. Instead, Donal opened his suit jacket and let it fall open as he sat back, allowing the shoulder-holstered Magnus to show.

"You want to explain what just happened?"

"Ah. Perhaps I should apologize for the graphic demonstration—"

"Perhaps you should."

"—but it was in the common good, I assure you. That bone you just touched was part of a common intake, ordinary bones destined for the reactor piles."

Donal shook his head. He knew he shouldn't have come here.

"But our staff is dedicated," Malfax Cortindo continued, "and highly trained. All bone shipments pass through necroscopic examination procedures. If a gifted artist has died a pauper's death, this is the final chance of our discovering their existence."

The cylinder had sunk into the floor, become integral with it, and was hardly noticeable now.

"Who was that?" said Donal. "Whose bone did I touch?"

"It was an ulna"—Malfax Cortindo gave a precise smile—"from Jamix Holandson, whose works now command exceptional prices. Several of his pieces are on show in the Federal Center for Modern Art, in Fortinium."

"Oh. Him."

"Our procedures are rigorous and our staff is highly trained," Cortindo repeated.

"Too bad this Sorenson—"

"Holandson."

"—Holandson didn't get famous before he died."

"As I said"—Malfax Cortindo rubbed his gray goatee with one finger—"it is the artist's *final* chance."

"More like the postultimate chance," said Donal, "if there is such a word."

"I don't believe there is, my good fellow."

Donal looked at him. There was more to be discovered here, but how much of it related to his job, Donal could not tell. He had a strong desire to get the Hades out of here, but he forced himself to slow down.

"What has this got to do with murders?" he asked.

"Isn't that obvious?"

"I don't know. Explain it to me, Mr. Cortindo."

The plaques on the wall indicated that he was Director Cortindo or Doctor Cortindo—or in the case of Donnerheim University, *Herr Doktor Direktor* Cortindo.

"If you were a certain kind of collector—a rich and influential collector, you understand—would you not pay a considerable amount of money to take possession of such bones?"

Donal stared at him. "Perhaps."

"Well, *perhaps* if you were a certain kind of dedicated

collector, you might not be able to wait for the natural course of events, let's say, before your favorite artist's bones became...available."

"Oh, shit."

"After all, there's no guarantee that you'll outlive the object of your desire, is there, Lieutenant? Does any of us know when he's going to die?"

Donal stood up.

"Thank you for the tea. And the...enlightenment."

"Why, Lieutenant." Malfax Cortindo also stood. "It's been my absolute pleasure."

They shook hands.

"I hope to see you down here again soon," added Malfax Cortindo. "Oh...I mean socially, of course. Not—"

"I understand."

Donal picked up his overcoat from the secretary's outer office. The black liquid-metal gloves were still in the coat's pockets. For a moment Donal considered putting them on, going back into Cortindo's office, and stuffing the dead artist's ulna down Cortindo's throat.

But Donal had a job to do, and beating the crap out of a civilian adviser was not the way to go about it.

"Thank you very much, Lieutenant. I hope you had a wonderful visit."

"The tea was great. Thank you, ma'am."

Donal left through the door to the spiral stairs and descended the black iron steps to the cavern floor. The same three men in gray coveralls were there to escort him back to the surface.

"Nice seeing you guys again."

"This way, Officer. You got no car?"

"I don't need one."

"The elevator for people, like, is this way."

The trio led Donal to a curved black door set in a stone pillar. The door rattled and slid open. Donal stepped in, finding himself on a scratched steel floor. Lanterns were set on short, stubby metal stands, forming a circle around him. Craning his head back, he could see only thickening shadows and total darkness overhead.

"Is this—"

But the door was already sliding shut.

"Oh, well."

The floor scraped a little as it rose, then moved faster, and in seconds it was accelerating hard, pressing his feet against the steel. The stone shaft wall went past in a blur; reaching out to touch it would be a bad idea.

Then the rising floor decelerated, and Donal's body weight felt normal as the floor clanged to a halt, jolting him. He was in a black hollow hemisphere.

"How do I—"

At that moment the metallic hemisphere split into flanges that folded themselves back, leaving him standing inside a small courtyard.

He stepped quickly off the disk, in case it was set to return below. Uniformed guards nodded to him—Donal recognized one as a former patrol officer who'd been kicked off the force for getting freebies in the Scarlet Quarter—and he gave them a light salute as he headed for a small exit door.

The door's height and width were for a single person, but when the door swung inward, Donal saw that it was foot-thick metal and could not imagine the weight of it. A small wisp of steam escaped from the powered hinges.

Donal gave a half wave to no one behind him, then stepped through the doorway and onto the sidewalk. Behind him, valves hissed and pistons swung the heavy door shut.

"Wonderful."

He was stuck in a dilapidated area, outside the fortress that served as the aboveground manifestation of the Downtown Core Complex. Few people ventured here except for work, traveling on the Energy Authority's own buses.

What Donal should have done was call a taxi or a squad car from the secretary's office, but he wanted to get out of the complex right away.

Several furlongs down the street, a dark finned automobile sat silently. Donal considered asking the driver for a lift, but as he turned his attention to it, the car started up. It pulled away from the curb.

"Damn it."

But the driver was a woman: Donal had glimpsed glossy pale-blond hair. There would have been no reason for her to offer a lift to a lone man walking these particular streets.

Beside him lay a derelict site, a scree formed of rubble from which skeletal ribs of rusted girders poked. Three pale lizards, scuttling across the ruins, froze when they realized Donal was staring at them.

He shook his head and looked up at the solid purple-black sky.

Then he pulled his coat around himself and began to walk. As he did so, a light quicksilver rain began to fall. Tiny mercury droplets spattered from the long coat.

I hate this place.

On the sidewalk, liquid-metal puddles were already forming, shining and glutinous. If it hadn't been for the regular injections Donal received as an active police officer, he would have been less blasé about walking down the street without a hat.

There was a scratching sound as the lizards scrabbled for cover.

Donal wondered where the diva, Maria daLivnova, was right now. Rehearsing in some swanky theater, or dining in a fantastically appointed hotel restaurant. Not walking alone down streets where lizards hid from the weather.

But as Donal walked, he remembered something more, against his will: the deep richness of the world seen through Jamix Holandson's eyes.

Through his lifeless bone.

3

Back in his own office, Donal beckoned Levison
to come and join him. Levison was tall and gangly,
bald save for patches of carrot-red hair over his protruding ears. As usual, his shirt's top button was open, his tie
loosened.

Picking up a folder from his desk, Levison entered
Donal's office, then pushed the door shut with his elbow. He adjusted the gun slanted forward on his left hip
as he sat. Levison's weapon had seen little action on the
street, despite the well-worn look of the leather holster.
Levison had never confused marksmanship with being a
good cop.

"You know," said Levison, "there are only twenty-five hours in the day. Perhaps you should have a word
with the commissioner and let him know."

"On account of how," said Donal, "me and him are
such great pals, right?"

"Yeah." Levison placed his folder flat on the desktop.
"This came down from above while you were out swanning around with the high and mighty. How was the
Energy Authority, anyway?"

"Filled with piles of bone, like you'd expect."

"Pleasant place." Levison shook his head. "Better
you than me, boss. Did you learn anything?"

"Only that certain sickos"—Donal remembered the

wonderful dreams: there was nothing sick in them—
"would have a great reason for offing the diva and stealing her bones."

"Wonderful."

"Or professionals working on behalf of rich sickos.
That scenario works."

"It sounds like a lot more effort, Donal, than guarding against one nutcase. This diva's landing in a week's
time at Tempelgard. It's all in there." Levison pointed at
the folder.

"Justice never sleeps."

"Naw, it just gets schizophrenic hallucinations caused
by dream deprivation and then blows out its brains with
a silver-loaded Magnus." The humor seemed to sink inside Levison's long face, leaving a serious mask. "You
heard about Peters, out at the Hundred and First?"

"Peters?"

"He did himself in last night."

"Shit, I was at his wedding." Donal stared out the
window at the rearing blackstone corporate building
across the street, seeing nothing. "His widow..."

"The guys are making a collection."

"Put me in for fifty florins, will you? I'll pay you tomorrow."

Levison nodded. "You're going back out?"

"Yeah." Donal pulled the folder to him and flipped it
open. "Need to check out the environment, the route
from the airport. Like that."

"She's staying at the Exemplar." Levison reached
over and turned back two pages. "There, see? Got her
own suite. No expense spared."

"Shit."

"Right. You want reasonable coverage, you'll need
guys in the room across the hall. You need full cover,
that'll be the rooms on either side, on the floor below—

that's three separate rooms, actually—and the one above. That's another suite."

"Thanatos."

"When I talked to the lovely Eyes on the phone" —Levison grimaced—"she passed on Commissioner Vilnar's favorite phrase."

" 'Tell them not to go crazy on the overtime'?"

"The very one."

"Accounts is going to go ballistic. I'd better go see the hotel first, see if I can charm them into giving us a better discount than usual."

"How about them paying us, considering we'd be saving them embarrassment?" said Levison. "Not to mention lost business."

"If you say so." Donal put his feet up on the desk. "Or maybe the public would come flocking in to stay at the place where the diva was murdered."

"Hades, Donal. Don't let anyone hear you say that."

"Yeah . . . I might give someone a bright idea. Or dark idea. Whatever."

Donal avoided Gertie's elevator and walked along the dark corridor to a colder shaft, where frost formed on the steel casing and the shaft's enslaved wraith carried out its duties in perpetual silence.

There was little time, but Donal hadn't practiced today, and if you let it slip once, then it would be easier to avoid practice the next time. Before you knew it, you'd end up a soft bureaucrat like Commissioner Vilnar, whose knowledge of street policing was based on ancient memories plus the reading of endless memos and precinct reports.

Inside the shadowed shaft, Donal plunged fast, feet-first. The icy slipstream whipped his coat upward, but he paid no attention. After thirty floors his descent

slowed. By the time he reached the minus-13th floor, his
downward motion was infinitesimal.

Donal stepped into a cold, half-lit chamber.

He pulled his Magnus from his shoulder holster,
slipped out the magazine to check it was full—chitin-
piercing load with silver-crossed bullets—then slapped it
back in and reholstered. Donal took in a deep chestful of
cold air and expelled a long calming breath.

In front of him was an ironbound door. Donal
pushed it open. An empty counter stood to one side.

"It's Riordan. You there, Brian?"

"Sure, Lieutenant." A bald man with bluish skin and
a pot belly levered himself up from behind the counter.
"What can I do you for today?"

"I need"—Donal glanced at his watch: he would
have to make this fast—"a box of fifty rounds, that's all.
The usual."

"Okay." Brian reached underneath the counter and
came up with a three-inch cardboard box filled with
shells. "You wanna sign?"

"Sure." Donal pulled the nearby clipboard toward
him. "Six targets, please."

A howl echoed from the corridor outside.

"What's going on?"

"Little combat-shooting competition." Brian slid out
flat drawers from the wall behind the counter. "The
boys from the Seventy-third are up against our guys.
You weren't thinking of making an illegal bet now, were
you, Lieutenant?"

"Wouldn't dream of it. If, hypothetically speaking,
someone *were* taking bets, what odds would they be offering on our boys winning?"

"Evens, is all. Woulda been three-to-one against, but
them Seventy-thirds had a lotta gang trouble last year.
Sharpened 'em up."

Donal shook his head.

"Some other time."

"Your loss, boss." Brian pulled out several sheets from the drawers. "Awright, we got yer basic roundel—one of those?—and some outlines. One ghoul-with-human-hostage. One human-with-ghoul-hostage. One—"

"I'll take two of those."

"Okay. And for the last . . ." Brian slid the two-foot-by-four-foot sheets of paper across the counter. "I heard someone's been sketching well-known figures on big pieces of paper, y'know? Like various aldermen, including Finross and O'Connell. Maybe even the comm—"

Donal reached across the counter and clapped a hand on Brian's shoulder. He smiled, keeping it friendly, as his grip tightened and his fingers dug in.

"Now, Brian, you know why we don't just shoot round targets anymore?"

"Um . . . no, boss. Listen—"

"It's because it makes it easier for us to shoot real people. Or real . . . whatever. They call it operant conditioning, and it helps keep cops alive. Because we don't freeze on the street when it goes down hard."

"Ugh, sure. But you're hurting—"

"So we don't ever make a joke of it, or use individual people on the pictures. Do we?" Donal released his grip. "Do we, Brian?"

"No, Lieutenant. I mean, *no,* for Hades's sake. Wouldn't dream of—"

"Good. Because when the inspection comes tomorrow, this place will be shipshape. And if I hear rumors of anything else . . . But I won't, will I?"

"No, sir."

"Good man." Donal gathered together the four sheets of paper. "I'll need two more targets, please."

In silence, Brian took two more standard targets from a drawer and laid them down.

"Thank you very much, Brian."

* * *

It took fifteen minutes to unload sixty rounds into the targets: the magazine clip plus the fifty rounds he'd gotten from Brian. That was a long time, but the ceiling cables used to carry the targets out to varying distances in the subterranean range were slow.

Silver sea, gentle breakers on a pink beach, while transparent birds sing overhead . . .

Donal was right-handed but with a dominant left eye, which meant he had to tilt his head down to his right shoulder when he aimed. It looked odd—when he was a rookie, fellow officers called him Cockeye Riordan—but it stabilized the head and made him a better marksman.

That, and the daily training.

On the last magazine, Donal sent the target right back, turned away, then squeezed his eyes shut before swiveling around to fire ten rounds in even succession.

When he opened his eyes, the target was in tatters.

"Good enough."

You didn't always get good lighting on the street. Sometimes the bastards came at you from darkness.

A series of loud percussive bangs echoed down the range. Donal had thought he was the only person here. Whatever the load the other guy was using, it was heavy-duty. Donal felt curious, but . . . He checked his watch. He still wanted to visit the Exemplar Hotel tonight and check out the floor where the diva would be staying.

Another sequence of bangs sounded.

"Just a peek," Donal told himself.

Walking slowly, not wanting to startle the officer with sudden movement at the edge of his vision, Donal passed seven empty lanes on the gun range until he could see the shooter.

The man was huge, nearly seven feet tall, with massive

shoulders stretching his dark-burgundy leather jacket. Round blue glasses perched on his long nose.

He fired a heavy silver gun single-handed. The weapon was designed for a two-handed grip: an abbreviated machine gun.

"Ha." The big man put the emptied weapon down and pulled out his earplugs. Donal did likewise.

"What kind of...Hades. Look at that." Donal peered down the range, then placed his hand on the green retrieve button beside him. "Can I?"

"Go ahead, Lieutenant."

So the man knew who Donal was. Well, that happened. A drawback of rank: they knew you, and you didn't know them. Donal pressed the button and held it in as the target holder whined its way back along the ceiling.

But there was little target left. By the time it reached Donal's position, he had verified that only a few flapping ribbons of paper remained.

"Not bad. What kind of beast is that?"

"Oh, her?" The big man ran a finger along the weapon, which lay flat on the shelf. "I call her Betsie. She's a Howler-Fifty."

"I thought it—she—might be. I've read about them. Not bad."

"You want to give her a try, Lieutenant?"

"Er...damn it, I'd love to. But not tonight. I've still got stuff to do."

"But you made time to come down to the range? Understood, sir."

The man was unshaven, and his face was tanned and ugly. Donal had already decided to like him.

"What's your name, Detective?"

"Viktor Harman, sir. I work out of the, uh, Seventy-seventh. They call me Big Viktor."

"I'm not surprised. You'll be around here again?"

"Oh, yes, sir. You can count on it."

"See you then."

"Lieutenant."

Out on the street, Donal had no trouble in flagging down a purple cab. Earlier, after leaving the Energy Authority complex, he'd walked over a mile before finding a phone booth that worked so he could call a taxi. It had come surprisingly quickly.

Now the driver pulled into the heavy flow of traffic and halted. Donal regretted not having chosen the subway. On the other side of the street, farther down, he could see two prospective customers—a couple of tourists from Kaltrin Province, judging by their blue coats—talking to a cab driver.

The driver was shaking his head: they weren't going far enough to make it worth his while.

Welcome to Tristopolis.

The driver of Donal's cab stared impassively ahead. He hadn't asked where Donal was going until Donal was inside the vehicle. That was one advantage of picking up a ride directly in front of police HQ.

Donal crossed his arms and leaned back, settling for a moment's calm. He thought about the big officer—Viktor . . . what was it? Harman—and the way he'd handled the .50-caliber weapon with ease.

"I work out of the, uh, Seventy-seventh."

That's what Big Viktor had said, but Donal wondered now at the precinct number. Had he meant to say "Seventy-*third*," implying he was with the team competing against the local cops? It would have furnished an excuse for an uptown-precinct officer to be here in the mid-Tristopolitan district.

Brian, on the desk, was competent enough on security. And Eagle Dawkins, the range safety officer, was always around, observing. An impostor could never make it into the practice range.

Donal came back into the moment. The taxi had moved less than a block before traffic congealed once more.

Digging into his wallet, Donal said, "I'll walk. But here's the fare." He handed over two florins.

"Aw, man, how am I—"

Donal leaned over, eyes hardening. "You hook a U at the end of the block and go back. There was a couple in blue coats standing there."

"Um, I saw them."

"Take them wherever they want to go, Mister"— Donal's eyes flickered toward the municipal license tag on the dash—"Boudreaux, driver number fourteen-oh-three. You got that, right?"

"Yes, sir. My pleasure."

"I thought so." Donal reached inside his pocket and found a seven-sided half-florin coin. He reached through the partition and dropped the coin on the seat. "You're a good man, Boudreaux."

The driver swallowed.

"Thank you, sir."

Donal slid out of the cab.

His first stop was the Exemplar Hotel on 99th and 201st. It was a grand old dark-gray building that rose fifty stories before reaching over and staring down in the form of a massive granite eagle's head. The east and west walls represented furled wings.

At street level, the originally plain talons were now decorated with upturned brass bowls in which eternal orange flames flickered and danced. Moving patterns swirled across marble steps leading up to the foyer.

Donal had never been inside.

Entering the polished reception hall, he passed gothic bronze dragons gleaming with reflected dancing flames. Slender women in fur stoles, brandishing long cigarette holders, were waiting for their portly, rich husbands.

A bellwraith, almost corporeal, said, *Can I help you, sir?*

Donal stared into the darkness where its eyes would have been. "You got a house detective here?"

Um...why would you—

Donal flashed his badge, replaced it. "I'd like to chat with him, if that's all right with you."

Right away, sir. The wraith began to float away, its cap maintaining a constant height above the brass floor. *This way.*

Behind the reception desk, one of the people in dark-green suits had exceptionally white skin. He looked up at the wraith's approach.

The wraith bent close, leaning inward until its face partly melded with the pale man's head. It was the most private way to whisper.

As the white-faced man nodded, the wraith drifted back. The man approached Donal.

"I'm Shaunovan. Sounds like you want to talk to me."

"Can we do it on the move?" said Donal. "While you show me around?"

"No problem." Shaunovan led the way to the rear. "The restaurant and kitchens first?"

"Sure."

"So I'm guessing it's the diva. She's the highest-profile guest checking in soon."

"You keep an eye on bookings?"

"Part of my job, Officer. Um, Fred didn't say what your name was."

"Riordan. Donal Riordan."

"Oh, Lieutenant. Of course."

They walked through the bar area. Two glasses

floated past, twisting and shivering: airborne cocktails, heading for one of the secluded booths at the rear.

"Who else works as detective here?" asked Donal. "Got a replacement for other shifts?"

"Just me." An odd look passed through Shaunovan's eyes. "I'm here twenty-five/nine."

"Never sleep, huh?"

"No." Shaunovan's voice went cold. "I never do."

Donal was impressed with the building's layout, which combined safety—easy access to fire exits and emergency-evacuation wraiths—with security. But the management had drawn the line at the use of in-house seers: the Exemplar's guests expected privacy.

"Come back tomorrow afternoon," said Shaunovan, "and Whitrose will sort out the bookings for your people. He's the senior manager, and he's got more . . . discretion . . . on rates than he'll admit to."

"Claims to have no leeway when he's negotiating?"

"Right. But Whitrose can reduce the rates all the way—if you can persuade him."

"You're a good man, Shaunovan."

"Are you sure of that?"

"Well . . . you're good, anyway." Donal held out his hand. "Nice meeting you."

"Likewise, Lieutenant." Shaunovan's grip was like frozen steel. "Likewise."

It wasn't a long walk to 92nd Street. Close to the Hoardway intersection loomed the massive construction that was the Théâtre du Loup Mort. From across the street, Donal watched a party of schoolgirls gathered outside the main entrance: a school outing.

The play was one that Donal had studied in school, a

study of warriors who were facing their last battle, and he remembered the spears flying across the stage in the final scene and the howling as the heroes died.

It had been shocking then and still seemed dreadful all these years later, despite the real terrors he'd experienced on the street.

Through a window up top, Donal caught a glimpse of a woman's outline and her perfect, bouncing breast, strawberry nipple against pale skin, and then it was gone. *Hades* . . .

One of the high windows opened onto the actresses' changing rooms, and the evening's performance was less than an hour away. Donal blew out a breath, watched the window for a moment longer, then forced himself to turn away.

Side alley. A lane at the back and a loading bay for trucks large enough to transport scenery. Fire escapes. This was going to be hard. There were so many opportunities for a trained hitman to—

Another actress walked past the window high up, pulling her blouse over her head as she walked. If Donal didn't move on, a beat officer would arrest him for peeping.

He walked to the corner of 205th, stopped in a small café-bar, and ordered an espresso. It came thick and dark in the tiny cup, and he shuddered as he drank it.

Then he walked to the glowing amber P-shaped sign that surmounted the iron steps leading below. Donal descended into the Pneumetro station, along with hundreds of other commuters forcing their way down to the platforms.

He looked for the red signs indicating the Z line—he didn't usually travel from 205th—and made his way there just as seven big slugs arrived, one after the other.

Donal wondered how often the guests at the Exemplar traveled by hypoway.

The tube was convex and sort of transparent against the platform, though the hexiglass was scratched and stained and maybe five years overdue for replacement. Each red slug held two hundred people, and Donal made his way to the third opening—Z3 was his branch line.

He was one of the last people to squeeze inside before the door wheezed shut. Everyone waited, crushed together and sweating. Then there was an explosive cough, and all seven slugs shot out of the station together.

It was a twenty-minute ride back toward Donal's neighborhood, but at least he didn't have to change trains. The slug flicked onto the third branch of the Z line without incident, and it only took seven more stops, and seven more explosive bursts of acceleration, to reach Halls.

No one greeted him as he walked down the street amid bluestones and converted temples, until he reached the apartment block. He opened the outer doors just as old Mrs. MacZoran was leaving, laundry bag in hand.

"I'll pop by the washeteria in a while," Donal told her. "Check everything's all right."

"Don't worry about me."

"Then I won't. I'll just—"

But Mrs. MacZoran was already gone, head bent and hearing only the voices in her head, memories of days long lost.

"—go out for a run."

Donal climbed upstairs, let himself into his fifth-floor apartment, and locked the door behind him. Moving quickly—because to pause and sit down would be to make the discipline more difficult—he used the tiny bathroom, then stripped and pulled on a long one-piece black running suit and his old black shoes.

He performed stretches and lunges on the bare floorboards and used the exposed ceiling pipes to haul himself up through a series of chin-ups, interspersed with push-ups performed with his feet up on the bed. Sit-ups and leg raises on the hard floor followed.

Donal rose to his feet, picking two splinters from his clothes.

The gun had always been problematic, and tonight he decided to run without it. Leaving the shoulder holster slung over the bedpost, Donal went out and locked the front door: all three locks. Keys and badge clutched in his left fist, he went downstairs.

Out on the sidewalk he jogged slowly to the corner.

Darkness was starting to close in, the purple sky deepening. The washeteria, known as Fozzy's Rags, shone its lights hard and white. Mrs. MacZoran was in there, sitting side by side with another of the neighborhood's old biddies. Wicker baskets, for transferring clean wash into the big dryers, waited at their feet.

None of the neighborhood derelicts appeared to be lurking around the place. Not this evening.

Good.

Donal jogged on to the next corner, where a dank stone pedestal stood, slightly wider than a man and about eight feet high. A stone door's outline was scarcely visible on its side, but the hand-size opening beside it was clear of obstruction.

Donal inserted his police badge, waited a long moment, then pulled the badge back out. This was what you might call a perk of the job.

The heavy door ground its way open.

Inside, the pedestal was hollow, revealing the beginning of a stone staircase that spiraled deep underground. Donal went down the first five steps and waited. The door groaned shut behind him.

Nodding slightly, he continued downward. Phosphorescent runes cast enough ghostly light for him to make

out the steps. In any case, he had been down this way
thousands of times before.

It took maybe ten minutes to descend to the tunnel
and step onto squelching gray ground: fine particles of
stone, wet, on top of worn flagstones. Donal's foot
splashed in a black puddle.

No automobiles moved down here, polluting the air
or taking over the streets. Generally speaking, no people
moved in this place. There might be guards, but the
newer mausoleums were farther downtown. Everything
here was ancient: relics of once-powerful families, now
forgotten.

These were the catacombs, cold and quiet.

End of another day.

Donal began to run.

Pounding now, ten minutes into the run and warmed up,
Donal raced along a winding tunnel that dipped and
widened out into a low cavern where half a dozen stone
sarcophagi were interred. Each sarcophagus had melded
with the stone floor and wall, like some kind of cocoon.

Donal ran past, feeling the faintest of whispers like a
spider's web slide across his skin.

Then he was out of the chamber, into an unmarked
tunnel, and the sensation was gone. He followed one of
his three usual routes, looping back until he was eventually at the stone steps once more: chest heaving, body
slick with sweat, ready to ascend.

Climbing the steps forced him to slow the pace, and
the tension in his thighs and calves was a kind of joyful
pain as he reached the top. He stepped out onto the sidewalk.

Donal half-jogged past Fozzy's Rags, reached his
apartment block, and took his time climbing the final
stairs.

Home once more, he rinsed off in the shower and used one of his old scratchy towels to dry with. Then he pulled on fresh underwear and a shirt and the same suit he'd worn earlier but with a different tie, dark-green. He went back out.

There was a secondhand (and third- and fourth-hand) bookstore two blocks away, and that was Donal's first stop. He went inside and picked up a battered copy of *Human: the Revenge,* one of a fantasy series set on a parallel Earth where the only sentient beings were human and necroflux was either undiscovered or nonexistent: he hadn't figured out which.

"Thirty centals, for you."

"Hey, Peat. How's it going?"

Peat was well named, from the spongy aspect of his skin to the dark woody scent that wafted from him. Not that Donal knew much about the countryside.

Each of Peat's hands ended in three stubby fingers, currently holding a massive stack of old books. He weighed about four hundred pounds, was three times stronger than a human, and knew every epic poem and sonnet of the last three centuries by heart.

"Well, Donal, as always."

"Good." For a man—a being—with such literary knowledge, actual conversations with Peat had a tendency toward brevity. "Listen, I need to get some dinner. But—"

"Later, my friend."

"Yeah." Donal put the coins down on the counter. "Later."

He left with the book in hand and crossed the street to Freda's Diner. There, Marie, a short waitress with missing teeth and a gentle manner, took Donal's order.

Sipping weak coffee—after all, he had to sleep soon—Donal read from the book until his food came. Then he continued to read while shoveling eggs and tubers into his mouth. It was greasy and filling and he ate too much.

Then he went back home, stripped off his clothes and hung them up, and lay on his bed, reading. It was the end of a normal day.

But when he finally put the book down and slid into sleep, the dreams that visited him were of a rich, colored texture such as he had never experienced before: meadows of impossible emerald brightness beneath a sky that was pale instead of dark, where winsome fantastical semitransparent creatures out of legend grazed on blue lawns. Finally a black crack appeared across the sky and Donal began to run, ever faster without covering any distance, while words—or were they fingernails?—scraped across his skin.

We are the bones, the grass beneath his feet seemed to say.

Donal ran faster in his sleep.

We are the bones. We know you now.

4

Nine days later, Donal was sitting in his office with Levison, checking his watch and wondering whether the diva's flight could possibly land on time. All of yesterday, thick summer fog had cloaked Tristopolis, until virtually nothing was moving. Today it looked like more of the same.

"Accounts will have my hide," Donal said, "if our guys have gotten an extra night in the hotel and the diva isn't going to make it here today."

"She'll make it." Levison looked up from the puzzle in his folded newspaper. "I'm telling you."

"Uh...okay." Donal leaned sideways in his chair, trying to see outside. From here, he could not see the sky, but he could judge the light in the artificial canyon of buildings and note the silver-lilac reflections in the windows. "I'm tempted to bet on it."

"Listen," said Levison. "You haven't been up to anything you shouldn't, have you, boss?"

"All my life." Donal focused on Levison's serious expression. "Nothing illegal, though. What's on your mind?"

"Nothing."

"Right."

"It's just, er, I was talking to Helven in Records—"

"And how is she? Have you asked her out for coffee yet? Has she asked you? Does your wife know?"

"—anyway, so I happened to notice this woman among the personnel files."

"While you should have been paying attention to Helven. Come on, Lev."

"Your dossier, Donal. That's what this nice-looking blonde had in her hands."

"Huh." Donal's chair creaked as he swung his weight back. "So?"

"So she had a weapon and she wasn't no bureaucrat." Levison's accent reverted to the streets and to his childhood. And Donal's. "Got it? Looked like IntSec to me."

"Ain't no reason for Infernal Security to worry about me, pal."

"Well." Levison nodded. "Good."

"Apart from those millions I got stashed away . . ."

"Hades, Donal. Don't joke about this stuff."

"All right. Have you got a car arranged?"

"For the airport? Yeah." Levison checked the small clock on top of Donal's bookcase. Inside the bichambered clock, dark fluid dripped from the lower chamber to the upper, causing the second hand to move. "Fifty-five minutes, downstairs."

"Great. You go on." Donal climbed out of his chair. "I've got stuff to do."

"Okay, boss."

Donal picked up his suit jacket and pulled it on as he left the office. That was mostly in case he ended up talking to a civilian before returning: hiding the gun usually made conversations proceed more quickly. Except during interrogation.

The elevator shaft opened while he was still ten feet away.

Hey, lover. Missed you. And as he stepped inside: *How long's it been?*

"All of an hour."

Feels like longer.

"Range, please, Gertie."

Invisible fingers seemed to cross his torso. *Where would you like me to range?*

But Donal was already falling down the shaft.

"Behave."

All right. The hands began to slow Donal's descent. *Behave well, or behave badly?*

"Hades."

Mind your language. Gertie exerted horizontal pressure on Donal's back. *Bad boy.*

The force expelled Donal into the corridor. He turned to say something, but the shaft had already sealed up. His snappy retort would have to wait.

Flat bangs sounded from the practice range. Someone was hard at work.

When Donal reached the entrance, Brian was sitting behind his desk, wearing a smart shirt and tie, his fresh skin bluer than normal. Behind him, two blank-faced men were flipping through folders and the boxed records of who'd signed equipment in and out.

"Hey, Brian. How's life?"

"Got my IntSec pals visiting. Right, boys? Other than that, biz as usual, Lieutenant."

Brian dropped Donal a wink, as if thanking him for the warning that Internal Security was going to be here. But it was Donal who had called IntSec and told them to check out the range, and if Brian had failed to get rid of his stupid targets, then the man would have been out.

Donal leaned over the counter. The IntSec men looked up.

"Don't take any crap from Brian," Donal told them. "Okay?"

"We won't, Lieutenant." There was no humor in the reply, just leaden fact.

Neither of the IntSec guys matched the description that Levison had given: a nice-looking blonde who'd been holding Donal's personnel file in her hand.

"Gimme two hundred rounds," Donal said to Brian. "And a pile of targets, ghouls and humans mixed."

"You got it."

"Er, Lieutenant..." One of the IntSec men held up a folder. "You signed for ammunition yesterday. Can you remember how many rounds that was?"

Brian's blue skin began to shine paler. Donal shook his head. Was Brian really that stupid, to change numbers of rounds handed over, overstate the expenditure, and pocket the surplus?

"Sorry," Donal said. "Can't remember."

Donal fired off the two hundred rounds and went back to the counter. The IntSec guys were still there, peeking in the target drawers and archive cabinets. Donal got Brian to give him another hundred and went back into the range and shot his targets into shreds.

When he returned the second time, Brian was alone.

"Your IntSec pals," said Donal. "They gone for the day?"

"Er...sure. Why wouldn't they be?"

"I definitely know the inventory's fine. It is fine, isn't it, Brian?"

"S-sure."

"You worked the streets a long time. I appreciate that—"

"Thanks, Lieutenant."

"—but if I think ammo or weapons are going astray, I'll put a bullet between your eyes myself. You got that?"

Brian's mouth dropped open. It was all the answer Donal was going to get.

"Shit." Donal turned his wrist over. "And now you've made me late."

"S-sorry."

Donal strode out of the range office and headed for the elevator. Gertie's door whisked open, and she bore him up to the garage level with only the faintest saucy humming in his ear, snatches of an old song he barely recognized and could not have named.

Coming out into the echoing concrete garage at a run, Donal spotted a squad car idling with its rear door open. Two uniformed officers sat up front, and Levison was in the back, on the far side.

"Airport," Donal muttered to the driver as he got in. "Quick as you can."

He pulled the door shut with an unnecessary slam.

The uniforms got the message. They pulled the car out into the traffic flow, using the black-light strobe and switching the siren from *wail* to *maximum thunder.*

For several blocks, the traffic was too heavy for it to make a difference, but then they were out onto streets where cars were moving—this was late morning, not rush hour—and frightening other drivers became a valid time-saving tactic.

Flashes of blackness reflected back from the buildings as the car accelerated, weaving in and out of half-filled lanes. They ran three stoplights in succession before reaching the Orb-Sinister Expressway.

All nine lanes flowed directly toward the center of the two-thousand-foot-high skull that marked the eastern boundary of midtown. There, the lanes peeled upward into the left eye socket of that vast construct—or maybe relic, no one really knew. They entered a mile-long round tunnel lit only by disembodied flamewraiths, dancing overhead.

The wraiths were indentured for short periods these days. The stress of passing traffic was great, and everyone remembered the tunnel crash of '93 in the Orb-Dexter Freeway. Then, a kind of group hysteria had seized the flamewraiths, many of them into their second century of servitude. Wraiths discorporated explosively into showering sparks; drivers swerved in sudden shock. The hundred-car pileup killed dozens.

Soon the squad car was out into the open. The sky was heavy with purple-gray clouds, and Donal still felt closed in. They passed through the mercantile district of Prismatic Trance, with its rainbow ads and myriad illusions.

Finally they reached the turnoff for the airport, and the driver pulled the car out into the fast lane and floored it.

Fog was thickening overhead by the time they turned through the glowering twin-panthers gateway of Brody Airport (named after Fisticuffs Brody, still remembered as the best mayor the city had ever had). They slowed as they came to a police-only entrance, then turned and went down a ramp into the depths of Terminal Aleph.

"Good work, guys," said Levison. He looked at Donal.

"Uh, yeah. Good job."

"Sir." The driver wheeled them neatly into a parking spot.

"You reckon the flights are on time?" said the other uniformed officer.

"Not with this fog," muttered Levison. "Gives us more time to check around. Right, boss?"

"Right." Donal sat unmoving for a moment longer. His unease might have been kicked off by some subliminal perception.

"You okay?"

"Yeah." Donal retraced the drive in his mind, the route into the airport, and felt no specific reaction to any part of the route.

Shit.

It was the entire operation that worried him. A killer could strike from anywhere.

"Let's get going."

They slid out of the squad car.

Whatever Commissioner Vilnar had said about keeping overtime payments down, there was only one way to stop the hit, and that was to ensure a visible presence. It would make two things clear: the killer would have to give up his (or her, or its) own life; and no one would be stealing the body afterward.

There was an escalator formed of rising glass slats, their lev-runes solidly encased and glowing darkly. Levison stood on the step above Donal as they rose through a seven-story atrium.

Donal scanned the crowds, soon spotting half a dozen men with fedoras tipped down over their eyes, hands in their overcoat pockets, standing at corners and pillars and other vantage points.

"They're all ours," said Levison.

"Good."

"But you want I should take a walk later, right, boss, and check them out personally?"

Donal glanced up at Levison. "I hate being predictable."

"I knew you'd say that."

"Fuck off, Lev."

"And I also knew you'd—"

"I mean it."

But Lev was grinning as they got off the escalator. They both knew he'd won that round.

*   *   *

The flight arrived late. Thick, pale-gray fog was everywhere when the four-propeller Dagger Airlines plane
came to a stand near the terminal building.

Ground crew wheeled the steps into place and rolled
out the long strip of crimson carpet. Reporters and pho-
tographers crowded as close as they could, held back by
officers of the 1005th Precinct. Several local dignitaries,
including Alderman Alexei Brown, were there to greet
the diva.

The props were rotating slowly, and finally they
stopped, one by one.

Magnesium bulbs popped white as the diva appeared
at the open door and paused on the top step. From the
small crowd's edge, Donal looked up and saw the triangular, fine features he recognized from the magazine articles he'd read during the week.

He hadn't realized how beautiful Maria daLivnova
was, but as she descended, a kind of iron elegance ruled
every motion, and when she paused once more at the
bottom of the steps, the sense of her presence was over-
whelming. Her smile as she looked around was wide
and white and shining with the message: *I'm full of joy
being here.*

Her gaze passed over Donal without pausing.

Expecting her to cavil at the arrangements had been
one thing, but this was worse: her failure to recognize
Donal's existence.

But why should he care? This was work, the diva was
a commodity to be protected, and if he had to step between her and an assassin's bullet, well, that was what
he'd become a cop for, what they paid him to do.

"What's it like to be in Tristopolis?" called out a re-
porter. He wore a dark hat and held his notepad and pen
ready for the diva's reply.

"Nice fog you people have here."

There was a round of laughter among the reporters.

After the handshakes, three black limousines with black windshields pulled up on the tarmac. The alderman's aides escorted the diva to the center limo. She got in and perched, half-sitting but with one stiletto-shoed foot on the crimson carpet outside, for a final round of bulb-popping photographs.

Then she pulled her foot inside, an aide closed the door—and Donal let out a tiny breath. This was the first possible fixed ambush point, and they'd gotten through it. If everyone could just maintain highest-level vigilance, nerves strung taut for the next eighteen days, they would make it.

Two weeks.

At least the time would pass quickly, because there'd be no time to stop and rest. That was Donal's theory as he got into one of the cruisers that pulled up, while the remainder moved into formation before and after the limos.

He looked back at the plane. The journalists were dispersing, the dignitaries were in the limos, and now the ordinary passengers were beginning to descend the steps, allowed to disembark.

No one was waiting to take their photographs or ask them what it felt like to be here.

There were outriders on low-slung motorbikes, officers with helmets and leather jackets, over-and-under spitguns clipped to the sides of their fuel tanks. They swung in on either side of the motorcade.

All the cars slid into motion. Donal watched in every direction.

He had wanted a helicopter overhead, but the fog was even better, providing visual cover from rooftop snipers: not so much here as when they reached the high midtown skyscrapers.

Except that in those architectural canyons the fog would be thinner.

Damn it.

Opportunities to make the hit were everywhere.

The diva's limo pulled up before the Exemplar. Here, not just journalists but fans had gathered on the sidewalks. Donal's nerves tightened as he exited his car fast and held his badge out for the uniforms to let him through.

"Nice to see you, Lieutenant," said one of them, a gray-haired veteran whom Donal recognized. "Looks like everyone's here to get your autograph."

"It's your picture they're taking." Donal gave a half salute while scanning the windows high up across the street. "Okay, here goes."

The diva was exiting her car, and the officers linked arms against the increasingly chaotic pressure of the crowd, as those farther back jostled. The dancing flames above the steps cast golden highlights on the diva as she stopped to wave at the crowd—*don't stay in the open, damn it*—and then ascended the steps so she was under the decorative canopy in front of the door.

Even here a Seeker round would pick her out through the obstacles. Donal waved at the doormen to usher the diva indoors. One of them bowed and murmured a greeting as he gestured inside, and the diva seemed to flow into the foyer.

Inside, Donal's own men were already posted at vantage points. He began to feel happier.

While the diva took the elevator—operated by a human attendant, suitably humble-looking—Donal went up the stairs three treads at a time. By the time he reached the third floor, his breath was coming in big, loud inhalations, and his body had sprung a layer of sweat: reacting to the promise of a hard run.

But the diva's suite was on the forty-seventh floor, too high to sprint, so Donal walked along the corridor to the laundry elevator, where Levison was already waiting, holding the brass door open. Levison had come here ahead of the cavalcade, and he was looking almost sleepy as he said, "Which floor, sir?"

But he had already pressed 47 and was hauling the door shut before Donal had finished stepping inside. The elevator car lurched, ascended a few feet and rattled, then rose more smoothly as it gathered speed.

"Nice to see you looking calm," said Donal.

"If Commissioner Vilnar's got every confidence in you"—Levison spoke with a straight face—"then who am I to argue?"

"You're absolutely right." Donal pulled his Magnus a quarter way out of his shoulder holster, then pushed it back in. No problems there. "In your place, I'd be calm too."

"And what about you?"

"I'm scared shitless. I'm looking forward to the whole thing being over, the diva off somewhere else on a plane, heading to Rio Exotico or someplace."

"Ah." Levison nodded as the dial needle swung through 40 and the elevator's ascent slowed. "That's why the rest of us are relaxed. When you're strung out, everything's in control."

"That's nice to know."

The elevator car clanked to a halt, and Levison hauled the brass door open. "Looks like we're ready."

Twelve uniforms were posted along the corridor. Detectives on the floors above and below were already in place. Two of Donal's squad opened the door of the suite across from the diva's and grinned.

"Hey, boss, Lev. You want anything from room service?"

"For Hades's sake..."

"Just kidding, Donal."

"Where's the—"

"She's coming now." Levison touched Donal's arm. "Here."

They walked down to the main elevator bank just as the diva's elevator arrived and the golden doors slid open. She stepped out, Maria daLivnova, diva extraordinaire.

The hotel's general manager, Whitrose, was beside her, fawning.

"Um, Miss daLivnova, you'll have met Lieutenant, um, Riordan? In charge of the...arrangements for your visit."

"No, I've not had the pleasure." Her gaze on Donal was amused, nothing more.

But she stopped his lungs and maybe his heart.

So beautiful...

And a target, unless he did his job properly.

"Honored, ma'am." Donal made himself speak. "If we could talk some more about the security prec—"

"A glamorous detective. For me. My, how I'm touched."

Then she swept past him, followed by her two female assistants. Both women were employees of the Théâtre du Loup Mort, assigned by the management. They'd been in the limousine at the airport to meet the diva. Donal had interviewed both of them; afterward, Levison, who was much better at forming a rapport with strangers, had talked to them individually. Neither seemed to be a security risk; both of them were already looking as stressed on the surface as Donal felt inside.

Glamorous detective.

Donal watched the door to the diva's suite swing shut. He blew out a breath.

That'll be me, all right.

The first performance changed everything.

Donal was standing in the shadowed interior of a box on the top level. Commissioner Vilnar was one of six dignitaries seated officially inside it.

Down below, armed officers were obvious outside the actual performance hall; in here, two department snipers in plainclothes were in another box, their rifles at their feet. Levison was seated in one of the stalls. Other members of Donal's team were scattered among the audience.

The visible presence outside presented the first layer of deterrence, but Donal assumed that a trained killer might spot the two snipers: their grim gazes continually swept the audience below. Neither one looked like an opera lover, despite the tuxedos.

They were the second, also visible, layer. The third layer was Donal's squad. If Levison hadn't told him, Donal would not have guessed that the overweight gray-haired lady with the diamonds and fur stole was Sergeant Miriam Delwether, one of the department's finest shots.

This was the opening night, and if there was to be an attempt on the diva's life, this would be the most dramatic time to stage it.

The lights went down, shadows growing unevenly inside the auditorium, and Donal was alert for any shifts of movement, any gleam of reflected light—*there*. He had to force himself to relax—*just opera glasses*—and to keep scanning, looking for any sign of a weapon being brought to bear.

Onstage, the production swirled into life. Colorful

costumes were bright, almost blazing at the edge of Donal's peripheral vision: the *Mort d'Alanquin*'s opening scene took place in a royal court amid pageantry.

None of it helped Donal's vision to remain dark-adapted. He continued to scan the audience.

Donal was half aware of the dancing onstage. As the scene progressed, the cast tended to stand still more and the singing became more important. When the diva stepped out onto stage left, at the entrance to the royal court, Donal's gaze snapped back and forth across the auditorium: stalls, circle, boxes, flicking to the stage itself, then back to the seats below.

And then she opened her mouth to sing.

Oh, my Death . . .

The diva sang, her voice pure and crystalline, pulling the audience to her with her innocent inquiry: *"Is this where the great king holds judgment?"*

When the solo was finished, the diva lowered her head as waves of applause washed through the auditorium. Donal rubbed his hand across his face and realized he had been aware only of her for the past several minutes as the aria proceeded.

Minutes that could have been a lifetime.

Just keep focused.

It wasn't only the danger to the diva. If bullets started flying through the audience, if his own people opened fire, he would be held accountable. And if someone important died and their relatives claimed blood money, it was Donal, not Commissioner Vilnar, who would be served up as payment.

But during the next solo from the diva, Donal—though he kept pushing himself to look elsewhere—kept returning his gaze to her, like an exhausted man whose chin keeps falling to his chest no matter how often he jerks it back upright, trying to maintain wakefulness.

So much for security.

During the intermission, Donal faded out of the box. He went downstairs and made his way backstage, past two hulking uniforms he knew well: the Brodowski Brothers. In the weight-lifting room, their fellow officers called them the Barbarians.

"All clear, guys?"

"Sure, but I think Al cried during the last song."

"Like you didn't."

Hades, they were as bad as him. Donal climbed up a flight of wooden steps and stepped through the heavy overlapping curtains.

Men in brown coveralls were pushing heavy facades—castle battlements—on industrial-size casters. Cast members who had not spent much time onstage were murmuring to one another; the others would be sitting down and rehydrating in the changing rooms.

A lithe young woman walked past, half naked, pulling on a peasant's blouse. Donal swallowed before forcing out a long exhalation.

"Can I help you?" asked a stagehand.

"No ... Yeah. You see anyone here that doesn't belong?"

"Er, don't think so." The stagehand glanced at the young actress straightening her blouse, then back at Donal. "Apart from you, Officer. The rest of us are used to this."

"Must be a hard life."

"Don't talk so much about *hard*." The stagehand winked. "Some of the boys might get excited."

Hades ...

Donal took a last look around the stage. Up top, beyond the overhead spotlights, a gantry allowed objects to be lowered on near-invisible cables. There was a heavy man up there, script in hand, ready to call down: he was to be the ghost's voice in the next act.

There were also two plainclothes officers, one of

whom waved Donal a half salute, which Donal returned.

All clear.

Donal went back out to the Brodowski Brothers. "Guys, it's a good job you're holding the fort out here. It's hell backstage."

"Why's that, Lieutenant?"

"All those naked actresses getting changed. Bosoms bouncing everywhere. My blood pressure's gone through the roof."

"Aw, man . . ."

Third act.

The plot was beyond Donal's comprehension, but he wasn't being paid to follow the story. Still, he kept glancing down at the stage.

Commissioner Vilnar was equally entranced. The diva—whether singing solo or as now, part of an intricate duet as she called out the prince for his impetuous treatment of the populace—had captivated Donal along with everyone else in the theater.

Fourth and final act.

The entire company was onstage, enacting the battle scene and then the coming together of both sides to mourn. When the diva sang that heartrending farewell to the slain prince, Donal felt his nerves hooked out of his body, his soul dragged out by talons.

Tears ran in silent floods down his cheekbones.

No shots rang out. No one sprinted onto the stage and ran a dagger through the diva's heart. It was just as well, because neither Donal nor any of the officers, not even the spellbound snipers in the opposite box, could have processed the danger or made a move while that pure sublime sound continued to emanate from the diva's perfect mouth.

And then the aria was ended.

Donal bowed his head in silence. Backing out of the box, he wiped tears from his face with the back of his hand, and by the time he reached ground level he was practically normal. The two detectives stationed at the side entrance to the auditorium were still damp-eyed.

"Be professional," said Donal as he went through.

"Sir."

From the side, Donal watched as multiple bouts of applause rose, ebbed, then washed higher once more. The company took bows, but the loudest cheers were reserved for the diva (and secondmost for the prince, or rather the man who sang that part, whose name a quarter of the audience and none of the police knew).

Flowers arced through the air, hurled by enthusiastic operagoers, and Donal winced each time one of the snipers moved up in their box. But neither of them raised his weapon over the balcony's edge.

A young girl brought a huge bouquet, taller than herself, up onto the stage. The diva accepted it and kissed the girl's cheek, which brought a fresh wave of applause.

Finally, the curtain went down and stayed down. The lights came up, the sudden brightness forcing Donal to squint. Happy people, murmuring and chattering, threaded their way up the aisles to the exits, while Donal's tension was strung tight.

He had been relieved in the emotional aftermath of the final aria. But now everyone's guard was down, and this was a danger moment. No one had said the diva had to be onstage for the killing to occur.

"Stay alert, damn it," he said to the two Brodowskis as he climbed backstage.

"Huh? Right."

"Got it, Lieutenant."

*   *   *

There was a press of well-wishers in the diva's dressing room, champagne in a silver rune-chased bucket, woven heptagrams of blue orchids and indigo roses, and a chattering cacophony of congratulations. Levison, in his unassuming way, stood in the background, assisting with the bouquets.

"Thank you so much," Levison murmured to the florid son of a well-known businessman, owner of the Black Viper supermarket chain.

The businessman's gaze didn't even flicker in Levison's direction.

From the doorway, Donal watched and raised his eyebrows as Levison took charge of another bouquet. The slightest of quiet smiles passed across Levison's face: it meant everyone was ignoring him, unaware that his presence ensured the diva's safety in this room.

Donal eyed the diva's visitors. Platinum skull-shaped cuff links, white-gold torques with diamond insertions... No overt weapons. And no body language that betrayed anything more urgent than the need to bask in the diva's presence.

For a second, the diva noticed Donal and gave the tiniest of nods. He felt a sensation like a multitude of sprite fingers playing down his spine. Then the diva's attention was on a large woman in an ivory-white gown who was offering congratulations, and the moment was past.

Donal forced his way back into the narrow corridor. Then he went back to the stage, checking angles and examining shadows. All clear. The Brodowski Brothers were now at the side exit, and Al—the slightly taller one—opened the metal door for Donal.

Outside, the limo was ready. Two of Donal's squad, Petrov and Duquesne, dressed in their best suits, were standing by the vehicle. Their gazes roved the rooftops as well as ground level.

"So far, so good," said Duquesne. "We got Avram up on the roof. No problems there."

"No relaxing yet."

"Right." Petrov spared a second to look at Donal. "And how many nights do we keep it up for?"

Donal didn't answer. The question was rhetorical, and Petrov's tone was mild: not a complaint but an observation.

Damn, damn, damn.

Because no one could keep alert forever.

At the official reception afterward, there were canapés and hors d'oeuvres and who-knew-what savories on the buffet. Commissioner Vilnar looked resplendent in his cummerbund and even congratulated Donal on the arrangements so far.

"Thank you, sir" was all Donal said, ignoring the final words: *so far.* He circulated around the party's edges, stopping to talk to Levison, who was nibbling from a plate of finger-size *things* that each appeared to end in a single black eye.

"What are you eating, Lev?"

"Haven't a clue, but they're lovely. Try one?"

"Not a chance."

As he moved on, the diva noticed him and beckoned. There was a tight half circle of important-looking people focused on her.

"And this," the diva said, "is my glamorous personal detective. See how the city treats me?"

"That's our pleasure," said a Tristopolitan councillor, who wore his platinum chain of office atop his frilled dress shirt. "And you'd be Captain..."

"Lieutenant Riordan. Glad to be of service, Councillor."

"Talent and beauty like this"—with a soft-fingered gesture—"must be preserved, no matter what."

"Oh, Edward. You flatter me."

Donal gave a tiny bow and stepped away. As he did so, the diva glanced at him, and perhaps he saw irony move inside those dark and perfect eyes. Then she returned her attention to the councillor, resuming their decorative and meaningless conversation.

Glamorous detective.

Staying on the periphery until the party ended at two A.M., Donal followed as the diva finally went down to the limo. The streets were eerie valleys almost devoid of people or cars as they drove to the Exemplar Hotel.

At this hour, the flames dancing above the entrance moved slowly, as though tired, but the doormen were alert enough as they opened up for the diva. She and her two assistants climbed the steps, with Petrov and Duquesne on either side and Donal following.

The night shift was in place, and Donal's duty was over. Still, he could not help taking a last walk around the hotel's deserted corridors, the darkened restaurant, and the quiet (though not entirely empty) residents' bar. Everything was clear.

Donal took the hypoway back to his apartment, ignoring the drunk who stared at him for most of the trip. No one disturbed him as he walked to the apartment building and let himself in.

Once in his own place, despite the lateness of the hour and the groan of the ancient plumbing, he showered with soap in the old tin stall. The water cut out before he had fully rinsed off.

Donal toweled himself dry, then sat at the single unadorned wooden table with a bottle of Jacques Dauphin liquor. Twisting the cap off, he saluted the shadows of his room and drank a slug.

It tasted like fire as it went down.

Two more slugs, and he screwed the top back on. Then, feeling scratchy and unclean, he forced himself to lie down on the plain bed and look up at the ceiling, waiting for sleepiness to manifest itself.

Some kind of glamour.

At five A.M., on a deserted street two blocks from the Exemplar Hotel, a supine body moved along the sidewalk. Head supported by nothingness, heels dragging along the ground, he moved.

Waves of dark refraction shimmered. *Something* was dragging the unconscious man.

It pulled him around the corner, then released him. The man's head fell to the sidewalk with a sickening thud. His nose had been smashed, and there were torn gashes in his cheek.

Beside his head, two expensive, elegant shoes glistened black. Their owner wore a gray skirt suit, and her hair and skin were pale.

"What's this?" she said.

Lurking near the exemplar. I found him.

"And that's all?"

Hardly. Take a look in his pockets.

The woman glanced into the shadows. Then she went down on one knee and inserted her gloved hand into the beaten man's pockets, retrieving a dart gun, its loaded bolt coated with a dark fluid whose scent she recognized immediately.

"Moonshade. Fatal dose."

The injured man also carried a stranglewire noose, treated so that it would tighten of its own accord when tossed around a victim's soft throat. It would contract to a fist's diameter—but *slowly*. Not a pleasant way to die.

Straightening up, the woman held the weapons in her hand. The man moved a little, eyelids fluttering, then lapsed into stillness.

"You got any suggestions, Xalia, as to what we do with him?"

The darkness rippled, then:

Nothing at all.

"What do you mean?"

Just that.

The woman looked up and down the street, and then she saw it: two pairs of amber eyes glowing briefly in black shadows.

"Just leave him? For them?"

Come on, Laura. He was going to kill the diva.

"I know. But he's not Black Circle. Just a lone sicko."

My point—the words seemed to float on wind—*precisely.*

The woman, Laura, looked down at the injured man once more. "Shoulda stuck to beating off with your fist. You know, been a *harmless* pervert."

Then she walked away and, after a moment, the disturbance in the darkness floated after her.

5

Donal woke at five twenty-three, seven minutes before his alarm was due to go off. In the tag end of his nightmare, swirling out of memory like fluid down a drain, he imagined a fading scream. Then it was gone.

He used the facilities, drank brackish water from the faucet—at least it was working—pulled on his old black running suit, and left the apartment. No one moved on the street, not this early.

A hundred feet overhead, a department scanbat moved in a straight line, and Donal gave it a wave. Perhaps later one of the surveillance mages, absorbing the bat's memories, would recognize Donal.

At the stone pillar on the corner, Donal did the usual thing with his police badge, and the door scraped open. He descended the spiraling stone steps.

Do you feel it?

Donal stopped, shuddering, and then told himself to stop being stupid. This place was empty. He continued going down, until he reached the catacombs.

There, he began to jog along the ancient stone floor.

Do you feel the song?

Coldness raked Donal's skin as he ran, forcing the pace before his muscles were warmed up. Then he was into the chamber where sarcophagi stood melded into the earth.

Do you hear?

Donal pushed himself to run faster, while talons that were pure imagination raked at his nerves, dragged like hooks through his body.

Do you hear the bones?

Donal's arms were shaking by the time he returned to the stone steps, and the big muscles of his thighs felt soft as he ascended, fearing he might fall at any time. The door opened partway, then jammed momentarily before freeing itself, and a sensation of dread swept downward through his body.

He staggered onto the sidewalk, heading for home.

Donal made time in the afternoon for a nap in the back of a cruiser. There was no opportunity to practice in the range at HQ, so after he woke, before opening his eyes, Donal sent himself into a trance.

He visualized a training session where he fired straight into the target's vital points. Then, with a long, deep, shuddering breath, he returned to reality.

"Hey, Lieutenant. Need coffee?"

"Only if there's doughnuts."

"We can manage that."

The two uniforms, Belden and O'Grady, had left him alone in the car while he slept, staying within earshot of the radio in case it squawked for them. Now they got back in and drove out of the alleyway. They pulled up on the ultraviolet no-parking lines in front of a Fat'n'Sugar. Belden went inside.

"He prefers Tarantula Creams," muttered O'Grady. "Make your teeth black."

"Wonderful."

But Belden brought back plain and redberry, just

what Donal would have ordered, and big snakeskin cups filled with coffee that was so-so. Volume over taste.

"You getting cultured, Lieutenant?" Belden, in the front passenger seat, pulled back the little snake-mouth opening on his coffee-cup lid. "All that opera and all?"

"Absolutely, my good man. Getting cultured up the wazoo."

"Hear that diva's a real honey." O'Grady, sitting behind the wheel, took a mouthful of doughnut and a large slug of coffee, and commenced chewing. "She as gorgeous as they say?"

"Oh, yeah." Donal's voice went soft, and he put his coffee down. "She is that."

The second performance bettered the first. The audience, affluent but not the city's most influential folk, were less restrained in their applause. That triumphant mood fed back to the opera company, raising them to a new level.

Not just the diva but everyone sang their hearts out. Several of the soloists reduced the audience to tears, capturing that ability to entrance the listener and weave patterns with their soul.

This time, the Brodowski Brothers were stationed backstage—it turned out they'd had a word with Levison—and after the performance, Al Brodowski pulled Donal aside.

"Hades, Lieutenant. You were right. Twenty bare bods, big titties everywhere. Bud's had to lie down."

"Er ... glad you were paying attention."

Then Brodowski left, leaving Donal to wonder whether they really had seen twenty naked women or whether they were torturing him in revenge.

"Hey," said Levison. "What's up? You were staring into space."

"Thinking strategic thoughts. Have Petrov and Duquesne got her car ready?"

Her meant the diva.

"All set. She still going to the Five Seasons?"

"Yeah. Seven-course meal." Donal and the others would get to stand around and watch. "All the trimmings."

Levison said, "You managed to eat already?"

"Sure. You?"

"Brought a bean-sprout sandwich in with me. Tilly made it last night. What about you?"

"Two redberry doughnuts and a Fat'n'Sugar max-size coffee. With Belden and O'Grady."

"Fat'n'Sugar?" Levison sighed. "Lucky bastard."

The diva left shortly afterward, trailing a cloud of hangers-on and admirers. Donal wondered if she ever grew sick of it.

Sitting in the back of Belden and O'Grady's cruiser, Donal watched the streets, his stomach sour, not from the bad coffee but the knowledge that a killer could be anywhere.

Once more the team had deployed to vantage points. That included three men who had spent the day at the Five Seasons, getting in the head chef's way, or trying not to get noticed by diners. Donal roved around the positions and the streets outside, watching for anything out of the ordinary, anything to break the pattern, finding nothing.

Three hours later it was back to the Exemplar.

Donal was technically off duty now but could not resist wandering through the corridors and facilities. He chatted briefly with Shaunovan, the Exemplar's house detective who never slept or—it seemed—left the building.

It was late when Donal finally went home.

Next morning, he rose at seven, itching to go for a

run. Although traffic was beginning to take over the streets at this hour, he chose to run along the sidewalks, not the catacombs. Nothing whispered to him at ground level.

Donal showered—in hot water that lasted as long as he wanted—had scrambled eggs for breakfast, and pulled on a clean shirt and his other suit. He'd had the suit steam-cleaned at Fozzy's Rags.

Today felt like a good day.

There was a matinee performance, which drew a different crowd: children accompanying their parents. They sobbed and laughed at the right places, though the plot surely had to be beyond them.

Donal was finally getting the hang of the intricacies of the story, which mixed innocence with ambition, social justice with revenge. He had learned to be in the deepest shadow when the diva sang that final aria over the body of the dead Prince Turol. That was when Donal's professional instincts failed and unearthly grief poured through him.

Afterward, the diva returned to the hotel to rest, and while she remained there, Donal walked the streets around the Exemplar. Once he saw a dark Vixen among the purple cabs and remembered the automobile that had been parked near the Energy Authority complex that time, more than a week ago.

It was an unusual vehicle but not unique, and by the time he drew near, the lights had changed. Donal saw nothing of the driver as the Vixen drove off.

After darkness fell, it was time for the diva to return to the Théâtre du Loup Mort. Once again the limo, bracketed by two unmarked cars and two cruisers, made its way across midtown.

At this hour the traffic was heavy, and Donal had

insisted that Levison and Duquesne—the department's finest shot in close conditions—ride in the limo with the diva. She had been furious, calming only when Levison asked her about what breathing techniques she used to hold such a range of tones.

To Donal, the change of subject seemed forced and obvious, but something in the way Levison did it—as always—let the conversation flow the way he wanted. Perhaps it was just that Lev was so focused. You knew he *absolutely* wanted to learn the answers to his questions.

The Brodowski Brothers were out front tonight—"We had to change position, Lieutenant. All that flesh, we couldn't concentrate." Donal went through the drill, checking the windows in the opposite buildings, scanning the crowds for unusual body language.

This was the third night in a row. It was beginning to feel like routine.

Dangerously like routine.

To the family who had seats in the top-right box, plush and comfortable, Donal pretended he was part of the theater management, here to see that everything was just right for valued guests. The husband preened, his chest swelling as he told his boys that influence was what life was all about.

His wife nodded quietly, absorbing everything, but there might have been an amused sparkle in her eyes as the family took their seats. The children looked more like her, which Donal could only think of as a good thing.

The lights dimmed.

Drums rolled, and the orchestra began the overture.

The first two acts proceeded with the same magic as before. During the intermission, Donal walked around the auditorium and went backstage. Everything looked clear.

No. Check again.

Because he felt as if he were going through the motions. This was *serious*. So Donal backtracked, checking every stagehand and performer he walked past. He checked the overhead scaffolding and the spaces behind curtains. He went back out into the auditorium, using the internal staircase, taking a tour of all the boxes.

Still clear.

Intermission over, the audience filed back into their seats. Donal remained at ground level, standing by the door with one of the ushers. When the third act commenced, Donal remained in the shadows, captivated as before by the diva's performance.

He applauded along with everybody else, and when the fourth act proceeded to Prince Turol's inevitable death, he was even more stricken than before. With the prince's body draped across the stone bench where he had declared his love to Lady Arla, the diva stood and faced the audience.

Hands spread wide, she commenced the aria, and that was when it happened.

Something black moved through the air, and every member of the audience sat rigid.

Donal did not react.

The small group of singers onstage, the prince's erstwhile allies who had betrayed him, were frozen like statues... but the diva continued to sing, not realizing anything was wrong.

But a second later, the first three rows of spectators stood up *in exact unison,* as if they were a single body. Donal could do nothing but watch, frozen as all the rest. The front row took a step forward, and the next two rows began to file out into the aisles, their footsteps in time.

A note faltered in the aria.

Trance. Have to—

When all the standing people were free of their seats, the entire aggregate, some hundred men and women, took a single step forward. And another.

Like the start of some macabre dance.

—break it.

Ensorcelled, the hundred people advanced, blankness in their eyes. The music died and the diva's voice trailed away. She stood paralyzed: not by a spell but by fear.

This was what had happened in the other theaters. Some part of Donal's captured mind realized that every report and article he had read in preparation had been a lie. Any power great enough to ensorcell a hundred people in public had enough capability to alter the memories of everyone here.

Something clicked inside Donal.

NO.

It felt like a sound, a wooden click inside his head as the trance training broke in, and sheets of ice seemed to slide away from his body, and then he was free.

Move.

Donal crouched, scanning the auditorium, but everyone—even his officers, even Petrov, who was in theory trance-shielded—was frozen in place.

Move now.

The orchestra remained unmoving. But a hundred people were advancing as Donal sprinted across the intervening space and leaped into the orchestra pit, heading for the stage.

It was like some sort of signal: every musician's head swiveled toward Donal, eyes dead. Hands reached for him, but he elbowed a cellist in the temple, thrust-kicked a woman violinist out of his way, and grabbed the edge of the stage.

He pulled himself up, kicked out at grasping hands, and rolled up into a crouch.

"Come on! Maria!"

The use of her first name seemed to break the diva's stasis. She whipped her gaze from side to side, breathing fast in panic, and backed away with shuffling steps. Behind her, the prince sat up, and the other performers took a synchronized step forward.

Shit.

Donal ran to the diva, grabbed her around the waist, and said, "We have to run. Do you understand?"

"Yes..."

He wanted to tell her to stop taking shallow breaths, but then something, perhaps her singer's training, made the diva take a single deep, calming breath as she kicked off her shoes.

"Which way?"

"Left."

Donal kept his arm around the diva's waist as they ran to the side of the stage and through the wing, where a stagehand reached out and Donal whipped an uppercut elbow under the man's chin. Then they were sprinting past, clattering down the steps, and reaching a fire exit. Donal kicked the bar mechanism open.

There was a dark alleyway outside, but three men reached out from behind them—spear-holders from the previous scene—and grabbed the diva's gown.

Donal spun, throwing a hard overhead left into the side of the nearest man's neck—*got it*—and that man was down, but more were advancing in the shadows. Donal kicked the second man in the knee, collapsing the leg, then grabbed hold of the man's head and twisted him aside.

The diva was struggling with the last man, but Donal whipped his Magnus from his shoulder holster and hammered the butt into the back of the man's neck, dropping him.

"Come on."

A hand reached from the floor—one of the fallen men—but Donal stamped down, heard a liquid crunch, and then he was pulling the diva through the exit.

Out in the alley, he crouched. A man at the corner, who had been walking by, now shivered and took a stiff step into the alleyway.

Ensorcelled.

Thanatos. How far can one spell spread?

"This way."

Donal ran, around the back of the theater with the diva keeping pace. The ground was cold and hard, and she was in bare feet. They skirted shards of broken glass, remnants of a dropped beer bottle that sparkled with reflected light.

In front of them was another alleyway: too narrow for them to walk side by side, and one hell of a potential trap, but there was no choice. Donal ran first, dragging the diva along.

Then they were out onto the sidewalk of 92nd Street.

Bright lights, moving cars, and a crowd of passersby: for maybe twenty seconds it seemed as though they were safe. Donal was starting to flag down a purple cab when he saw a group of Zurinese tourists, cameras in hand, shudder and grow blank-eyed.

The ensorcelled tourists turned their attention on the diva.

She's the locus.

Wherever they went, the trancing spell would coalesce and fall upon anyone who could see her. It was like some kind of infection. Donal batted aside a tourist's grasping hands and tugged the diva—"Ow!"—into motion.

Her ivory gown had slipped and Donal caught a peek

of her breast—Hades, there was *no* time for this—and
then he spotted a stone pillar wider than a man, across
the street on Hoardway.

Donal reholstered his gun, took hold of the diva's left
wrist, and ducked under. He straightened up with her
weight across his shoulders in a fireman's carry.

"Hold on."

Then he ran.

Horns blared and someone shouted, then two cars
crunched together in a shower of broken glass as ensorcelled drivers turned their attention to the fleeing pair.
But Donal had run every day for twenty years, and a
kind of joy flared through him as he dodged the vehicles,
leaped up onto the opposite sidewalk, kicked out—
hard, despite the diva's weight on his shoulders—and a
heavy man fell.

Twenty more yards, then Donal crouched down, almost throwing the diva off him as he felt for his wallet,
got it, and pulled out his badge. He slammed it against
the stone slot.

The metal door moved, revealing steps leading down.

"You first." Donal pushed the diva inside. "Hurry."

Blood shimmered on the diva's bare foot. She might
slip, but there was no choice. Donal pushed her again,
but gently, then followed her inside and worked the
door mechanism. Dozens of people were advancing, and
the door was slow—

Shit shit shit.

—but it closed in time. For now they were clear.

"They're going to—to—"

"No. Keep moving. Distance and stone will shield us."

It was the only thing that would stop the ensorcellment: getting clear of people.

"Where to?"

"Just keep going."

It took maybe two minutes to reach the rough-carved tunnel at the foot of the stairs.

"Is this—where are we, Detective? The catacombs?"

"Call me Donal. And, yeah, this is the catacombs."

They moved along at something between a fast walk and a jog. Donal would have preferred to move faster, but the diva couldn't maintain the pace.

Sound...

Donal stopped dead.

"What's wrong, De—Donal?"

A distant rumble emanated from somewhere up ahead.

"We need to go back the other way. Now."

"Oh..."

The diva broke into a stumbling half jog as he pulled her back along the tunnel and took a turn to the right. After a moment she pulled away from him but continued staggering forward.

"Don't you even know your way around?"

"Not these particular catacombs."

"Shit."

That sounded un-divalike.

The city's catacombs weren't all joined up, but any given network was likely to stretch for miles. Occasionally they linked through to the hypoway or sewage system.

In the distance, a thump sounded.

"Can you go faster?"

"Oh, Hades..."

"Can you?"

"Yes."

Here, some sarcophagi were so ancient they seemed mere geological bumps in stone. Others looked freshly carved, just decades old. Donal and the diva ran past them.

Do you feel the bones?

Donal shuddered. "Ugh."

"What is it?"

"Nothing. Run."

They moved faster.

Do you kiss her bones?

Terrible feelings tugged at Donal as they passed into a wider cavern. Odd, fragmented images assaulted him. There was *hunger*, as if every cell in his body needed to absorb . . . something.

Or do you taste the song?

But then they were through the worst of it, leaving the sarcophagi behind. A closed ceramic door in front of them bore a red mu-sigma-tau logo on an alpha-shaped shield. The Municipal Subterranean Transport Authority.

Once again the emergency lock responded as Donal rammed his police badge into the slot. He leaned back, tugging at the door until it groaned and began to shift.

"You first."

"It's dark."

"I know. Go."

The diva stepped inside and Donal followed, hauling the door shut. There was a soft pressure wave against his face as the door clicked. They were into the subway system, and it was total blackness.

"Grab my hand. Okay, stretch out with the other hand, with your fingertips."

"All right."

"Feel anything?"

"No."

"With me, then."

Donal led the way. There were no obstacles until his reaching hand felt for the tunnel wall and found it.

For a long time—or maybe just ten minutes—they traveled like this, until his fingertips touched a sheet of heavy, flexible material that might have been rubber. It formed a curtain to hold out dust.

Donal found a vertical slit in the sheet and pulled it open. His eyes blinked, stinging at the sensation of distant light.

"Safe . . ." murmured the diva.

"Perhaps." Donal helped her through. "Let's try to stay out of sight. There are MSTA workers over there."

"The ensorcellment—"

"Can reach down here." Donal's tone was rough.

"What can we do, then? Will it wear off?"

"Not while you're alive." Donal took hold of her shoulders. "Trust me, all right? I'm going to find somewhere isolated with a telephone. One call, and they'll be flying in federal spellbinders from Fortinium. The feds can break any enchantment there is."

"All right."

"They can have a chopper airborne in minutes. What I need is—"

"A phone. That way?"

"That way."

There was a flat cart on a dark section of the subway track. Donal thought the cart might be called a bogey, although in the orphanage a bogey was something you picked from your nose, synonymous with *booger.*

At any rate, the cart looked as though it drew power from the rail. It was obviously for maintenance, but there were workers farther along, in the lighted area, and Donal did not want to steal the thing unless it was necessary.

Flying headlong through darkness, possibly straight into an oncoming train, was not the kind of safety he'd promised the diva.

Her hand grasped his upper arm and squeezed: a primate response, a youngster clinging to an adult for protection.

Just then a hammering series of thumps echoed down the corridor, and a thunderous compressor started up. Several pneumatic drills, powered by the compressor, added their own noisy contribution to the din.

Donal and the diva continued to advance along the dusty tunnel, keeping away from the live rail. Finally they reached a length of platform on the right: an unused station. Beyond stood portable floodlights and a big compressor, with the workmen farther inside the tunnel.

Do you hear the bones?

In the cacophony, some strange combinations of tones must have—No. Donal pushed that from his mind. He had work to do.

He climbed onto the deserted platform and pulled the diva up after him. They moved into a short corridor, looking for a maintenance engineer's office, and that was when Donal bumped straight into a barrel-chested mustachioed man.

Hades...

Donal slammed the palms of both hands against the man's body, knocking him against the hard ceramic-tiled wall, then ripped an uppercut elbow, harder than a punch, into the man's sternum. The big man fell, his mouth working like a landed fish.

He lay there, groaning.

Donal considered tying the man up, but there was nothing obvious in sight for the task, and they had to move fast. He stepped over the man and pulled open a plain door. An office. An empty phone socket was on the wall, round and black like a mocking eye.

"Why..."

This was the diva.

"What is it?"

"...don't you kill him?" Hand shaking, she pointed at the fallen man.

If the bastard wakes up, we're done for.

Donal had no proof, but he had an idea that if the ensorcellment took hold of this man, it increased the chances that the maintenance team farther down the tunnel would change, slip into trance, and that would be the end.

"Is he the enemy?"

"I . . . I don't know."

A blue-and-white schematic was pinned to the wall, and a true-scale map lay flat on a worktable.

She didn't even remember my name.

Irrelevant. He had to work out where they were and where they could go.

Not until I told her again.

This seemed to be an unused branch off the 23rd Street Line.

She's probably forgotten already.

Donal traced the intersections. Police HQ was less than two miles away, but there was *no* tunnel in the right direction. It would take three changes—no, four—to reach the place.

Every crowded train, every packed platform en route, would contain a multitude capable of transforming into murderous parazombies.

"Shit shit shit."

"What's wrong, D-Donald?"

He hated being called Donald.

"Nothing." He could see it now. "We've got a route out of here."

But the man on the floor was looking up at them.

Thanatos.

Donal kicked the man in the temple.

"Y-You said he wasn't the enemy."

"Yeah. But"—Donal stared down at the unconscious man: overweight, his breathing unsteady—"they might be able to see through his eyes."

Donal thought back. He had said nothing about where they might run. The small logo on the map, the skull-and-Ouroboros, did not particularly stand out. If the enemy had linked in to the man's perceptions, they would not know...unless they could read the man's own knowledge of where he was.

"We're moving now."

Ten minutes later they were on the bogey, using its head-lights now that they'd rounded a bend in the tunnel. They sped south, Donal keeping the throttle handle pushed all the way.

At some point they hurtled through another aban-doned station where men were working. Several heads looked up, but then they were through.

The diva placed her cheek against his shoulder.

Ha.

Earlier, she'd paid no attention to the man who'd risk everything to protect her, but now...

Do you taste the song?

...he had to pay attention, that was all, and he counted unused stations as they passed through them. These were truly abandoned, save for a twenty-foot white snake curled up on one of the platforms.

Then Donal cut back the power, letting the bogey de-celerate by friction. A faint patch of pale gray up ahead was growing brighter.

They coasted to a halt.

Here stood a clean platform, its indirect lighting growing stronger as Donal and the diva climbed from the bogey. Was this in use? There were no exits up to ground level—not according to the map he'd seen—but perhaps freight slugs used these places.

"Where are we?"

Donal pointed. Where the station name should have

been, an Ouroboros worm encircled a skull, headband-like, swallowing its own tail.

"Energy Authority," he said. "Downtown Complex."

"Is it safe?"

"I hope so." At the platform's end, Donal saw a man-sized door bearing a smaller version of the logo. "I sure as Hades hope so."

6

They passed along a horizontal shaft and came out at the edge of the vast cavernous complex. Rows of huge reactors stretched back, filling the immense dark space.

A million fingers seemed to slide across Donal's skin, and the diva moaned.

"There's shielding here," Donal whispered. "Look. See up there?"

He pointed to a small shape set high on the left-hand wall: the director's office. His fingertip traced the path of the rising black iron staircase that led upward.

"All right." The diva clasped his upper arm, released it.

They stepped into an aisle and commenced walking. It was more like a roadway, and they kept to the left, walking close to each reactor base, as they moved from one pile to another. No one was—

Damn.

A man in a bulky protective suit was working on a reactor casing, maybe twenty yards down the cross aisle to the right. But he didn't look up, and then Donal and the diva were past.

"He didn't notice us," the diva whispered.

Donal lowered his voice to a murmur, which was less likely to carry. "His protective gear. It might have blocked the spell."

It had been part of what he'd counted on, taking her to this place.

They walked on, passing seven more reactor piles, and the staircase up to the director's office was within sprinting distance when everything went to Hades. Four men in gray coveralls stepped directly into their path.

"Um...hi. I'm Lieutenant Riordan, here to see..."

But their eyes were blank. Donal glanced at the diva. Her pale, beautiful face was bone-white now.

Had she noticed that the men didn't shudder when they saw her? Almost as if they were *already* en—

"Move it." Donal whipped a circular kick into the first man's thigh, paralyzing the leg and dropping the man. He punched the second man twice, then grabbed hold of the diva and ran, pulling her *through* the foursome, raking another man's eyes, and then they were clear.

"Fast..."

They began to accelerate, but then a larger group—seven, eight men—was blocking their way. Donal stopped, looked back—reinforcements there as well—and dragged the diva sideways, quickly, jerking her arm in its socket, pulling her into a cross aisle—

No.

—and stopped, because the way down here was blocked too.

"I'm sorry."

Every route was a no-go.

Donal's shirt was soaked with sweat. He'd run hard, but the diva...Her feet were bloody, her dress ripped, and yet her face and body were the most sublime creation of the universe. She was so beautiful.

"Save me, D-D—Please. Save me."

Donal swallowed and pulled out his Magnus. He raised it up, lowered it, and squeezed off a shot. The diva yelped at the loud bang.

One of the men fell.

He was innocent...

But the other ensorcelled men did not hesitate. They continued to walk toward Donal, closing in from both ends of the aisle. Donal glanced upward. It might be possible for him to scale the side of the reactor... but with the diva? No chance.

Thanatos.

Donal fired into the advancing group, swiveled fast, and shot down two more men from the other contingent.

Then both groups swelled with reinforcements, more men wearing Energy Authority coveralls, bearing heavy shotguns. Now they had no chance.

Donal lowered his Magnus.

"Save..."

Do you taste the song?

"...me."

There were six rounds left in the magazine before he needed to reload. There were more than twenty men advancing on him; half were armed with shotguns that could blast him into redberry spray. It was over.

The men advanced closer.

"Please..."

Donal was tempted to ask the diva if she remembered his name. Such a petty thought to have before dying, before his personal universe blanked out, like wiping down a blackboard back in the orphanage school.

He remembered Sister Mary-Anne Styx drilling him in math and bandaging him after he took down the three bigger boys who—

The men shuffled to a halt.

What's happening?

One group parted slightly, allowing another figure to advance. The man was narrow-bodied, with a gray goatee, and Donal had a bad feeling he should have expected this all along. It was Malfax Cortindo, director of this place.

There was nothing blank about Cortindo's dark and sparkling eyes. Nothing blank at all.

"Ah, Lieutenant. How nice to—Careful."

As Donal's Magnus came up, all the ensorcelled men who bore shotguns brought them to bear on the diva. With the two groups facing each other, the men were likely to blow away one another's legs at best, but ensorcelled men care nothing for their own safety.

They were kamikaze pawns.

Donal lowered his gun, then let go. It clattered on the flagstones.

"Did I come here of my own free will?" He hadn't intended to say this out loud.

"Aren't our own motivations"—Malfax Cortindo's voice was courtly, devoid of tension—"an eternal mystery to us all?"

"Screw you."

"Oh, please." The derringer that Malfax Cortindo pulled from his silk-vest pocket was a gleaming antique. The ends of its twin abbreviated barrels were dark, malevolent. "A sense of style, if you would."

Cortindo swung the derringer around to face the diva.

"Time to die, my loveliness."

Do you feel the song?

"No."

That was the moment.

Do you touch the bones?

The ensorcelled men held their shotguns steady, but that was not the reason. In the name of Death, fear could never be the reason.

But that was the moment.

"S-Save . . ."

"He can't."

The moment when Donal could have moved.

Do you taste the . . .

The derringer banged, flashed strontium-red.

Crimson was the spray of drops from that pure ivory neck as the diva spun, toppling to the stone floor as arterial blood arced forth.

And died.

. . . bones?

Too late.

The moment when—

A second shot, red flame, flat bang, a third eye appearing in the diva's forehead . . .

—when Donal could have saved her, but it was too late, would always be too late, a lifetime and a universe beyond the second when he could have acted and made a difference.

"No!"

. . . and dark blood pooled, spreading from her shattered skull.

Then Donal *did* move.

He flowed into motion, and Malfax Cortindo circled, fast with the pa-kua moves, but he wasn't the only one to have studied the internal arts. Donal followed with a palm change of his own, flipping the derringer aside, then stabbed fingertips into Cortindo's eyes, whipped an elbow into the bastard's throat and a knee below the ribs, targeting the spleen and finding it.

Wrapping one arm around Cortindo's neck, Donal spun, keeping their bodies close like lovers, because that's how fulcrums work. Donal whipped him toward the flagstones, and Cortindo was down.

The ensorcelled men were frozen.

Do you feel the . . .

Down but not dead. Cortindo was a threat. Donal raised his knee.

. . . song?

And stamped down.

Hard.

All around, ensorcelled men dropped and lay sprawled on the hard floor in thaumaturgic coma. Not dead.

Only Malfax Cortindo and the diva were corpses now.

Expected me to save her.

Donal wiped hot fluid from his face. It might have been sweat; it might have been blood.

To save her. Couldn't even remember . . .

It was blood. Some injury he hadn't noticed getting.

Bitch couldn't remember my name.

But she was so beautiful, even now, splayed with eyes open on eternity, pale skin splashed with red, that fine dress soaked with the hot slick fluid of life. While all around, the reactors seemed to glow black, to howl silence.

Do you hear the bones?

Slowly, slowly, Donal retrieved his Magnus and reholstered, all without removing his gaze from the diva, the beautiful diva.

He squatted down beside her perfect form.

So lovely.

Donal slid his hands beneath her body.

Perfection.

Steadied himself.

Do you taste the . . .

And then he pushed himself up to standing, the limp weight of her across his arms. He took one step and then another, and then they were leaving this place for good.

. . . song?

He used the personal elevator that he remembered from before, standing proud with the diva in his arms, one of her arms dangling, as the steel disk rose through the shaft.

Then it shuddered to a halt inside the dome formed of black flanges. The metal folded back on itself. Donal was in the small enclosed courtyard.

In the internal wall, an iron door stood half open, two men collapsed on the ground beside it. Like their comrades below, they were the ex-ensorcelled, so deep into coma that only thaumaturgic intervention could save them.

But that was not Donal's concern.

Perfection.

He stepped over the fallen men, carrying the diva into the larger courtyard, where three finned black cars were parked, each with a raised black skull-and-Ouroboros on the doors. No one was moving.

Half-squatting, Donal tried the door handle of the nearest car. It clicked open.

Good.

So he carried her around to the rear, his perfect diva, half-squatted again to twist the handle—*careful, don't drop her*—and stood back as the trunk lid rose up. Then, with perfect care and a tender smile, he rolled the diva's wonderful body into the trunk.

And slammed the lid down.

Donal went to the gatehouse, where he found two more slumped men. Three sets of car keys hung from hooks, and he took them all. Then he wrenched down the series of brass levers that would cause the outer gates to open.

Crossing back to the car, he tried the keys, and the second set fit. The huge steel gates were groaning back as Donal walked over to a drain in the ground and dropped the two remaining sets of keys through the grille. There were two viscous splashes in darkness.

He climbed into the car, pushed the skull-embossed

lever into first, and drove forward through the huge gates while they were still opening, then turned onto the empty road where derelict buildings stared at him.

Overhead, the sky pulsed dark purple as he drove.

It took two hours to clear the central Tristopolitan districts, using backstreets and odd alleyways where possible, staying off the main grid. Donal kept under the speed limit, drove courteously . . .

So beautiful.

. . . and tried to keep his attention on his driving, despite the flawless wonder in the trunk of his car. It was difficult, and he wanted to stop and allow the stupefied trance to swallow him. He needed to go back to touch his beauty . . . but not yet. Not yet.

Beautiful.

And not just beautiful, but *his;* wasn't that the point?

Once past the city limits, Donal turned the car toward Black Iron Forest, where few people ventured and fewer lived. Perhaps that was why the orphanage had never sold the cabin for their own gain, or perhaps it was Sister Mary-Anne Styx who had arranged things to Donal's advantage.

Although Donal's parents had died when he was a week old, his grandfather, dour and solitary, had survived for thirteen more years. Unwilling to raise a grandchild, he nevertheless acknowledged Donal. When Jack Riordan died a year before Donal's "graduation" from the orphanage—before they kicked him out on his fourteenth birthday—Donal received title to the cabin, plus the small amount of savings that had allowed him to continue in school and work toward the military entrance exams.

As far as Donal knew, none of his department colleagues was aware of the place. He had never mentioned it, rarely visited, and for sure had never brought anyone here.

Not until now.

The long car growled along ever-darkening roads, the trees becoming odd-patterned shadows against night, twisting perspective. There was a long period when Donal drove without any conscious thought, lost in beautiful dreams—*oh, my diva*—and when he came back into the moment, he was entering the Dispersed Vale.

They—he and the dead diva—were deep inside Black Iron Forest now. Someone would have discovered the mess back at the Downtown Complex. Scene-of-crime diviners might already be at work.

The time when he could have given it up and returned to police HQ was hours past.

It's all right, my love.

It was better when the path was clear, all choice removed.

The time on the skull clock—the hands fashioned in the form of slender bones: one femur, one radius—passed twenty-five o'clock. It was the early hours of the morning.

He continued to drive.

Eldritch howls and half-perceived shadows with amber eyes moved in the darkness. Donal branched off the already-narrow forest road onto the Tartrous Trail, dropping his speed. Grit seemed to have gathered in his eyes.

By four A.M., he was in familiar surroundings. Donal drove the car quietly down to a clearing and stopped.

And waited.

He switched the engine off.

* * *

Lost in trance for a time, Donal eventually came to. He inhaled, then forced himself to move, pushing the car door open and stepping out onto dark mud. The sky was a featureless purple. Looking downslope, he could see the lake.

It was a massive shadow that would never grow lighter. The lake had no name, and its waters were permanently black, perpetually still. Donal had never seen it any other way.

He walked to a wide silvery tree that stood on a hillock, dragging a key out of his pocket. Donal inserted the key into a knothole in the bark. There was a hesitation, then a cracking sound.

The slope's mulch slid back to reveal the cabin's steel windows and the carved blackwood door.

Grandfather Jack's legacy.

Donal opened up the front door, then went back to the car and hauled the dear diva from the trunk. Gently he carried her to the cabin, *their* cabin, and laid her down on the long dining table.

He snapped the flint switches on two oil lamps. Their yellowish light danced and flickered before growing strong and steady.

Perfect ...

No. There was work to be done.

Forcing himself not to look at the perfection spread out upon the table, Donal looked around the low-ceilinged room, avoiding the overhead beams, searching for something heavy.

He stopped when he came across an old Zurinese stone skull, some beloved totem of his miserable old grandfather Jack, who had never come to visit his grandson, never mind take him away from the prison that was ...

Irrelevant now.

So beautiful.

Stone skull in hand, Donal made his way downslope to the car. He pushed down the trunk lid and climbed into the driver's seat, the skull in his lap as he drove in first gear, bypassing a large tree root. Then he stopped but left the engine running.

Directly below, the nameless lake was thick and dark as ever.

Donal slid out from the driver's seat, jammed the stone skull down on the accelerator, let go of the clutch pedal, and leaped back. The car bumped its way down toward the waiting lake.

It's going to stall.

For a second Donal thought he had failed, but then the car was over the edge into the lake with a heavy plop, no more. Black water surrounded the car's roof, pulling it under, and then it was gone.

One long curved wave moved across the viscous surface like a satisfied smile, then attenuated into nothingness. Lake and forest had returned to dark normalcy.

After a moment, Donal turned and made his way back to the cabin. To the object of his dreams.

For the next three days and nights there was no sleep—no true sleep—for Donal. He slid in and out of strange half-waking dreams, where the diva sang arias that were purely his, amid impossible white sands by a quicksilver sea born of the memory of that other artist, Jamix Holandson, whose dead bone Donal had touched.

But it was the diva who remained with him, laid out on the long table beneath the low ceiling, her flesh pure and radiant ivory.

So beautiful.

Donal washed the wounds and scraped dried blood from perfect skin—a spatula from the kitchen served for that. He cut away the bloodied portions of her dress—*oh, Thanatos, such perfection*—and wrapped a white bedsheet around her body.

Afterward, he pulled the only armchair close, turned it away from the table, and used it to kneel upon, his forearms across the chair's back. He contemplated the drying perfection of his desire.

Soon she would be ready for the flensing.

Do you hear the bones?

Not every moment was spent in contemplation. For the beautiful dark act to take place, it was necessary that the diva—and Donal—remain undisturbed. So he was able to drag himself into the kitchen, drinking cold canned soup as he dug through the old toolbox and equipment chest.

In a forest such as this, Grandfather Jack had needed to prepare for dangerous times. There were thirteen old iron life-wards: narrow, heavy objects the length of his forearm, ending in a rough spike so they could be jammed into the ground.

Designed primarily to ward off packs of deathwolves, the devices would repel all living organisms above the level of plants.

The life-wards were heavy as Donal lugged them outside. When he pushed them into the hard soil and leaned on them, the life-wards' spikes slid easily into place. It took an hour—as far as he could tell; time seemed to be moving strangely—to set them all in place, in a rough ring around the cabin.

As the last ward entered the soil, a great shimmering hemisphere descended, shielding the entire cabin from invasion.

Safe.

Donal went back in to contemplate the diva.

After a long, rapt period, Donal shook himself into awareness. He was kneeling on the reversed armchair. When he pushed himself to standing, his sinews ached with unaccustomed use.

He wiped his hand across his face, feeling rough stubble. Then he moved toward the bathroom, and each step was hot agony.

Finishing, he drank brackish water from the faucet. Then he walked, still in pain but with more mobility, to the kitchen. He opened another can of soup, took three cold sips from it, and put it down.

There was something important he had to do.

What is it?

The toolbox.

From it, Donal drew the rusted scythe that Grandfather Jack once used to cut back the tall, dark grasses. He found the stone sharpening block, poured seven drops of moth oil upon it, and began the long, careful process of sharpening the scythe.

Soon the flesh would begin to soften with a hint of liquefaction.

Beautiful. So ...

Then, only then, Donal could begin the slicing and cleansing process, which would culminate when he polished those dear bones, one by one, with every ounce of skill he possessed.

Donal worked until he could stand it no more: the presence of perfection in the next room while he scraped blade against stone in here.

He went back into the lounge and resumed his kneeling position upon the armchair, contemplating the diva laid out upon his table.

So perfect ...

And that was the position he was in, kneeling and frozen in rapt awe, when the front door blew apart in splinters and the windows exploded inward.

No ...

Dark-clad troopers in hexlar armor stormed inside, dropping to crouch, some rolling and coming up with weapons trained on Donal.

You cannot ...

Donal's hand moved toward his shoulder holster.

... have her!

He clasped the butt of his Magnus, drawing it out.

And in that moment a woman clad in a pale-gray skirt suit stepped through the splintered remnants of the doorway. She raised a heavy dart gun, aimed at Donal's heart.

The world was moving so slowly.

"Too late."

She fired.

The ceiling spun past and he was flat on the floor, limbs rigid, ribs paralyzed, scarcely breathing. Darkness circled and shifted around the edges of his vision.

"How . . ." It was so hard to speak. "Wards . . ."

"That was your mistake. They're *life*-wards."

The woman leaned over him and brushed back her white-blond hair with one gloved hand. Donal's lips moved to ask the next question, but only a gasp came out.

"The ward shield keeps out"—she smiled—"only living beings."

Donal's eyes shifted toward the troopers.

"Oh, *they're* alive, all right." The woman tapped Donal's forehead with one finger. "It's me you didn't count on."

Darkness was closing in.

"—take the diva and—" was all he could hear of the troopers' voices.

A hush surrounded Donal, blanketing him.

No. She's mine.

Even the air was thicker, viscous. It was difficult to drag the stuff into his lungs.

Do you hear the . . .

Silence.

A shadow fist closed around the world and snuffed it out.

8

Delirium followed chaotic dream followed a thrashing in his bed, limbs screaming with pain as Donal—or the near-mindless thing that had been Donal—fought against the restraints and howled. Then he would lapse into comatose darkness.

Afterward, liquid fire would spread along each fine nerve, igniting it with agony, as the cycle of torture began again.

For nine long days and nights, nurses with vertically slitted eyes watched over Donal, their skins shifting through hues of violet as Donal's writhing body threw back refracted energy from the thaumaturgic field. They were immune to the field's effects: Night Sisters with delicate fangs and elegant limbs, revealing hints of their feline aspect.

They watched and cared for him.

On the tenth night, something burst inside Donal, something in his mind...and he gave a great agonized gasp and fell back, slipping into peaceful sleep. Above him, the ten-foot-long shield casting the healing field glowed strongly and then began to fade. The thaumaturgic field shifted hue and became a pale-blue volume that smelled of ozone and lilacs.

Two of the Night Sisters looked at each other, the vertical slits of their eyes growing more circular as the light faded once more.

"He'll be fine, don't you think?"

"Yes. You did a good job, Sister Felice."

"Thank you. Shall I phone the commander, or do you—"

"I'll let you make the call."

The younger Night Sister, the one known as Sister Felice, walked along the central aisle of the shadowed ward. The room was in darkness save for one of the beds, which glimmered with a sapphire glow: radiant energy from an ensorcelled victim trapped deep within the paralyzing influence of a deathmoth's bite.

Other sleeping forms were just lumps beneath the bedclothes, unmoving, while tiny monitor sprites hovered over each pillow, ready to flare with brightness should any vital signs drop below the parameters that the Night Sisters had set.

In the nursing station, Sister Felice picked up the phone. With one long retractable fingernail, she rotated all ten combination wheels to a memorized sequence. She listened for the ring. Though it was the middle of the night, someone picked up the phone immediately at the other end.

"Hello?"

"Is this Commander Laura Steele?"

"Yes."

"You wanted to know when a patient called Lieutenant Riordan underwent a phase shift in his condition?"

"What's happened?"

"It's an improvement, not a decline. Although, not having died in the first three days, he had a good chance of—"

"He's going to live?"

"Yes, that's—"

A burr sounded.

Sister Felice held out the receiver.

"You're welcome." Her voice was a predator's whisper. She put the receiver down.

On the seventeenth day—after Donal had woken for an hour at a time, three times in twenty-five hours—Sister Felice hauled him from the bed, onto a wheelchair whose frame was formed of interlocking silver heptagrams.

"For luck," she murmured, as Donal ran his fingertips along the soft metal. "And for healing."

"Where..." His voice was a croak. "Going...where?"

"Rehabituation." Sister Felice pushed the chair into motion. "Don't believe what they say about mystical therapists."

She let go of the chair's handles and walked in front, heading through open double doors and into an empty corridor. The wheelchair trundled after her, bearing Donal's pain-racked form.

"What do they...say?"

"Oh"—Sister Felice looked back over her shoulder at him—"that they're evil and sadistic and delight in torturing you until you scream."

They continued on until they came to a floating handshape sign hanging in midair in a five-way intersection of corridors.

"Rehab," said Sister Felice loudly.

The hand swung left.

"Everything moves around in this place." She shook her head, then headed into the indicated corridor. "Come along."

The wheelchair followed.

"The...therapists." Donal's voice was tight, but he had to ask. "Don't...torture patients?"

"Oh, they torture you, all right." Sister Felice slowed

before a set of black opaque doors labeled *RD*. "It's just they don't enjoy doing it."

Then she grinned, showing needle-fine white fangs.

"Only kidding."

The doors swung open of their own accord, and Sister Felice stepped aside as Donal's wheelchair rolled forward and took him into Rehab.

A soft feminine chuckle sounded as the doors closed behind him.

"Ah, so you're our latest vic—patient." The androgyne in white tunic and trousers had wide shoulders and ten-inch-long fingers. A smile stretched its long features. "That's our little joke. Don't you worry."

"Thanatos." Donal was not up to this.

"All right, my name's Jan, and the first thing we have to do is restore some basic thought and movement patterns. You with me?"

"Uh, if you say s—"

A strangled gargling sound came from one corner of the Rehabituation Department. Donal was confused by the strange geometric shapes of apparatus designed for Hades-knew-what functions, but then he saw the patient trapped inside.

Gross distortions rippled across the man's body. His right hand flared to maybe four feet in length, and he moaned in pain.

Then, just for a second, his whole form pancaked outward to ten or twelve feet in diameter, amoebalike, before retracting into a normal human shape. The man bent forward on his couch, retching. Another androgynous therapist held a cardboard bowl beneath the man's mouth.

"That's Andy"—Jan used one frighteningly long finger to indicate the patient—"and the therapist is Alyx."

"Very good," Alyx was murmuring to the wretched Andy.

"Are you trying to tear him apart?" Donal felt an urge to get off his wheelchair and run, but when he commanded his muscles to move, only hot pain resulted. "You're killing him."

"No. Relax." Jan ran its long fingers, ending in soft padded tips, down Donal's face. "Andy's been infected with an attenuation field. We're teaching him to hold himself together."

"Oh." Donal's eyelids fluttered.

Again Andy's hands ballooned, the right more than the left, and his face grew larger and larger.

"See the natural precursor to complete expansion?" Jan gestured, and Donal's wheelchair rolled closer to Andy's couch. "That's how your nervous system views the world, in terms of touch. The hand and face are more sensitive than—"

All of Andy's body started to rip outward, to flow across the room, but Alyx shouted at him, "*No!* Pull yourself together!"

"Can't..."

"Now."

With a whimper, Andy sucked his body back into normal configuration. Then he looked over at Donal and gave a tiny smile, ignoring the tears flowing on either side of his mouth. "Some people would pay good money for this."

"I'd pay a shitload to be somewhere else."

"Don't"—a painful ripple spread across Andy's chest and face—"make me laugh."

Then Donal's chair swiveled away. It was time for his treatment to begin.

Back in the ward, body aching in what might have been a good way—Donal hovered in that strange place between hurt and joy—he was sitting up beside the bed in a hard wooden chair when he heard strange voices coming from the nurses' station.

"... Commander? I'm not sure he's up to it yet."

"But it's just me, and I'll keep it low key."

"You mean"—this was Sister Felice's voice, and she gave a soft hiss before continuing—"the both of you?"

After a moment: "Very perceptive, Sister. I can see that Lieutenant Riordan is in good hands."

"Ha. Come this way."

Sister Felice came walking down the wide aisle between the beds, her feline eyes slitted, her ears flattened against the sides of her head, and her hair flowing straight back, not hanging down. Behind her walked the pale woman who had shot Donal with the dart gun, wearing a pale-blue skirt suit today, with dark-blue gloves. And behind her...

Something?

"Yes." Sister Felice bared her delicate fangs. "That's right, Donal. Call me if you need anything." She placed a green stone in his hand. "Squeeze it, and I'll be here in a second."

Behind the woman, the air rippled. But if Donal turned his head and closed his eyes nearly all the way, the wavering became almost human-shape.

"Thank you," he told Sister Felice. "You're the best."

"I know." She gave a soft laugh. "Remember, you just need to squeeze the callstone."

Then she walked away, silent and elegant. Both Donal and the pale woman watched her go. After a moment, the woman said, "Do you remember who I am?"

"Yeah." A knot of pain was forming over Donal's right eye. "Not your name, but I remember in the cabin, when I..."

Do you hear the bones?

But the words were distant, no longer clinging: just an abstract memory. It was the image of the diva stretched out upon the table—the *dead* diva—that made Donal's gorge rise. He turned to one side, grabbed a trash can, and vomited into it.

"Perhaps this is too soon."

"No, it's all right." Donal wiped his mouth with the back of his hand. "So who are you?"

"Laura Steele." She held out her gloved hand. "Nice to meet you properly."

"Er . . ." Donal sniffed. "We should shake when I've cleaned up. And does that mean you're *Commander* Laura Steele?"

"That's right. And this"—Laura nodded toward the wavering in the air—"is Xalia. She's a member of the federal task force that I'm heading up."

"Ah." Donal leaned back against the hard chair. "Are you here to cheer me up or to interrogate me?"

"Neither one. We're here to recruit you."

"You're joking." Donal closed his eyes and remembered the long drive into the forest and the blur—how many days?—that was his stay in the cabin, while he kept the diva's corpse laid out and made his preparations for scraping clean the bones. "How many laws did I break?"

"You were effectively ensorcelled."

"Yeah, but not actually. Doesn't that make me *effectively* guilty?"

"No, it makes you a damned victim, especially if you keep acting like one."

"Thanatos." Donal looked at her, then at Xalia's near-invisible shifting form. "Nice bedside manner you got. You say you're heading up a task force. So what are you working on?"

"Well, it's a task . . ."

"That is so fuckin' funny."

"We're investigating the exclusive little club that

Malfax Cortindo belonged to. We call them the Black
Circle—"

"That's original."

"—because their real name is a secret only they know."

Then a soft whisper that might have just been a
breeze sounded:

I wanted to call them the Pink Collective.

A smile twisted Donal's face, despite himself. "How
about the Lilac Conspiracy?"

Xalia's form rippled.

"So how big is it?" added Donal. "This conspiracy?"

"Let's just say"—Laura's glance flickered toward the
end of the ward, where Sister Felice sat at the nurses'
station, drinking hellebore tea—"the BC have gone for
quantity over quality when it comes to recruitment."

"But not just in Tristopolis."

"Why do you say that?"

"Because you're federal, even if you're based here.
And because of the background to my screwup. We
were supposed to be on alert because of what happened
in other cities. Including overseas."

"Hmm." Laura walked over to the bedside cabinet.
On top stood a cheap stained vase containing two black
dandelions. "I think Sister Felice likes you."

"It's her job. She's good at it."

"Whereas you let your principal die seconds before
killing the chief suspect."

Donal consciously relaxed his shoulders. "You said
you were here to recruit me, and now you're telling me
how badly I performed. Interesting tactic, Commander."

"The thing is, we"—Laura nodded toward the near-
invisible wavering of the air that was Xalia—"understand
more about ensorcellment and the ways of manipulation
than your superiors do. Or more than they'll pretend to,
for the sake of political expediency."

"You mean I'll be a scapegoat? But it *was* my operation, didn't you know?"

In lucid moments, Donal had wondered what might have happened to his career. Or whether he was going to jail, or worse.

"You were the only person in the whole theater, cops included," said Laura, "to break the trance. If you hadn't been there, the diva would have died anyway, with police protection all around. The story that everyone remembered would not have been what happened."

"So I resisted the influence." Donal looked down at the floor, remembering. "One kind of influence, anyway."

"Cortindo sowed the seeds of what happened to you," said Laura, "when he showed you the artist's bone. He did show you the bone, didn't he?"

"Thanatos, yeah. How did you know?"

Another ripple moved through Xalia's discorporate form. This time, Donal sensed no amusement in her.

"We investigated his office." Laura nodded toward Xalia. "Every nook and cranny. It was no big extrapolation to work out what happened. We already knew you'd been ordered to go there."

Donal stared at Laura's pale face, trying to read between her words. Without using Commissioner Vilnar's name, was she accusing him of being a member of the conspiracy? Or of abetting it without realizing?

Sister Felice was a long way down the ward, but Donal already knew how sensitive she was, how acute her hearing. It was best not to discuss specifics.

"So the only reason I've got for joining your team," he said, "is because my current bosses are going to leave me twisting in the wind."

No. Xalia's insubstantial form drifted closer. *That's not the only reason.*

"And the other is . . ."

Laura answered for Xalia. "She's talking about revenge."

"Ah. That."

After discussing a few specifics about the job offer, Laura said she wanted to check with Sister Felice regarding Donal's progress. Laura walked with Xalia beside her down to the nurses' station.

There was a brief discussion, which Donal observed, watching without making judgments. Then Laura returned, while Xalia remained hovering by Sister Felice.

"Nine days or nineteen," Laura told Donal. "Or ninety, if that's what it takes to get you rehabituated. What's rehab like, anyway? Rewiring-body-and-mind thing, right?"

"Exercise and illusion, to restore the old patterns of thought and movement," said Donal. "With plenty of pain, so you know it's doing you good."

"Sounds . . . interesting."

"Uh-huh." Donal wondered what she was thinking. "You understand, I still haven't agreed to join you."

"There's no rush."

"All right."

"So I wondered . . . You understand Xalia's nature, right?"

"What? That she's a freewraith?"

"Exactly. She's not bound to a crane or an elevator or a . . . wheelchair. She's a member of the team, not some kind of *device*."

"Obviously. Though I think you don't know Gertie very well."

"Who's Gertie?"

"Elevator Seven at HQ. Next time you ride up, tell her you know me."

Laura's pale eyes narrowed. "A lot of cops wouldn't feel that way."

"So they're assholes. It's 'cause they don't know any better."

She opened her mouth to speak, closed it, then spoke up. "I hope you decide to join us, Lieutenant Riordan."

"Thank you." Donal wondered what it was she hadn't said. "Thanks for coming out here."

He watched her leave, accompanied by the wavering of the air that was Xalia. The heels of Laura's shoes were high stilettos, and the fit of her skirt was snug; her motion caused him a certain feeling in his gut that was unexpected.

"Oh . . ." Sister Felice was standing beside Donal's bed, her slit eyes widening into roundness. "I guess the lady commander made an impression on you, huh?"

"Not really."

"Ha." Sister Felice gave a tiny cat smile, allowing her claws to flick in and out a centimeter. "You are such a liar, Lieutenant."

"Shit."

"Oh, do we need to use the bedpan?"

"No, *we* don't." Donal swung his legs over the edge of the bed. "But *I* am going to walk to the bathroom by myself."

"Really?" Her eyes were slits once more.

"Yes." Donal's voice was tight with pain.

"Good for you. If you fall over, just shout."

On the following day, the liquefying patient called Andy, the man who had difficulty maintaining his normal form, began to scream softly. The sprites floating around his bed went wild, emitting banshee yells of their own, flaring from bright orange to blazing white and back again.

Sister Felice came running, stared at the silver bands wrapped around Andy's bed, and checked the intricate device that appeared welded into the bed frame. She hurried to the wall phone.

"Get Thaum Support here, stat. We have morph-support equipment failure."

Donal sat up in his bed, watching but unable to do anything. Even Sister Felice appeared helpless now, as she reached toward Andy's bubbling form, then drew back, unwilling to disturb his equilibrium further.

Donal wondered what would happen if Andy's skin burst.

Soon a young man with pale, smooth Asian features was walking quickly into the department, with two older, gray-haired men following. All three wore rust-and-brown jerkins embossed with brass-colored runes.

Sister Felice said, "Thank Thanatos you're here, Kyushen. Can you fix it?"

The younger man, Kyushen, carried a steel toolbox. One of the older men nodded as Kyushen took a silver forked rod out of the chest and ran it above Andy's bed.

"The hex-flux integrity failed." Kyushen looked up. "We can handle that."

The three men worked swiftly, muttering about resonant frequencies and shifted octaves, replacing a blackened valve with a shining amber new one.

Suddenly a clear sheet of light passed across the bed, and Andy's suffering form shivered into stillness. His body was still distorted, but static.

"Good work," said Sister Felice. "I'll call Dr. Drax, and we'll take it from here."

"But it's fixed," said Kyushen.

"I know. But"—Sister Felice pointed at Andy's twisted, elongated body, frozen in the bed—"he isn't."

"Oh. The patient."

"Just a little detail," said Sister Felice, but she was smiling. "Like I said, leave it to us ordinary mortals. You thaumies go back to your labs."

"All right."

*   *   *

By the end of the week, Donal was hobbling around the silver lawn in thin mist (while mistwraiths floated around in odd patterns, murmuring encouragement) beneath a dark-purple sky. You couldn't call his motion running, not yet.

His firearm was in a secure locker somewhere—according to Sister Felice—so Donal did the next best thing. He stood at the lawn's edge, using an imaginary gun, visualizing the attacking figures in his mind's eye, feeling the imaginary pressure of the trigger and the recoil as he fired again and again into the shadows advancing on him.

Rehabituation continued, using pressure and psychic stress to reestablish the neural patterns of the preensorcelled Donal. Jan told him that the old patterns would reemerge stronger than before: a virtual guarantee that he would remain free of senility in old age.

On the third morning he hobbled to the nurses' station and asked Sister Lynkse if he could use the phone.

"Sure."

She left him while he made the call. Silvery fingers seemed to play around the handset: he'd used a secure number.

What can I do for you, Lieutenant?

"Put me through to Commander Steele, please."

One moment.

A strange sighing drifted down the line. Perhaps the countermeasures ached for the chance to defend against spikewraiths infiltrating the network.

Putting you through.

"Hello?"

"Commander Steele, this is Donal Riordan."

"Lieutenant. Have you considered the job offer?"

"Yeah, and I'm accepting it."

Again, the line sighed.

Then: *"Good,"* said Laura. *"Report for duty as soon as you're discharged."*

"All right."

"I won't send you into anything strenuous until you're fully fit."

"That's all right, I didn't expect to—"

The line went dead.

"Nice talking to you too," said Donal to the silent receiver. "Rats."

Sister Lynkse, returning, gave him a strange look.

"Just renewing my membership," Donal said, "in the Rat Fancy Club."

Half-revealing her slender fangs, Sister Lynkse gave a silent laugh.

"Kill some of those rats for me, okay?"

A black low-slung ambulance came to take him back to the city. The vehicle was wide, with flared housings along the running boards.

Sister Felice pushed Donal in the wheelchair he no longer needed, while Sister Lynkse walked alongside. They stopped at the edge of the dark-blue gravel drive.

The ambulance rear door rose up, and Donal stood. He kissed Sister Felice on the cheek and patted Sister Lynkse's hand.

"You're wonderful," he said. "Both of you."

"Well, we *knew* that."

"Yeah." He smiled at Sister Felice. "Look after yourself."

"You too, Lieutenant."

Two black-suited paramedics with bone-gray skins descended from the ambulance.

"I can climb in," said Donal, "by myself."

The paramedics watched in silence, unblinking, as Donal hauled himself into the rear compartment. He sat down on one of the stretchers that were fastened in place. The two paramedics locked gazes, exchanged some form of silent communication, then bowed to each other.

One of them climbed into the back and sat down on the opposite stretcher from Donal; the other returned to the front and slid into the driver's seat.

Sister Felice waved.

Donal blew her a kiss, and then the rear door lowered itself into place and clicked shut.

And that's that.

The ambulance rolled into motion, scrunching its way along blue gravel until it reached the road. The driver hauled the vehicle through a tight turn—the paramedic sitting opposite Donal gave a tiny grin—and then they were accelerating smoothly, back toward Tristopolis.

When they were a mile from the hospital grounds and the road was wide enough, the housings alongside the chassis split open. Bat wings unfurled, stretching to either side.

The engine note dropped as the front of the ambulance tipped up, gathering speed.

And the ambulance rose into the air.

T he bat-winged ambulance howled low over
  dank marshes until it reached the city limits, where
the density of thaumaturgically charged airborne particles forced the vehicle down to the ground, for fear of a
flameout in the engines.

Slowing to a normal crawl, the paramedic driver took
the black ambulance through desolate west-side streets
before reaching midtown.

"You live in Lower Halls, yes?" asked the paramedic
riding in the back with Donal.

"Yeah, but . . . take me to HQ, why don't you?"

"HQ?"

"Police headquarters. It's Number One Avenue of the
Basilisks."

"Yes." The paramedic's voice grew oddly sibilant.
"We know where it is."

He blinked: a slow, wet motion of nictitating membrane preceding the flicker of his eyelids. In the driver's
seat up front, the other paramedic gave a slow nod.

Neither spoke a word for the remainder of the
journey.

Donal exchanged greetings with FenSeven and another
deathwolf that he didn't know well, FenNineBeth.

FenSeven sniffed, tasting the air for evidence of Donal's health. Then his tongue lolled in a lupine grin.

Once inside, the first thing Donal did was descend to the gun range. Gertie made no smart remarks during the descent, and she was gentle pushing him out of her elevator shaft and into the corridor. It disconcerted Donal more than anything else might have.

Brian, behind the counter, his skin a healthy medium-blue, waved to Donal. "Hey, Lieutenant. How's life?"

"I've still got one," said Donal. "And yourself?"

"I'm in the pink." Brian patted his bald pate. "Or in the blue, at least."

"And in the clear?"

"Lieutenant. Everything's clean. Really."

"Good. Gimme two hundred rounds and a bunch of targets, mixed."

"None of the, uh, *specials*?"

"Brian..."

"Just kidding. We're all legit here."

Donal took the targets through to the range, sent the first of them back to maximum distance, then whipped out his Magnus and blew the target to shreds. He changed targets, reloaded, and got to work again.

Over and over he fired, blowing tightly clustered shots into the targets, until the air stank and his ammunition was gone.

Good enough.

Donal walked back to the elevator bank.

"Something new for me, Gertie. Down to minus twenty-seven."

Have you been a bad boy, Donal?

"New job. I'm going to be working out of there from now on."

So you have been a bad boy.

Donal said nothing more during the descent. Finally,

Gertie brought him down slowly, slowly, toward minus 27, as if giving him time to reconsider.

At the doorway, Donal floated for a long moment while Gertie hesitated. Then:

Your funeral, lover.

She pushed him through.

A hulking figure was waiting for him. Donal recognized the guy from that time at the gun range, from before the debacle with the diva. Viktor Harman, who had claimed to be from the 77th Precinct.

"My name really is Viktor Harman," the guy said now. "But I've never been inside the Seventy-seventh."

"Okay . . . I'm guessing we have the same boss."

"You're guessing right. Laura's looking forward to seeing you."

Laura Steele's office was a glass-walled cube inside a large, gloomy workspace. When Donal entered, she looked up, and just for a second her eyes looked as gray and metallic as her name suggested. Then a change shifted inside her gaze.

"I thought you were only being discharged this morning."

"I am. Was. I came straight here."

"So what do you expect to be doing on your first day on the team?"

Donal looked out at the communal office: dark polished desks and ancient phones and Viktor Harman's hulking figure chatting to himself—no, to the wavering in the air that was Xalia.

"Don't tell me," he said. "You have a bunch of really interesting files for me to read."

"You got it."

"And stuff you don't have written down?"

"Some of that too. But this"—Laura pointed at her

own head—"isn't guaranteed indestructible. Most of it's down in writing somewhere."

"Well, that's something." Donal looked at her. "Who are we investigating?"

"We call them the Black Circle."

"Yeah, I remember that much."

"You looked woozy. I wasn't sure how much you'd recall."

"Uh-huh. You mentioned Malfax Cortindo."

Like some attenuated echo, he half-remembered a whispered *Do you feel the bones?* Then the disconcerting memory was gone, and he was back in the moment.

"Don't worry about the flashbacks," said Laura. "They'll—Never mind. Not my business."

She was right: this was none of her business.

"Malfax Cortindo," said Donal. "You said he was part of the club. Part of the Black Circle."

"Yeah, well. The BC—the name *is* embarrassing, right?—seems to include your favorite alderman. Some of the paper trail is in the files, as you'll see."

"You mean Finross? I haven't had any dealings with him. Er . . . not directly."

Donal's visit to the Energy Authority had happened because Alderman Finross had made the arrangement. That was one thing Donal would not forget.

"I'd guess they were trying to figure out how much you knew or how hard you were going to work to prevent the kill."

Donal shook his head. He *hadn't* prevented the kill, had he? But his own remembered actions seemed like a stranger's.

"It was Commissioner Vilnar who contacted Finross initially, I think. You can't suspect the commissioner."

Laura cocked her head to one side, saying nothing.

"Thanatos," muttered Donal. "But he was the one who briefed me in the first place."

"Well, he had to, didn't he? Once he'd been assigned to protect the diva. The orders didn't originate with him but the City Council."

"Oh."

"And that thought is most certainly *not* in writing. How well do you get along with the commissioner, Donal?"

"We're like"—Donal pretended to have difficulty crossing his fingers, as if they were repelling magnets—"that. Damn. Just like that."

"Good answer. I should've asked you earlier."

"Perhaps, Laura—If I can call you that."

"What I think is, if you have to ask—"

"—it's probably too soon. So can I get you a cup of coffee, Commander?"

"Yeah. Black and strong."

"You got it."

Donal fetched coffee in ectofoam mugs and left one on Laura's desk. She was deep in phone conversation with someone now, but she'd left the door open, so it clearly wasn't confidential.

Going back out into the main office, sipping his too-hot coffee, Donal nodded to Viktor. Then he made his way to the only clean desk.

That's mine.

Suddenly the air was wavering in front of him.

Yours is the messy one over there.

A faint outline of a raised hand pointed.

"Thank you so much."

Donal sat down, kicked a gray metal trash can into position, and slid the papers from the desktop, plus the old-fashioned blotter, straight into the can. Then he pulled open the tall lower drawer, designed for hanging files, and stuffed the trash can inside.

"There we are. All tidy."

Donal pushed the drawer shut with his foot.

Aren't you going to ask why I need a desk?

Donal looked at her.

"Xalia, come on. I can see right through you. You're fishing for compliments."

Like I haven't heard that one before. But what do you mean?

"You're solidly beautiful. You're gorgeous. Why wouldn't you have somewhere to sit?"

Ha. You're a piece of work yourself, Donal Riordan—

"Back at ya."

—But you're not fooling me. I know who you've really got your eye on.

"I don't—"

But his gaze had already shifted toward the door of Laura's office before he could stop himself.

"Shit."

Ha.

Then Viktor was returning to his desk with a flimsy report clutched in one big hand, and Xalia faded into near-invisibility. Donal pretended to find something interesting in the upper drawer of his new desk.

A detective, not part of the team, passed through the office. He was big, almost as big as Viktor, and his eyes were the color of slate—in fact, they appeared to be *made* of slate. Donal had seen stone lenses before, during his army days: they were sniper implants, and they were for life.

"Hey." The big man stopped by Donal's desk, and offered his hand. "I'm Kresham."

"Donal."

Kresham's grip, like Viktor's, felt capable of crushing Donal's hand. "Good to meet ya."

"Likewise."

Kresham nodded, as though a one-word reply was a point in Donal's favor. Given the reticence of most snipers, that was probably the case.

Viktor said, "Who's on Blanz, then?"

"Harald's got him."

"Long-range?"

"Yeah. I'm going back to my own desk, for some peace and quiet. Don't call me."

Donal looked from one to the other.

"You guys wouldn't be talking about Sherman Blanz, would you?"

Viktor shrugged. "Why not?"

"Senator Sherman Blanz."

"Right."

"You have a visiting federal senator under surveillance."

"Uh-huh."

"Shit." A slow smile spread across Donal's face. "I think I'm going to enjoy it here, if we all stay out of jail long enough."

Ain't the jailhouse we have to worry about. It's the graveyard.

Donal stared at Xalia, whose form seemed to grow as opaque as mist just for a second. He remembered that smartwraiths like Xalia would be classified as nonhuman under Blanz's proposed Vital Renewal Bill, with no more legal rights than a piece of furniture.

"But we wouldn't do anything illegal or bad to Blanz, would we?"

We're professional police officers.

"Even though Blanz is a cretinous bigoted motherfucker who deserves to die in long-lasting agony."

Even though.

Donal let out a long breath.

"You guys got any other interesting surprises for me?"

"Dozens," said Viktor. "But if we told you, they wouldn't be surprises."

"Shit."

*   *   *

That evening brought a different kind of surprise into Donal's life: the sudden experience of being homeless.

When he arrived at his neighborhood, no one paid him any attention, but that was business as usual. Walking past the washeteria, Fozzy's Rags, he saw old Mrs. MacZoran give a start at his appearance; then she turned and said something to the large woman sitting beside her. Behind them, the washing machines churned on.

Donal would have gone in to chat with her, but he'd drunk too much coffee and his guts were still shaky: he needed the bathroom. When he reached the apartment block and climbed to the fifth floor, he knew right away that something had changed, even before he saw and smelled the fresh coat of black paint on his front door.

A tiny handwritten label said *Davinia Strihen,* which meant it was no longer *his* front door, exactly.

For a moment, hand inside his jacket and resting on the butt of his Magnus, Donal was tempted to kick the lock out of the jamb. But this Strihen woman probably knew nothing of Donal Riordan, and she might be an old dear, liable to drop dead of a heart attack if he burst in.

"For fuck's sake."

He went downstairs, pushed his way between cardboard boxes in the ground-level hallway, and made his way back to the super's office at the rear. That was a door he could kick in, and did.

It crashed open with a satisfying sound of splinters ripping from wood.

"Hey—"

"Right, fuckin' hey. What's up, Ferd?"

"Oh, Hades, Loot . . . er, Lieutenant. It was the landlord. Bastard made me."

"Made you do what, Ferd?"

Ferdinand was old and fat and hadn't shaved for ten or twelve days. If Donal needed a decent opponent to fight, Ferd wasn't it, and this wasn't the place.

The landlord lived a long way uptown from here.

"They said you was in the hospital. Didn't think you'd come out again."

"Nice of everyone to care."

"Yeah, well . . . we did. Old Mrs. MacZoran wanted to send flowers, but I didn't know where the hospital was."

"Where's my stuff?"

"Oh, Thanat—Sorry. It's . . ." Ferd's voice trailed off, and he swallowed.

"You trashed it?"

"Hades, no. It's outside."

"In the backyard."

"No—I mean, yeah, but it wasn't my idea. Honest."

Donal started to raise his fist, then turned away and slammed the rear door open with the heel of his hand. It bounced back from the wall, and he kicked it. Then he went out into the narrow alleyway of broken concrete.

Small black ferns were growing in the cracks. Four dented cardboard boxes lay there, stained in the aftermath of quicksilver rain. One of the boxes was torn. Donal's old brown jacket looked shredded.

He went back in to Ferd's room. Ferd had pulled on his coat, trying but failing to button it across his globular stomach. He stopped, swallowing, as soon as he saw Donal.

"I was just, er, just—"

"About to phone for a taxi for me. Right?"

"Er, right, Lieutenant. Right."

The rent hadn't been paid for a month, that was true. But beyond that . . . Damn it, Donal would sort it out tomorrow. But he needed a place to stay for the night.

He stared around Ferd's tiny room, with torn wallpaper hanging in triangular patches from the walls. It was filled with an old, dank, rotten smell, and the couch was torn, its springs exposed. He could have forced Ferd to let him stay here, but he'd rather sleep in the open.

"Taxi. Outside. As soon as possible. Got it?"

"Got it. Thanks, Lieutenant."

Thanks for what? For not punching his head in?

Donal went back out and picked up two of his four boxes—half of everything he owned, how wonderful—and headed inside. Ferd was already dialing, and Donal pushed his way through to the front hallway.

He set the two boxes down just inside the closed front door. Going back to fetch the other two, he heard Ferd say, "Please, Joe, for Hades's sake. He'll kill me otherwise."

Donal felt the anger rise inside him, and for a blinding split second he could feel himself ripping out the Magnus and whipping it backhand across Ferd's flabby face, cutting open the skin. Then he throttled down and pushed the anger back inside him, where it belonged—coiled up, ready for use when he needed it.

Ready for when he met the true killers responsible for the diva's demise.

Out on the sidewalk, he waited for the purple cab to appear. While he did so, he wondered where the Hades he was going to stay for tonight and the nights to follow. A month's unpaid rent was the equivalent of, what, two days in a hotel?

Just as a cab appeared at the left-hand end of the street, a Vixen slid around the corner of the opposite end, its curved, finned shape out of place in this neighborhood. It slowed, cruising. Then Donal recognized the blond-haired silhouette behind the windshield.

He held up his hand in a static wave.

"Hey, bud." The taxi driver leaned out his window. "You Riordan?"

"Never heard of him," said Donal. "That's my lift over there."

"Hades, I hate this rat-damned place. Lower Halls." The driver stared at the apartment building's scratched and scabby door, obviously debating the merits of going inside to raise hell while leaving his vehicle exposed on the curb.

On the far side of the street, two shifty youngsters with yellow eyes (nephews of the Fozzy who owned the washeteria) slouched against ruined brickwork, watching Donal and the taxi. That was enough for the driver, who gunned the accelerator and said, "You want my advice, you get far away from this dump."

Donal said nothing as the taxi pulled away from the curb and twisted into a U-turn, engine growling as it headed back the way it had come. Then Laura's Vixen pulled up, and the taxi was forgotten.

"You throwing out the garbage, Lieutenant?"

"I *am* the garbage, Commander. Me and my worldly belongings here are headed for a hotel."

She stared at him for a moment. Then: "The trunk lid's unlocked. What are you waiting for?"

"Thank you."

Donal went around to the back of the car. Low and solid, it appeared to purr as it sat there idling. Donal had to use both hands to twist the twin handles; then the lid raised itself up on the sprung hinges, revealing the near-empty compartment.

He hesitated, then transferred the first of his boxes from sidewalk to trunk, squashed it into one corner, then followed it with the remaining boxes. He slammed the lid down, walked around to the side of the vehicle, and slid in on the passenger's side.

"You've booked a place?"

"I thought I might try the A." The Agnostic Men's Association ran hostels, as well as the jailhouse gyms that Donal often trained in. "There's one on Thousand Third."

"That'll be a no, then."

"I—Right."

"I've got a spare room. More than one." Laura slipped the car into gear. "But you'll have to fend for yourself when it comes to food. I have nothing in stock."

"No problem." Donal watched the apartment building slide away. It felt as though a chunk of his life had come loose and fallen into a wild, cold ocean. "I'm not used to . . . Well. Thanks."

Laura nodded, her mouth tightening, as though she was engaged in some kind of internal argument with herself. Donal decided he should keep quiet.

So why was she driving this way in the first place?

The old, damaged neighborhood disappeared behind them as the Vixen arced upward onto a curving overpass, slipping among fast-moving cylindrical motortrucks, ignoring a blast of horns as she pulled in front of a triple-decker transporter stacked with five-wheeled quin bikes.

They pulled onto the Midtown Expressway, and Donal's pulse quickened. Laura was astonishingly beautiful. She was also a coworker, acting on a charitable impulse toward a subordinate. And if she owned a Vixen, she was a lot richer than he was. When he left the orphanage, he'd vowed never to accept charity again.

Do you hear the—

Shut up.

They soared into the heart of the city, among the hard-edged Gothic-deco towers, then pulled into a helical off-ramp.

Oh, shit.

Donal hated these things.

"You're all right with thaumatunnels, right?" Laura was already taking them off the main overpass and into the mouth of the spiral. "Right?"

"Yeah . . . sure."

The car flipped upside down as it spun through the helical descent.

Shit shit shit.

Then it was righting itself as it slid into a basement garage, screeching echoes bouncing back from stone walls carved with malevolent hard-angled protective runes.

Most of the parked cars were bigger and grander than the dark-but-sporty Vixen, but there was one thing every vehicle had in common: Donal could never afford to rent one for a weekend, never mind buy one.

"Home bitter home," said Laura, with no trace of emotion, and slammed the car into a decelerating turn that pushed Donal to the side, pressing him against the door. "Here we are."

And screeching and yowling—

What's she trying to do?

—the Vixen pulled to a halt, its nose just inches away from a wall of dark polished granite.

Give me a heart attack?

Then Laura gave him a sideways look.

"Sorry," she muttered. "I forgot, you're just an ordinary—Never mind."

Perhaps that dismissal—of Donal as ordinary—was the most devastating thing that had happened in a confused and disturbing night.

A black baggage cart pulled up beside the car, and Laura popped the trunk before stepping out. By the time Donal had walked back to the rear, all of his battered boxes were already in place on the cart's flatbed, held in place by four fat, pulsing arms.

At the cart's front end, two large yellow eyes turned

to look at Donal and gave a long, slow blink. Then the
cart rolled into motion.

Donal began to follow, but Laura said, "The people
elevator is this way."

"Uh . . . okay."

He watched the cart make its way past a gigantic
Nebula limousine to what looked like a blank concrete
wall. An opening drew apart and the cart rolled forward
into a darkened, empty shaft. It hung in midair as the
wall clamped shut behind it.

Where the Hades am I?

Laura was heading for a buttress of the same shining
granite-and-quartz rock, in which a silver elevator door
was set. Over it was a dial, its needle currently indicating the 227th floor.

A flare of blue light traveled down the door at Laura's
approach. The needle began to swing, indicating the elevator's descent.

Soon the doors were sliding open to reveal a steel-
floored elevator car with walls that curved inward to a
point overhead. As Donal stepped forward, metallic
thorns slid like cat's claws from the walls, but then
Laura touched Donal's arm. The thorns retracted.

Security system.

At least Laura had identified him as a friend. Donal
wondered just what the building would have done otherwise.

Sealing itself up, the elevator rose fast, its floor pressing against Donal's feet. It hurtled upward with relent-
less speed, then began to brake. The ascent slowed, they
bumped to a halt, and the doors slid open.

They were in a twenty-foot-high lobby with only one
doorway: massive black steel double doors, which
swung inward as Laura walked toward them. Donal
hung back.

Beyond was a huge reception area decorated in steel-gray and matte-black metal. On twisted helical stands, metal cups bore dancing blue flames whose motion matched the near-subliminal music of Illurian harps seeping through the obsidian floor.

A pale ethereal hand at the end of an insubstantial arm headed toward Donal, its fingers lengthening as it drew close, reaching for Donal's Magnus in its concealed shoulder holster. At a tutting sound from Laura, the hand froze, then withdrew back toward the wall, sank inside, and was gone.

"This is just like my old neighborhood." Donal looked around the chamber. "They try to steal your weapons there too."

Laura half-smiled. "Don't worry. I'll look after you."

"Yeah . . . you're not doing a bad job so far."

"You're welcome. The apartment's through there." She inclined her head toward the solid-looking wall, its surface decorated by a twelve-foot-high steel mask: a man's face, hook-nosed, eyes shut.

"The apartment? So what's this place?"

"Kind of a hallway, I suppose. A . . . what, antechamber?"

"Antechamber," murmured Donal.

The mask's eyes opened and stared at Donal for a moment, then it opened its mouth, wider and wider like gaping jaws, splitting apart to form an entranceway into a large room with a dark-blue floor that looked like solid glass. Laura led the way; Donal caught up with her, glancing back as the steel mask folded and slid into place.

Here, the air was chill.

"Sorry," said Laura. "I wasn't expecting—Well. You know."

"What are you sorry for?"

"I meant, it's cold, isn't it? That's all."

At her words, shafts of orange flame slid up the walls

from controlled vents at floor level. Waves of warmth washed over Donal as he wheeled around, checking out the huge room: bigger than his old apartment, almost as big as the entire apartment building.

"You're rich," he said. "I mean really rich."

Laura shrugged. "Are you asking why I'm a police officer?"

"No, but...why *are* you on the force? I take it you don't need to earn a living."

"A living..." Laura shook her head, an odd look in her eyes. "That's one way to put it, I guess."

She led him across the forbidding high lounge to the dark twenty-foot windows that reared upward, looking out onto the night-bound city towers. In the distance, a lone smartbat sailed against the background of a moon-illuminated cloud.

"Tristopolis," she said. "Is it worth it, do you think? Should we even try to save it from itself?"

Donal shook his head.

"I don't even know what you're talking about."

"Excuse me?"

"A city might be a thing in its own right, like a living being, but it ain't the city we're here to protect, y'know? It's your average man or woman struggling through life, who doesn't deserve to become a victim as well—that's who we're here to help."

Donal could not stop himself scanning the high room, the black iron-and-quartz chandeliers, the tall twisted sculpture of what looked like a melting warrior standing in one corner.

"You've got a problem," said Laura, "because of my wealth. Because I'm so well off, is that it?"

"No." Donal blew out a breath. "I don't figure you for a career politician. Not if you're running a task force that's investigating federal senators—unless you're *really* figuring to make a name for yourself as a moral crusader."

"Thanatos, me, a crusader. I've enough trouble just—Well." Laura crossed her arms. "If I let you stay here until you sort yourself out, we're not going to have a problem with each other, are we?"

"You run the task force. You're the boss. Although if I'm stuck here until my life's sorted out"—Donal couldn't help grinning—"we're going to be putting up with each other for a long time."

"Ha." Laura uncrossed her arms. "Come on. I'll show you around."

10

The place was huge, and *apartment* seemed such a tiny word for the wide Gothic dwelling that Laura kept. She owned the whole 227th floor of the building, Darksan Tower, which was the uppermost residential level; the higher, narrower levels housed maintenance rooms and the huge motors and drums of the seven elevators that serviced the building.

The rooms were cold, simultaneously grim yet palatial, and Donal's breath steamed as he stood in a huge bedroom with a clean, polished obsidian floor and a four-poster bed. The bed's coverings were silver fabric interwoven with dark-purple runes of a kind he had never seen before.

Black vaselike constructs, dotted around here and there on low tables, sprouted dancing pale-blue flames when Laura snapped her fingers near each one in turn.

"Not flamewraiths." Donal frowned. "I'm not sensing...There *are* no boundwraiths here, are there? Of any kind."

"You think there should be? That I should have spirits enslaved inside my household appliances?"

Donal thought about the moans echoing through the subterranean avenues of reactor piles, spill-off from necroflux waves passing inside the bones of the dead.

Do you feel the—

No, not anymore.

"Maybe it's no worse," Donal murmured, "than whatever's waiting for the rest of us."

The expression in Laura's eyes was unreadable.

"I should show you the kitchen," she said after a moment. "You'll be able to fix yourself some supper. This here is your room, and there's a bathroom through there."

She pointed at a wall decorated in vertical ten-foot-wide panels of alternating gray and black. "Third panel's the bathroom door."

Donal's four cardboard boxes of belongings were already stacked in one corner. The cart—which *was* a wraith container—must have used an alternate route, perhaps through some kind of maintenance shaft, to reach the room. There was no sign of the cart now.

Perhaps it belonged to the building management rather than to Laura.

He followed Laura into the ice-cold kitchen. Cupboards opened at Laura's command, revealing a stasis pantry full of food cartons and chinaware stacked away as though it had not been used for ages.

"I'd forgotten about the cartons," Laura said. "Help yourself. I'll see you in the morning."

"Um . . . okay. Thank you."

Donal felt let down, knowing it was an unreasonable reaction.

Do you—

Never.

After all Laura had done for him, sharing supper was too much to expect. She would be going out to dine with her rich friends, moving in strata that would be alien to any normal working cop.

"I appreciate this," he added, as she left the kitchen.

"You're welcome."

The door—simply ensorcelled, not requiring a

wraith—swung shut of its own accord as Laura's heels clicked along the hallway floor, fading from Donal's awareness.

"Well," he murmured to himself. "Let's see what's for supper."

In fact, Donal no longer felt hungry, but he had a brief memory of Sister Felice back at the hospital, telling him to eat or his recovery would take longer. He supposed that still applied.

Donal found a waxed-paper-wrapped brick of Alcadian pink cheese and a cardboard carton of black-sprout broth. Some black crackers from the pantry. And that was it. He searched for a saucepan.

There were none that he could find.

"Bleeding Thanatos."

In the end he settled for drinking the soup cold, straight from the container, standing at the counter. The cheese and black crackers tasted . . . interesting.

The wrapper on the cracker box bore a date: *Sextember 22, 6604.* At least they were all right to eat: the stasis pantry looked top-of-the-line, guaranteed against decay.

But what kind of luxury apartment was this, where the rooms were kept icy cold and there was no fresh food, only three-year-old crackers and frozen cheese?

Donal ate slowly, cleaned up the crumbs he had spilled, and stacked the dishes in the sink—which coughed up rust-colored water, as though unused to working, before the water flowed through long enough to clear. Then the sink swilled the dishes, small extruded arms washing and polishing the plates before setting them to one side to dry.

Donal walked back through the echoing hallway to the tall, dark bedroom. He stared at the four-poster bed for a long time before stripping down to his skivvies, finding the right cardboard box, and retrieving a bat-

tered book with the covers torn off. It was the copy of
Human: the Revenge that he'd started before the job
with the diva.

Do—

No.

He took the book into bed with him.

Donal sat propped up against silk-covered pillows
with a mercury sheen, reading by the light of flickering
pale-blue flames, finding some comfort in the words of
an imaginary story. Real life and the actual world had
slipped far away from logic and ordinary purpose.

And at some point he closed his eyes to rest, laying
the book on his lap. He drifted into a warm, blank, orange dream.

Donal woke thirsty. Still in his skivvies, he went back
out to the kitchen . . .

And stopped.

Do you feel—

Oh, my Death, yes.

Laura was in the hallway, totally nude. Behind her,
tall windows stood open to the icy night. Quicksilver
rain fell almost horizontally through the powerful wind.

And Laura's perfect, pale skin was silvery. If Donal
didn't know better, he'd think she'd been outside.

"You're so warm," she whispered. Her eyelids fluttered. "I didn't mean to—"

Part of Donal's mind cried out a warning, but most of
him thrummed with a resounding affirmation as he took
a step toward her.

"So close to the living. All day, at work . . ."

"You're perfect." Donal's voice was rough.

Feel the song?

Something, some powerful force, washed through
Donal's being.

I don't know.

Perhaps he struggled against that tidal attraction for

a moment, or perhaps he imagined that, and he gave himself up immediately to what was happening.

His hand cupped one cold breast. Her nipple was erect and frozen, like steel.

"Thanatos."

And they were embracing, desperate to cling to each other, and the time for thought was past as they stumbled toward her bedroom.

Laura straddled him, pale and strong, laughing as he came inside her, a novaburst of white joy as he cupped her small breasts. He rolled sideways, bringing her down to lie on the bed, and kissed her icy nipples as he hooked his fingertip inside her, and in a moment she screamed aloud, shuddered, then laughed once more.

Do you—

Not now.

Donal kissed her soft skin, so cold against his lips, his body. In minutes Laura was aroused again, arching back as Donal used his tongue, and then he was inside her once more, climbing to that pinnacle of explosion, which this time occurred simultaneously for both of them.

"Oh, Death . . ."

"You're wonderful," he told her, suddenly able to speak.

"And you, lover."

They snuggled close, holding each other.

"Shit." A cramp seized his ribs. "Sorry."

He rolled away from her.

"You all right?"

"Yeah." Donal stretched, even though it hurt. "You wait 'til I get my full strength back."

He rolled back over and kissed her cool lips.

"Yes. You should sleep, dear Donal. Or you'll be no good to me in the morning."

Did she mean at work or in bed? Smiling, he meant to ask her, but he was lying in a bed more comfortable than he had ever known, exhausted from ongoing trauma and recent lovemaking.

Do—

Dunno. Can't remember. Who cares?

Donal slipped into a state that might have been sleep or might have been trance but was in any case disconnected from the ordinary world. It was bliss, and nobody experiences that often in their life.

Donal drifted.

When he woke, the room had grown chill once more. It remained dark, lit only by one pale-blue flickering flame. Laura was not in the bed.

What have we done?

Desire had overwhelmed them. But how had that happened?

"Laura?" Donal blinked and pulled himself half upright on the bed. "Are you—"

She was there.

Oh, black Thanatos.

Still nude, Laura sat cross-legged on the floor. A narrow black cable, hanging in a catenary curve, connected her to a power valve in the wall. The cable pulsed with necrotonic power. But on her left breast—

No. I didn't realize.

—a large flap of pale skin hung back, a triangle of that perfect skin he had kissed and run his tongue and fingers over—

Or did I? Did I know?

—revealing the hollow in her chest and the slick black wetness that pumped and beat in a regular, never-changing rhythm, recharged for another night and day.

A repressed memory rose up.

"The ward shield keeps out only living beings." That was Laura, back in the cabin with the troopers who had burst in.

Now Laura's eyes were shielded by shadow as she watched him watching her.

Then, "What's the matter?" she asked, her voice harsh. "Haven't you ever fucked a zombie before?"

Donal tried to speak. Something clutched his throat, and it was exactly like being strangled. He tried to tell Laura that it didn't matter, but it was impossible as she stood up, pulled the power cord from her beating black heart, flicked the cord aside, and sealed up her thoracic cavity. She pulled her breast skin back into place.

The edges joined up and faded so that her skin was whole once more.

"I—"

"Don't worry yourself, Donal."

Laura walked nude from the room, her perfect convex buttocks clenching and relaxing in rhythm. Then she was gone and Donal was cursing himself.

"Ah, Death."

He swung his legs off the bed and came to his feet in one fast motion.

She regrets it. It just came over her too, that desire—

Donal was used to moving athletically, but not in his current state. Blood drained from his head. Donal swayed, tottered, and then the bedsheet seemed to rise to meet his face—*Hades, I'm fainting*—and he was falling forward but could not stop himself as everything went.

Black.

In the main lounge, Laura stood shivering, but not from the chilled air. How could a dead thing feel the cold? She stared back at the hallway and the bedroom door—her own bedroom, where Donal lay.

The room she had not used since...since it happened.

There were six guest bedrooms, but the seventh bedroom was her own: though she had not consciously planned to make love to Donal, some part of her must have known all along that it was going to happen.

Thanatos. Balls.

Giving Donal a moment longer to follow her and apologize—*Death, he was so warm*—she gave up—*but I'm his commander*—turned to the massive open windows, and climbed out onto the sill.

So I found myself a real man at last.

Laura was 227 stories above street level. The night was blacker than ever; even the moon was shrouded behind impenetrable cloud, the only hint of its presence a silver outline to the cloud mass.

Too bad I'm not a real woman.

She grabbed hold of a skeletal head carved in the wall and pulled herself upward. Using other carvings—here of a Zurinese komodo, there a Balkran carnivulcan next to a ghouleagle—she climbed steadily, naked in the night.

Great stone demonic heads, part of Darksan Tower's massive superstructure, stared at her with dark-green eyes bigger than automobiles. They followed Laura's ascent to the next, narrower level.

Finally she reached the roof that ringed the final, tall spire rearing up to the sky.

Laura sat down, her buttocks pressed against the root of one of the four great demons' necks. She stared, seeing nothing beyond the depths of her own stupidity.

A gray cat padded toward her.

"Hey," Laura murmured.

The cat's eyes glowed scarlet.

"Will you sit with me for a while?" she added.

Silence, then:

+Yes, I will.+

The cat sat next to her, blinking its shining scarlet eyes.

Across the human- and wraith-built canyon that was the street, Laura's dark-adapted sight focused on the opposing towers and the narrow spars of stone that linked them: channels for necrotonic cabling as well as phone lines.

No person could traverse within the spars—the internal spaces were too narrow—but wraiths could, and did, flow along the wires from building to building as required. And, externally, if they chose to risk the turbulent winds that battered the heights, other creatures might walk (or occasionally slither) atop the stone spars, crossing the spaces and the vast drop below.

Now, on other rooftops, pairs of scarlet eyes blinked, feline and knowing, at Laura sitting at the base of Darksan Tower's spire, staring into the night.

The night to which she belonged.

Donal slipped back into wakefulness. It was morning, but very early. He padded into the bathroom, drank musty water from the faucet, then left it running. A second glass, after a few minutes, tasted fresher.

No sign of Laura.

He went back to the small stack of cardboard boxes, searched inside, and pulled out his old jump rope. The cord was black and slick and shiny with age: a narrow length of manticore gut, well worn.

Dressed only in his shorts, Donal skipped slowly, beginning with the simple two-footed jump, then alternating feet. He interspersed the steady rhythm with bursts of high-speed footwork. His old boxing coach would have been proud.

It was half an hour later, with Donal just about to finish up, when Laura walked into the bedroom, fully clothed. She was wearing one of her severe skirt suits, this one navy with matching high heels. Her iridescent lipstick shone as blue as the cloth.

"I see you're fit enough," she said.

"Fit for anything"—Donal whipped the rope around himself fast, spectacularly, then tossed it onto the bed—"you'd care to attempt with me."

"Excuse me?"

"I feel much better now."

"No."

Donal let out a long breath.

"I'm..."

No. He would not apologize.

Do you feel the—

All the damn time.

Donal wanted to tell her that he loved her, even as the rational part of his mind yelled that it was a hangover from ensorcellment, a rewiring of his basic animal drives.

"We don't need to talk about it."

"No," he said.

They stared at each other.

Do—

And swallowed.

Laura unbuttoned her jacket and blouse, took hold of his right hand, and cupped it against the black lace of her bra, covering her heart. "Do you feel the black pump...slithering...inside me?"

"Yeah." Donal closed his eyes and shivered. "Yeah, I feel it."

"Oh, Thanatos."

They pulled each other into a unifying embrace, as

though every cell in their bodies was sucked toward the joint organism they formed together, as though they could be one single being, filled with the joy of lust and love, sweaty and salty mingling fluids. And then he was pulling off her clothes and his shorts were off, yet there was a gentleness here, not the rapid urgency of last night.

It was deeper and far more satisfying, and they cried aloud and laughed as they came: once, twice, and a third time. They lay back naked atop the tossed silver sheets and laughed again, soft and satisfied.

"Well," said Laura. "I guess we've done it now."

"I guess we have. You're seducing a minion, and I'm—"

"—involved with a nonperson, at least by Senator Blanz's criteria."

"Fat lot that bastard knows."

They stared at each other.

"Is it always going to be like this?" Laura said.

Donal shook his head. "I don't know anything."

"Me either."

He could guess at the origin of the desire sweeping through him. But why would Laura feel that attraction to him?

I don't know.

But he knew that she *did* feel it, that was the thing.

Donal propped himself up on one elbow and looked down at her, tracking his fingertips along her cool and flawless skin. Her icy nipples peaked and crinkled at his touch.

"So why are you on the senator's case, Laura? Why is Blanz your enemy?"

"Besides the obvious? I didn't say he was my enemy." Laura's lips curved, and she raised her head up to kiss him, then lay back. "Of course he *is*—I just didn't say so. He's the enemy of all my kind, mine and Xalia's."

"Xalia's a smartwraith. That's hardly in the same category as you—"

"You think she's less than human, then?"

"No, I don't. How can you ask that?"

Laura shook her head, her blond hair swirling across the silvery satin pillows. "Sorry, I'm still not used to... The world's not supposed to change in an instant."

"Yeah, but it can."

And had she known this would happen? Had she planned it?

I don't care.

"Right." Laura rolled herself up to a sitting position and checked the angular needle hands twisting into position on the bedside table, indicating the time: 11:07. "Death, do you have any idea how late we are?"

"Yeah. We'd better travel to HQ separately."

"No."

"Or you can drop me off maybe five blocks away, somewhere discreet. I can pick up some take-out coffees. Anything has to be better than the muck that Viktor makes."

"I don't think so."

"You can't like Viktor's coffee. Tell me you don't."

"I've never tasted it," said Laura. "Never felt the need. And I don't feel the need to disown you either."

She touched her fingertips against his chest, and for a moment a hint of steam played around her fingertips and evaporated.

"Er... I don't hurt you, do I?" Donal realized consciously for the first time how different his body temperature was from hers. "I mean, my skin doesn't burn you, does it?"

"Yeah. But not in a bad way."

"You said"—Donal responded to her kisses, blood leaping back into his manhood—"we're late for work, remember?"

"Mmm. Lucky I'm the boss."

They slid together, forming one being once more.

"Lucky, lucky . . ."

And they headed for the novaburst that awaited them.

Laura drove the Vixen, which seemed ideally suited to her. Even the crescent-shaped steering wheel was fitted to her exactly, as if she could steer the car through massive turns with the tiniest fingertip pressure.

They slid through the half-busy streets, enjoying the respite from rush-hour traffic. Only near police HQ did the cars grow packed together, and then Laura used her Vixen's black-strobe light—bands of shadow flitting across the street as the siren moaned. Pedestrians retreated as Laura eased one tire up onto the sidewalk and drove along the edge of the street.

At the cross junction the lights were red, but the drivers had seen the strobe, and everyone pulled to a halt as Laura's car streamed through.

"I want you to take the diva trail," she said, hauling the car into a right turn across three lanes of traffic, ignoring the horns. "All right?"

Steel doors carved with dragons' heads slid apart to either side at the Vixen's approach—moving improbably fast for such massive constructs.

"That's like, what, some kind of cross-country hiking route?" Donal forced his hands to relax—he'd been about to tense them into fists—as they swung past carved stone pillars that bore brooding, stylized eagles' heads. "Or what?"

"If the trail takes you across the country, then that's what it does." The tires screeched and howled as Laura pulled the Vixen through another tight, fast turn, startling a uniformed chauffeur who was starting up his big armored limo. "But I was thinking of paper trails, the boring, unglamorous kind."

"What about the diva?" Donal was amazed there was no pain left when he said her name, or rather her title. Donal was only now realizing: he hadn't known Maria daLivnova at all.

And how little that mattered now.

"Malfax Cortindo," Laura said, slowing the car at last, wheeling past bronze pillars and descending a long red metal ramp that led into a bowl-shape parking area.

The parking spaces were arranged radially as tear-shape depressions in the floor, like a potter's marks in clay, and three of them were occupied with rich-looking empty cars.

"You'll need the paper trail there. See why Alderman Finross was so keen to send you to him in the first place."

"You don't want me to talk to Finross."

"Not yet, Donal. Let's not reveal our thinking at this stage. The bastard probably thinks he's gotten away with everything—and I'm not even sure what he *is* guilty of. I think he might have brokered a deal....I don't know."

"Cortindo was a middleman." The Vixen rolled to a halt, and Donal closed his eyes and let out a gentle breath, then opened his eyes again. "But that doesn't rule out your theory on Finross—one man brokering a deal with another broker, two layers of indirection between the crime and whoever paid for it to happen."

"Hmm. Like I said, that's your job." Laura leaned over to kiss him, then winked and pushed open the door, stepping out with one foot. "Come on, Lieutenant, we're not hanging around here."

Donal gave a crooked half smile and exited. As he stood on the hard parking garage floor, the door pulled itself from his grasp and swung itself shut. It locked with a loud click.

"Er . . ." He hadn't realized the Vixen was wraith-enabled.

"Don't worry about it. She's quite tame." Laura patted the already-shut driver's door. "Aren't you, dear sis?"

"What?"

Laura shrugged. "A story for another time. But we're only half sisters, so it's not as strange as you might imagine."

Thanatos.

Life really had taken a sudden swerving turn for Donal. But there were richly suited men accompanied by overdressed wives heading for the trio of silver limousines nearby. Donal kept his thoughts to himself as he and Laura walked past.

"We're not in HQ yet," he said instead, staring up at the curved red-brown ceiling with bas-relief designs of what looked like smiling parrots. "Which building is this? The Redburn Center?"

"Yeah, you got it. The Five Seasons is two hundred floors up, if you want to eat dinner with senators and aldermen and similar fauna from the fish tank of local politics."

"Nice description. I don't think they'd let me in." Donal walked alongside Laura, shoulder close to her but not holding hands. "Not with my suits and ties."

"You're probably more welcome in there than I am. And I'd be happy to take you there once for the experience, you know?"

In his mind's eye, Donal imagined some portly maître d' attempting to stop Laura from entering his restaurant, and her iron reply: "*What's the matter, haven't you ever served a zombie before?*"

They walked past the entrance to the upper levels and continued along the silver-and-white tunnel marked

Deepway Fast 17. Secondary notices bore a list of buildings it linked to, including police HQ.

There were shops and small eateries, but the prices behind the counter were enough to make Donal wince.

"I guess I'm moving in new circles now."

"Huh." Laura shook her head. "Not much of a social circle, hooking up with me."

"Is that what we've done? Hooked up?"

They walked on in silence. Donal wanted to hold her hand but knew he should not—Laura was a senior officer, and he was on her team, and that was it.

At the silvery subterranean entranceway to HQ they stopped. An openmouthed wolf formed the design, some thirty feet high, the upper fangs raised above their heads, and the long tongue forming a ramp.

Donal nodded to the real deathwolves stationed on either side.

"Hey." He moved slowly, pulling out his wallet and flipping it open to reveal his badge. "Riordan."

"Don't know...you." The deathwolf on Donal's left raised its head and focused its amber eyes on his face. "Lieuten-ant."

"FenSeven is my friend." Donal held up his hand and allowed any microscopic residual scent to waft into the warm air. "Can you tell?"

"Ah. Yes-s-s."

The other deathwolf was already staring at Laura. She looked back at it in silent exchange. Then the deathwolf growled, ducked its head, and padded away inside the building. When it came back, two more deathwolves accompanied it.

"This is Donal." Laura nodded toward Donal, then to each deathwolf in turn. "He's my—"

"Mate." The biggest wolf, old and silver gray, pulled back its—her—upper lip in a lupine laugh. "We know."

Then the pack parted, two to each side, and watched

as Donal and Laura entered the building. It was oddly ceremonial.

He dared not look at Laura.

Seconds later, they were ascending in an elevator shaft—not Gertie's—headed for another day at the office.

Donal felt an odd thrill—except that it seemed not so strange, given the sudden shifts in his life. It was that familiar start-of-semester sensation, that feeling of entering another year, another adventure. They walked through the team room together, heading for Laura's office.

Viktor was seated at a desk, his fingers encased in wire claw gloves as he wrestled with a compositor framework, like a 3-D abacus, harder to use than a typewriter. A pale woman whom Donal did not know appeared, her eyes serious.

"Alexa," said Laura. "I want to introduce you to—"

"It's Sushana," the woman, Alexa, said. "No one's seen her for thirteen days. Last night she was supposed to meet her cousin and never turned up."

"Shit." Laura looked away. "Shit."

"We're backtracking, as quietly as possible, but you know how hard it is."

Donal looked from one to the other. "What was she doing?"

"Undercover sorcerer," said Alexa. Then, when Laura did not intervene to prevent further explanation: "It was a mixed coven, thirty-seven acolytes, meeting over a used-tire garage uptown. Rumors were that Sally C—Sally the Claw—funded the place."

"The coven or the garage?"

"Both. You know of Sally?"

"I met his brother Al once. Al Clausewitz."

Alexa blinked slowly. "I didn't know Sally had a brother."

Donal waited a beat.

"He doesn't," he said. "Not anymore."

Laura's cold lips tightened in a smile. "You're the right man for the job, I think."

"Tracking down this Sushana?"

"What about Harald?" said Alexa. "If he gets his network looking for Sushana, she'll turn up. One way or the . . . other."

"Look, she's undercover," said Laura. "Once Harald's tame pimps and fortune-tellers start spreading the word, they'll know we're taking a special interest in Sushana. If they think she's a made woman from Selvikin City, like her cover story says, then no harm done. But if they think she's a snitch . . ."

"Or that she's a cop." Donal shrugged. "She's dead either way."

"The missed meeting is one day old," said Alexa, "but it's thirteen days since anyone's seen her."

Laura said nothing for a moment. Donal knew what he would do, and he'd suggest it if Laura asked.

"Do it," Laura said then. "Get everything going that you can. Any hint of someone who knows Sushana, if we don't already know the person, we snatch 'em and sweat 'em."

Alexa whirled away, back to her desk, and ripped the phone from its hook.

"That's a go," she said, and slammed the handset down. Then she looked up at Laura and gave a bright girlish smile. "I had it all arranged, because I *thought* you'd say that."

"I hate being predictable."

"Remind me to introduce you to my pal Levison sometime," Donal said to Alexa.

But the humor was a coping mechanism, no more.

A missing undercover cop, on the first full day that
Donal was on the team . . . Luckily he didn't believe in
omens.

 Do you hear the—
 Oh, for Death's sake, not now.

11

The task force sent their contacts, their snitches and sympathizers, their paid informants and the weaklings they threatened, searching the unofficial labyrinths that defined the city for Sergeant Sushana O'Connor—or, rather, Sorceress Shara Conrahl, who had expressed such an interest in exploring the darker sides of her professed art.

That night, Laura remained in the office, coordinating. Donal's eyes were drooping, and she finally said he should go home. There were cots he could have used, but that seemed more conspicuous in terms of staying here all night with Laura.

Finally, he gave up and did what she suggested. He descended to ground level, where he chatted with FenSeven for ten minutes until the purple cab arrived.

The streets were empty and it took little time to reach home. His new home.

Darksan Tower's guardians were eight-foot behemoths with single slit eyes, who stood aside to allow Donal entry. An elevator whisked him up to the apartment, where he wandered around its metallic Gothic-deco spaces before collapsing into bed.

Dark dreams enveloped him.

Donal woke late, a sign that he was not yet fully recovered. He changed into his old running suit and took

the elevator down to the basement levels. A maintenance worker with grease-stained skin and two wraiths
hovering behind him showed Donal how to access the
deep stairwells that led into the catacombs.

He ran along routes that were unfamiliar to him, the
length of twisting long-abandoned ways. Then he was in
a cavernous area where newer family mausoleums, some
of polished brass and silver, were ringed with pale amber
lanterns. Running on, he finally entered a region that he
knew, and he grew certain that he was not imagining it.

Something had changed.

Catacombs persisted for centuries or even millennia. If
there was a change, it could not be in them. Yet odd whispers began now, falling silent whenever Donal neared a
sarcophagus or a mausoleum. It was almost as if—

Don't be insane.

As if the dead were afraid of him.

Back at the apartment, Donal's breakfast consisted of
cold blacksprout soup and coffee. If this arrangement
was going to last longer, he was going to have to see
about shopping and cooking. He checked his Magnus
load, then dialed down to the concierge and asked him
to call a taxi.

"I could get used to this," Donal muttered after putting down the phone. "Maybe."

The elevator that he rode down in was like a giant's
bullet, very fast. It stopped at the fifty-ninth floor to take
on two passengers, a man in a dark suit with a sine-wave
weave, and a woman with ballooning features and too
much jewelry, all of it real.

The man wore a monocle. Both he and his wife stared
at Donal with superior mild curiosity, as though wondering what sort of new servant had been hired by the
management.

When the elevator reached the ground floor, Donal pressed his palm against the elevator's steel wall and murmured, "Thanks."

The couple sniffed and frowned, passing through the doors before Donal. But the elevator wall delivered a cold shiver, and Donal knew he had been right: it was a wraith capsule. He wondered how long the wraith had been in service.

When Donal told the taxi driver where he was going, disappointment descended down the driver's features. Probably he'd figured on a big tip from one of the rich bastards who lived in Darksan Tower, but a hard-faced man headed for police HQ didn't fit the type.

At the corner of Fifth and Avenue of the Basilisks, the traffic was thick with the rush-hour crowd, and the taxi slowed to a halt. The driver frowned, thought for a moment, then turned and said through the partition, "Know what, Mac? It'll be quicker if you walk."

Donal looked at the sidewalks. The driver was unlikely to pick up another paying fare for a while. It was a fair assessment.

"Right," he said, and counted ten bills from his wallet and handed them through the gap in the partition. "Keep the change."

"Really?"

"Yeah." Donal slid out and slammed the door shut behind him. " 'Cause I'm a soft touch, really."

The sky overhead was a medium purple, with no scanbats in sight. The faintest hint of quicksilver was upon the air, but it wasn't raining yet. Donal pulled up the collar of his overcoat and walked fast for five blocks, until he reached the familiar tower that was HQ.

"Hey, FenSeven. Met one of your cousins yesterday."

"Yes-s-s." Amber eyes glowed. FenSeven pulled back his upper lip, slobbering. "You are . . . mat-ed."

"Thanatos, does everybody tell everyone everything in this place?"

"Not the . . . hu-mans."

"Well. Good."

Another two deathwolves rounded the nearest pillar and sat down next to FenSeven.

"Loo-ten-ant Riordan." FenSeven performed the introductions. "FenSevenThree. GrimwalTwo."

Both deathwolves looked young—too young for this assignment.

"Good to meet you both." Donal tipped his forefinger against his forehead in salute. "And any daughter of FenSeven has a lot to live up to."

The smaller wolf, FenSevenThree, ducked her head and gave a low growl of acknowledgment.

"See . . . you." FenSeven nodded to Donal.

"Later, pal."

Donal climbed the dark steps, passed through to the hall with the purple-and-white-checkered floor, and skirted a bickering group of young-looking, scarred whores from the dockside. On the granite desk, Eduardo—his lower body long melded into the granite—waved a hand toward Donal.

"You're wanted upstairs," Eduardo called out.

"The commissioner?"

"That's the upstairs I was thinking of."

One of the whores raised a finger and said, "Climb upstairs this." A thin man who might have been her pimp backhanded her across the face. "Dumb pig, shuddup."

A uniformed cop kicked the pimp in the side of the knee.

"Hey—"

As Donal turned away, Eduardo called, "Good to see you back."

This from a man turning into granite. Perhaps Donal's

experiences with the dead diva and the hospital could
have been worse.

"Thanks, Eduardo. Good to be here."

From the floor, the pimp called, "Ooh, Edu-*ar*-do.
What a lovely name. Are you a man or a statue up in
your—mmmph."

There was a dull crack, and the whores fell silent,
while the pimp uttered a tiny moan.

Donal continued to the elevators without looking
back.

Commissioner Vilnar's secretary, the lovely Eyes, turned
toward Donal but continued working. Silvery fibers
clamped against her eyes joined her to a switchboardlike
console filled with tiny levers, which in turn linked her
to the citywide network of rooftop surveillance mirrors.

Donal had never seen Eyes any other way. It occurred
to him that if he passed by her in the street, he would
never recognize her.

"The commissioner will see you right away, Lieutenant."

"Is he in a good mood?"

Eyes's fingers paused, hooking the air, as though using imaginary controls to parse meaning from Donal's
words. Then, saying nothing, she turned back to her
console.

The doors to the commissioner's office parted.

Do you feel the—

No. Never.

It seemed to take an age for Donal to pass through
the doorway, as if something were dragging at his skin.
This was new.

Or I've changed.

Secure sites sometimes used time-distorting hex fields
as one layer of protection. Such fields could slow down

intruders long enough for deadlier countermeasures to swing into action, or for the intended targets to make an escape.

But here, inside police HQ? Were such defenses really necessary?

Commissioner Vilnar, fat unlit cigar in hand, pointed toward the black iron visitor's chair.

"Sit."

"Sir."

"You're on this task force, Riordan, which I am not fucking happy with, understand?"

"Um ... okay."

"What's that supposed to mean?"

"I mean I understand now, but I didn't before ... Sir, I volunteered."

"That zombie, what's her name—"

Donal felt his voice drop an octave. "Commander Steele."

"—right, she led the squad that broke you out of the cabin, so I couldn't refuse the request. But..." Commissioner Vilnar let the sentence hang there. "I could have shit-canned you. That possibility is still there."

"Sir? Am I under internal investigation?"

"No." Vilnar placed his big pale hands flat on the desktop. "You called in IS to check out the gun range, which doesn't mean you're clean yourself, but it helps. Still, you allowed yourself to be ensorcelled in a high-profile assignment that I gave to you."

"Yes. I remember."

"There are people who weren't happy how that turned out." Commissioner Vilnar meant important people, high enough in Tristopolitan society to matter. "Some of them tried to give me a hard time."

"Oh."

"Which is why I'm giving you a chance, because I don't like being threatened. By anyone."

A smile tugged at the muscles around Donal's mouth. Underneath it all, the old man had this kind of iron strength. That was what Donal admired about him.

"If anything strange crops up in your investigation," Vilnar continued, "anything that might affect the security of our city"—he meant the safety of his own career—"you'll let me know here, in private, as soon as you can."

"Right, sir. I'll use my judgment on that."

"Okay, you can go, Riordan." Vilnar raised his scarcely existent eyebrows. "I gather there's some kind of commotion going on at present. Hammersen's network is causing waves."

"There's an officer missing."

"Right. Sushana something? But the street networks are shaking"—Vilnar gestured with a fat hand at his office—"from what I can gather up here."

"I don't know anything about Hammersen's snitches," said Donal. "Only that he has them."

Harald Hammersen sounded like the most impressive of the team members that Donal had yet to meet. An ex-marine with the most widespread network of underworld contacts that any working police officer had come across: that was Harald's reputation.

"It would be interesting," said Vilnar, "to learn more about that."

"Yes," muttered Donal, getting up from the chair. "I suppose it would."

And if Vilnar thought that Donal was going to hand over any details he might learn about another cop's private network, then the commissioner was insane. After a moment, a tiny glimmer appeared in Vilnar's eyes: it might have been anger or amusement.

"Go," said Vilnar. "And keep in touch."

"Yes, sir."

He went out, passing Eyes, who was bent over her

console, fingers flickering across the tiny levers. Just as well. If Donal had said anything, it might be a bad decision.

You want me to spy on Laura?

Donal really didn't think so.

In Gertie's elevator, Donal muttered, "Take me to the gun range, will you?"

What's the matter, lover? Need to pull your trigger desperately?

"Just do it, Gertie."

Well.

She dropped him fast down the shaft. At the subterranean level of the range, she dragged him to a bouncing halt.

Go play with your bangs.

The invisible hands that expelled him into the lobby were rougher than usual.

While Donal was blowing targets apart on the range, an army of informants was working the labyrinthine byways of the less-than-legitimate world. The people involved ranged from fruit-stall owners in Mixnatine Market close to the docks, who turned a blind eye to the odd carton that slipped away from the delivery trucks belonging to the large chain stores, to a corrupt enforcer working for Sally the Claw.

This enforcer had been exposed by Harald Hammersen three years before, with photographs taken by city technicians. Harald sent him back to work in Sally C's organization with the understanding that spying on his own boss was preferable to the official Tristopolitan execution pit, where wraiths with ravening, insane minds manifested hard talons and claws and beaks to satiate their hunger on the living.

"Dropping the hammer" was what Harald threatened as the last resort. He looked pale and thin, with dead white hair and strange eyes, and there was a rumor that he had once eaten an informant's eyes when said snitch failed to notify Harald of an arms shipment arriving at Buldown Docks inside crates of herring.

Whether the stories were true or not, Harald made tactical use of their implied threat. That was one of the reasons that Brijak Nelsan, a hard-faced stevedore with hooks for hands, was willing to share a bottle of vodka with Harald in the untidy "office" space at the rear of his warehouse. Nets strung across old boxes formed a kind of swing in which Harald sat, watching Brijak's face grow redder as he drank.

"You?" Brijak offered the vodka bottle.

"No. You finish it."

"Ha."

"So what have you heard?"

"Nothin'."

"Brijak . . ."

"Nothin' about why there's a bonded warehouse in North Dock that's going to be empty tomorrow night. I mean, no guards at all."

"A robbery?" Harald was disappointed. Sushana was missing and he was learning about a stolen shipment of cigarettes or booze.

"Dunno. Maybe a transport."

Harald ran his fingers through his white hair. He had the skin of an eighteen-year-old and the hair of a grandfather, but he was neither. His hands were slender but iron-hard.

"Tell me about it," he said.

"The transport? You wanna get on a ship to, I dunno, Zurinam, how would you go about it?"

"You mean, other than buy a ticket like a normal person would?"

"Normal?" Brijak smirked. "Don't know much about what that means."

"Tell me."

"Stuff's en route to another dock, just passing through here. Steal something, and eventually someone notices. But add a little extra shipment, who's gonna find out? 'Specially when you can just fill in some blank paperwork to make it right."

Harald thought about this. "You mean, someone's breaking in to put a crate *inside* the warehouse? Not to steal one?"

"What I said, ain't it?"

"Huh." Harald pulled out his billfold, counted out three blue twenty-sevens, a single three, and an eleven, and passed the notes over. "Interesting story."

"Was it what you was after?"

"No, but you've done well, all the same."

"Told ya. Sure you don't want a swig of this rotgut?"

"Some other time."

Harald went out quietly. Outside, on its stand, his bone-colored motorcycle stood waiting. Its ceramic duckbill snout was close to the ground, the headlights like angled eyes, the handlebars swept back like twisted horns.

When Harald drew closer, he saw a smear of bright red across the bill.

"What happened?"

Something faint glimmered inside the headlights. Harald crouched down, breathing in the dockland scent, and then he saw it: the faint trace of blood, dark upon dark. Two hundred yards away, two figures, bulky in shapeless clothes, were helping each other to limp away as fast as their broken limbs could manage.

"I don't like thieves much myself—"

The headlights flared amber, then dimmed.

"—but I'm glad you didn't kill them."

Harald swung his leg over the saddle.

"You ready?" He took hold of the raised handlebars, which reconfigured themselves as he gripped, bringing his hands lower. " 'Cause I am."

The bike growled into life.

"I need to talk to you," said Donal, waving at Laura. "If . . . that's all right."

Viktor and Alexa looked up from their desks. Whether they sensed something was happening between Laura and him, Donal had no idea.

"Can it wait?" Laura was standing over a purpleprint of some building.

"I've just been chatting with Commissioner Vilnar."

"So did you shoot the old bastard?" Alexa's tiny nostrils flared. "I smell smoke and cordite." She licked her lips. "Yummy."

Donal looked at her for a moment, then turned and followed Laura into her office. The door swung shut behind them, deadening the sound from outside.

"Thanatos," Donal said. "Am I the only normal one around here?"

For a moment, Laura's face was a pale mask. Then she relaxed and half-smiled. "If you're the most normal person we've got," she said, "then Death help all of us."

Donal glanced at the visitor's chair, decided he would remain standing.

"How would you rate me as an undercover operative?" he asked.

"If you're asking could I send you in as Sushana's replacement"—Laura's face was a mask again—"the answer's no, even *if* I could find a role for you. You're not a sorcerer, and she was specifically—"

"That's not what I meant. Vilnar wants me in here so I can spy for him. On you."

"Oh." Laura blew out a cold breath, steaming faintly in the warm room. "That makes life interesting."

"Yeah. I don't suppose Eyes is a spy *you've* planted on *him*?"

"I wish. That cold bitch is a mystery to me." Laura's breath steamed again, and she saw Donal looking at the dissipating vapor. She half-grinned, half-looked about to cry. "Shit. I'm just so funny. What do you see in me?"

"The most amazing person," said Donal, "that I've ever met. Or just about, anyway."

"Hey." Laura blinked. "What do you mean, just about?"

"I had quite a crush on Sister Mary-Anne Styx, back in the orphanage. Everyone else thought she was a hard bitch."

"Oh." Laura looked at her desk, as if its blank surface had become interesting. "Guess I can't compete there, then."

But there was more to it than that. If Donal had known the words, he would have asked Laura about the traumatic transition into paralife—but not here, and not now. Not in the office.

Instead, he told her, "I'm going to do what you said and follow the trail. If Vilnar's dirty, there'll be a link between him and Alderman Kinley Finross somewhere in the Archives. All I've got to do is wade through several lifetimes of boring shit to look for the shining nugget, right?"

"Right."

"And—"

Donal threw his fear aside. Life, and paralife, were too short for nervousness or complexity.

"I l—" He closed his mouth.

Laura's eyes widened in surprise, as she processed the words he had almost spoken.

Death. It's too soon. Or something.

He blinked, not knowing what had come over him.

Do you hear the—

Not now.

Donal turned and banged into the door, moving fast enough to take it by surprise. It recovered with a jolt and swung open, letting Donal into the office, where Viktor and Alexa were staring at him.

The door shut behind Donal, and he passed through the office, heading for the elevators. He was almost there when applause sounded back inside, along with laughter, and Alexa called, "Way to go, Riordan!"

The muscles of Donal's face tightened in what might have been a grin as he stepped into the shaft and began to free-fall. For perhaps twelve seconds he dropped, heart thumping as he tamped down his fear and refused to yell, and then invisible hands surrounded him and slowed his descent.

Where you going, darlin'?

"All the way, Gertie. The Archives."

Then I'll forgive you. Maybe.

She continued to lower him, under control, inside the two-thousand-foot shaft.

You got a real hankering for dead things, don't you, lover?

Strong feelings roiled in Donal, preventing his reply.

12

Vaults filled with obsidian sheets of runic transcriptions floating among the racks, vibrating against their tethers; strange half-physical, half-discorporated bird forms who cried out and wept as they recited the recorded conversations of long-dead men in the exact tone of voice—so the Archivists claimed—of the original speakers.

There were pits of magma fire where the researcher could chain himself (or herself) and relive the Farseers' visions of distant events, for as long as they could stand the pain. There were sealed-off shafts from which subtle rustling and the occasional inhuman groan emanated, with no explanation provided to the ordinary visitor.

Worst of all were the Vacua, those zones of nothingness that could drive even a federal spellbinder into madness. They promised the wisdom not of fact but of intuition, to any who could withstand the nine-day torture it took to traverse a Zone.

Such was the outer ring of the Archives.

Donal's coat flapped in breezes of alternating cold and hot vapors as he passed along the half-lit colonnade that ran alongside the Junior Archivists' pit. The wizened, gray-skinned forms mostly sat, bent and unmoving, poring over ancient records written on faded skin, some of which was not human.

They all appeared to be working on the same project, but Donal knew better than to stop and ask them what they were doing. One of them looked up, his eyeballs crawling with tiny red mites, each giving and receiving the blood of the Archivist's fellows, sharing the stuff among the thirty-seven-strong team. Lines of the tiny mites stretched across the desktops, in their endless march among the ancient-looking Junior Archivists.

Just why the Archivists shared their blood, and in such a way, was another mystery closed off to outsiders.

"What the Thanatos are you doing here?"

The voice was harsh and loud, causing Donal to stop and scan to every side before looking down at the ten-inch stone figure standing near his foot, gesticulating.

"My job," said Donal, drawing out his Magnus. "What about you?"

"I'll accept that answer," said the little homunculus, and then it began to shiver . . .

"Hold on."

. . . and melt, as it slipped down and soaked into solid rock and was gone. Donal reholstered his Magnus.

"Nice place you've got here," he muttered to no one and nothing.

In the distance, there might have been stones falling into dank pools, or perhaps the sound was of laughter, mocking Donal's presumption in entering the Archives.

Donal continued until he was in a chamber of razor-edged glass sheets arranged in a haphazard fashion at every possible angle in three dimensions—and possibly beyond. Occasional twistings occurred at the edge of Donal's vision field, where he glimpsed geometrically impossible arrangements of glass that blurred or became invisible when he tried to stare at them directly.

"Lieutenant Donal Riordan," he said, "badge number two-three-omicron-nine, requesting Bone Listener assistance for Archive exploration."

Around him, huge glass sheets seemed to rearrange themselves, although he could not actually track any motion. It was as if the glass moved without moving.

There was the potential for the new arrangement to slam into existence where Donal stood, carving him into geometric blocks of meat. The Archivists' criteria for acceptance often seemed arbitrary to the outsider, and cops told rumors of investigating officers chopped apart for no reason, except perhaps that the Lattice required fresh bones.

The air shifted—somehow, in some direction not easily perceived—and then vibrated in Donal's ears, with deep harmonics he felt only in his gut.

~~We require this knowledge: Why are you here?~~

Donal clenched inside and fought his reaction to the subharmonics. To show fear was to lose: the orphanage had taught him so.

"To track down a network of corrupt sorcerers and politicians," Donal said, "and take the bastards down."

There was a silence like the false calm of water flowing massively fast but without surface turbulence to reveal its power. Beneath, there was the sense of dark beings carrying out portentous unheard conversations. Donal's safety meant nothing here.

Laura had expected him to follow the paper trail, not the bone trail, but the real information was held in the Lattice. It always had been. There was every reason to suppose it always would be.

~~The diva's killers?~~

"Yes. Among other things."

~~Do they not sing, the bones?~~

Were the subharmonics mocking or sympathetic? Donal could not tell. Those words disturbed him, yet he had half-expected them, in this place.

"If you say so."

~~We taste them on you still.~~

"Fuck off."

The sound that echoed among the glass sheets now *was* laughter, but not from any human throat. Donal felt the blood draining from his face, from the skin of his torso.

"Are you going to fuckin' help, or what?"

Now the sound that washed around him was a torrent of strange whisperings, layer upon layer of them, building up a thunder that drowned even the blood rush in Donal's ears.

Then:

~~Yes.~~

A pale white light floated in the air at his head height. It shifted shape: first a tiny winged human, then a kind of wriggling, featureless white caterpillar, then a convoluted tangle of finger-thick cords, like some form of living knot. Whether it was alive, Donal could not tell.

As he focused on the knot and took a step forward, the glowing shape morphed once more, turned itself inside out, then glided through the dank air to Donal and stopped.

It hovered.

"You want me to follow?"

Donal stepped one pace in its direction, and the glowing shape drifted a yard farther. Donal followed again, and the shape began to move steadily, into an arched, darkened tunnel formed of cubic stone blocks that were worn and distorted with the centuries.

Somewhere, something screamed. Donal forced himself to ignore the sound.

There were steps leading downward, which Donal descended carefully; it would be easy to slip and end up lying there with a broken leg. In this place, there was no certainty of help.

Then there was a series of twisting tunnels, some that were intended to be straight but had warped into irregular configurations, others that deliberately wound back on themselves. In one place, where a fluid that smelled like blood trickled between the stone blocks, the tunnel was a slanting spiral that corkscrewed downward.

This was deeper into the Archives than Donal had ever wanted to go. And all the time, the glowing shape led the way, occasionally morphing into bizarre forms, always to return to the knot that perhaps approximated its true shape.

In an area floored with sandy dirt, ringed by openings to seven dark tunnels, the knot stopped its onward motion and twisted in place, hanging there.

"This is as far as you go, right?" said Donal.

The shape gave one final twist, then creased over in the middle as if bowing, shot off into one of the tunnels, and was gone.

"Thank you," Donal called out after it.

"You're welcome," said a dry voice behind him.

Thanatos . . .

There had been no footstep, no sensed presence, but when Donal spun around, the woman looked solid enough: tall, pale skin, a bald forehead, and lank milk-colored hair that began halfway back along her scalp and hung to the small of her back.

The woman was lean, but her wrists looked thick and strong, her jaw square, her gaze calm but redolent with something more, as if she had looked upon things that Donal could only half-imagine. Those eyes had dark-brown irises that were double the normal diameter, so that only tiny hints of white appeared at the corner of her eyes.

She was a Bone Listener.

"I'm Feoragh Carryn," she said. "You can call me Feoragh, Lieutenant."

"In which case I'm Donal to you."

Feoragh acknowledged this, inclining her head. Then: "Do you have a worthwhile search goal? Something worth bothering the Lattice for?"

"I don't know," said Donal. "I know nothing of the Lattice, but it's worth a lot to me. The case is... political..."

Feoragh frowned.

"...which I don't give a rat's ass about," Donal continued, "but it makes it hard to track down the killers. And if I do find the triggermen, the principals are going to be protected by massive layers of indirection."

"Killers," murmured Feoragh.

"Including the killers of Maria daLivnova, the diva. They tried to take her bones."

"Ah."

When Feoragh blinked, her eyes went momentarily black. Donal shivered.

"Tell me more, Donal. Tell me everything you know."

Donal related what he remembered. The period before his hospital stay was a little blurry, and the final days in the cabin, before Laura broke in and pulled Donal away from the bones' spell, formed a traumatic pain buried in his subconscious, but he could remember enough.

There was the meeting with Commissioner Vilnar that had started it all, the newspaper clippings from foreign cities about theatrical celebrities dying unexpectedly. Donal surprised himself by recalling all the names and locations—or at least he *thought* he remembered them all.

Then there was the meeting with Malfax Cortindo—

"Oh, yes," said Donal. "I nearly forgot. There was a letter from Alderman Kinley Finross, who arranged for me to visit the Energy Authority. He obviously knew Cortindo..."

Beneath Feoragh's dark and steady gaze, Donal found he was able to recall the letter word for word.

Then he told her of the visit itself. When he talked about picking up the bone and slipping into dreams, Feoragh sucked in a breath. And he told her of Cortindo snatching the bone from his grasp, dumping him back into the real world after three hours had passed, though it had seemed only a minute.

Finally, voice unsteady, he related the diva's final performance, the ensorcelled audience, and his flight with the diva down through the tunnels that led to the Energy Authority.

"That was a mistake." Donal's chest was heaving now, his skin covered with a slick layer of sweat as though he had been running. "Because, of course, Cortindo was behind it."

He told of the confrontation among the reactor piles, surrounded by ensorcelled workers, and Cortindo giving the order to fire.

"I could..." Donal's throat felt as if the diva's ghost were strangling him. "I hesitated. I could have saved her, but I froze for half a second..."

"Ah."

"...as if I *wanted* her to die. As if I wanted to touch her bones, caress them. Shit. You know..."

Do you feel the bones?

Yes.

Always.

Donal stared at the Bone Listener.

"Yes," murmured Feoragh. "I do know."

And Donal realized that Feoragh Carryn knew exactly what he was talking about.

"Malfax Cortindo," he said after a moment. "Thanatos. I didn't check the autopsy report."

"I can find out," said Feoragh. "Come with me."

They walked along a sand-floored stone tunnel and

stopped before a plain green door. Feoragh opened it and went inside. There was a simple wooden desk, sealed document boxes on a shelf, and a solitary telephone. Feoragh picked up the phone.

"Padraigh Fasheene," she said. "If you would."

Donal shook his head, smiling at his own preconceptions. He'd been expecting some kind of esoteric device, not a telephone.

Feoragh covered the mouthpiece with one hand. "Padraigh's my cousin. Works for Mina at the OCML."

"You mean Wilhelmina d'Alkarny?"

"Who else?"

"That's—good." He'd been about to say it was an interesting coincidence, her cousin working at the Office of the Chief Medical Listener, but then he realized that perhaps it was no kind of coincidence at all. What did he know about Bone Listeners?

"Could you ask your cousin," he said, "what the—"

Feoragh held up her hand.

"Padraigh, the autopsy on Malfax Cortindo... Yes, the one from the Energy Authority."

Donal watched, trying to read something into Feoragh's tense pale features.

"You're sure," said Feoragh: not quite a question.

Again there was a delay while Donal failed to guess what Feoragh's cousin was saying on the other end of the line.

"Yes? All right... Could you get her to notify Lieutenant Donal Riordan when it happens? *If* it happens... Fine." She glanced at Donal with those too-dark eyes. "Thanks, Padraigh."

She put the handset down.

"Don't tell me," said Donal. "They've lost the report."

"Hardly." Feoragh shook her head. "They haven't

done the autopsy yet. Cortindo's body is suspended in a stasis hex."

"But...that's impossible. I was in the hospital for two weeks." Donal knew there couldn't be that many bodies in the morgue. Not even the lowest-priority case could be held back this long. "What's going on?"

"Nothing."

"I don't believe—"

"By order of Commissioner Vilnar's office," said Feoragh in a hard tone, "absolutely nothing is happening."

"Oh," murmured Donal. "Like that."

"Exactly like that."

Donal stared at the wall, seeing nothing. Vilnar had put him on the diva assignment originally, but Laura believed that had been because Vilnar was under political pressure.

Could Vilnar really be holding back his own department's investigation?

Except that the task force had federal authorization. It wasn't truly under departmental jurisdiction.

"All right." Donal was trying to work out whether he could ask Feoragh to circumvent the restriction, to somehow get the OCML to carry out the autopsy anyway. It seemed unlikely. "What about the information trail? In the Lattice?"

An odd smile pulled at the muscles of Feoragh's face.

"Well, that's why you're here, isn't it?"

"Yes."

"Then let's go."

It was impossible to tell how big the Lattice was. Donal followed Feoragh along a convoluted route that led in the end to a long low chamber filled by struts and nodes—the struts made of titanium-wrapped bones, the nodes formed of carved bone inlaid with strips of some green-and-black mineral.

The chamber reminded Donal of a wine cellar. It was arranged so that Feoragh, provided she was willing to crawl on hands and knees or to stretch up onto tiptoe, was capable of touching every bone node with her bare hands.

But that was only one chamber, one tiny cell among thousands—maybe tens of thousands or more.

They had used a stone bridge to reach this place, and Donal had stopped at the midpoint to look over the edge, into the shadowed abyss. It plunged down as far as he could see, and the police department's medics had always rated Donal's distance vision as excellent. There were narrow bridges everywhere, entering the vast subterranean edifice that contained a three-dimensional array of bones many times bigger than the greatest buildings Donal had ever heard of.

Far below, on separate bridges, Donal had made out the figures of three Bone Listeners: two entering the Lattice, one shuffling and bent over, stopping to catch his or her breath partway across the bridge's span. Did they pay a price for working in the way they did?

"I'm ready."

Feoragh's voice brought Donal back to the moment, to the cold chamber in which they stood. This close to the Lattice, Donal felt as if the air was fractured and his body was brittle. He thought if he turned too quickly his eyes might fall out.

"For the information quest," Feoragh added. "You might want to listen to anything I say. Because if I speak it means I'm not retaining what I hear."

The atmosphere was different from the Energy Authority with its rows of reactor piles. There, a form of chaos had lapped at the edges of Donal's awareness, threatening always to explode, but here in the Lattice cell, it was more as if glass razors filled the air. There was a sharpness, a *density* that scared him.

"We need links," he forced himself to say, "between the diva and Alderman Finross, and between—"

"That much I remember."

Whether Feoragh was offended, Donal could not tell. She was slipping into some form of trance state, though not a relaxing kind: her limbs twitched, a short-lived rictus jerked several times across her face, and her eyelids fluttered for longer than seemed probable.

Then Feoragh's dark eyes snapped wide open, and she was expressionless as she walked into the midst of the Lattice and reached out toward a node. Her sleeve dropped back, and as she reached, a sharp-edged node cut a thin red arc on her pale skin. Tiny beads of blood glistened as Feoragh's fingertips touched the node.

The blood drops grew smaller and sank inside the bone, like water into a sponge.

Feoragh's mouth stretched open as she screamed—except there was no sound. To Donal it seemed that she was howling in agony, but the sound failed to reach him: something in the air cut the vibration apart and fed on it, absorbing it.

Then Feoragh bowed her head, and Donal thought he saw some dark vibration ripple along the struts, play across the nodes, and flow outward into the greater Lattice.

I'm sorry.

But this was what Feoragh did for a living.

It hurt her—in fact, it seemed to be torturing her—but Donal knew that he would ask her again to engage on an information quest if it was important. In fact, it seemed to him that a touch of ruthlessness was required in order to be a successful candidate in the first place: the Bone Listeners did not respond to everyone.

And there were rumors of candidate clients who had

entered the depths of the Lattice buildings—if not here, into the core—and simply never returned.

Feoragh shuddered once more.

"Going—"

Her voice reached Donal as if through ocean waves, attenuated and broken.

"—to Ill—"

Strange ripples broke up the air.

"Illurium. That's where—"

Feoragh clamped her mouth shut and now stood catatonic, unmoving save for the blood that started at her lip and trickled down toward her chin.

"Wake up," said Donal, changing his mind. "Whatever it is, I don't need to know this badly."

But it seemed his decision was too late. Feoragh began to shiver, and her hands sprang off the bone nodes as though she'd been burned. Then, stiff as a two-by-four, Feoragh toppled to the floor.

For a split second Donal thought that he wouldn't be able to react fast enough, but his body had already shifted and, the next thing he consciously knew, he was kneeling with Feoragh in his arms. Her head was two inches from the hard flagstone.

He laid her down onto the too-cold floor.

"Shit."

Now what was he supposed to do? Did this happen to Bone Listeners all the time? Or was Feoragh ill? Could something she had discovered inside the Lattice have *made* her ill?

Donal shifted Feoragh into the recovery position, checked that she had not swallowed her own tongue, then got to his feet. There was nothing in the chamber— or cell—that would let him communicate with the outside world: no phone, no alarm button. Nothing.

He went out to the colonnade, which led to other cells. No one was there.

"Hello? Can anybody help?"

From the balustrade he leaned over to stare down into the shadowed abyss crossed by thin stone bridges. Again, no one. He looked up at the undersides of further bridges, but there were no sounds of movement.

"I have a Bone Listener in trouble!" Donal's voice echoed back at him. "Feoragh Carryn needs your help!"

The shadows were still.

"Thanatos," he muttered, and went back inside.

But Feoragh was already sitting up on the floor. When she saw Donal she stretched out one hand so that he could help her to her feet.

"It happens sometimes," Feoragh said before he could ask. "When the depth of information is too great, when there are thaumaturgical safeguards to navigate, we pay the price."

"I'm sorry."

"It has nothing to do with you."

"Oh." Donal stared at the bone nodes, the titanium-and-bone struts that supported and linked those nodes.

Do you feel—

Yes, and I wish I didn't.

"This isn't," said Donal, "what I sensed near the reactors. They were dangerous and I knew it. Fragments of agony . . ."

"Yes."

"This is different."

"We have clear information, incised deeply." Feoragh paused, then: "The bones are a medium with a vestigial trace of their memories from life. New bones are formatted first, utilized later."

Donal nodded, only half-understanding what she meant.

"Surely it's fuzzy," he said. "The information. Unfocused."

Feoragh shook her head.

"Information etching is a precise process," she said. "There's nothing fuzzy about the results. Nothing at all."

She rubbed her fingers across her forehead in what Donal thought was an unconscious gesture.

"What is the process?" he asked her. "The etching—how does it work, or are you not allowed to say?"

Feoragh stared at him for an extended moment. Then: "Suffering," she said. "That's where the focus comes from."

Donal had no idea how to respond to that.

13

The information quest did more than disturb Donal. Bloodied, Feoragh seemed matter-of-fact about what it took to be a Bone Listener; and she had uncovered some positive results.

She told Donal as much as she'd been able to discover about the people-behind-the-people-behind-the-people involved in the diva's and the other performers' deaths. There were "unfulfilled links"—as she described them—to Zurinam and other countries.

Feoragh recited a short list, which Donal memorized.

"But the clearest trail," Feoragh said, "leads to Silvex City. Councillor Gelbthorne is the name you need. I rate him at ninety-three percent likelihood of belonging to the same group as Cortindo."

"Silvex City? That's in—"

"Illurium, yes. And one of your colleagues is Illurian. Though she has no meaningful contacts that I can discover, she should be able to brief you on what life is like in Silvex City, when you decide to go there."

Donal scarcely noticed the "when" rather than "if." The colleague that Feoragh referred to was Xalia, and what a wraith could tell Donal about surviving in the city, he was not quite sure.

"Senator Blanz has been dealing with someone in

Silvex City," Feoragh added. "I can't track down the name. I'm sure that Malfax Cortindo knows it."

This made a kind of sense.

"Cortindo's dead," he said. "But why is his body still in stasis?"

"I didn't pursue that question," Feoragh answered. "There's no point in looking inside the Lattice for information that fresh."

"Shit."

Donal needed to get an autopsy scheduled. Perhaps Laura's influence . . . but even she couldn't move openly against Commissioner Vilnar. And if Vilnar really was dirty and suspected that Laura's task force was investigating him, he would have the power to shut them down, provided he resorted to dirty tricks.

And Donal suspected that Vilnar, if he were fighting for his own survival, would have little hesitation in pulling out every nasty tactic he knew, from discrediting Laura or her officers to having them arrested or worse.

There were many bad things that could happen to a police officer whose own superiors had turned against him—or her.

"Talk to Padraigh," Feoragh said. "Tell him I sent you."

"All right."

"That's not a promise that he'll be able to help you."

"I understand. Thanks. And thank you for—" Donal gestured toward the cell. "You know."

Feoragh bowed her head. "What else could I do?"

"I don't know. But thank you anyway."

Harald was crouched low over his Phantasm Mk IV, traveling at a hundred mph along the overpass. This late at night there was little traffic, though it was still dangerous as he hurtled from the orbit opening in the two-thousand-foot skull that overlooked the city's midtown.

He accelerated, weaving between three freight trucks and their loads of scared-looking lizards in their crates, destined for the food markets. The Phantasm's handlebars had already morphed to their lowest configuration, and the engine growled, certain in the knowledge that there was more power to give should Harald need it.

Then there was a spiraling down-ramp and Harald took it at speed, feeling the bike's joy as he banked the continuous turn through some thousand degrees of curve until he was on the level. The bike shot forward between two vast supporting pillars, screaming through blood-red stoplights as horns honked—even at this hour there were people to be scared by his tactics.

He slowed, followed a zigzag route through nine city blocks, then turned into the gentle off-ramp that led onto Avenue of the Basilisks. It was the same street but several miles away from police HQ: the avenue stretched for over a hundred blocks.

There. He could see the green headlights now.

Brijak, his snitch, had been telling the truth. There was a bonded warehouse exactly where Brijak had said.

A lone low-slung car was pulled up at the gate. Its driver got out and talked to the security guards for a couple of minutes before getting back inside the car and driving off. The driver had been wearing a dark suit, and he had scanned the streets—security conscious—before walking over to the guards' booth.

But there was no way he had spotted Harald.

When the car moved off, Harald waited nearly two minutes before setting the stealth switch, turning the engine into mumbling life, and moving slowly in the correct direction. There was only one sensible direction for someone leaving the warehouse district.

Harald didn't open the engine up to normal power

until he was on the expressway. Red strontium-vapor streetlights turned the highway into a glistening blood-red river as Harald gunned the Phantasm, bringing the car into sight.

He remembered the way the driver had checked the surroundings. Damn it. As Harald followed along the high expressway, the bastard had to have spotted the Phantasm trailing him.

When the car took the off-road that ended five miles later at the Avenue of the Basilisks, Harald took the penultimate exit, the spiraling ramp that rush-hour drivers crawled down carefully in their complaining cars. For a minute, he would be out of sight of the car's rearview mirrors.

Now Harald manipulated switches and spoke the keywords that he preferred not to use: they made the Phantasm uncomfortable. It stretched out, wheels rotating as it elongated its chassis in preparation, then it hunched back and raised its handlebars into a vertical attitude.

A shivering change washed over its bone-pale skin. The fairings broadened and darkened toward green. It no longer looked like a Phantasm.

To a motorcycle enthusiast, its outline was closest to a Maleville 7, a low-performance classic. It was the best the Phantasm could do for disguise.

Up ahead, a car swung into view. Green headlights, a cautious driving style—yes, that was the bastard.

"Let's go." Harald laid his hand flat on the fuel tank. "And thank you."

The first stop was at the rear of a garment store that should have been deserted at this hour. In the alleyway around back, the car stopped.

The driver got out and crossed to a metal door, then

spoke a password that Harald was too far away to lip-read. Silver sparks flickered across the metal as a hex field dissipated. The man opened the door and went inside.

Harald left the bike. It was gently thrumming in stealth mode and fully armed should anyone touch it in Harald's absence.

On foot, Harald went down the alleyway, keeping to the edges as it opened out to a yard paved in black oily gravel. Despite the footing, Harald moved with scarcely a sound. At the lighted, barred window, he peeked inside.

Two short men with square jaws and massive shoulders and arms were shifting a coffin-size container into position on a table. The man in the suit was standing in an internal doorway, only partly in Harald's line of sight.

They said something more, then the dark suit disappeared from the doorway and Harald realized the meeting was already over. He moved fast, disappearing into the narrower alley just as the metal door banged open.

"—course it's light when it's empty," a rough voice was saying. "Obvious, ain't it?"

"Then you won't have any problem being there." This man's voice had a trace of an accent. "Will you?"

"Er . . . No, boss."

Harald waited in case they might say something obvious, like a place or time. If they did, he would have to evaluate whether it was the truth or a fabrication—the latter would mean they'd spotted him.

But there were no further words as footsteps crunched across gravel and the car door opened and slammed shut almost in time with the building's metal door. Harald was already moving. Beneath the car engine's sound, he could hear a deeper rumble as the bike switched itself out of stealth mode in readiness for the chase.

"Well done."

By the time the car pulled out onto the Avenue of the Basilisks, Harald was already riding the still-altered bike in its Maleville form, following from in front. The car overtook him but not at high speed; this was close enough to police HQ that the driver would not want to be stopped. Not tonight.

Then the car pulled off to the right, into Kilbury Circle, and Harald had to think fast, taking the bike into Melville Square and cutting through a small alley, knowing that he could no longer afford to be spotted. He'd thought the car would pass him, but this was the way life turned out: there was no use worrying about it.

There.

Harald caught a glimpse of the target car, saw the wash of its lime-tinged headlight beams play across a garbage can—they were into a residential area, five-story town houses from the turn of the millennium replacing the huge towers—and he turned the bike to follow.

"I think you can relax," he shouted above the slipstream, and squeezed inward with his knees.

There was a warmth against his inner legs: a signal of gratitude as the bike began to morph itself back into default shape.

It lengthened and lowered its configuration, paling back to the color of dried bone.

Harald lay forward, close against the armored fuel tank, and the Phantasm growled its delight as its natural form returned. It banked over as Harald directed the hard-accelerating turn, and they arced into Pallas Heptagon.

Slowing now, the car had already passed along two sides of the heptagonal central park. On the other side of the road, although it was late, lights were burning in many of the grand old buildings. Outside two of them, soldiers in unfamiliar uniforms stood on guard duty.

This was the diplomatic district, where embassies and consulates had stood for centuries.

The motorcycle switched its lights off and slowed simultaneously with Harald's decision to do just that: it was no longer clear which of them was the rider and which the vehicle. Sometimes they acted together like a single being.

Coasting to a silent stop, the Phantasm-and-Harald reflexively chose the darkest spot. A large parked limousine with obsidian windows and flared fins helped obscure them. They quietly observed the target car slowing and then halting before armored gates that led into a yard beside one of the older and more luxurious embassies.

A white-helmeted guard came out of a sentry box, looked in at the car's driver, and nodded. At the same time the armored gate slid to one side on impressively quiet rollers—Harald assumed that diplomats liked to sleep soundly—to reveal a darkened yard.

The car slid forward and disappeared from sight as the gate rolled across and clicked into place. Pallas Heptagon was still once more.

Harald squeezed his knees and the bike slipped into stealth without his having to use the controls. Then it rolled backward until they reached the next corner of the heptagon, before spinning around and taking them out of there, heading for the nearest police phone.

It was late, but there was at least one person that Harald knew would not be asleep. Every member of the team had Laura's home phone number, and the police HQ switchboard had it set up as if it were an internal extension.

Harald wondered what he was going to say.

Sushana was missing, that was the thing. Was any of this going to help? A bonded warehouse, a covert shipment—it might have nothing to do with Sushana's disappearance.

There was an all-night convenience store on the corner. Here the houses were dark and crumbling. Harald stopped and parked the Phantasm.

"I'll just be a moment."

The engine purred.

Inside the store, Harald nodded to the owner, a tall man with pale-brown skin and three purple scars along his left cheek.

"Have you got any maps?" Harald asked. "Local maps?"

"Yes, I think we have—" The man started to point, then his gaze flickered toward the street outside. "Is that your motorcycle?"

"Uh-huh."

"Please, shall I call the police? I think a man is trying to steal it."

Harald felt himself relax, listening.

"Everything's fine," he told the store-owner.

"But he is going to take your motorcycle!"

Flicking through the maps, Harald found the one he wanted. He pulled it open, checked the index, turned to the *Tristopolitan Midtown* section, and found the page that showed Pallas Heptagon. As he'd hoped, the embassy names were marked.

The man he'd followed had entered the Illurian embassy.

"Please, sir, I'm thinking I should really call the—"

A scream echoed from the street.

"No need to panic," said Harald.

*   *   *

There was no need for the switchboard to patch Harald through to Laura's home. She was in the office, as was Donal. He'd found a small cot to sleep on from among the four set up in the supply room at the end of the corridor.

Viktor and Alexa were in the squad room, bruised arcs beneath their eyes, showing the strain. Waiting was worse than being on the streets.

After a while, Viktor pulled on his leather coat and said he had to get out. Alexa, staring into space, scarcely acknowledged the words.

When the phone rang, Donal was standing in Laura's office, while she sat, flicking through the same reports she'd already read twenty times. Donal felt sweaty and unclean, his shirt rumpled and his suit in need of a drycleaning, his tie half undone.

Laura picked up the handset.

"Harald? You've found something?"

There was a pause.

"Sounds thin," she said then. "Sounds like you were following a different kind of lead. . . . No, I don't blame you: a bonded warehouse job is big news. Coincidence?"

Laura listened some more, then glanced up at Donal.

"We might be in luck," she said into the phone. "Let me talk to Donal a moment. Just so you know, Donal's uncovered another trail, and it also pointed to Illurium. To Silvex City."

Laura covered the mouthpiece with one hand.

"Harald's found a driver from the Illurian embassy," she told Donal, "who's connected with a bonded-warehouse job. They're going to deliver some container to the warehouse." She continued with the details that Harald had given her. "What do you think?"

Donal was used to running his own team. It was good of Laura to recognize that.

"Go with it," said Donal. "But don't commit all our resources."

For a few moments, Laura considered.

Into the phone she said, "Sorry, Harald. Just planning. D'you have any input?"

She listened, eyes hardening.

"Intelligence," she said then. "Damn it."

Donal guessed what they were talking about. "You want to call in the spooks?" Even to someone used to freewraiths, some of the DIO's operatives were hard to take. "They'll crawl all over the place and shut us out."

Laura tapped her desk with her diamond-hard fingernails.

"That's not good enough. . . . Look, Harald." She switched her attention from Donal to the phone. "You know Alf Zentril? From Robbery-Haunting? Good. I'm going to call in a favor. Expect to see his team at your location shortly. If not, we'll send our own people. Got it?"

She listened a bit, then nodded. "Sounds good. Make sure you're not spotted." And after a moment: "Good luck."

Laura put the phone down.

"I didn't figure you for a territorial animal," she said to Donal. "We have an officer's life at stake, and the Distributed Intelligence Organization has resources we could never—"

"It's not Sushana I'm thinking of," said Donal. "Ah . . . I don't mean that the way it sounds."

"You don't?"

"The driver that Harald followed," Donal said. "He's not an Illurian agent."

"Why not?"

"Because if you needed to ship something—or a dead someone—out of the country, and you're a foreign intelligence officer, you'd use the diplomatic bag."

"Diplomatic bag..."

"That's just what they call it. The 'bag' could be a shipping crate." Donal was sure of himself now. "If it's from an embassy, Customs doesn't open it."

"Damn it," said Laura.

"It's as if the embassy mail room were a bonded warehouse all by itself."

"All right. I've worked it out. But someone official in the embassy might want to run an operation off the books. I've heard people do that sometimes."

A tiny smile tugged at Donal's mouth. "That's terrible."

"Right. We'd never do that."

"Thanatos forbid." Donal sat himself down in the visitor's chair. "So what are we going to do, boss?"

"We're going to track down whoever's got Sushana," said Laura, "and deal with the fuckers."

"On or off the books?"

"Either way."

Harald's network of snitches was huge, but he wasn't the only one with resources. Big Viktor had contacts of his own, and right now he was busy bouncing one of them, hard and repeatedly, against a brick wall.

Still, Franz was refusing to talk. His eyes had widened at the blue-and-white photograph that Viktor had shown him: the photo of Sushana. But Franz had shaken his head, clamping his mouth shut.

This was unusual for Franz. Unfortunately, his reticence guaranteed that Viktor would keep hammering until he got answers.

"How's business?" asked Viktor, using a paper towel to wipe blood off his fist. None of the blood was his own. "Well enough to miss it when it's gone?"

They were behind Franz's largest gambling joint. In a

parlor at the front were stone couches where wraithing addicts slid into trance, their disembodied viewpoints hooking on to wraiths and following them in their races through channels beneath the city.

Viktor hooked his fingers into Franz's collarbone and pulled downward, tugging at the friable bones and bringing a wince to Franz's face. Then he hammerlocked Franz's arm and propelled him indoors, through the dingy hallway to the parlor.

No clients lay on the deserted stone couches. Each couch was a single hollowed stone, shipped from up-state Orebury, quarried from the Resonant Caves.

Viktor bared his teeth in something that was nearly a smile. He pushed Franz away from him, then, crossing his arms, reached inside his leather jacket and drew out two square-edged Grauser automatics.

He took aim at the nearest couch.

"No." Franz swallowed. "Don't you know how much they—"

Viktor pulled both triggers.

Shards of stone blew in all directions. One sliver cut Viktor's cheek, but he ignored it.

"*No,*" Franz whispered.

Viktor swiveled and took aim at couches on either side of him, arms spread dramatically: a calculated stance. Intimidation is a skill best learned on the streets.

"All right." Shoulders slumped, gaze weakening, Franz said, "The woman—there was one like her."

He meant Sushana, from the photograph.

"Tell me."

"I heard . . ." —Franz swallowed again—"she was in the docks, with Tax Silberman's crew. You know them."

Viktor nodded.

"It was a snifferwraith." Franz spoke quickly now, as though some internal dam had broken. "What I heard, anyhow. They scanned her, found she was a plant, and..."

"What?"

"Either they dumped her straight into the Plax with chains on, or they took her to Sally the Claw and he did it. I ain't sure which version is true, and I didn't try to find out."

There was a rage building up inside Viktor, but now was not the time to release it.

Sushana, my love.

Franz looked up, regaining a little of his composure. "Was she one of yours?"

"Was..."

Then it burst out, a black flood that Viktor made no attempt to rein in. His hands raised of their own accord and the twin Grausers thundered loudly, shot after shot crashing through the air as stone couches blew apart into sharp-edged fragments.

Franz was on his hands and knees, crawling back toward his office for safety beneath the maelstrom, then giving up. He crouched on the floor like a facedown fetus, shivering while the world disappeared in the cacophony overhead.

"*Sushana,*" Viktor whispered.

The guns clicked empty, half a second apart, and Viktor's rage dissipated more quickly than it had come, blowing away like smoke in a sudden wind. What remained in Viktor's core was something harder and darker, and as patient as it needed to be.

It would take time to reach Sally the Claw, past all the cutouts, the lieutenants, and the foot soldiers, but Viktor would do it. What happened next would be up to Sal, but Sal was not the kind of man to submit to arrest.

Viktor was counting on that.

*   *   *

Donal looked ready to fall over. Alexa had already gone, finally giving in to Laura's order to get some rest. Nothing more was likely to happen tonight, or this morning.

It was already twenty-five o'clock, and the only thing Laura had achieved since Harald's phone call was to dispatch a team from Robbery-Haunting to act as Harald's surveillance team.

Now she told Donal, "You need to go home."

"What about you?" He was too tired to argue much but had no wish to leave her here.

Laura looked around the office, then decided quickly, rolled up two charts from her desk, and tucked them under one arm. "I'll come with you. All I need is a phone, and the switchboard can patch through to the apartment."

"All right."

Picking up the phone, Laura waited for the internal operator to come on, then gave her instructions, thanked the wraith, and put the phone down.

"Let's go via the street," she said. "I need some air."

"Me too." He thought perhaps it was for his benefit, because Laura looked exactly as she always did.

Donal and Laura descended in the elevator shaft side by side, borne by Gertie, who remained silent all the way, giving them only an impersonal push to assist their exit from the tube.

At ground level, they passed along the stone halls that became the outer reception area, where Eduardo was on perpetual duty, melded into the stone block of the reception desk.

"She'll be all right," Eduardo said, meaning Sushana. "I'm sure of it."

Donal nodded, but Laura shook her head. She was obviously sure—or almost sure—that Sushana was already dead.

Out on the street, the sidewalks were slick with puddles through which fine silver threads swam, glinting orange or crimson where they caught the streetlights' reflections. Donal and Laura walked in silence, until a purple cab appeared and Laura flung her arm out.

"It'll be quicker than retrieving the car," she said.

"Um . . . all right."

Perhaps she was too tired to drive. Or perhaps it was just that she wanted to be out of contact for minimal time. Donal followed her into the cab and told the driver to take them to Darksan Tower, fast.

It took only minutes to reach the tower.

"Good man."

Laura paid before Donal could move. They got out and passed the entranceway's guardians. Laura's heels clicked on the black-glass floor as they crossed the lobby to the express elevator and ascended straight to the apartment.

At first Donal thought he was too wired to rest, but once inside the bedroom he pulled off his jacket and sat down on the edge of the bed to pull off his shoes. He felt the lure of the bed and lay back and slipped into relaxation, and then he was asleep.

"Very good," he might have heard Laura murmur.

After she had kicked off her shoes, taken off her jacket, undone her skirt and blouse, and allowed them to slip to the floor, Laura stood there for a long time, staring at Donal as he slept.

It was hard for Laura to remember sleep, and dreaming.

Clad only in black lingerie, she walked out into the hallway and stopped before the mirror-hung wall. Clapping her hands softly, she spoke the keywords that activated encrypted spells inside the hidden mechanisms.

She stopped, listened—no sound came from the bedroom save the softest of snores—then clapped once more.

This was the quickest way up, faster than ascending the outside of the building. That was something she did only when she needed to feel alive—or to try recapturing that feeling.

The mirror shifted, then swung back, revealing a narrow portal. It led to a darkened shaft. Inside, a slender ladder formed of struts that might have been bone glimmered with a gray-green luminescence.

Laura stepped through the portal and directly onto the ladder. She grabbed hold with both hands, swung her other foot onto the same rung, and waited. The door swung shut behind her, the concealing mirror once more in place.

After a quick glance down—the ladder disappeared into the black depths—Laura craned her head back, focusing on the faint heptagonal outline high above. She returned her attention to the ladder.

Slowly at first, Laura climbed.

Ten minutes later she was at the hex-guarded hatch, muttering the keywords that would let her through. In moments, the hatch flared silver and swung itself up and back. A sudden vicious draft caught hold of Laura, but her grip was tight. After a moment she moved, pulled herself up onto the roof, and stepped into the turbulent night.

The hatch swung shut behind her.

Laura was high above the streets now, on the complex Gothic-deco spire that rose high above Darksan Tower proper, hundreds of feet above her apartment on the 227th floor. As always, necrotonic cables hung in dark catenary curves, linking her building to the other towers that stood like giant sentinels high above the city streets.

Hunkering down—not against the cold, simply to

present a lower profile to the capricious wind that could tug her straight off the roof at any time—Laura watched the night and waited.

Soon, pairs of glowing scarlet eyes were visible amid the darkness, where Laura's enhanced vision could scarcely make out the cables and skywalks. The tiny scarlet beacons moved through darkness, drawing closer.

Laura's cats were coming.

14

One by one, the small shapes slipped across the narrow stone bridges, the hanging cables, and the tiny translucent filaments that normally bore only sprites engendered by the splitting off of insubstantial fragments from large wraith forms.

Now the cats moved steadily across these narrow byways, their forms undulating as necessary to counteract the turbulence that swept these high places. Their eyes glowed powerfully scarlet when a distant reflection caught them.

Once, as a scanbat glided past overhead, two of the cats hunkered down on the skywalk they were traversing, alert to the opportunity to catch new prey, but the bat was past soon enough, and after a moment the cats continued on toward Darksan Tower.

If Sushana was alive, Laura needed to know. She had lost officers before, but not in this team, not during this job. What Laura did for a living—or whatever she should call it now—had always defined her. And now that she had allowed Donal into her life—unlife—the job mattered more than ever.

Not the politics, not the checking of boxes when cases cleared or budgets were secured. The real people.

The first of the cats licked her hand and settled down beside her to wait.

While Laura thought about the ways she could direct her friends of the night, which buildings they might investigate, which people they might observe unsuspected from the darkness, the cats themselves gathered in a widening circle around her on the rooftop. Behind her rose the skeletal needle that was the final upthrust of Darksan Tower, making its mark in the night sky.

Then the cats were gathered, and Laura began to speak.

While Donal dreamed—bizarre, broken images that might have been a nightmare, might have been a way of dealing with the dark reality *without* frightening himself—and while Laura laid out her plans for the cats' approval, the rest of their team was busy.

Alexa, after calling in at a cops' bar and sinking back three flame tequilas in rapid succession, was now in her own apartment, inhaling lilac clarity smoke from broken twigs burning in a copper bowl. She was attempting to reverse the drunkenness and cough her way back to sobriety.

But the other members of the team were more active. Harald, though he had not slept in three days, looked entirely alert as he sat astride his stationary motorcycle and told his new colleagues, the team from Robbery-Haunting, everything he knew about the embassy's layout and the driver who was their target.

"When he moves, we follow, hanging back but not enough to risk losing him." Harald's gentle eyes did not change as he added, "If he spots us, we'll need to shut him down."

"Shut down? How permanently?"

"An officer's life is at stake."

The R-H guys looked at one another. "That explains it," one of them said.

"What?"

"Why our boss is doing your boss a favor."

"And," said one of the others, "why none of us is on duty right now, unless we have to be. No reports."

"Off the books?" asked Harald.

"Completely. Unless something exposes us."

"Good," said Harald. "Let's try to keep things quiet. I like quiet."

Around him, the R-H team nodded. They had lives and families to return to when this thing was over.

While this was happening, Harald's friend Viktor was on the west side, near the dockyard district, only a few miles away from the bonded warehouse where Harald's trail had begun. But Viktor's target was something else.

There were several acres of concrete beyond the chain-link fence. Stacks of pallets and crates stood haphazardly between a half dozen block-shaped office buildings and warehouses. They provided reasonable cover from the swinging silver beams cast by slow-gliding jelly lights overhead.

In the office, a surprising number of windows were lit. Men in ties and shirtsleeves were going about their business (most of which, Viktor knew, would be legitimate, for this was a real trading company).

Strange ripples of darkness moved across the chain-link fence. Atop it stretched razor wire that slowly twisted and turned, animated by tortured wraiths whose forms had been dragged thread-thin along the wires' lengths. They screamed forever in a realm where no human could ever hear, hanging on only so that they might catch a living person and deliver agony of their own.

At the gateways, guards stood smoking and watching the street outside and the unlit buildings beyond, occasionally fingering their weapons. As Viktor watched, an older, gray-haired man approached them. The men dropped their cigarettes and ground them out with their heels.

Alertness was everything.

But still, thought Viktor, as the older man retreated to one of the buildings, the setup was less secure than it looked. That was partly because Sally the Claw was running a mostly legitimate business here. But it might have been a miscalculation, or an overreliance on Sal's reputation as a stone killer with an organization of psychopaths at his back.

To Viktor, the outer defenses looked strong, but once inside the perimeter, the site was poorly guarded.

Even as he thought this, Viktor noticed the gray-haired man reentering a building without having to use any kind of password or submitting to personal inspection. The building's doors were not even locked.

From his hiding place inside a blackened alley mouth, Viktor smiled, cold and predatory.

In the apartment, Donal sat bolt upright on the sweat-soaked bed, sheet falling away from his bare torso. His eyes snapped open, seeing nothing but the fading tails of his own nightmares. The bedroom was empty save for him, with no sign of Laura's presence.

"Oh, Thanatos," he said.

Then his eyelids fluttered, and he lowered himself onto the mattress, shivered once, and slipped straight back into his dreams. He smiled briefly, but it was cold and flat.

Donal slid deeper into sleep.

Viktor remained standing in the alleyway, knowing he should take action, not knowing why he wanted to stay as he was. But he had worked the streets for long enough to trust himself, to trust his own subconscious, which saw more of the world than the surface mind.

After a few minutes he got it.

On the very edge of his peripheral vision, five stories overhead in what had seemed a deserted building, a shadow shifted within darkness: just the tiniest of movements.

Snipers.

Well, one sniper at least, in this building. Even if the man was solo—which was probable—he would not be the only man stationed around the perimeter. Other buildings would have their watchers armed with rifles, observing the surrounding streets and watching the compound fence from the outside.

There was a chance that this was some enemy of Sally the Claw, whether police or criminal, watching the premises with much the same intent as Viktor himself, but that seemed unlikely.

Victor began to move his feet slowly, carefully, down the alley's length, just above the broken concrete surface.

Once, he touched a half brick with the toe of his shoe and stopped himself from scraping the brick across concrete. Instead, he circled the small obstacle with his foot and took another silent step. With such slow motion, he took an endless time to reach the back of the building.

The rear entrance was of metal, rust-patched but solid enough.

Digging deep into his pocket, Viktor's hand came out with the set of hex keys that he always carried. A pale-blue phosphorescence washed across the keys.

The door was protected.

A chain of tiny glowing heptagons appeared around the threshold. They spread along the rust-covered lintel and down both sides. That was where Viktor got to work first, scratching tiny antipatterns to dissolve the geometric setup that stood against him. It was painstaking work. It could collapse in an instant if he made a mistake.

In that case, would he sense the final flare of light that accompanied his death? Or would his world already have blanked out forever?

Viktor let experience guide his hand, working around the edges of the doorway. Then he scratched a knot shape on the concrete threshold. His key flared blue and white, burning him, freezing him...

Bastard.

...as chain and anti-chain writhed together, grew brilliant...

Bloody bastard.

...and collapsed, fading from existence.

The first barrier was down.

There were three more barriers that Viktor could detect. There might be further shields inside. But Viktor was the best, and this was what he enjoyed.

Sushana. I'm coming.

He moved on to the second layer of defense and got to work.

Wilhelmina d'Alkarny, known as Mina to her few friends, walked the long stone passage that led to the underground labs. Deep below street level, they were arranged in two concentric heptagons around the central morgues.

Earlier, one of her most promising young employees, a junior Bone Listener called Padraigh, had mentioned that Feoragh Carryn was inquiring about one of the many bodies stacked up in morgue storage. They were held in nondecay stasis, awaiting the decision: post-mortem or disposal.

Usually, any pressure came from none-too-subtle hints from the Energy Authority that their stockpile of bones was becoming depleted, and could they have some more as soon as possible? It was a request that Mina normally ignored.

Her distaste regarding the necrofusion piles was born of a deeper understanding than a normal person's. Mina knew how much suffering remained, intensified beyond anything a living person could withstand, inside the reactor piles filled with standing waves of necroflux that provided heat and power for every living citizen of Tristopolis.

It was a form of balance, of paying back for the luxuries of life once that life was over. It was not a form of fairness that appealed to Mina.

In this case, the strange inquiry had come on behalf of a Lieutenant Riordan, whom Feoragh had referred to as Donal (a familiarity unusual enough in its own right). When Padraigh had investigated, he found that the hands-off stasis order had originated in Commissioner Vilnar's office.

While that request was not totally unusual, it wasn't an everyday occurrence. What interested Mina was that one of Vilnar's own senior officers was questioning the ruling.

None of that would have necessarily caused Mina to undertake a personal investigation. She was chief here, with the whole OCML to worry about—not just the postmortems, but salaries and staff morale, whether they had enough cleaners and whether the plumbing worked, and the myriad other bureaucratic administrative tasks that came with being the boss.

But there was something else unusual here: the identity of the body in question.

The dead man's name was Malfax Cortindo. Until dying at the hands of one Lieutenant Donal Riordan, this Cortindo had been the unpleasant, manipulative City Director of the Energy Authority. He had supervised the Downtown Complex, where he kept his office amid the necrofusion piles that groaned with replayed agonies.

Why wasn't he reactor fuel himself?

Two uniformed officers stood at attention, shoulders pulled back and gaze straight ahead. Mina could taste the subliminal pheromones of their fear—to her, noradrenaline was bittersweet with a hint of almonds: a synesthetic illusion—but she did not smile. After all these years, Mina no longer cared what ordinary humans thought of her.

She was a forensic Bone Listener, the best of her generation. That was enough.

"I need to go inside," she said.

"Yes, ma'am."

Behind them, the big circular steel door looked impenetrable and probably was. Wisely, no one had ever attempted to break the security in this place. Pale waves passed through Mina's tall, lanky form. The scanwraiths finished their check and approved her entry.

On the door, complex heptagonal wheels and cogs rotated in different directions—one of them appearing to circle through an impossible arc that existed outside of normal geometry—and a sudden draft tugged Mina's limp hair forward as the metal door swung inward, sucking air from the surrounding corridors into its cold low-pressure interior.

Mina hesitated a moment, reflecting for perhaps the ten-thousandth time that she was lucky to be here, in what others found a forbidding place. It was the ultimate calling for a Bone Listener.

She went inside, and the big door swung shut, generating

a pulse of air pressure that propelled her steps. Mina walked through a thin sheet of shimmering coldfire—a second-layer defense that could turn nova-incandescent—and entered the outer chambers.

Two junior Bone Listeners, neither of them Padraigh, were at workbenches in the admin area, filing cards in the metal cases that would go into the vaults before scanning for Archive entry. Both Bone Listeners wore purple robes streaked here and there with black where some corpse had spilled its decay fluids as they cut into it.

It was the bonework that was important, not the cold flesh. In any case, Bone Listeners were almost impervious to normal infections: wearing stained robes in this place was business as usual.

"How goes it?" Mina asked the two young men.

"Well, ma'am," said one, pale-faced with a dead expression. "We're just filing the results of yesterday's intake. Nineteen incomers."

"Excellent," said the other, a froglike grin distorting his bony face. "Picked up a resonant trace from a young girl who was flamewraithed. Thought they'd destroy her bones, but we"—he glanced at his companion—"managed to drag out the perceptions we needed."

"Good enough to make a match?" asked Mina, meaning a visual ID of the killer.

"Done already, ma'am," said the serious one.

But something in his voice told Mina that it was the enthusiastic guy who'd done the real work, not the plodder who was sharing the credit. These were two people she needed to keep an eye on.

"All right," Mina said. "I'm going to make an inspection of storage. No need for you to help," she added, seeing the enthusiastic Bone Listener starting to rise. "I like to wander 'round the place alone."

His answering grin was immediate, and Mina realized that he did exactly the same thing: allowing the low vibrations of the bones' trapped memories to play at the edges of his awareness as he walked around the morgue labs and repositories. It was a way of getting a feel for the atmosphere of the place, of noting anything unusual in advance, of being prepared when the postmortem began.

"You're Lexar, right?" said Mina.

"Uh—yes, ma'am."

"Keep up the good work." Part of Mina laughed at herself for using the trite phrase. "I mean it."

"Thank you."

When Mina stepped through into the interior tunnel, she remembered that the other young man was called Brixhan and realized that he had scowled as she left. Did he think that Mina wouldn't notice?

Thanatos save her from such subordinates... but it was unwise to make enemies, even junior ones. Especially when you were planning to break the laws you were supposed to help enforce.

Mina entered the metallic space they called the Honeycomb. Heptagonal steel cells contained the bodies of the dead awaiting analysis. The ends of those cells were sealed with a mistlike wavering of the air: a side effect of the stasis hex that filled each cell.

Stasis prevented degradation of the interference patterns laid down in bones, the same interference patterns that the most experienced of forensic Bone Listeners might deconstruct and reconstruct as they relived the final moments of the dead person's life.

Most often the interference patterns merely confirmed a medical diagnosis, at least within the normal parameters of a physician's ability. Down here, the Bone Listeners knew better than most how much guesswork filled medical science.

By definition, Mina and her colleagues only met the patients who had died.

The metal floors were gently sloping and suffered sudden reversing turns, so that they zigzagged deep down into the subterranean volume of the Honeycomb. Five levels down, Mina came to the section she wanted. She slowed down, checking the numbers on the labels that bore the deceased's details.

Here were some of the long-term stasis cells, where bodies were preserved for years or even decades, usually waiting for some judicial process to complete, so that a body's ownership could be established. There was one corpse, known affectionately as Fat Fredo, who had been in stasis for over 120 years while generations of lawyers argued with their counterparts in distant Zurinam.

Fredo had been some kind of junior diplomat killed in a bar brawl, but there were complications due to the Tristopolitan mayor's daughter, who had been the cause of the fray, and allegations that Fredo had used his position to illegally influence certain business deals. The battery of entwined legal cases dragged on with a life of their own, with the original participants long gone.

Then Mina found the cell she was looking for. The name was written in an ornate script that most Tristopolitans could no longer decipher.

It read: *Malfax Cortindo.*

Mina stared at the shimmering stasis field, thinking about what she was going to do. Most forensic Bone Listeners needed the fully resonant chambers that were the autopsy rooms in order to work.

But Mina was aware of her own capabilities, straightforwardly and without a sense of ego. With the right tools—a scalpel and a bone cutter, perhaps a platinum divining scope—she could analyze Cortindo's skull right here.

The question was whether the powers that be were going to insist on holding the corpse in stasis indefinitely—in which case Mina would be safe, because no one ever looked in on the bodies once the stasis field was plugged. Not until it was time for the autopsy.

But if the postmortem decision was made soon, then the interference would be obvious. So would the trail of blame.

"Shit."

Mina's colleagues would have been surprised to hear her now. She was renowned for her equanimity in difficult circumstances and her insistence on clean language, even when there were only corpses to hear.

Mina placed a hand against the steel rim of the heptagonal cell, as though gaining strength from the metal. Then she pulled away and headed back up the long sloping floor, climbing toward the autopsy rooms, where she kept her own personal set of tools and devices.

Cats moved across the rooftops, searching, comfortable in the darkness, lithe and agile, enjoying their own abilities as they slipped through the night. They hunted tiny silvermoths that flickered in the air. As they spread out across the city, they were alert for any sign of the people that Laura Steele was tracking.

Sometimes the cats met others of their kind and spread the word in a manner undetectable to humans (though Laura might have sensed a little of the phenomenon, had she been present).

That was why one of their number, a scrawny little silver tabby called Spike by the humans who sometimes fed him, was perched on a damp brick wall near the docks, watching a big man in a leather jacket working on the ensorcelled rear door of a mostly deserted building.

Mostly deserted, but not entirely. Spike's feline senses revealed the rifle and the hidden sniper deep inside as sour tastes or bitter scents in the air. And he sensed a compressed violence barely kept in check by the need for discipline, along with the fear of punishment from someone more evil than the sniper himself.

Lights flared across the door, dissipated, and were gone, leaving no defenses behind. The leather-clad man, Viktor, drew the Grauser from beneath his left armpit, leaving his left hand free to push open the door. He held the weapon close to his chest, where no assailant could grab it.

As Viktor entered the building and was lost from sight, Spike hunched on the wall, a tiny ball of fur, and commenced a tiny buzzing purr.

Donal rolled awake off the bed, stumbled, then hauled himself vertical and stretched hard, vertebrae and tendons popping. Barefoot, he walked around the bedroom, looking for signs that Laura was there, knowing she was gone.

He padded out to the kitchen, which he still hadn't stocked, detecting no sounds in the apartment anywhere save the soft, ongoing sibilant hiss of the internal systems that kept Darksan Tower operational. He called out Laura's name, got nothing back except a micro-echo of his own voice.

Definitely gone.

Perhaps she had scarcely been here, for Donal remembered only that Laura had stood outside the bedroom as he fell onto the bed and into sleep. Perhaps she had left right away and gone back to HQ, having made Donal get the rest he needed.

"Shitfuckbugger," Donal muttered. "Laura, for Thanatos's sake."

Picking up his discarded suit jacket from the floor, Donal searched through the pockets until he found a scrap of notepaper he'd stuffed there earlier. It was a list of phone numbers, some of them home numbers, which he could use to contact members of the team at odd hours.

Donal squinted at the steel-handed clock on the wall: it was eleven minutes past two in the morning, but at times like this, normal standards failed to apply.

He took a guess, set the rotary wheels on the bedside phone to Alexa's number, and waited for the ring.

The tone sounded twice, and then there was a click and Alexa's voice said: *"Hello?"*

"Hey, it's Donal. I'm glad you're up."

"Right." Alexa sounded hoarse. *"You going in to HQ now?"*

"I would, but"—Donal looked at the tangled bed-sheets where he'd slept alone—"I have a feeling no one's going to be there, not even Laura."

"Why? Aren't you two—" Alexa coughed. *"Sorry. Forget that. None of my business."*

"Maybe." Donal's laugh came out easily, surprising him. "I *am* at her place. It's just that she isn't. I think she just wanted me to crash."

"And then what? She went out on the streets?"

"Yeah, I guess. Where would she go?"

"Hang on a minute."

Donal listened to coughing on the other end of the line, then some muted sounds followed by a faucet running, filling a glass. After a few moments Alexa came back, her voice clearer.

"Two possibilities," she told Donal. *"One, she went to Harald's location to join the surveillance team. Second . . ."*

"What?"

"Something else. She followed up some lead of her own. She's . . . Well. She's like that."

"Thanatos."

"Yeah, precisely. You okay?"

"Not really. See you near the Illurian embassy?"

"*Yeah. See you there.*"

Donal put the phone down, found his Magnus, and checked it over, ejecting the magazine and snapping it back in before reholstering.

Time to go to work.

15

Viktor moved farther into darkness.

There was a stairwell, and he tested the narrow treads carefully. They were old and prone to creaking, but the edges seemed solid enough. Viktor began his ascent, feet parallel to the treads, using cross steps to climb. He moved carefully, slowing when he reached the first landing. Were there trip wires?

None. Not that he could detect.

With his left hand Viktor drew out his picklocks and continued to climb, knowing that the keys would fluoresce at any hint of a hex field. But there were other, equally dangerous traps. As the gloom intensified, he slowed the pace once more.

The sniper was four more stories up. At this proximity, if Viktor tripped something and the trap itself wasn't fatal, the sniper's response would be. He would come out of hiding and fire down into the stairwell, and that would be it.

Slowly...

But there were tricks you could play with time. While part of Viktor's mind remained in the moment and alert to the smallest stimuli, other layers altered their time perception, slowing down to a leisurely pace, to a kind of moving meditation.

Viktor moved upward, farther and farther into the

danger zone. Finally he was on the fourth landing, and everything clicked into place inside his skull. The night burned with a dark and silver life.

Where the stray moonlight was coming from was impossible to tell. It was enough to cause the hairs to rise on the back of Viktor's neck as he saw the sliver—*Thanatos and Hades*—like a single thread spun by a nocturnal spider. It stretched across the floor and touched, just touched, the material of his trouser leg.

Trip wire.

Another millimeter and he would have tripped the thing.

Viktor retreated three paces.

Beyond the wire was a shut door, which would open inward. As always, there were two choices: to creep in slow or charge in fast, hoping that momentum would take him beyond whatever trap waited inside. A third choice was to kick in the door and then retreat, ready for what would follow—but the man inside was a sniper, and the last thing Viktor wanted was the sound of a firefight.

On the other side of the street lay several acres of yard and buildings owned by Sally the Claw. While many of the people there were office workers, there would be a couple of dozen foot soldiers at least, all of them ready to shoot.

Viktor's keys remained dull, so there were no hex shields to contend with. Perhaps the elaborate hex alarm down below had seemed enough for the sniper.

With no time left for deliberation, Viktor moved. His foot crashed into the door just below the handle, smashing the lock apart. The door flew inward. Viktor leaped, clearing over ten feet as the prone sniper jerked himself upward.

Down below on the street, the gates to the complex had swung open, and a glimmer of bright yellow indicated an unlikely sight, which Viktor would later think had distracted the sniper for those few extra milliseconds.

But Viktor's own momentum saved him the necessity of processing what he saw. He swung his leg forward powerfully and kicked the sniper in the ass: a move that might have looked comical but crushed the man's coccyx and caused him to arch back, voice frozen. In that moment Viktor descended.

He knee-dropped onto the sniper's spine, hammered the Grauser butt into the back of his neck, then slipped his left forearm under the sniper's chin. Viktor pressed down with his right elbow and applied a sleeper hold, hard.

The man was probably unconscious before the strangle went on, but this would make sure—though it added the risk that he might never wake up. After thirty seconds, Viktor released the hold. He stood up.

The sniper remained prone, unmoving.

As part of checking the environment, Viktor allowed himself to sink quickly, deeply, into a trance, checking for ensorcellment. If the various parts of his mind were no longer in synch with one another, then it might indicate that some form of hex was distorting the neural patterns in his brain, causing hallucination.

Nothing.

That meant several things: not just the lack of hidden, subtle booby traps in this place, but also that the vision Viktor had glimpsed earlier was real.

Just why the gates outside had swung open to let out two dwarves riding a canary-yellow tandem bicycle was unclear—but that was exactly what Viktor remembered seeing. Either that, or twin children wearing false beards.

The sniper began to groan and shake.

Good.

*   *   *

Meanwhile, Spike the alley kitten was already on his way, moving among shadows. He darted across a wall surmounted with fragments of broken bottles. They were fastened in place to discourage human intruders; Spike circumnavigated the sharp-edged shards with ease.

Then he was scrambling up a long-dead tree and slipping along one dry branch that led to a rooftop. High above, a noxeagle glided below moon-tinged clouds, but Spike was aware of the danger. In seconds he was hidden beneath a rusted water tank, waiting for the flying hunter to pass.

Yellowish eyes regarded him from across the roof. It was a parafox, not a deathwolf, but the look in its eyes was nothing like friendly. But even as Spike began to realize the danger he was in, two pairs of eyes suddenly glowed scarlet, followed by a third pair, and a fourth.

The parafox blinked at the appearance of more cats, these rangy and muscular. With one flash of his bushy tail, the parafox turned and slipped away. After a moment, one of the cats, old and gray and torn-eared, made his way across to the water tank where Spike crouched.

The other cats maintained their watch. They were far from familiar territory.

Ducking low, the tomcat peered in at Spike. Spike stared back, and the two cats—the old warrior male and the determined youngster—locked on to each other. Information passed along the entangled channel of feline communication that slips through the deepest geometry of space-time.

Spike began to purr.

Then the older tomcat turned and moved away, accelerating across the rooftop. It took a few seconds for the other cats to realize what had happened, then they, too, were on the move, into the night, heading for their rendezvous with Laura Steele.

There was a spare medical robe in her locker. Mina drew it out and pulled it on over her ordinary clothes. The robe was clean and smelled good. She ran her finger across her instrument case, then rejected it. The damned thing was too heavy to cart several stories down.

Mina had a smaller, zipped traveling case of instruments, which had been given to her by Aldinov, her boyfriend back in graduate school. Aldinov had lost interest in direct proportion to Mina's success and prospects outshining his. Aldinov had been rich—or rather his parents had been—and a useful-but-expensive present like the portable instruments had been a clever idea.

After their affair's bitter ending, Mina had almost thrown away the instruments rather than continue with a reminder of her stupidity. In the end, though, she kept the case and settled on using it only when carrying a full kit was impractical.

Mina slipped the small instrument case into the pocket of her robe. She stared at herself in the small mirror fixed inside her locker door, then swung the door shut. She exited and found herself in Autopsy Room 3, where concave steel benches with built-in drains and antiseptic nozzles were empty and shining.

No stains marked the tiled floor, no scents hung in the air that could penetrate the eternal mist of disinfectant pervading this cold place. Perhaps a hint of steam marked the exhalation of Mina's breath.

Mina crossed the autopsy room and pushed her way through the triple sets of doors. She did not look back as the steel floor began its downward slope toward the Honeycomb, where Malfax Cortindo's corpse waited.

Something rumbled deep beneath her feet. Mina stopped.

"What the Thanatos—"

Mina held herself still, expecting something more. There was nothing. It had felt like a distant train, but no tunnels ran beneath this place. If it was a freak trick of geology and happenstance, then that was all right, but Mina decided she would report this.

All the more reason for doing what she had to do quickly, quietly, and privately.

Her pulse began to beat visibly beneath her thin skin. She took out the instrument case and unzipped it as she walked, drawing out a long, slender scalpel.

She neared the heptagonal cell containing Cortindo, then stopped to look up and down the steel corridor, sensing nothing save the clammy sweat coating her narrow body. Another tremor passed through the floor. This time she was certain.

Whatever was happening, there was danger, and she was its target.

"Fuck you."

All the decades of medical training, of playing politics with the high and mighty—and immersing herself in the most painful Bone-Listener disciplines—fell away now, leaving only her native toughness.

"Just . . . fuck you."

Mina hammered her fist into the crystalline ward set at the edge of the cell and watched as the hex shield flared, then began to fade. Inside that dying glare, the unmoving form resolved itself into a dead body, no different from any of the thousands that had passed through here before.

Except this time someone wanted the body back.

Someone who was capable of breaking into this place—but this was *her* place. Mina sliced savagely into the inanimate head of Malfax Cortindo, the scalpel coming away sticky with semiliquid blood.

There was no time to retrieve the other instruments, but that was all right, as Mina hooked her fingers into the flap of scalp and ripped back. She threw herself inside the cell as far as her shoulders, desperate as an explosion banged through the corridor outside. Metal ripped open amid showering dust and noise.

I hear you.

The corpse's exposed skull tasted raw and salty as Mina placed her tongue against it.

Cortindo, I hear you now.

Then Mina pulled her head back. Splaying her fingertips against the bone, she began her quest for one particular song amid the inchoate patterns laid down inside his—

Hands clasped Mina's ankles.

"No!"

Strong hands, hauling her away from Cortindo.

"No—"

She shivered as the contact was broken....

"Please, don't—"

... and they pulled her into the cold, dusty air. The two small figures who stared at her were ordinary thick-boned men, less than four feet tall but strong. Mina knew in the instant she saw their stone gazes that the rules she had broken, and the rules she had lived by, were of no consequence, not any longer. This was the day her own life ended.

One of the dwarves raised an ax that shimmered with coherent hex waves, its edge capable of slicing through the hardest stone or metal. Biological matter was no kind of challenge. The dwarf drew back his lips; you couldn't call the expression a smile.

Concentrate. Replay.

Mina squeezed her eyes shut, remembering the disciplines.

Remembering the pain.

Concen—

The universe blacked out.

Was finished.

The Robbery-Haunting team was professional. By the time Donal and Alexa arrived, the R-H guys were well settled in place.

They had formed two concentric circles of observation posts around the Illurian embassy. Harald, his gentle eyes beginning to show his exhaustion, took Donal and Alexa on the tour, walking the quiet streets.

"And the limo," Harald said, as they crossed one of the narrow avenues that led into the heptagon. "R-H impounded it from a counterfeit ring."

Alexa grinned. Donal checked the vehicle from the edge of his vision, not turning his head, just in case their suspect or someone working with him was mounting a surveillance of his own.

In an area like this, where the grand old houses were owned by diplomats and embassies and occasionally a rich old Tristopolitan family, the normal kind of surveillance vehicle would have stood out: a baker's van, for instance. But the dark-windowed limousine was perfect.

"Who's inside?" Donal asked.

"Guy I know vaguely," said Harald, "called Ralfinko, and an older guy, a sergeant, who looks like he knows what's what."

"All right."

Alexa touched Harald on the arm. "You need to get some rest."

"No."

"Er . . . I know you and I have only just met," said Donal, "but I think she's right, pal."

"Balls." Harald spoke softly as always. "All right. My old sergeant used to say, it's only your comrades who can tell you when you're screwing up."

They were standing under a streetlamp. Harald dug inside his pocket and pulled out a small food box. He flipped back the lid and held out the open box. "Hungry?"

"Um . . . no thanks," muttered Donal. Inside the box were layered flower petals, orange and darkest purple predominating. "I don't know how you eat that stuff."

"It's all he ever eats," said Alexa. "Mr. Gentle, we like to call him."

"Right." Donal looked at Harald, who nibbled at one of the petals. "Which sergeant was this that you mentioned?"

"Oh, Bastard Balrooney, we used to call him."

"And this was in—"

Harald looked at Alexa, then at Donal, and smiled peacefully. "The Fighting Sevens."

Donal had rarely come across the men of the 777th during his own military career, but those few had always lived up to the reputation of their brigade, known widely as the Cursed Commandos. He had once seen a one-eyed old sergeant of the 777th take down six military policemen, before walking back to barracks and handing himself in for punishment.

"Mr. Gentle," Donal said.

Harald smiled again.

"So what do we do next?" asked Alexa.

"The usual." Harald closed his food box and tucked it away. "We pick the most comfortable surveillance spot and wait."

That was the way of things. Surveillance consisted

mostly of watching and dying to take a pee. The biggest
challenge was boredom and the tendency to doze off.

From somewhere behind them, an engine started up,
then revved with power.

"Did you say we were going to wait?" muttered
Donal.

"I am occasionally wrong," said Harald.

A dark car turned into the avenue, its headlights a liquid malevolent green. Then the driver accelerated hard,
and the car sped past them. Startled, a reptilian gekko-
bat launched itself from a stone tree and flapped away
into the dark, featureless sky.

"Shit," said Alexa.

The limousine parked at the curb started up, as the
passenger window rolled down. "You guys want a
ride?" The speaker was square-jawed and gray-haired:
the sergeant that Harald had mentioned. "Better hurry."

The driver had the limo pointing the wrong way, but
he swung away from the curb in a tight U-turn and
jerked to a stop next to Donal and Alexa. Donal pulled
the door open and pushed Alexa inside, then followed.

"Go ahead," said Harald. "I'll catch up."

"Okay."

Donal pulled his door shut, and acceleration slammed
him back into the seat.

"Don't let him see you," he muttered to the driver—
what was his name again? "Uh, you're Ralfinko, right?"

"Yeah, and you gotta be kidding. The bastard's already out of sight."

Tires screeched as Ralfinko hauled them through a
left turn and piled on the acceleration.

At the corner of Silvan Avenue and 504th rose a blood-red
craggy tower, famed locally for its twisted architecture,

black oval windows that looked like rows of eyes, and the odd visitors who passed through its doors.

On a windowsill on the thirteenth floor, near the junction where a necrotonic cable disappeared into the wall, a gray cat hunched. Its crimson gaze followed the embassy car speeding past below, followed by a dark limousine, then a small car, and finally a bone-colored motorcycle, taking up the rear but accelerating hard.

The cat blinked.

After a moment, it leaped lightly onto the hanging cable and walked on toward the next roof, dismissing the chase it had seen developing below. Two other cats had relayed the message since the hard-bitten tomcat, Dilven, got it from the young Spike, but it was the goings-on at the docks that would concern Laura Steele.

The place where she awaited news, Darksan Tower, stood tall against the purple sky.

Viktor pressed down with his thumbs, and the sniper gave a strangled scream, all that his paralyzed vocal cords would allow. At this stage, the sniper didn't even know what information Viktor was after. This was only to establish that Viktor was willing to cause suffering.

Willing, and able.

"A short woman." Viktor's voice was low and throaty, designed to reinforce fear. "With green eyes. Have you seen her?"

"No . . ." The sniper could only croak a whisper. "Haven't—"

Viktor pressed again, hard, and the sniper's back arched off the floor, though his limbs remained helpless. Viktor had worked on the shoulders and hips first, and those joints must be burning in agony by now.

"Is there a prisoner? A woman?"

"I—Yes!" A finger twitched: all that the sniper could

manage as a warding-off gesture. "There . . . Sal. Got some . . . one."

Viktor glanced at the window. "In the compound? Sally the Claw's in there?"

The sniper nodded, eyes wide.

"With a prisoner?" Viktor's jaw muscles flexed. "Tell me."

"Brought her . . . in. Tonight."

"Her name. What's her—"

But the sniper was already shaking his head. If he knew the name, he'd say it: Viktor was sure of that.

"Which building?"

"Block . . . Three."

Viktor didn't know which building that was, but he wasn't going to ask—to maintain dominance, he had to appear to already know almost everything.

"What else can you tell me?"

The sniper shook his head.

Viktor stared down at him. As the sniper regained consciousness, fear and bewilderment had cracked his conscious defenses, and direct questions had elicited answers. But now Viktor had run out of specifics to ask about.

"Next time," said Viktor, "choose your employer more carefully."

"No, you—"

Viktor's fist hammered down.

Afterward, just in case he had missed something on the first search, Viktor went through the beaten man's pockets with care, finally extracting a small brass ID strip. It was stamped with the dragon-wing logo of CalTransPort, the main holding company of Sally the Claw's near-legitimate import-export group.

There was no personal identification to go with it. For a moment Viktor considered stripping the sniper of his armored hexlar vest and impersonating him, rifle in hand. But there was no way of knowing whether the guards down below knew the sniper by sight, or even by name.

Or perhaps Viktor was too attached to his own leather jacket to want to leave it in this infested joint.

Shaking his head, he picked up the unconscious sniper's rifle, checked the balance, and ejected the magazine. It held a clip of five long, slender bullets. If the sniper had a spare clip, he must have hidden it somewhere, and he was in no position to divulge that information now.

Viktor put the cartridge clip in his jacket pocket. Then, with a last inspection of the sniper—the man would live, provided someone found him within the next few hours—Viktor left the bare room. The landing and the rest of the dilapidated building looked clear. He stepped carefully over the trip wire, and went down the old treads quickly but almost silently.

At ground level, he stepped over broken shards on the floor, ducked under the stairs, and groped around until he found a suitable hiding place. He slid the rifle into the gap between a tread and a broken shelf—this had once been a cupboard, but the door had long since been ripped off, probably used for firewood.

There. Good. The rifle was too conspicuous to take inside the complex, but if Viktor had to retreat, this would be a good place to grab a long-range weapon. Five shots would drop one or two pursuers, maybe more.

Viktor hefted the brass ID strip in his left hand and walked out of the building, pulling the door shut behind him. If someone was expecting the door to be hexed but had no detector, then everything would look as before. If they *did* have a detector, they'd know the defenses had been breached. There was nothing Viktor could do to help that.

In the broken alleyway beside the building, Viktor paused, scanning the street, the blackened pits that were paneless windows in other buildings. Then he took a deep breath, held it, and let it out.

Viktor walked out into the open street and headed for the main gate, his walk loose-limbed and confident, projecting ease. Inside, his nerves crawled. Perspiration speckled his skin as the fine hairs rose across the back of his shoulders.

Someone behind the wire fence swung a flashlight beam in Viktor's direction.

16

They hurtled through the streets, not yet in open pursuit. If anything, the man they were tracking should be suspicious at the lack of cops. Twice he'd gone through stoplights at speed.

On the other hand, this was the early hours of the morning, and they were into the less-than-salubrious district of Vulkan's Vale, otherwise known as Blood Alley. Here, police cruisers traveled in convoy or not at all.

"I don't like this," muttered Alexa, sitting on Donal's left.

"Ralfinko knows what he's doing," said the sergeant from the front.

"Yeah." Donal gave a grin that lasted half a second. "We can see that. But why's the target going so fast?"

"Because he can," said Ralfinko. "Looks like he's got diplomatic flags flying."

"Or—"

Donal stopped as the radio squawked beneath the dashboard. The sergeant pulled the mike from its clip.

"Car oh-seven-niner. What's up?"

"Is Lieutenant Riordan with you?"

"Yeah, affirmative."

"Could you put him on, please?"

"Er, sure."

Donal leaned forward as the sergeant passed the mike

back. The coiled cable just reached over the back of the passenger seat. Donal clicked the mike to transmit.

"Riordan."

"Sir, Bone Listener Carryn said we needed to tell you this. There's been a break-in in the OCML."

"What?" said the sergeant, while Ralfinko muttered, "Impossible."

"There are four fatalities reported so far, sir, including Dr. d'Alkarny."

"Say again?" Donal glanced at Alexa. "Did you say Wilhelmina d'Alkarny?"

"That's correct. We have possible sightings of a green van leaving the vicinity, possibly with stolen goods aboard."

"Stolen goods? From the morgue?"

"Sir, Bone Listener Carryn says to tell you, the missing body belonged to Director Cortindo."

"Damn it," muttered Donal, with the mike still set to receive. He clicked to transmit. "Can you contact Commander Steele?"

"Sorry, sir, but no. We've been trying."

Outside the window, buildings were streaming past. Then Blood Alley was dropping away as the car climbed the steep on-ramp to the ten-lane skyway. Donal realized that Ralfinko had floored the acceleration by the way the engine howled.

"What is it?"

"Your man from the embassy is up ahead."

"Yeah, but—"

"And he's driving parallel to a green van."

Donal stared at Ralfinko for a moment, then clicked the mike. "Control, do you have any more description on the green van? From the OCML incident?"

"Negative, sir."

"Shit."

Alexa said, "We need to coordinate with our other cars. Can we get a roadblock across the skyway?"

The traffic was sparse, moving fast. There was one more exit ramp before they reached the two-thousand-foot-high skull intersection passing into the mouth.

"Control," said Donal. "Stand by for all points. Listen, have you got any cars down on the flat that can block Exit Forty-seven North? We need a barrier."

"Sir." There was a loud crackle, then: *"Done it. Two cars moving to block off."*

The freeway curved and banked, and just for a second Donal glimpsed the white-and-purple flashing beacons ahead and down below, as the cars closed off the exit at ground level.

"Nice work, Control. We have a possible match for the green van, linking up with our own suspect."

"I'll relay that information."

Up ahead, white-and-purple flashes showed from inside the empty right orb of the great skull. More cruisers in position. But on the route that Ralfinko was following, no obstacles were visible. The green van and the Illurian embassy limo increased their speed, drawing away from the pursuit.

Then a long, low bone-colored motorcycle swept past in the fast lane, as if the cars were standing still. Ralfinko flinched.

"What the Thanatos—"

"That's Harald," said Alexa.

At the edge of the dock complex, a dark-finned low-slung automobile drew close to the wire fence. It was a Vixen, top of the line, and more. The vehicle seemed to shrug as it drew close to the wire.

Silvery waves passed across the fence, then faded from sight as the Vixen's door swung open. Laura stepped out onto the cracked asphalt.

"It's hexed, sis," Laura muttered. "Can you do something about it?"

A glimmer grew in the headlights. The car rolled forward, edging closer to the fence, until its passenger side was touching the wire. More silver pulses passed along the wire, arcing downward as if tugged by gravity. Soon there was a dark area of fence directly above the Vixen:the car was diverting the hex flow along her chassis.

"The hood's safe?" Despite her skirt suit, Laura climbed up onto the hood, her high heels morphing into combat boots. "Nice one, sis."

Laura checked the pistol holstered at the small of her back, slung her handbag diagonally over one shoulder, and leaped lightly from the hood toward the fence. She landed like a cat about to scramble up, hands and feet fastening into the wire mesh.

At the top of the fence, razor wire writhed and swirled. But as Laura neared the uppermost portion of the mesh, she was deep in concentration, preparing herself. When she reached the wire, she grabbed with both hands simultaneously. The wire bucked and thrashed, and then the section between her hands grew limp.

After a moment, Laura scrambled over the top and descended to the other side.

That's one thing I couldn't have done when I was alive.

By the time she reached ground level, the razor wire was stirring again, though feebly.

"If I don't come back—"

The Vixen flashed her headlights.

"Yes, I will be." Laura opened her handbag and checked the larger gun inside: a Grauser .23. It was a smaller caliber than Viktor carried, but still a man-stopper. "Don't worry so much."

She moved into shadow.

* * *

Inside the Vixen, a small furry shape stirred, then curled up into a ball. Spike closed his eyes, whiskers spreading as he slipped into sleep.

He had done all he could, passing on the message to the network and keeping watch on the man, Viktor, as he entered the compound. He had told Laura which building Viktor had entered. Everything else was up to her.

The air in the car's cabin was warm, soothing. In seconds, Spike was breathing softly, paws twitching as he dreamed of the chase, before growing relaxed once more.

But the car herself maintained a watch, tracking Laura's progress for as long as she was able, until Laura slipped among piles of shipment pallets and was lost from sight.

They'd blocked the off-ramp, so the green van and the limo were constrained to remain on the skyway. No one had thought to block the next on-ramp, even if there had been cars available, but as soon as Donal caught sight of the second big truck he knew there was a problem.

There were six of them, approaching the skyway at improbable speed, though they were hauling huge trailers. The trailers had to be empty.

"Speed up," Donal told Ralfinko. "Get past those bastard trucks."

A light silver rain was beginning to fall. Slippery road surfaces were not what they needed.

"I see 'em, but I can't get there," muttered Ralfinko. "Not before—Shit."

Already the first three trucks had pulled alongside one another in the fast lanes and were beginning to slow.

Harald on his bike was just behind them, and then he was level with their tailgates.

Just as Harald started to accelerate into the gap between two trucks, they drove closer together, dangerously close, blocking Harald's bike. Harald fell back.

Two more trucks moved into position, blocking the road. The sixth was backup, and it pulled in behind one of the others as the whole formation slowed.

"Damn it."

The sergeant was using the mike, describing the situation to Control. Alexa watched Donal pull out his Magnus and check it before reholstering. She bit her lip.

"What is it?" said Donal.

"They're well organized." Alexa was staring forward. "So far. What have they got in mind for up ahead?"

The sergeant put down the mike. "We got barricades across every lane beyond the skull. Once they're in, they ain't leaving."

At that moment, Donal saw something: a shadow high in the sky.

"I don't think," he said, "they're planning to leave by road at all."

"You've gotta be—"

"There goes Harald," said Alexa.

The motorbike shot forward through the narrow gap, and then Harald was clear of the trucks, accelerating in front of them. Behind the trucks, civilian cars were braking, pulling over; in front, one car was driving too slowly, while the other three drivers that Donal could see were making use of their mirrors and speeding up, drawing farther ahead of the steadily slowing trucks blocking the skyway.

A truck nudged the slow car in the rear, jolting it. The driver panicked, swerving across two lanes before regaining control and flooring the accelerator. Far ahead of him were the green van and the dark limo, with the bone-colored Phantasm motorcycle fast catching up.

Then a sequence of white flashes brightened the night, reflected as silver threads in the thickening rain.

"What the hell is Harald firing?" Donal leaned forward, trying to make out what was happening.

"Don't ask," said Alexa. "I'm sure it's regulation issue."

Ralfinko snorted.

"Sure," he said. "So you got any ideas on how to get past these guys?"

The trucks were still slowing down. Civilian cars had already stopped. The sergeant looked back at Donal; both men nodded and turned to roll down their windows. Ralfinko's face grew masklike with concentration as he drove close to the trucks' tailgates and kept the car steady.

It took a magazine full of shots from Donal and the sergeant firing in parallel to blow out the rear tire, but when it happened, it was spectacular. Ralfinko swung the car left, hard, just as the truck swerved and bounced from the neighboring truck on one side to the other, the skid setting up an oscillation.

Then Ralfinko jerked up the hand brake and slammed his heel into the brake pedal, turning the car sideways into a skidding deceleration as the colliding trucks bounced off one another. The crash became catastrophic as four of the six trucks entangled and the fifth lurched and toppled. Only the sixth managed to brake as the remainder collided, smashed, and swerved across the lanes, one going through the central barrier and into the opposing lanes.

Flame belched from a truck that was lying on its side.

The car stood still.

"Can you get through?" Donal pointed to a path through the wreckage. "That way."

"Got ya." Ralfinko gunned the engine.

Donal had already slammed a replacement clip into his Magnus.

More white weapons fire flashed from Harald's motorcycle up ahead, and the dark limo swerved but corrected its course. They were less than a minute from the orange-lit mouth of the great skull, and the chase was getting serious.

Donal leaned out the open window, eyes squinted against the slipstream, and stared up into the sky. Nothing. He must have imagined the—

There.

"Shit." He pulled himself back inside the car. "It's big, maybe a pterabat."

"What the Death have they got going on?" said the sergeant.

"I don't know," said Donal. "But let's make sure they don't get away with it."

The sergeant had the mike again and was telling Control to get air support organized any way they could, but things were moving fast: everyone knew there was no time left.

White fire flashed up ahead once more, and this time the dark limo screeched across the fast lane and ricocheted from the central barrier. It swerved back, and for a moment Donal thought the driver had regained control, but then the limo wobbled, Harald fired twice more, and the rear tires went.

The limo swung wide and spun as it headed for the hard shoulder and hit the balustrade.

Concrete exploded and the limo went straight through, sailing out into the air. Donal shut his eyes, trying to listen for the impact, hearing nothing amid the ongoing roar of motor and slipstream and the shocked voices of Alexa and Ralfinko.

"Impossible!"

"What kind of—"

"It was molyscarab armor," the sergeant told them. "The limo's body. I've seen the stuff before. Goes through anything."

Up ahead, the green van—looking black as it slid into the orange sodium-vapor light—was entering the tunnel, through the great skull's mouth.

"You're not saying the limo survived that drop?" Alexa was staring back at the gap in the balustrade.

"The bodywork might," said the sergeant. "But the wheels 'n' axles are a different story, and the driver's probably a mite squished by—"

"This is it." Ralfinko was pouring on the acceleration. "Crunch point coming soon."

"Apt term," muttered Donal, flicking the safety catch on his Magnus. Even with his finger outside the trigger guard, a sudden jolt could cause an accidental discharge.

"Here goes."

Ralfinko brought the car swerving through a tire-burning arc across the asphalt, blue-gray smoke rising from the wheel arches, and then the car was still, diagonally placed across one lane from the green van. The van was stationary, all its doors thrown open. Up on the safety path for pedestrians, a metal emergency exit door banged shut.

Donal was first out of the car, drawing his Magnus as he ran. A hundred yards farther along the tunnel, a bulky man who had left his own car to see what was going on stopped, jerked so fast his jowls wobbled, and then ducked back behind the steering wheel and pulled his door shut.

There were stone steps a few yards away, but seconds mattered, so Donal used the hood of the parked van as a springboard, caught the iron safety rail one-handed, and vaulted over, landing crouched on the concrete walkway. The walkway was for evacuating the tunnel in case of emergencies, which meant the stairwell beyond the metal door led downward for safety and also up to the higher tunnels.

To the skyways that fed through the empty orbs of the great skull, hundreds of feet above.

Behind Donal, Ralfinko shouted, "The van's empty. Except for a yellow tandem."

"A what?"

"A bicycle made for two. You know?"

"Shit."

If the suspects were carrying Cortindo's body, it would slow them up. Donal kicked open the metal door, then ducked back. The auxiliary lighting inside the stairwell was dim amber, pushing back dark shadows.

There was a red alarm button on the wall. Donal slammed the butt of his Magnus against it.

"Hey!"

A shower of artificial rain poured down inside the tunnel as the sprinklers—in fact, they were high-powered nozzles—came on. Purple lights strobed. More important, the inside of the stairwell shone with magnesium-white light.

Donal ducked into the doorway and then back out.

"Which way?" called Alexa softly. "Up or down?"

Donal shook his head. They might be lying in wait with guns at the ready, but he'd caught no glimpse of gun barrels, and no one had fired. And he was ninety percent sure that he'd seen a pterabat earlier from the car. That would make one hell of an expensive diversion.

Donal pointed up.

The sergeant pointed toward the ground, and Donal nodded. Just in case, it was best if one man went that way.

Ready . . .

Donal ducked into the stairwell.

No shots fired.

Ah, Thanatos.

Gun at the ready, Donal stepped onto the first tread and began to run up.

Viktor crouched on the seventh floor of the office block he'd entered, listening to low voices coming from behind closed double doors. A brass label read *Boardroom,* but the soft moan from inside the room indicated this was not the usual kind of meeting.

At four o'clock in the morning, that was a given.

To get into the building had been both more and less trouble than expected. From outside, the doors had appeared completely unguarded, with no locks and no watchers. But once he'd pulled open the outer door, things had changed.

Viktor had first spotted a small orb floating near the ceiling in one corner. Then he realized that floateyes were hovering at every choke point.

But they were one of the things that Viktor was prepared for. He pulled out his big handkerchief, inspected it—grimaced—then tied it around the lower half of his face. From inside his leather coat he produced two small gray atomizers and took a few deep breaths through the handkerchief.

Viktor had sprayed a little of the eyesleep mist into the corridor first, letting it drift along to cause inattention in the floating eyeballs. Then he stepped fully inside and sprayed straight into the first floateye.

Its nictitating membrane slipped across the glossy orb, and the eye was asleep and dreaming.

Viktor had continued to spray as he penetrated the building farther. At a glass half wall he peered into an open office space where a few tired-looking workers were bent over stacks of invoices and bills of lading, processing the legitimate transactions of Sally the Claw's business.

Reaching an inner stairwell, Viktor had climbed past a series of unlit floors, finally reaching the seventh story. Now Viktor crouched outside the door.

Another moan sounded from the boardroom.

Sushana!

He was sure of it.

Viktor checked the door. It had a long brass handle, not a knob. Good. Crossing his arms, Viktor cross-drew both Grausers from his shoulder holsters. Then, crouching, he brought his left elbow slowly down on the door handle.

It turned.

And what happened next went very fast.

Through the door, rolling diagonally over his right shoulder, Viktor came up with weapons ready.

Seven, no, eight men were already reaching for their guns. A bulkier figure stood at the far end of the room, clad in a pearl-gray suit, and the bloodied form of Sushana sat tied in a chair, her clothing torn, two of her fingers bent and twisted back at sickening angles.

Viktor began to fire: both guns, swiveling his stance, blasting continuously, an overlapping series of loud bangs in the room, deafening. But the corpses dropping around the conference table would never hear anything again.

Maybe one shot in three hit what he was aiming at, but Viktor had seventeen rounds in each clip, and that was more than enough. Cordite smoke hung in the air as Viktor moved quickly around the room, checking the fallen bodies, firing once as a dying man twitched, hand reaching for a dropped, bloodstained weapon. All down.

A stray round had blown apart Sushana's left shoulder, and her eyes were wide with shock, face whitened by blood loss. But there was no time for Viktor to help her, because the bulky man in the rich suit at the end of the room was Sally the Claw, and this was the moment he lived up to his name.

Sal's right hand was normal, but his left was a huge, shining pincer. His left arm came up fast, and Viktor fired at the movement, rounds ricocheting from the carapace protecting the limb, but the claw swept both weapons from Viktor's grasp.

Viktor tried to duck and spin away, but Sal was faster, and the claw opened, moved, and struck in a tenth of a second. Then it was fastened around Viktor's neck, and he knew that he was too late.

"Who are you?" asked Sally the Claw.

Donal pounded his way up the echoing stairwell. Twice he stopped, breath sawing, thighs pumped and beginning to burn. A layer of slick sweat coated his skin beneath his clothes, and so far he'd run up only three hundred steps—a part of him insisted on keeping count.

There were scrapes up ahead, but no shots came firing down the stairwell at him. The suspects were headed for the roof of the great skull—they had to be.

"Thanatos. Come on."

Donal pushed himself back into motion, breathing hard. Then, involuntarily, a semigrin pulled his lips back as he ran upward, a primordial reaction to the hard physical work and the sense of mortal danger: he was in the moment where he belonged, all doubts gone.

He pushed harder.

Laura was hunkered down beside a drain when the gunfire banged out and a series of flashes showed between blinds on the seventh floor of the nearest building. She moved into cover, next to a stack of pallets.

She checked her handbag, which hung at her hip, the strap still slung diagonally across her shoulders. Her firearm was inside.

Then something ripped through the air, parting the handbag strap as other hands tugged the bag away from Laura's grasp. She launched herself forward, but two big figures leaped from behind the pallet, grabbing her arms.

Yet another bulky man stepped out in front of her and raised a shotgun to her face.

"What shall we do?" asked one of the men.

"I suggest," muttered Laura, "that you damned well—"

"Tell me what," came a sepulchral voice, "is in the bag."

The man—or kind of man—was seven feet tall and gray-skinned, and a scar ran diagonally across his squarish face. His gaze, when he looked at Laura, was devoid of feeling.

"Automatic," said one of the men, pulling open the handbag. "Pretty small. And ID. She's police."

Another team of guards was moving toward the building. If Viktor or Sushana was still alive, then the chances of their remaining so were diminishing fast.

"A *commander.*" The gray-skinned man checked Laura's badge, then put it in his pocket. "We're honored."

"You won't—"

"Kill her." The gray-skinned man turned away. "Now."

Laura squeezed her eyes shut.

Donal . . .

Then Laura felt a jerk and heard a gasp. Her eyes snapped open to reveal a misty form rising up through the cracked pavement.

The being reached insubstantial hands inside the rifleman's head and chest . . .

"Xalia!"

...and then Xalia manifested her extremities into corporeal existence and squeezed.

Squeezed hard.

Even as the man dropped his weapon and gasped with mortal shock, Laura was spinning aside, flicking back her jacket and ripping her second gun from her back holster, firing three times before the team of guards had even processed her movement.

Then they broke formation, scattering to every side, only two of them returning fire as they ran. But Laura was already ducking and continuing her tactical movement, while Xalia was insubstantial: the bullets passed through her wraith form.

Then Xalia was upon the two men who were still firing. Blood bubbled from their mouths as she solidified her grip, crushing their hearts, and they, too, dropped dead onto the asphalt.

The gray-skinned man simply ran, but his gait was controlled rather than fearful, and Laura had to decide her responsibility. His back was toward her, but he was running for help, not escape, she was sure of it—and there were officers' lives at stake. There was no choice for her to make: no choice at all.

She squeezed the trigger, the small .23 jerked back, and the back of the man's neck blossomed dark fluid. He fell and did not move.

There was still a great deal of danger, and Laura rolled sideways across the ground, next to another dead man. She picked up her bigger handgun. But the remaining guards had fled—other than one who'd chosen to face Xalia, soon regretting it as Xalia's fingers became talons like steel, slashing downward.

The man fell, whimpering, tendons severed so that all four limbs were useless. He could only shiver as blood spurted out of torn arteries and death closed in.

Laura scanned the environment as Xalia drew closer.

There was no immediate danger, and for a split second Laura grinned at her own continued survival. Then, "Where did you come from?" she asked. "How did you know I'd be here?"

Xalia's wraith form drifted as though on a breeze, yet the cold air was still.

Same way as you.

"What's that supposed to mean?" Laura went down on one knee, reloading her automatic. "The same way as me?"

Why, Laura.

Xalia rose a few feet up, appeared to sniff the air, then descended.

You think you're the only one who talks to cats?

Then another shot fired from inside the building. Laura and Xalia moved fast toward the doorway, alert for more armed men.

17

Donal was two flights down when he heard the roof door bang open. There was a glimpse of two short figures carrying something gray-wrapped and bulky—Cortindo's body—and then the dwarves were out onto the roof, and Donal was cursing.

Even as he redoubled his pace, sprinting up the last thirty or so steps, he could hear not just the wind from up above but also a deeper grumble, a near-subsonic vibration of total power. It was the pterabat, coming in to hover above the top of the great skull.

Come on.

Donal's breathing was harsh and wheezing now.

Push it.

There was no possibility of silent pursuit as he clattered up the final steps and half-stumbled to the landing, stopping inside the doorway. Outside, the flat expanse of the skull's top reached for two hundred yards before curving down and beginning the sheer descent. The suspects were nowhere in sight.

Donal ran as hard as he could—his legs felt like molten rubber—out onto the wet, slippery surface that was the top of the great skull. Rain was heavy in the gusting wind, and Donal had to squint to see the two powerful figures dropping their burden and scattering to either side as Donal raised his Magnus.

"Desist or I will fire!" The legal words were tugged away by the wind. At least Donal was observing correct form. "Stop!"

Overhead, the pterabat filled half the sky as it dropped lower. An incision in its abdomen puckered and pulled open, and narrow black ropes rippled from it. In seconds, dark-clad hooded figures were rappelling down.

Donal fired a single warning shot, but the descending figures did not hesitate.

Thanatos . . .

Squatting low, he took aim at the figure closest to the roof surface—*no, watch out*—then spun away as one of the dwarves leaped through the air feetfirst, just grazing Donal's forearm. The Magnus banged out once more, another shot wasted, and Donal swung the weapon down butt-first, but the dwarf was already cartwheeling away.

A heavy impact took Donal in the small of the back, and he pitched forward.

Donal threw himself into a twisting fall, firing at the dwarf who'd kicked him. The fabric of the dwarf's heavy pullover ripped apart. But it was a surface wound, and a small but heavy foot was swinging for Donal's eye—the other dwarf—and he rolled away just in time.

Hardness thumped Donal's brow. Fluorescent yellow spots rippled across his vision as he came up on one knee and cupped his left hand beneath his right, aimed, exhaled—*calm*—and squeezed the trigger.

No shot sounded.

Misfeed . . .

The dwarves were upon him, teeth sinking into his forearm, and a small hard fist took him in the groin.

He punched the one who was biting, turned his hip against the second, then pumped three more hooking punches into the side of the biter's neck. The dwarf fell.

The other dwarf advanced again, head forward as he came in to tackle Donal at the knees—*not a coward*—but Donal snap-kicked once, catching the dwarf just under the chin.

Then Donal struck with his knee to the same target, followed by an uppercut punch to the same spot again, and the little figure was down.

The first dwarf was already stirring—*what do they feed you guys?*—but Donal took a running step to kick him in the face, knocking the dwarf back and rolling him over. For the time being Donal was clear.

But the dwarves hadn't needed to beat him, only distract him long enough for the hooded figures to wrap their ropes around the bundled form of Cortindo's corpse.

Donal raised his gun, then remembered the misfeed—*clear, rack and hammer:* that was the dictum Rangemaster Ryan had drummed into Donal—and he clawed back the slide, banging the Magnus with his left fist to fling the unfired cartridge out.

Ready.

It took less than a second, but that was too long. The pterabat rose slightly, and the corpse of Cortindo came off the roof surface.

"No, damn it."

A dwarf reached for Donal's ankle, but Donal kicked the fingers aside and moved away, swinging the gun up.

Donal could not reach the hooded figure with his hands, but he could shoot them.

He took aim.

For a moment the sight blurred as Donal's focus shifted to the target. The hooded man's eyes were trained on Donal. The man knew he was about to die.

Steady . . .

Donal exhaled, tightening his abdomen and trigger finger together.

"Fuck."

Then he pulled his finger out of the trigger guard and lowered the gun. He sucked cold wet air into his lungs.

Do you hear—

No. There was no point in killing the man, that's all.

The pterabat continued to rise.

Perhaps Donal might have fired into Cortindo's already dead body, but what was the point? There wasn't much you could do to a corpse, and it was already tied to the ropes, borne aloft by the pterabat. Killing one of the hooded figures, who were unarmed, was not Donal's idea of legitimate force.

He checked the dwarves again—one of them was on hands and knees, shaking his head, dripping scarlet blood mixed with rain—and looked back up. The ropes were withdrawing into the body of the pterabat as it ascended and began to wheel away.

"Oh, sweet Death." Alexa's voice carried through the pterabat's subsonics with a disconcerting clarity. "Those steps killed me."

She bent over, left hand on her thigh to keep steady, her lungs wheezing. But none of that prevented her from taking steady aim with the gun in her right hand on the nearer of the two dwarves.

"Don't you fucking..." She sucked in a breath. "Ah...don't...move."

Then Ralfinko staggered out of the doorway, clutching his coat around himself against a sudden squall of rain, and took aim at the second dwarf. Donal checked them both, then reholstered his Magnus. He looked back up into the dark sky.

Cortindo's body had been drawn into the hold, and the hooded figures were already out of sight. The opening sealed shut as the pterabat banked, dived into the turn, then pulled up, ascending into the cloud layer. Its outline grew indistinct, and then it was gone.

One of the dwarves began to laugh.

*   *   *

The claw tightened around Viktor's throat.

"I said"—Sal's voice clenched as though he were the one being strangled—"who the Thanatos are you? And what is the woman to you?"

"My . . ."—Viktor forced out the lie—"sister."

The claw that grew from Sal's left arm could snip shut and part Viktor's head from his body in an instant. If he did that, the headless corpse of Viktor would reveal the subdermal police ID tag, beneath the skin at the base of his throat.

Even drenched in blood, Sally the Claw would see the badge right away for what it was. But every second that Sushana remained alive was a kind of victory, and perhaps that was the best Viktor could—

Sally the Claw screamed.

A wraith's arm was reaching inside his groin, and Sal reacted as a normal man would, bending over, chin coming up, and his grip weakening. That was enough for Viktor. The claw's sharpness had pierced the skin of Viktor's neck, and it was his own slick blood that allowed him to slip out of that grip now.

Then a pale figure in a skirt suit stepped through the doorway, raised her gun, and fired. Sal's right eye exploded.

Xalia grew insubstantial as Sally the Claw's corpse toppled through her and dropped to the floor with the cold thud of dead meat. She drifted to one side and partially manifested, her outline growing steadier.

Are you all right?

Viktor's answer was a croak, scarcely audible: "Never . . . better."

"Damn it." Laura quickly checked the corpses scattered around the floor—making sure they *were* corpses, not wounded men about to revive and reach for their weapons. Then she tried to free Sushana from the ropes that bound her to the chair.

Viktor dragged himself over to where his Grausers had fallen.

"Allow me."

He picked up the guns, walked over to Sally the Claw's body, and opened fire, aiming at the wrist and blowing it apart in a hail of chitin-piercing rounds. Finally Viktor holstered his weapons, took hold of the near-severed claw, and tugged.

"Almost . . ."

Viktor pulled again, and the claw came free with a liquid sucking sound. He dragged the thing over to Sushana and swiped at the ropes, cutting them apart.

"Well done," said Laura.

Sushana fainted at last, toppling from the chair. Laura and Viktor caught her before she hit the floor.

I guess . . .

Xalia drifted over them.

. . . we should call this a success.

Laura looked at the bloody bodies strewn across the floor.

"Yes," she said. "We damned well should."

Three hours later, every member of the team except Harald was gathered around a table in an interrogation room on the hundredth floor of HQ. Lying on its side atop the table was a stained canary-yellow tandem bicycle.

"What?" said Viktor. "We should threaten the bicycle until it talks?"

Xalia wrapped a near-invisible hand around the frame, the rest of her body drifting like smoke.

There's no wraith in here.

"That was a joke," Viktor growled.

Alexa smirked.

"You said you saw a tandem like this"—Laura was at the back of the room, leaning against the wall with her eyes closed, thinking—"at Sally the Claw's place. Before Xalia and I turned up."

And rescued you.

"I was doing all right."

You were what?

Viktor grinned. "What, are you feeling underappreciated, Xalia?"

"Peace," said Donal. "And we all know the chances of two yellow tandems making an appearance in two different locations last night. This was in the back of the van that the Ugly Twins used to carry Cortindo's body. Sally the Claw is part of the network we're tracking down."

"The Ugly Twins with steel-trap jaws," muttered Alexa.

That referred partly to Donal's bandaged forearm, partly to the way the dwarves had clamped their jaws shut and said not a single word since their formal arrest. Nor had they struggled once the cuffs were on: merely went limp and forced the uniformed backup officers to carry them down the many flights of stairs inside the great skull to the waiting police van.

"No surprise." Laura opened her eyes. "Sal had his fingers—well, claw—in a couple of dozen different pies."

"Nice if we could backtrack."

"Yeah. Nice," said Alexa, "if the OCML get something out of Sal's corpse."

Donal blew out a breath, and Viktor muttered, "Shit."

"Right."

The whole team now knew that Wilhelmina d'Alkarny, the chief forensic Bone Listener, was lying on one of her own steel autopsy tables in the depths of the OCML. Viktor and Harald had known her—well enough to call her Mina—and that was why Harald was at the OCML right now instead of here.

"None of this makes sense," said Donal. "Why use the dwarves to blow open the place just to get Cortindo's corpse?"

"How else would they do it?" Alexa reached for the tandem as though to push it off the table, then stepped back. "Who'd have thought anyone could mount an attack like that?"

"No." Laura looked at them. "Donal's right. If the opposition could mount that kind of strike, why do it now? Why reveal themselves because of one dead man?"

"Because Cortindo knew something." Viktor's voice was like gravel spilling in an iron bucket. "Because if Mina performed an autopsy, she would have learned something about the Black Circle."

"The name of Cortindo's contact? Maybe," said Alexa, "his direct superior. Or someone higher still."

Everyone was silent for a few moments. Then Donal put his hands in his pockets and looked up at the ceiling.

"You know," he said, "it might be interesting to find out why Cortindo hadn't been autopsied yet. I mean, there's a waiting list, but it can't be that long, right?"

Laura said, "You're thinking someone ordered him put in stasis?"

"Someone important." Viktor looked from Laura to Donal. "Someone who could override Mina's authority."

"Right."

"Someone," said Viktor, "that we should have a little word with."

Harald was in an outer chamber of the OCML. A young Bone Listener called Brixhan had brought Harald a cup of rose-and-blackthorn tea, then scowled when Harald asked him to stay for a moment.

"You know—knew—Mina, right?"

"I worked for Dr. d'Alkarny, yes."

"What the Thanatos happened, do you know?"

"I believe that Dr. d'Alkarny must have decided on an unauthorized—"

Another Bone Listener was entering the room. "It was her prerogative to check the Honeycomb," said the newcomer. "In fact, it was her duty, Brixhan, don't you agree?"

"Um...technically, yes."

"Well, *technically* is good enough, wouldn't you say, Officer?"

"What's your name?" Harald's voice went very quiet. "I didn't catch it, Bone Listener."

"Lexar Pinderwin. I hope you catch the bastards who did this."

"I think we already have. At least the ones who carried out the physical act."

Brixhan frowned.

"You mean," said Lexar, "you've got the foot soldiers but not the principals who hired them."

"Yeah," said Harald. "That's what I mean."

"Well, that's a start."

"It is." Harald blinked. "Any hints that you could give me might help us to track down those principals."

"Dr. d'Alkarny did nothing wrong." Lexar was staring at Brixhan.

"That's good." Harald touched Brixhan on the shoulder. "She had a day diary, right? A list of appointments and such?"

"Um...Yes, I think...Well, yes, she did. It should be in her—"

"Go and fetch it for me, will you?"

"I don't—"

"Right now."

Brixhan swallowed.

"Um, sure, Officer."

"Take your time."

With a last glance toward Lexar, Brixhan left. Harald counted to twenty, then walked over to the door and checked the metal-lined corridor outside. It was clear.

"All right." Harald came back in, sat down, and waved at an empty seat. "Sit with me, Lexar."

Lexar sat.

"And talk."

"I won't gossip," said Lexar. "Dr. d'Alkarny was the best examiner who ever—"

"And Mina was a friend of mine." Harald leaned forward, and suddenly his gentle eyes went as hard as steel. "A close friend. I want to know *everything*."

Lexar swallowed, then blinked several times, his eyes growing damp.

"I shouldn't have looked," he said. "But she . . . There was a body in stasis, under orders. Dr. d'Alkarny wondered why."

"Whose orders?"

"Um . . . I'm not sure. Is it important?" Lexar started to rise. "I can get the—"

"In a moment," said Harald. "What is it you didn't want Brixhan to say?"

"He knows nothing. He only half-suspects, and that's because of something I said. He doesn't have the sensitivity to have felt it for himself."

"What are you talking about?" Harald's tone took the sting out of the words. "Sensitivity to what?"

"To the traces left on her fingers, in her bones . . ."

Harald drew back. "Excuse me?"

"Dr. d'Alkarny did the autopsy," said Lexar, "even though she was forbidden to by executive order."

"You're sure of that?"

Lexar hesitated, then, "Yes, I'm sure of it."

Harald stared around the room. If Brixhan came back, Harald was going to cuff him to a table and take Lexar outside, because this was important.

"Mina had focus," said Harald. "Wouldn't you say?"

"Yes. Better than anyone I've met. Any Bone Listener."

"Enough focus to hold a dying thought?"

"Oh, Thanatos . . ."

"To burn a dying image into her bones?"

"Yes." Tears began to trickle down Lexar's cheeks. "Oh, yes. She was the best."

Harald stood up.

"I want you to perform the autopsy."

"No." Lexar swallowed. "I'm only a junior—"

"I want you to carry out the autopsy right now."

The rest of the team would arrive an hour later, while the autopsy was in progress. First they had to stop in the lowest subterranean level of cells, where the dwarves were fastened against the cold stone walls with silver bands.

Neither of them looked about to talk, not even when Xalia drifted close and ran her fingertips across their brains, reaching through their bony skulls. Donal reckoned, as he watched, that it was all Xalia could do to restrain herself from manifesting her long-nailed fingers and squeezing hard.

It just wouldn't have done anyone any good.

Donal made a phone call first, direct to the Archives, and spoke briefly to the Bone Listener he'd consulted with, Feoragh Carryn. There was a sadness in her voice overlaid with something more, but it took a minute for Donal to work out what it was. Feoragh was guilty with the knowledge that she'd caused Mina's death, or at least that was the way she saw it.

"No," said Donal. "You talked to Dr. d'Alkarny because of me, to begin with. Let's not have any survivor's guilt here."

"Please..."

"I'm sorry, but realize this. At one end of the causal chain are the people who carried out the attack, at another are my actions, and you're somewhere in the middle. There is no blame."

"Yes." Feoragh's voice sighed down the line like a breeze. "But while I know the theory behind your words, right now I believe none of it."

"Then what will help?"

"Finding out who killed Mina, and why. And ... dealing with them."

"Good," said Donal. "Then that's what we'll do."

He put the phone down, seeing Feoragh in his mind's eye, imagining her going down into the Lattice and immersing herself in the bones' Archived memories, digging deeper and deeper. Whatever other result Mina d'Alkarny's death might have, it meant that one Bone Listener at least was probing the Archives with a resolution no one could match.

And whatever the Black Circle—or whatever the opposition called themselves—had intended, they were going to find a task force on their tail that would not stop.

Donal went down to the ground level of police HQ, past the glowering deathwolves on the main steps. FenSeven turned to Donal with a smoldering anger in his amber eyes: he'd heard of Mina's death at the Archives. Donal nodded.

The Vixen was waiting at the curb. She swung her passenger door up, and Donal climbed inside. Laura was already at the wheel, and as the door came down and clicked shut, she put the car into motion.

"Have the others left?" Donal looked back as HQ slid away behind them. "Viktor looked surprisingly edgy, after all he's been through."

"What do you mean?"

"I'd have expected an adrenaline crash, you know? In reaction to everything. Especially since . . . I'd say he's quite fond of Sushana."

The medics had taken Sushana away and made it plain that no visitors would be welcome for some time, probably days.

"Yeah," said Laura. "But he was fond of Mina too."

"Oh."

Laura reached across for Donal's wrist, then placed his hand against her left breast.

"More normal," she said, "than taking up with someone who has no heartbeat, wouldn't you say?"

"I love you."

"Damn it." Blinking, Laura shook her head. "That's not supposed to happen."

Do—

Shh.

Donal withdrew his hand.

"And?"

"And, for Thanatos's sake, I damned well love you too. Good enough?"

"Yeah," breathed Donal. "More than."

The Vixen came to a halt and opened her doors.

"This is the place," said Laura.

Aboveground, the Office of the Chief Medical Listener was a hunched blue stone building, with a smaller extension attached to the main body of the place. Only the twenty police cruisers parked at odd angles around the perimeter gave any clue to the events that had taken place in the subterranean levels of the

Honeycomb, deeper down than the autopsy level, where even now Mina's body was cut asunder, where the young Bone Listener who had admired Mina so much laid his hands upon her still-warm blood-slick bones, trying to read the message inscribed by agony within.

18

I can't do it." Lexar laid aside the marrow saw. "There's nothing I—"

"You can." Harald's voice was muffled by the surgical mask he wore. "Try again."

"No . . ." Shuddering, Lexar forced his hands inside Mina's splayed-open corpse once more. "Ah . . ."

Lexar's eyelids fluttered.

"Shit." Harald caught Lexar as he toppled over. "For Thanatos's sake."

But Lexar stirred immediately and pushed himself away from Harald. He stood on his own feet, swaying.

"Two squat men," he said. "Dwarves."

Harald let out a breath. It confirmed what Laura had said on the phone about the two prisoners that Donal and Alexa had captured. Whether it could be used as evidence in a trial would depend on whether he could retroactively get this autopsy declared official.

"Ax," Lexar added. "They had an ax."

Harald shook his head.

Wonderful. Now we can interrogate every hardware supplier in Tristopolis.

This was less than useful.

Can't be more than a couple of thousand of 'em.

But Lexar's eyes cleared and he focused on Harald.

"No ordinary ax," Lexar said. "This was a coherent hex-wave resonator. They don't exactly grow on trees."

"Okay." Harald stared down at Mina's corpse. "Good. That's something."

"Looked Illurian to me," said Lexar. "Well, to Mina..."

There was an odd pain in Lexar's voice, and Harald suspected that there were agonies involved here that only a Bone Listener could appreciate or understand. Then fingernails tapped against the clear-glass window inset in the autopsy-room door. It was Laura, standing outside.

A misty form drifted through the closed doorway.

"What?" Lexar's hand reached reflexively for one of his surgical cutting tools.

"She's a colleague." Harald nodded. "Xalia, this is Lexar. He's a good man."

Xalia drifted six feet away and rose a little toward the ceiling.

Nice to meet you, Lexar.

"I'm...pleased to meet you, Xalia. Pardon my reaction."

But Xalia was already floating over Mina's corpse, and the shadow and hollows of her near-invisible face were as expressive of grief as Lexar's own.

She was a good person.

"Yes."

Xalia rotated to face Harald.

Viktor won't come in.

"Can you blame him?"

No...

After a moment, Harald said, "I'll go out to him. Lexar?"

"I'm all right here. There's nothing more to do, except to...tidy her up, you know?"

"Make her look presentable."

"Yes." Lexar reached out to touch Mina's dead, intact face. "Presentable."

A single tear grew in the corner of Harald's left eye.

Are you—

"Hardly."

Xalia said nothing more but drifted almost to the ceiling as she watched Harald leave the autopsy room, trying to keep his feelings under control. He looked like someone who needed to be alone, and as a wraith who could float through walls and watch anything unobserved, Xalia had an unbreakable rule.

You did not spy on friends, ever.

We'll track them down. She spoke to Lexar, who was hunched over the corpse, hesitating before closing up the great incision that split Mina's torso. *Eventually we'll get them, including the ones who gave the orders.*

"Probably."

Lexar's tone was empty, and Xalia understood what that signified: revenge meant nothing, justice in the courtroom sense meant nothing, because the only true justice would involve bringing Mina back to life. And that was something no Bone Listener or thaumaturge could ever do.

Perhaps they'll end up here. On your table.

At this, Lexar looked at Xalia.

"Yes. And if they're not quite dead, I can live with that."

Xalia wondered what a Bone Listener could do with the feelings and nervous system of a person—an enemy—who was still alive.

I'll see what I can do.

Then she bowed her head, drifted upward through the ceiling, and was gone.

* * *

Laura was using the office that had been Mina's to make some phone calls. The first was to the hospital, where it took three transfers and several minutes of holding on the line—one nursing supervisor in particular was unimpressed by Laura's rank—before learning that Sushana was "critical, doing as well as expected." Laura tried to think of a reply that expressed what she thought of that categorization, failed, and hung up.

Then Alexa came through the door and pushed it shut behind her.

"What's up?" said Laura, looking up from her chair.

"Um...I may be speaking out of line here." Alexa paused.

"Or not."

"Excuse me?"

"You're not speaking, Alexa. So what *is* up?"

"You and Donal." Alexa swallowed, then continued quickly, "Was recruiting him your idea?"

"What are you getting at?"

"I know you're close. We—everyone—we think that's great, see..."

"Thanatos, Alexa. Will you spit it out?"

"It's just...I'm wondering about the timing. We get deeper into the Black Circle than ever before and trip something that causes a massive reaction. Breaking into this place." Alexa gestured at the steel-covered walls. "That's bringing things out into the open, don't you think?"

Laura crossed her arms.

"What's Donal got to do with this? Other than the way he's cracked the case."

"I'm not jealous of his success, if that's what you're thinking." Alexa rubbed her eyes, and Laura reminded herself that living people require sleep.

"So what? I think you've got cause and effect mixed

up." Laura's voice sounded tenser than she'd intended. "Donal joined us first, and *then* we started unraveling threads."

"Following lines of inquiry we'd already started." Alexa shuffled her feet. "Sorry, but that's why I had to ask about Donal. Cause and effect..."

Laura held herself still, then: "Xalia and I virtually dragged Donal from a hospital bed. We had to work on him. Persuade him."

"Well...thank you," said Alexa. "You could've just told me to fuck off and mind my own business."

"I nearly did." Laura smiled, and waited until Alexa smiled back. "But you're really asking if Donal could have played me, manipulated me. And the answer is no."

"Okay."

Laura waited again. Then she pointed at an empty chair. "Sit down, why don't you."

Alexa sat.

Laura stopped breathing. For the undead, respiration is unimportant.

"Shit," said Alexa finally, and fumbled inside her jacket pocket. "Here. You take this."

She pulled out a bent pink file card and handed it over to Laura. The writing on the card was in purple ink, a Gothic style embellished with heavy curlicues. It read: *Placed in stasis by order of the office of Commr. A. Vilnar, Quintober 3, 6607.*

Underneath, a different hand had added a note in burgundy. *Duration: indefinite.*

Laura placed the card down on the desktop beside her.

"No need to ask whose body this referred to."

Alexa bit her lip. "You trust Donal."

"You were with him, chasing the body." Laura frowned, strange highlights shifting through her eyes. "You're not saying Donal held back? That he could have caught them?"

"I . . ." Alexa blew out a breath. "None of the rest of us was even close. I think he did better than anyone could expect."

"Well. Good."

"And there's something else."

"What's that?" said Laura.

"I did watch him run up those steps in the great skull, while I tried to follow."

"So?"

"So he's got a great ass, and he's fit as hell." Alexa grinned. "I'd say you're a lucky woman, boss."

"Thanatos," said Laura, but she was laughing despite herself. "Will you get the Hades out of here?"

Just as Alexa was rising, there was a knock on the door. It swung open, and Donal looked inside.

"Hi," he said. "Am I interrupting something?"

Laura and Alexa looked at each other.

"*No,*" they said in perfect unison, then lapsed into sputtering laughter.

"Sorry," added Laura.

Donal looked at them for a moment, shook his head, disappeared back into the corridor, and closed the door. But he was smiling as he did it.

The smile faded as Donal continued down the corridor. He was glad that Laura and Alexa were friends, and Alexa seemed like a good person, or at least a good cop. Whether those two concepts were the same was a discussion for a lazy day.

But there had been something in the atmosphere in the room, something that indicated the laughter he had caused was partly in reaction to earlier tension. And the cause of the tension had been visible: the pink filing card, faceup on the desk beside Laura.

Donal had learned to read upside-down, sharing

books in the orphanage. And his long-distance vision had always been acute. That was how, with a glance, he now knew that it was Commissioner Vilnar who had ordered Cortindo's body to be held in stasis.

"*Follow the paper trail,*" Laura had said.

The thing was, Vilnar *had* asked Donal to spy on the task force. And Laura suspected Vilnar. But none of this was proof.

A prickling crossed Donal's spine, and he turned around. A pale figure—a male Bone Listener—was watching from an open doorway.

"Can I help you?" said Donal.

"Um . . . it's about Dr. d'Alkarny."

"And you are?"

"Brixhan Dektrolis. I'm not sure, but I think that one of my colleagues might be carrying out a postmortem on Dr. d'Alkarny."

Donal said, "This is the OCML, isn't it? Where autopsies take place?"

"Of course it's—" Brixhan colored. "The person involved is not qualified, and I believe he might have had an emotional attachment to Dr. d'Alkarny."

"Goodness."

"Well, yes. It's a clear breach of professional—"

"I'll say. Listen, did you assist my colleague, Detective Ceerling? Alexa Ceerling?"

Brixhan blinked. "Yes, I unlocked the records room for—"

"And cross-checked with the"—Donal was going to say "the correspondence files," then quickly changed his words—"tags in the Honeycomb? Just to make sure we've got the right body."

"There's no mistake." Brixhan frowned, probably trying to look authoritative. "The records are accurate."

"Of course they are. You people do good work."

Donal let his gaze go unfocused. "Don't care for it myself."

"A lot of people react that way." Brixhan sounded smug. "We have the training, though."

"We certainly need forensic geniuses." Donal raised an eyebrow. "And people who know how to be professional. I think you're destined to go far."

"Ah. Thank you, Lieutenant Riordan."

So Brixhan had already learned Donal's name, though Donal hadn't introduced himself.

"Perhaps," Donal said, letting his gaze drift toward the steel wall beyond which lay the autopsy rooms, "you'll go as far as Dr. d'Alkarny herself."

Brixhan's mouth worked silently.

"Take it easy," Donal added.

He hitched his jacket, being careful to let the butt of his Magnus show for just a second—it made Brixhan take an involuntary half step back—then turned and walked away, letting Brixhan make of his remarks whatever he wanted.

Unpleasant asshole.

But being a creep wasn't a major crime, more like a congenital disease. It had been a long time since Donal let people like Brixhan worry him.

Conversely, Donal knew that making an enemy of Commissioner Vilnar would not be worrying: it would be terrifying. He had respect for the man. But if Vilnar was involved with the Black Circle, then someone had to take him down.

On the edge of the lab area was a kind of antechamber that acted as a waiting room for civilians who needed to identify a body or otherwise assist. Donal had been there several times with relatives of victims—or in one case, in the company of a fat old lady who examined the soapy-looking body of the man thought to be her son, poked it with one gnarled finger, and said, "Looks like a piece a shit, doesn't he? Too good lookin' to be *my* boy, though. Nice try, Loot."

He made his way there now, remembering the small acoustically shielded phone booth set against one wall. The room was empty, so Donal dug in his pocket for the seven-sided coins he needed, picked up the receiver, and fed the coins into the slot.

A woman's voice answered.

"Hello? Commissioner Vilnar's office."

"Hi," said Donal, realizing that he had no idea what Eyes's real name was. "Um . . . Is he in? This is Riordan."

"One moment." Eyes was too self-confident to lie and say that she would have to check. She was quite capable of telling anyone that her boss was too busy to talk. *"Putting you through, Lieutenant."*

There was a click and a scrape, and Donal imagined Eyes flicking a toggle switch on her console. Could she listen in on these conversations?

No matter. If Vilnar trusted her, then she could; otherwise, he would have taken countermeasures.

"Riordan."

"Sir. I'm at the OCML, where Cortindo's body was stolen."

"You think that's news to me?"

"The theft? No, sir. And I assume you know that Dr. d'Alkarny was killed during the break-in."

There was a long pause, longer than Donal would have expected.

"Is there any progress on that? On her death?"

"Almost certainly the two suspects we have in custody killed her. I'm expecting confirmation on that shortly."

"Confirmation?"

"Sir, Dr. d'Alkarny was a Bone Listener. She might have been able to visualize her dying moments in sharp focus, so that the vision could be . . . retrieved. Later."

"*You mean they're carrying out an autopsy.*"

"There hasn't been time," said Donal, "to get the magistrate's authorization for a PM."

"*And?*" Vilnar's tone was dry. He might not be a street cop anymore, but he understood bureaucratic systems and how to bypass them.

"Someone's doing the autopsy right now. Unofficially."

There was a sound on the line that might have been static, might have been Vilnar exhaling.

"*Good. Let me know how that turns out. Good work, Riordan.*"

"Er...One thing more, sir. Cortindo's body was in stasis."

"*It was? But his death was weeks ago, when you...*"

"When I killed him. Yes."

There was more that Donal could say, but this seemed the wrong time to say it. Instead, he added, "But that was just a bureaucratic hitch, I think. It's the dwarves who are the main lead."

"*Dwarves?*"

"The two suspects we have in the cells. They're four feet tall, if that, but powerful."

"*Ah.*" Papers rustled at the other end of the line: Vilnar checking documents on his desk. "*Yes. I see.*"

So Vilnar already had copies of the arrest-and-detention reports.

"*And the task force? Are they making any other progress I should know about?*"

Donal hesitated.

"Commander Steele is very capable, sir," he said finally. "But one of their other officers was kidnapped and rescued, and none of it looks like it's leading anywhere. I'd say the task force is...distracted."

Let Vilnar think that the trail had stopped instead of leading directly to his office.

"All right." Vilnar coughed. *"Keep me informed."*
"Yes—"

But the line was already dead. Donal listened to the oceanic wash of static hiss, learning nothing. He put the receiver down and left the waiting room, failing to notice the faint misty movement, nearly invisible, against the wall where the phone was attached.

Long wraith fingers curled back, the insubstantial hand palm up. Then the wraith raised her middle finger and gestured toward the doorway where Donal had disappeared.

Screw you, lover boy.

Xalia disappeared back inside the wall.

Harald addressed the rest of the team (Sushana excluded—it would be a long time before she left the hospital) with his eyes flatter than usual, his voice toneless. The results of the autopsy conducted by the young Bone Listener Lexar were conclusive as far as the task force was concerned.

Presenting the findings before a court of law would be a different proposition.

Donal leaned against the wall, his arms crossed, unsure why Xalia had moved away from him when he entered the room.

"Surely we can put the Ugly Twins at the scene. I saw them on the roof, for Thanatos's sake, while an unregistered pterabat took off into the sky."

"A pterabat," said Laura, "that not only failed to file a flight plan but escaped detection by any surveillance system. None of our launched copters managed to spot it."

"Damn it."

"Well, yes. The dwarves' green van wasn't identified for sure either. The only link"—Laura nodded toward Harald—"is Dr. d'Alkarny's dying memory of the dwarves attacking her. If we can retroactively get the magistrate's authorization for Lexar to perform the PM, then we'll be able to submit that much evidence."

Alexa held out both hands.

"Well, then. That *is* enough, isn't it?"

"To get the foot soldiers," growled Viktor. "Not the ones who ordered them to kill Mina."

Harald nodded slowly.

"Shit," said Alexa.

For a few moments, nobody spoke. Then Donal shifted against the wall. "You said something about a weapon, Harald? An ax?"

Harald shrugged.

"Lexar says it was Illurian."

"Another connection to Illurium," muttered Laura. "And you've got contacts of your own there, haven't you?"

Donal raised his eyebrows. Harald said, "I was there for nearly two years. In the military police, seconded from the marines."

"Yeah, like one ax," muttered Viktor, "is going to lead you to the shop that sold it. One shop from an entire country. Assuming it *was* Illurian...This Lexar can't be certain, can he?"

"It was ensorcelled in some way," said Harald. "Coherent flux thingy...I can't remember what he said."

"You weren't taking notes?" Alexa's tone was half joke, half accusation.

"No, there was a scribewraith writing an official record."

"Without a time stamp, I hope," said Laura.

If the wraith had time-stamped the record, it would flag the autopsy as having taken place before legal permission was granted. That would be enough to make the findings inadmissible as evidence.

Liquid waves rippling through a melting human body . . .

The sudden image passed through Donal's mind, and he shook it away, remembering his fellow hospital patient called Andy: the man with an inability to prevent his body from morphing into random shapes. The man who had nearly ruptured his flowing body, almost dying when the healing-field generator on his bed had failed.

"I might have accidentally discharged a sparkler," murmured Harald, "before the wraith sealed the entry." He looked at Xalia, and shrugged. "Sorry."

That's not funny.

"I know."

No, you don't. You're not a wraith.

"Sparklers hurt. I know that much."

Xalia drifted above the floor, making no reply. She obviously disapproved of Harald's using the sparkler to drive the scribewraith out of the autopsy room.

Laura sighed. "This isn't helping, gang."

"Sorry."

"Maybe it is," said Donal, ignoring the strange look that Xalia seemed to be giving him. "Are you saying, Harald, that this ax was unusually ensorcelled? And strongly?"

"Um . . . Yeah. That's what Lexar implied."

"So it would leave a strong trace in the Ugly Twins' auras, right?"

Harald nodded. "You're right. We should get Lexar to—"

"No." Laura slapped the table. "We don't use Bone Listeners to torture living people."

"Maybe we won't have to." Donal pushed himself away from the wall. "Maybe there's someone else who can follow the trail. Dig down inside the prisoners' auras."

His subconscious mind had delivered the memory of the unfortunate Andy melting on the hospital bed. When the healing field failed, Sister Felice had called in the experts.

What was the young genius called? Kyushol? Kyushen? Something like that.

Xalia drifted closer.

I want to be there when this interrogation happens.

Donal tried to focus on her wraith form, but it seemed to be slipping in and out of reality.

"All right," he said eventually. "If you want to."

I do.

"Then I'll make a phone call."

For a moment, Donal thought Xalia was going to say something. Instead, she shook her near-invisible head, and then her whole insubstantial form sank down inside the floor and was gone.

"I hate it," muttered Alexa, "when she does that."

Laura was staring at Donal.

Now what? Donal wondered.

"I'll see you all in a minute," he said, and went off to call the hospital.

19

Sister Felice sounded softly charming on the phone, and for a second Donal wondered why he had not tried to see her after leaving the hospital. But there was Laura, and the suddenness of what he felt for her was still startling.

Sister Felice sounded glad that Donal was well and only a little puzzled by his asking for the young thaumaturge's name. It was Kyushen Jyu, he learned, and technically he was Dr. Jyu—holder of a ThD, not an MD. He never used his title, in case someone thought he was a medic.

When Donal got through to Kyushen, it took a while to persuade him that a trip to the city would be interesting enough to drag him away from his normal work. It was only when Donal mentioned an Illurian artifact—an ax—ensorcelled with hex coherence that Kyushen became interested.

"Coherent hex waves? A resonator blade?"

"Um, yeah," said Donal. "I think that's what they said."

"Oh, man."

"But you can follow the traces inside the prisoners' auras?"

"Auras? Are you on something? There's no such thing as auras, apart from some people's visual metaphors. They're not, like, real."

"Oh," said Donal.

"*Look, modern thaumaturgical engineering is based on IIH, which makes procedural hex as antiquated as . . . as an antiquity. You know?*"

"Do I need to know what IIH stands for?"

"*You haven't heard of Image-Inclined Hexing.*" It was not quite a question. "*Everything in the world has qualia and propensities, and in IIH that's how we model it, in hex. We combine the two concepts, see, instead of separating out the teleological functions from the entities they act on. That's the old-fashioned way.*"

"Right," said Donal. "Well, obviously."

"*That makes all the—Look, I'll explain it all clearly when I get there.*"

"I'll look forward to that."

"*All right,*" said Kyushen. "*I'll be there at six* A.M."

"Six? That's a little—"

There was a click, and then the line buzzed. Donal stared at the receiver for a moment.

"—early," he said.

And put the receiver down.

Laura poked her head around the doorway. "You got through to your contact?"

"Yeah. We're going to try some Image-Inclined Hexing," said Donal. "I think."

"Well. That's nice."

"It's more fun than sex. Or so my contact implied."

"And does he have a girlfriend? Has he ever had a girlfriend?"

"I doubt it," said Donal. "And how did you know my contact's a he?"

"A lucky guess." A smile dimpled Laura's pale face.

"Well . . . you up for some hex later?"

"If you play your cards right, Lieutenant."

"I'll do my best, Commander."

* * *

Xalia moved from her concealed position inside the solid wall into the corridor where Harald was standing with a sparkler in either hand. Xalia shivered, which was the wraith equivalent of a living human jumping with fright.

What are you doing here?

"Watching you drift out of the stonework."

Xalia floated back a little, wary of the unlit sparklers.

I don't like those things.

"And how about Donal Riordan?" asked Harald. "Do you like him?"

Xalia shook her head, stopped, then nodded.

Like, yes. Trust, no.

"Alexa said he did a good job."

Like a slow tornado, Xalia corkscrewed around in the air. Then she untwisted herself and descended closer to Harald.

He's spying on us. For Vilnar.

Harald blinked and looked at Xalia with placid eyes. "That's not good," he said.

Back in HQ, Donal noticed that Viktor had disappeared. He mentioned it to Alexa, who stared at him for a moment, then said, "He went to the hospital."

"Oh, Thanatos," muttered Donal. "I'm sorry. Sushana."

"I know." Alexa relented. "You've never even met her, but some of us have known her for a long time."

"Undercover work is dangerous, in lots of ways."

"You're saying she was crooked?"

"No." Donal leaned against a desk. "Brave and determined and under a lot of stress. It takes guts to do that kind of work. I'm not surprised that Viktor's with her."

"He's not *with* her, not in the sense you mean."

"Okay."

"Everyone needs someone."

"Um, yeah." Donal hoped Alexa wasn't proposition-
ing him. It had happened before with other women on
occasion, and he hadn't always seen it coming. "The
thing is, with Laura—"

"If you hurt her," said Alexa, "one of us will kill you."

"Ah." Donal smiled. "I'm glad we've got that clear."

"Well?"

"I won't hurt her," Donal said. "And if anyone else
does, I'll kill them myself."

"That's good enough." Alexa held out her hand.

Donal looked at her, then reached over. They shook.

"What are you two up to?" It was Laura, coming
into the main office.

"Team building," said Donal.

"He'll do," said Alexa. "Just barely."

"I'm sorry I asked. Donal, are you sure you want to
do this?" Laura held up a long slim envelope on which a
stylized silver airplane had been embossed. "Incognito
and without official powers, you'll be in a lot of danger."

Alexa frowned. "You're not talking about undercover work for Donal, are you?"

Donal said, "We were talking about Sushana. But this
is different. I'm just visiting Illurium as—"

"The department will never pay for that," said Alexa.

"Er . . . What do you mean?" Donal pointed at the
flight ticket in Laura's hand.

"Ask Laura who booked the ticket," said Alexa.
"Ask her who paid for it."

Laura put the ticket down on the desk. "Does it matter? Really matter?"

"Come on," said Donal. "Laura, you didn't pay for
that yourself, did you? It'll cost a—"

"I live in Darksan Tower." Laura looked amused.
"You still haven't figured it out, have you?"

"At least," said Alexa, "he's not after you for your money."

"What are you two talking about?"

Alexa pointed at Laura. "Your girlfriend, Lieutenant Riordan, isn't just your superior officer. She's one of the richest women in Tristopolis."

Laura shrugged. "Stinking rich," she said.

Alexa pointed at Donal. "But you better still remember what we said."

Donal nodded.

"I won't forget."

But Alexa was frowning, and Donal thought that he understood: after talking about the dangers of undercover work, he was volunteering to do the same kind of thing across the border in a foreign country, where the justice system was swifter and harder than the one at home. And while he would not hurt Laura deliberately, if he got himself killed, that would be the worst thing that could happen to her. All this, Donal read from Alexa's expression.

"If we don't get a more specific lead," he said, "then I'm not sure it'll be worthwhile going to Illurium at all. Can you cancel that ticket without losing your money?"

Laura shook her head. "Doesn't matter. But you know that Harald has a lot of contacts in Illurium. You'll have resources to call on."

"Snitches," said Donal.

"Maybe. I think some are more highly placed than that."

Alexa said, "How can we get more leads? There's nothing to go on."

"The Ugly Twins," said Donal.

"They're not talking, are they?"

"Not yet."

*　　*　　*

Next morning at five o'clock, the smell of coffee woke Donal. Laura, already dressed in an olive-green skirt suit, was holding a silver tray with a poured cup of coffee.

"Uh," said Donal.

"Morning, sweetheart."

"Mmm." Donal took the coffee and sipped. It was hot. "Ah . . . Thanks."

"You sure you don't want me to meet the charming egghead for you?"

"Yeah. No." Donal rubbed his face. "You'd frighten him off, dear."

"Is that a compliment?" Laura leaned down and kissed him. Her cold lips felt extra-chilled this morning. "Or an insult?"

"Not fair. I'm defenseless."

Laura ran her hand down his cheek. "Easy prey."

"I—" Donal picked up his wristwatch from the crystalline bedside table. "Look at the time."

"You don't want me to join you in the shower?"

"Well, Dr. Jyu will wait for us, I'm sure."

"You're not sure at all."

"Um, no . . ."

Laura was already walking out of the bedroom. "Don't be late. I'll wait by the front door."

The Vixen pulled up just behind the purple taxi that was dropping off Kyushen Jyu, at the steps of police HQ. Donal and Laura alighted and turned to watch Kyushen, who hadn't noticed them.

As Kyushen passed the deathwolves, the wolves' eyes glowed amber—that was more or less normal—but then the entire pack, FenSeven among them, lay down on their bellies, front legs outstretched, and opened their mouths in lupine grins, tongues lolling and teeth bared.

"That's quite a display," said Laura.

Donal caught up with Kyushen in the main lobby. Kyushen had already caused a wave of diagnostic hex to pass over Eduardo's counter block where his lower body was melded into the desk itself.

Eduardo was grinning. "Why, thanks, Dr. Jyu. I never really thought of myself as special in that way."

"Are you kidding?" Kyushen gestured into being a silvery mist, which formed itself into floating runes. "Best hemimorph I've ever seen, and the integration gradient is spectacular. You mind if I write you up for one of the journals?"

"Uh, sure. I mean, no, I don't mind. Will my picture be in it?"

"Yeah," said Kyushen. "Definitely some TRS, maybe some—"

"What's TRS?" asked Donal.

"Oh, hi, Lieutenant. Thaumatic Resonance Scanning. Don't your forensic folks use it for analysis?"

"I don't know." Donal thought back to the shattered room in the OCML where Dr. d'Alkarny's body had been found. "The prisoners I wanted to, er, introduce you to—"

"Oh, the test subjects. Sure."

Eduardo frowned, but whether it was the reference to prisoners as test subjects or whether he resented Donal's taking Kyushen's attention, Donal could not tell.

"They killed the Chief Medical Listener."

"Surely she didn't try to listen while they were still alive. Why would she be amused by them, anyway?"

"Huh?" It took Donal a second to recognize Kyushen's misunderstanding. "No, I mean, they really killed her. Literally."

"They murdered Dr. d'Alkarny?"

"That's what I'm telling you."

"Awesome. I mean, really bad." Kyushen put his

hands in his pockets. "Like, how far do you want me to go?"

Donal said, "What?"

"Look, human thought is kind of transient, but it's formed from neural patterns that build up over time. Pattern persistence is...Say you have an image you form habitually in your mind."

Donal's eyes shifted to the left as he thought of Laura.

"That's what I mean," said Kyushen. "You've just instantiated a pattern that you've used before, though each instant—that's a technical term—is uniquely different from the previous instants."

"Um...If you say so."

"But you also learn, for example, strategies of learning. That produces metapatterns that are used to create patterns, which are then instantiated. Got it?"

Donal decided it was time to show that cops aren't stupid. "And there are metametapatterns, I take it, that produce metapatterns."

Kyushen smiled. "You've got it."

"And when you asked about taking it all the way?"

"When you look at the room around you," said Kyushen, "most of it is hazy background, but you build a mental model of what the room looks like."

"All right."

"But hidden parts of your mind might find details that the foreground patterns ignore. There are tricks to pulling new patterns out of background haze. You're filtering through a debugging frame because the whole point is you're stochastically analyzing apparent noise that the foreground didn't...sorry, am I losing you?"

"No." Donal stared into Kyushen's eyes. "You were trying to tell me how difficult your job is."

"Partly that, maybe...But the tracing tools dig deep into neural structures. Pain is entirely a neural construct."

"You mean, the deeper you dig, the more it hurts."

"Well, oversimplifying—yes."

"And you want to know how much pain the suspects should undergo."

"Yes."

"If you take it all the way, extract everything you can, will it kill them?"

"Unlikely. It's just . . ."

"What?"

"Well, they'll probably wish they *had* died. The process may last minutes or an hour, perhaps two hours at the most. But time flow is a matter of internal mental states."

"You mean it'll last longer for them."

"For years, or at least that's how it'll feel." Kyushen gave a soft smile. "Maybe even centuries. Longer than a normal lifetime."

"So you'll be doing them a favor. Making it feel like they live longer."

"In agony."

Donal shrugged. "Actions bring consequences."

Kyushen nodded.

"Yes," he said. "They do."

Harald walked into the task-force office and sat down at his desk. There, he stared into space, not speaking.

"Hey," called Alexa. "Are you all right?"

Harald looked at her. "I don't think so."

"So what can I—"

But Harald had already opened his desk drawer and pulled out yellow report folders. He placed them on his desk blotter and began to leaf through loose typed pages. It was movement for movement's sake: Alexa could see that Harald wasn't really reading the reports in front of him.

Laura came out of her office, pulled a visitor's chair into the gap between Harald's desk and Alexa's, and sat down.

"Any news on the pterabat?" Laura asked Alexa.

"Sorry." Alexa checked the list of official addresses and telephone numbers she'd written down on her notepad. There was now a line drawn through every number.

"I tried every official agency I could think of," she added, "starting with the Federal Air Force and the Civilian Flying Authority. I even tried the weather service, in case one of their observation balloons spotted anything."

The wraith-enabled sentient balloons were often referred to as Behemoths, an emotionally charged term that Alexa avoided, in case Xalia was offended. Not that anyone had seen Xalia for a while.

"What about the FAF? A pterabat can't cross into federal airspace without anyone noticing."

"Come on, Laura." Alexa tapped her notepad. "The border's thousands of miles long, in largely unoccupied territory. The chances of seeing an intruder are minimal if they keep low to the ground, beneath the scanseers' hex casts."

"Is that an expert opinion?" Laura gave a half smile. "You sound pretty definite."

Alexa colored a little. "I got one of the CFA officials talking. He's a nice guy."

"Oh, yeah?" managed Harald, though his voice sounded empty: ribbing Alexa, but unable to put his heart into it. Not with Sushana still critical.

"What did he tell you?" asked Laura.

"Just what I said. The broadcast masts send out their waves at a thousand feet. In bad weather at night, even a pterabat can fly below hexar altitude and avoid the banshee patrols."

Harald rubbed his face. "Did it definitely come from Illurium? The pterabat, I mean. Couldn't it have taken off and landed inside our own borders?"

"Well, David said—" Alexa stopped, and looked at Laura, then Harald. "Leave me alone. He *is* nice. He works for the CFA's safety board, and he said that a pterabat is too large for a normal small airfield, certainly not the kind of thing you can care for on an isolated farm or whatever."

"He's not married, is he?" said Laura. "This David?"

"I don't—Look, he might not even call me again." Alexa blew out a breath. "Thanatos. Anyway, David doesn't think you could arrange the flight from anywhere but an airport unless you were *very* well organized. And there were no flight plans of pterabats that could have matched our suspects. None at all."

"But it's not impossible," said Harald.

"No. A pterabat could have taken off and landed inside federal airspace. It's just not likely."

"Why do you ask?" said Laura. "You have any other information, Harald? A reason for discounting Illurian involvement?"

Harald shook his head.

"Just being logical, is all. Making sure we don't focus all our attentions on one trail, when it's not a definite one."

Laura said, "You were the one staking out the embassy."

"I followed the driver to—" Harald stopped. "I've got nothing against Donal."

Alexa looked surprised.

"What's wrong with Donal?"

"I just said—"

"What you said in words and how you tensed up your voice are two different things," said Laura. "I heard it, and so did Alexa."

Alexa looked unhappy. Then she nodded.

Harald closed his eyes, exhaling, then opened them again. "Vilnar assigned him here, remember? Whether you recruited Donal or not, it was still Vilnar who he reported to before and who agreed to second him to you."

"What are you saying?" Laura's voice was like ice.

"Nothing. Absolutely nothing. *You* asked *me*." Harald stood up, report folders in hand. "I'm going to the hospital. Give Viktor a break."

Laura looked at him for an endless moment, then said, "All right. Send Viktor home to rest."

"I'll try."

Laura watched Harald go, expecting the door to slam behind him. When it gently clicked shut, she gave a tiny jump nonetheless. Then she realized that Alexa was watching her with care.

"Do you think I'm losing it?" Laura asked Alexa.

"I hope not," said Alexa. "Because if you are, so am I."

Unsure what to make of that, Laura nodded and returned to her own office, where she could stare at the big wall map of the city she'd pinned up and wonder what to do next.

20

It resembled dissection.

When Donal entered the interrogation room, the sights that hung before him were not what he'd expected. Instead of a screaming, twisting body streaked with wet, glistening blood, he saw a still, pale, dwarfish body almost obscured beneath the multitude of bright, multicolored images suspended in the air throughout the room's space. The suspect looked to be in a coma, his face rigid.

Meanwhile, Kyushen sat against the far wall before a small table, manipulating a rack of delicate equipment such as Donal had never seen.

Still, it looked like vivisection: but of the mind, or perhaps the soul, rather than the body. Frames of golden light hung in the air, bearing legends such as:

```
[[image schoolJourneyDaily [
qlist: [duration: variSec dftval=30min,
        painLink: Beating* dtfval = new
        Beating(severity:=3.2),
        adrenalDump: seq<glandExcrete> =
        new seq[dftlen = 5]
        tempList: seq<Stratagem> =
        getDump(dumpType.stratagem
```

```
            .levelOne).
            ]
plist: [ flee (inp SurroundPic: minGestalt, inp
         Howling: audioChord)
         [
         initRun(speed:=currentState.physio
         Max()),
         attempt [
         executeStratagem(nearFit(tempList))]
         success [ wait(22), watch(maxPoss),
         continue]
         otherwise [ initRun(speed:=recalc())]
         self.propensityElasticity:=sub1.
         ]
    ]
    ] end_image]]
```

None of which made sense to Donal. The frames
were stacked into patterns linked by rune-labeled arcs,
like *containment-materialization*, *precursor*, and *conju-*
ration.

"Oh for fuck's sake."

Donal deciphered what the shining frames meant by
remembering his own childhood.

That bloody orphanage.

Because these were the prisoner's memories of being
beaten up while traveling to and from school. These were
the behaviors that had turned him into what he was.

Kyushen leaned back in his chair and wiped sweat
from his face.

"Sorry, Lieutenant. Tough work. He's been neatly ensorcelled with protected hex."

"Er . . . You mean you can't get into his mind?" Donal
gestured at the images. "But aren't these—"

"Part of Dilvox's soul, yes."

"Dilvox?"

Kyushen pointed at the strapped-down dwarf. "That's his name."

There was a glowing light in Kyushen's eyes that had nothing to do with the flame script reflected and dancing across his corneas. He was a knowledge seeker. This was his drug of choice.

"So . . ." Donal looked around at the glowing frames. "Are you getting near the core of his thoughts yet?"

"Oh, no." Kyushen looked surprised. "That'll take hours, at least. These are mesolayer templates for recurrent behavior. I need to send him into deep trance."

Kyushen's fingers moved across the dials and tiny switches. New, complicated geometrical patterns of dark blue and dark green shifted into being among the flame-script frames.

"We can perform instant traces and step through the actions of his potentiated thoughts."

"Potentiated," said Donal.

"Yeah, stored."

More displays opened up, and then Kyushen's fingers moved across the equipment once more. This time the captive dwarf moved beneath his bonds. Then he screamed, a howl of awful agony that Donal had never imagined a human throat could utter.

Donal opened his mouth to tell Kyushen to stop, then saw the sardonic expression on the man's face: the expression that said, *All laypersons react this way.* Donal clamped down his feelings.

"Is that all you can manage?" he said. "A bit of pain? I can do that with my bare hands."

"Wait 'til you see this." Kyushen twisted three dials. "Now I have him reliving his memories of three nights back."

This time the howling was loud enough to make Donal curl up with his hands over his ears, and it continued until he could take no more. He stumbled toward the interrogation-room door, and it swung open at his approach. He stepped through, and the big door swung back.

Ensorcelled bolts clicked shut of their own accord. In the corridor outside, there was silence.

"Thanatos," said Donal, to no one there.

But perhaps a ripple of movement passed across the wall, just beyond the edge of his peripheral vision. Donal squeezed his eyes shut, then opened them.

"Shit," he muttered, knowing he would have to go back in.

My prisoner.

For no good reason, Donal reached inside his jacket to his shoulder and drew out his Magnus. He clicked open the catch, slipped out the magazine to check the heavy load, then pushed it back in place.

Donal grabbed the door handle and went back inside the interrogation room.

Xalia was in darkness, rising through cold stonework, aware of the vertical rivers of not-quite sound defined by a nameless sense that was akin to remote touching: a tactile sensation of icy metal pipes that were yards away.

Xalia's density in the material dimensions was close to zero, maintaining the minimum containment necessary to stop dissipation. She was on a knife edge no human could appreciate: rotate any more of her self out of the mortal universe, and she might never find her way back.

She had been in Darksan Tower and with Laura's permission had roamed up and down the shafts and communicated with some of the wraiths imprisoned there. The tower was a vast, labyrinthine, ancient place, but it paled beside the dark history and complexity of police HQ.

Ward fields repelled Xalia.

If it hadn't been for Sushana in the hospital and for the dead Mina, there was no way Xalia would have tried to penetrate this place.

The ward fields stretched horizontally across the whole of police HQ at this level. Layers of standing hex waves filled resonance cavities in the stone floors for only one purpose: to prevent quasimaterial forms like Xalia from passing through to the upper levels of the building.

To the levels where senior officers like Commissioner Vilnar had their offices and secret vaults.

Far below, other ward fields, beginning at the minus-fiftieth floor, prevented wraiths (and sprites and ectomists) from reaching the dark secrets of the torture chambers. Not to mention the entombed bones of earlier commissioners.

But Xalia was high up in the tower, higher than she had ever climbed. She floated with tortuous care between webs of high-tension hex, among intricate three-dimensional mazes of deadly energy. One lapse of concentration and she would be fried out of existence, in all universes.

Vilnar had sent Donal to spy on Laura—and worse, to seduce her. Once Xalia had proof that she could show Laura, there was no doubt in Xalia's mind about what would happen next.

Donal would suffer, perhaps die in some lonely alley, waiting for backup that would never arrive.

Xalia was slipping through the third layer of defenses when a fiery sentence sprang up in her awareness.

+Who are you?+

Xalia stopped her ascent. For a split second she began

a sideways drift, but there were HT hex lines close by. She brought herself to a halt.

Who's asking?

The reply came cold and loud.

+Have you ever considered the nature of eternity?+

What?

+The length of time that persists beyond your existence.+

It took a moment for Xalia to decide that was a threat.

Fuck off.

And for a few more moments, silence filled the solid stone. Then a cold rippling passed through everything, including Xalia, and she began to understand the nature of the being that guarded the upper layers. It was a tesselan, an aggregation fashioned from families of wraiths that were torn apart, twisted into new forms, and reprogrammed with a single quasisoul by master practitioners from the darkest schools of mind-control mages.

+I will eat you.+

I don't fuckin' think so.

+And tear you apart, and take you into myself.+

Xalia was already moving.

You and what horde?

+I need no other—+

But they were at the nova-bright webs deep inside the stone now, where lethal energies burned and a vast powerful form like the tesselan guardian dared not move. Sensing the huge capacity for resonance from the tesselan, the dumb, mindless energies of the fire webs were already closing in.

Xalia elongated her form and slipped *inside* the fire webs.

And now she was really in danger.

Ah, shit.

From behind, the guardian's words were bright.

+That was fatally stupid, little one.+

Xalia tried to move forward, but the ravening lines of energy beat her back, and a deep realization flooded through her: she was about to die.

Donal stepped back into the interrogation room. The original frames and glowing patterns were now obscured by arrays of flowing light, webs in which glyphs and icons moved.

Beyond the blaze, Kyushen was scarcely visible at his workbench. Equipment hummed and crackled. The dwarfish prisoner whose soul was being flayed was completely out of sight, hidden by the vast display of light and movement filling the stone-walled room.

"Thanatos, what are you doing to him, Kyushen?"

"This is the running soul." Kyushen's voice was made indistinct by discordant clicks and moans from his instruments. "The actual thoughts generated by the schemata and images. See: there's a propensity being invoked in order to return the qualia associated with—"

"You're insane."

"On the contrary. See." Kyushen's sleeve was painted in kaleidoscopic hues as he pointed into the midst of the visual maelstrom. "There. *That* structure is completely inconsistent with rational thought, at least of the human variety."

"Are you saying the prisoner's not human?"

"No, I'm telling you he's clinically insane. It would take some powerful mage therapists to work any kind of rechanneling to solve the guy's problems."

Donal stared at the shifting light for a few moments.

"We're not here to solve his problems."

"No. We're not."

"But I can't let you—"

"Hush. There. Bloody Death, I've got it."

"What have you found?"

"Wait. This is the trace I've got to follow, just stepping through these invocations..."

Donal started to ask a further question, then closed his mouth.

"There's a phone number," muttered Kyushen.

"You're kidding."

"It's a resonance impression." Kyushen looked up at Donal. "He didn't perceive it directly. I'm going to have to trace the impressions and build a shadow."

Donal shook his head.

"You mean it's guesswork, not memory."

"If we get a complete image, it will be accurate."

Donal wanted to ask how Kyushen knew that but decided not to. Kyushen's fingers flicked across switches and toggles.

"I'm getting it..."

Fingers moving faster across the console.

"No. Damn..."

There was nothing Donal could say or do to help.

"Ah...Hades."

"You've lost it," said Donal.

"Oh, no." Kyushen looked up. "I can tell you exactly where the call came from: seven-seven-seven, two-nine, three-five-one, seven-two-zero."

Donal stared at him, then nodded.

"Keep a log," he said. "Of everything you find."

"Of course." Kyushen shook his head. "What did you expect me to do?"

Donal said nothing, but his mind was whirling. This was the second piece of evidence.

I expect you would bury it, if you knew you'd just fingered Vilnar.

Because if there was a more dangerous enemy than a police commissioner, Donal could not imagine it.

*   *   *

Xalia tried, but the pseudofire that could destroy her wraith form, inflicting pain that would last a subjective century, beat her back. The fire web was squeezing and burning her out of existence: a time-dilating immolation.

Fucking bastard place.

Then a cool wave passed through the web, clearing a passage.

Who—

They call me Gertie.

Xalia recognized the wraith now. When Laura rode the elevator tubes upward—elevators that were irrelevant to Xalia—Xalia sometimes flew up alongside, so she'd gotten to know some of the captive wraiths.

Gertie? Aren't you trapped in elevator seven? Bound to it?

Well, there are binds and binds, aren't there?

Uncertain what to make of that, Xalia matched her own vector's rotational frequency with Gertie's: it was like two corporeal humans holding hands. Together, they slipped through solid matter, heading up toward the place that might unveil the truth.

Commissioner Vilnar's office.

Harald brought his bone-shielded motorcycle to an idling halt. The Phantasm extruded two curved stands, steadying itself as Harald swung his leg over and dismounted.

"Stay ready," he murmured. "And keep watch."

A sense of alertness seemed to radiate from the Phantasm as Harald left it behind him. He strode quickly down an alleyway, across which a row of low spiked posts was set: there to discourage bikes and cars from joyriding between the graffiti-decorated walls.

Tonight was too cold for the neighborhood youths to be out in force. Even so, a sudden burst of red-and-gold light washed across closed windows, and a series of loud cracks split the air: firecrackers and gunpowder candles thrown by young idiots who ought to know better.

As a rookie cop, Harald had nearly shot a fourteen-year-old boy for throwing a firecracker, when his galvanized nerves had reacted as if to gunfire. Now he knew the difference automatically—not just from his years on the street, but from the intervening years as a marine before returning to life as a cop.

And as a sergeant in the Fighting Sevens, he had once led his troop into a safe haven in the Kongal Rock Forest, in the disputed Fuerile Valley beyond the Zurinese border. Harald had used a native guide, one who'd lived in the military base with them and even cooked their food. The guide's name was Gam Sintil, or at least that's what they knew him as.

Fucking bastard snitches and traitors.

But no one realized that Gam Sintil's true sympathies lay with the separatists—until a crescendo of hexlar-piercing rounds crashed from among the fractal forest pillars, and half of Harald's troop were dead before they even recognized the ambush.

Kill the fuckers.

Harald had fought his way out with three wounded comrades. His only satisfaction had been when Billy—aka Corporal Bilken Flewelor—placed a round in Gam Sintil's spine. The bastard had been running and nearly got clear.

Billy's skull had exploded into scarlet mist a second later, from a sniper that Harald never saw. Harald just managed to get away.

Kill them all.

Just as Harald would do to Donal Riordan if it turned out the bastard was responsible for what happened to Sushana.

Harald used snitches. He was gentle and friendly

with them, when appropriate. But he distrusted and hated them all.

This was an immigrant area, where refugees from Illurium made their homes. Harald already knew where to check first: a café called Stelto's, where Birtril Kondalis hung out eight evenings a week (with Hachiday reserved for worship at the Temple of Xithros).

The usual haunting music drifted out of Stelto's, and Harald pushed aside the metal-beaded curtains and slid open the heavy rune-carved wooden door. Its runners were well-greased, so the door action was smooth and soundless. Harald stepped into the opium-scented atmosphere.

Three long-faced men were sucking from helical pipes in the far corner. When they turned their eyes toward Harald, the irises were fully contracted, their pinprick gazes focused on a dream world that had little to do with Harald himself: it was just a reaction to movement.

On the right-hand side, where a family was gathered to eat, a round-faced man with coffee-colored skin— that was Birtril—closed his eyes and swallowed. Then he opened his eyes and forced a smile.

"Hello, Sergeant," he said.

"Birtril. What have you got for me?"

"Huh?"

"Information. You know that's what I like." Harald dragged a spare chair across the cheap linoleum floor and sat down at Birtril's table. He nodded to the thin woman and two young boys who were sitting with Birtril.

"Mrs. Kondalis," Harald added. "Nice to see you. And the sons."

Birtril's wife, Laxara, nodded, but warily. She and

Birtril were all too aware of the true legal status of their marriage. Birtril's first—and by law, only—wife remained in Silvex City, back in Illurium.

The money that Birtril sent her every week was the only thing that prevented her from raising the matter officially. If Birtril's bosses at the embassy heard about it, his career in catering for diplomats would be ruined for good. And no one would get any money.

"There's, er, nothing going on. . . ." Birtril looked up as the café's owner, Zegrol (the original owner, Stelto, had passed away during a dispute in a nearby nightclub whose bouncers bore scimitars that they knew how to use) poked his head through the curtains at the rear.

Zegrol spotted Harald, observed his mood, and withdrew immediately. The curtains swung gently after he disappeared. Birtril gave a long liquid blink of unsurprised disappointment. "Honestly, Sergeant. No one in the embassy's up to anything."

"Not even the driver of XSA899-omega-beth-del?"

"Huh?"

"Limo driver. Lean, pale skinned, black hair. Get a grip, Birtril." Harald leaned toward him. "And concentrate, will you?"

"Um . . . Sure, Sergeant."

Harald checked the two sons for signs of anger, but they were not yet old enough to appreciate the bind that Harald held them in and to realize just how much their parents must resent him. Laxara's feelings remained deeply hidden.

"So what's his name? The driver?"

Birtril's gaze shifted to his left. "Ixil Deltrassol. He's an ex-army driver. Keeps to himself."

"And?"

Birtril glanced at Laxara.

"Um, can we take a walk, Sergeant?"

"Well." Harald smiled. "Of course. Let's get going."

He stood quickly and helped Birtril get up, as though he needed assistance. It was a matter of maintaining dominance. Harald ignored the opium smokers and Birtril's family—his second family—as he left with Birtril beside him. But he kept watch in his peripheral vision.

Nothing happened as they passed through the hangings and out onto the cold street. Two youths on the corner, one carrying an unlit gunpowder candle, caught sight of Harald and faded into Raxman Alley. Harald was known here.

That was the way he liked it.

"Talk to me, Birtril."

"I have no idea what he's done," Birtril said quickly. "Deltrassol doesn't make friends. Not enemies but not friends either, you know what I mean?"

"Only if you use simple words."

"Huh?"

"Never mind. What are you hiding?"

"I'm not—Shit." Birtril stopped by one of the metal posts. "I don't know about any crime he might have committed, okay?"

"Right, and who are his acquaintances, if he doesn't have friends?"

"I don't know. He spends time in Sir Alvan's offices, but then, he works for the man. That's all."

"And?"

Harald stared hard, maintaining psychological pressure.

"There were rumors, and . . . I've seen Deltrassol's car parked where they said it would be."

"Uh-huh. Continue, Birtril. All the way to the end."

"The See-Through Look 'n' Feel," said Birtril. "I happened to see him coming out of there."

"You're sure?"

"Yeah, and the doorman said good night to him by name, like he was a regular or something, y'know?"

"Good."

Birtril let out a sigh of relief.

"That's it, boss. Sergeant. That's everything I know about him."

"I believe you." Harald pulled out his wallet and slipped out three thirteen-florin notes. "Here, buy Laxara a new coat."

Birtril slipped the money quickly into his pocket.

"Much appreciated, Sergeant."

He waited, as if for permission to rejoin his family.

"Go on." Harald nodded back toward Stelto's. "Laxara's waiting for you."

"Thanks."

Harald waited until Birtril was almost at the café door before calling out, "And I won't mention anything to Laxara."

Birtril stopped, stiffening.

"About you being in Quarter Moon Alley," added Harald. "I wouldn't want to speculate on what you were doing there. Know what I mean?"

Birtril's head hung forward, and he stood there in front of the door to Stelto's. His face was in shadow against the light, and perhaps he was crying: it was impossible to tell. Then he straightened by a small amount, pushed open the door, and went inside.

It banged shut behind him.

Harald stood looking at the closed door for a while. Then he remembered Sushana's battered face, and his own expression turned to stone.

A rocket burst high overhead, throwing out silver and black stars, emitting a screeching howl.

Reaching his motorcycle, Harald swung his leg over the saddle and settled into position.

"If this Deltrassol's a principal," he told the

Phantasm, "I'm going to rip his nuts off. But if he's just a stooge..."

The Phantasm rumbled and growled, engine revving as Harald took hold of the handlebars. It rolled forward, pulling its twin stands back inside itself.

"...then I'm going to make sure it's Donal bloody Riordan who loses his testicles, and more. For Laura's sake as well as Sushana's."

The Phantasm accelerated into the street.

21

Xalia fought her way through further barriers that Gertie found easy to slip past. For over a hundred twenty years, Gertie had glided along elevator shafts and the lesser-known aspects of police HQ architecture. She knew where solid stone offered clear passage and where security concerns had resulted in devious defenses.

Now Gertie hung back before the final labyrinth, directing Xalia.

That way. See?

Yes. Thanks.

There were risks in helping a fellow wraith, but Gertie had a perverse streak, and in any case she had been bored for days. And Xalia worked with Donal, was part of his new team, and Gertie's fondness for Donal had been growing with the years.

Xalia, meanwhile, slipped and squirmed and attenuated her form to a dangerous extent, fighting to breach the barriers. She wanted proof of Donal's complicity to take to Laura. But this fire labyrinth was of expert design.

How are you doing, Xalia?

Gertie's message came through blazing curtains of hot hex like a distant echo. Xalia directed a narrow beam of communication back through the labyrinth, more to see if she could than because she wanted to answer. She needed to concentrate.

Fine. What did you think?

Whether it was the tiny distraction of making that reply, Xalia could not tell—but in the next few moments, the bars of hex floating among the thinner shields grew fatter and hotter, strengthening their manifestation. Xalia pulled herself inward and held still, floating in place.

Then the bars brightened and began extruding crescent-shaped horns of crackling energy, and Xalia knew she was done for.

Going farther into the labyrinth was out of the question. Secondary and tertiary labyrinths began to swing and rotate through from the orthogonal pocket universes in which they were stored. They inserted themselves into the mortal continuum, filling the labyrinth's gaps.

Vilnar, you mother—

Xalia's curse was cut off as the first two horns of energy pierced her half-ethereal form, and pain flared along the length of her paranerves: a twisting agony such as normal human beings could never experience.

Xalia?

It's got me.

A long, thin thread worked its way among the sprouting new bars of the overlaying labyrinths. It was Gertie, extending herself to reach Xalia—or trying to.

In a moment of clarity, Xalia understood what Gertie was doing, and why. She remembered the way Gertie joked with Donal and how Donal had not shown any hesitation in accepting a freewraith as a task-force member.

Damn it, Xalia liked Donal, but if he was in league with the enemy . . .

Gertie, I'm here to gather evidence against Donal Riordan.

For a second, the extruded portion of Gertie's form

withdrew, like a blind snake slithering backward from an electric shock.

Then she extended back into the ever-tightening labyrinth, questing, and after a moment Xalia understood that there was no sense in telling Gertie to get out of there. It would be quicker to show her how bad things were.

Xalia extended herself until her form impinged on Gertie's extrusion, wraith coexisting in the same space as wraith, just as two more crescent horns slipped inside her body. She howled, broadcasting agony along frequencies and energy fields unknown to humankind.

Gertie's form—such parts of her as Xalia could sense—throbbed and flared with shared pain as the cutting hex blasted along her own paranervous system. In the distance, a scream sounded.

Now will you for fuck's sake get out of here, Gertie?

After a hundredth of a second, Gertie's reply rang inside Xalia's paranervous system:

This is my damned building, and no one does this to me!

Then Gertie's form began to glow with a concentration of energy such as Xalia had never experienced before.

Donal, meanwhile, had the telephone number that he needed, the second link to Commissioner Vilnar's office, but with no hope that it could be offered as evidence in court. His technical expert, Kyushen, sat in shocked silence, unmoving, while stretcher bearers carried out the unmoving dwarf.

The dwarf's condition, if nothing else, made the evidence invalid.

It was not true death but a Basilisk trance, unbreakable according to every diagnostic Kyushen had run. Legally, such deep catatonia *was* death. No one in

Tristopolitan legal history had ever awakened from a Basilisk trance.

Kyushen stared into nothingness.

"You feel bad." Donal watched the stretcher bearers leave and the iron door swinging shut behind them. The displays that had flared so brightly earlier had faded to a few small, minimized, and dimmed-out ghosts. "And you could probably use your own instruments to change how you feel about that..."

Kyushen looked up.

"...but you shouldn't," continued Donal. "Because you *have* killed a man, and you don't get over it, you don't accept it—you just live with it."

"But I didn't mean to—you know."

"Yes," said Donal. "But it was always a risk, and we both knew it."

Kyushen began to shake. His skin was pale, and this was the aftermath of shock. Donal watched the fit of shivering take hold of him.

"Relax," said Donal. "Don't fight it. Let it pass through you..."

Kyushen closed his eyes and moaned.

"...because this is natural. Afterward, you will be okay."

Some of these words came from Donal's subconscious, from the mesmeric trance the police mage had taken him into after the first fatal street shoot-out that Donal had been caught up in. Donal had killed three men, not just one, after Fredrix's throat exploded in gouts of scarlet arterial blood.

Donal had watched Sergeant Fredrix Paulsen—the nearest to a father Donal had ever known—gasp and shrink as his eyes grew opaque, and that was it: nothing left of the man save fuel for the reactor piles.

Two minutes later (though it might have seemed much longer than that to Kyushen), the shaking fit be-

gan to fade to a tremble and finally was gone. Kyushen
slumped.

After a moment, Donal left.

Xalia screamed, rotating like laundry in a dryer, twisting
in and out of reality as Gertie dragged her through tiny
closing apertures of pain. Scalding agony defined the
tightening labyrinths as Xalia's wraith form was ripped
and torn.

Yet she remained essentially intact as Gertie's cunning
use of power and topology took both of them through
the fatal hex defenses, back to the perimeter. And then
they were outside, basking in cool solid stone. Above
them, the outer defenses roiled and burned.

Gertie's words rolled through Xalia's awareness.

So what point did you prove here today?

Suffering delineated every movement of Xalia's discorporate being.

What . . . do you . . . mean?

You were trying to accuse Donal Riordan. Implicate him.

Xalia billowed, her wraith form still ripped, insubstantial inside the solid stonework of the building. Her
ability to concentrate was gone; her communication was
weak.

Yes . . .

*Did you get any resonance of a personality in there? In the
energies of the labyrinth?*

Xalia twisted, trying to focus.

Resonance?

Yeah . . . what kind of wraith are you, anyway?

After a moment, Xalia drew enough energy into herself to be able to reply.

Fuck off.

Gertie chuckled.

That's better. Now, as soon as you can work out whose

flavor that was*—she meant flavor of resonance—*The sooner you can leave young Donal alone.*

You like . . . him.

Again Gertie was amused at Xalia.

I like puppies too. Have you been in the deathwolves' den?

If Xalia had had eyes, she would have closed them. Banter was too much. Everything still hurt.

Don't . . . understand.

Young Donal's like a pet to me. You're like a neighbor's kid. And it's time you straightened out your own feelings about Laura Steele.

Fuck . . .

Well, you're a wraith, so maybe you shouldn't. Not with humans.

This was too much. But the words that came next from Gertie were softer in tone, soothing, leading Xalia farther away from the burning labyrinth. The two wraiths began to sink downward, remaining inside the cool, solid, protecting stone.

Come on, Xalia. There are groves and grottoes no one knows about anymore. Some have healing energies.

I don't . . . know.

Gertie drew closer.

Trust me. I can heal you.

After a moment, Xalia replied.

Yes . . .

Then come.

Their descent through stone became faster.

Donal was in Laura's office. Laura had commanded the internal glass walls to darken so that she and Donal had privacy. They hugged and kissed, and she groaned when Donal ran his palms and fingertips along her thin blouse, across the silkiness of her bra, but they drew back from going any farther.

There were too many officers and other beings in the building capable of sensing powerful resonances; love-making would have to wait until they were back in Laura's apartment. Donal blew out a long breath.

"Oh, Thanatos."

"Yeah..."

Then Donal swallowed and looked at the now-opaque wall, as though there were something to see. He said, "I don't *want* to go, you know."

"You don't want to visit a foreign country?"

Donal shook his head.

"I *am* scared shitless of flying, if you want the truth, but I can always get drunk. Foreign trips weren't exactly a feature of the orphanage, so I would like to go abroad.... That's not it."

"I know." Laura's voice grew small and quiet. "It's scary, isn't it? How fast things happen, like you and me."

"Exactly."

"You don't want to be apart from me, and that's good." Laura gave a half-sad smile. "I feel the same way, love. But we both know you're going to Illurium because it's the only way to do the job."

After a moment, Donal nodded.

"I guess. Listen, I don't want you in danger, but you could come with me and—"

"No, I don't think so."

Donal rubbed his face. "Couldn't we make it a vacation for you, while I do the investigation work? I don't want you undercover—sorry, I know you're the boss—but we could set you up in a separate location. I'm good at shifting through alleyways without being tailed—"

"Oh, my beautiful man."

Laura stepped close, laid the palm of one cold hand against his face—it felt deliciously soothing to Donal—and kissed him gently.

"What?"

"You treat me just like any other woman."

"Well..." Donal smiled. "Not *exactly* like everyone else."

"Ha. But that's the point."

"Uh, what is?"

"What's in here." Laura gestured toward her left breast. "I'm *not* like other women. People like me are carefully tracked wherever we go. I'm not even sure I'd have legal rights in Illurium."

"Ah, fuck."

Laura smiled beautifully.

"Whatever you say. Just as soon as we get home."

Donal shook his head, squeezing his eyes shut. Laura laughed.

"All right," she added. "We'll get some initial planning done for your trip. Harald's contacts over there will be invaluable—Where is he, anyway?"

"Haven't seen him for ages," said Donal. "Maybe at the hospital with Sushana?"

"No, I just called there a while ago. Viktor's with her. I think he and Harald are taking turns to watch over her."

"Good."

Harald was leaning over his bike, accelerating hard as he retraced his route along the Orb-Dexter Freeway, knowing he was within minutes of potentially destroying Commander Steele's happiness. Laura Steele was the best superior he'd ever served under, his marine service included. When she realized that Donal was a creature of the Black Circle, she would be devastated.

But then Harald remembered Sushana's face, the evidence of things done to her by Sally the Claw and his men. Viktor had been closeted away with one of the hospital doctors for what seemed like an age before coming out with a dead look in his eyes and brackets of anger in the muscles beside his mouth.

Harald would make someone pay . . . make everyone pay, beginning with Lieutenant Riordan and not stopping until he'd taken down Commissioner Vilnar. He needed just one more piece of evidence. But he had always felt there was something wrong in Commissioner Vilnar's domain. Odd energies had flickered and resonated in the commissioner's office, just beyond the edges of Harald's marine-trained senses.

The Phantasm motorcycle leaned into a corner, took the bend while startling a finely dressed old woman about to cross the road, then straightened up and increased speed once more.

"Ixil Deltrassol," Harald's unwilling informant Birtril had said. *"He's an ex-army driver. Keeps to himself."*

Working in the embassy, unaware of the true nature of the Black Circle he ultimately worked for, this Deltrassol was probably a lowlife. He was a driver who scarcely ranked as a foot soldier in the extended army of morons and deviants (though their mid-rank officers could be real pieces of work: witness Sally the Claw) manipulated from above by unseen individuals.

But no one would dare to investigate their own police commissioner. If Harald had been halfway sensible, he wouldn't have considered it either.

They're going to pay.

It was Sushana who made the difference, Sushana who had always made the difference in Harald's sometimes bleak world.

Away from the ornate old town houses with polished brass railings, Harald slowed the Phantasm. They entered a pentangle fronted by former mansions long transformed into decaying hotels. There was a five-sided

garden that was no longer safe to enter at night, not unarmed or alone.

Then he took the bike down a series of narrowing
and darkening streets until the lights brightened once
more, this time with garish blues and reds predominating. He was into an area that the old rich lady they'd
nearly run over would be shocked to realize existed,
only half a mile from where she lived out her grand existence.

A tiny chained demonic form fluttered its leathery
wings over Sid's Scar Parlor, the curlicued rune-and-
knot patterns across its body a testimony to One-Eyed
Sid's considerable skill with a straight razor.

Here in Quarter Moon Alley, Sid's artistry was well
known, but Harald remembered the days of his and
Sid's youth, when they had run the streets in the same
gang and Sid's use of the razor had been for more immediate purposes than fiscal gain or artistic recognition.

Or perhaps there *had* been a kind of artistry involved
in the way Sid wielded the ultrasharp blade.

Slowing right down, the Phantasm mumbled with its
engine close to idling as they slipped past the black mul-
tifaceted windowless building known as Nameless, past
a betting shop, and past a nightclub whose failing business was driving it inexorably toward the status of hot-
pillow house, strictly illegal in Tristopolis and always
present.

Had there ever been a large city without prostitution?
Harald had often wondered at the nearness between this
and the Courts of Mercy, less than two miles away yet
worlds apart. At least, any supreme judge caring to walk
down Quarter Moon Alley to sample its facilities left his
robes of office back at the courts.

Past the glowing signs of three more establishments
on the right, Harald could see the ephemeral beckoning

hand that came through the wall and hung above the sidewalk, inviting passersby inside. The See-Through Look 'n' Feel appeared classier than many of the surrounding nightclubs, but there was only one type of person who frequented the place. Some of them turned even Harald's hardened stomach.

There was a purple taxi parked just ahead, and Harald pulled the motorcycle in behind it. The three young Zurinese sailors who tumbled from the taxi were laughing and half drunk, and Harald hoped that whatever adventures awaited them this evening, however sordid, there would be at least the illusion of happiness involved and no traumas to follow them through the rest of their lives.

But in this place, it could as easily be the flash of a blade or the glint of light from a spinning bullet case that would be the last impression to catch their confused awarenesses before darkness slammed in. They might never sense the fingers fumbling for their wallets and ID cards.

It happened here, and it had happened in the foreign ports that Harald visited as a young marine; it seemed to be the way of the world. For a second Harald considered flashing his own ID, his detective's shield, and warning them away, but they would only get in trouble somewhere else.

And then he remembered the state that Sushana was in, and the sailors faded from Harald's awareness. The Phantasm extruded one stand—tentatively—and that allowed Harald to lean sideways to check out the doorway of See-Through Look 'n' Feel.

There were four men standing there in deep-purple cloaks—the club's colors—and the largest of them was Stone. Harald had known Stone for a long time, and knew him only by that name. The street moniker was accurate enough.

"All right," Harald murmured to the Phantasm. "I'll be going in the front way. Let's just get you tucked out of sight."

The motorcycle rumbled in agreement and rolled on, withdrawing its stand.

In a darkened alleyway strewn with broken crates and shards of blue and brown glass, Harald brought the Phantasm to a halt. As it extruded both stands and Harald dismounted, he saw a pale child with reptilian scales across his forehead.

The child looked about five years old but might be as old as eight if his diet was poor.

"Hey," said Harald. "Could you do me a favor?"

After a second the scaly boy nodded. Harald dug inside his pocket and flung over a handful of nine-sided coins. The boy caught them.

"Keep people away from the motorcycle," Harald instructed. "And I'll pay you more when I get back."

A shimmer passed across the Phantasm's bony carapace. The boy's eyes widened.

"Yeah," said Harald. "It's kinda for their own good."

The boy grinned.

Harald grinned back. Then, gun held straight down at his side, he retraced his steps along the alleyway, heading back toward the club's front entrance.

Stone saw Harald coming a hundred yards away and stepped out into the middle of the sidewalk. He stood like some massive rock half-filling a strait. Passersby drifted past on either side, avoiding him subconsciously.

"Hey, Sergeant," Stone rumbled as Harald drew close.

"Hey, Stone."

"You gonna need that?" Raising one stone-encrusted hand, Stone pointed. "We expecting trouble?"

"I hope not." Harald kept the gun pointed down. "But I like to be prepared."

"You're not saying one of our clientele has been a naughty boy?" When Stone frowned, the flanges of interlocking granite that shielded his brow scraped together. "We got a classy establishment here, Sergeant."

"That's right," said Harald. "And I'm sure you want to keep it that way."

"So who's the miscreant?"

"Miscreant?"

"What?" The stones shifted around Stone's grin. "Ya think I can't use big words?"

"You won't hear me say that, big guy. The miscreant is called Deltrassol, though who knows what name he uses around here."

"Oh, that one." Stone's grin widened. "He likes the ladies ... insubstantial. Doesn't wrinkle his chauffeur suit, at least not from the outside, know what I mean?"

Harald knew pretty well what Stone was getting at.

"You ever thought about getting an honest job, Stone?"

"What, you mean like a police officer? Nice uniform, stroll the streets, nab perpetrators ..."

"We don't actually call them perp—"

"Not since I taught you how to say miscreant, obviously."

"Right." Harald smiled at the thought of Stone in police uniform, studying interpersonal skills and criminology at the academy. "So where's our Deltrassol?"

"Top floor," said Stone. "Right at the back."

"Nothing but the best for our miscreants."

"There you go, Sergeant," said Stone. "You don't do so bad—"

"—for a dumb cop," Harald finished for him. "Thank you so much."

Inside, Harald stepped through the ectoplasmic curtain that filled the hallway—it slid wetly across his skin—and then he was inside a corridor furnished in red and black. Tiny flamesprites danced in niches along the walls.

To Harald's right, an archway opened onto the dark interior of the club. Blue-lit booths were sparsely occupied by middle-aged men and their paid companions, some of whom were ordinary humans: the See-Through Look 'n' Feel catered to a range of clientele.

There were three wraiths dancing on the bar, their lower extremities just inside the top of the counter, swaying to the too-loud music. One of them looked over toward Harald, the darkness where her eyes should have been now focusing on him. She gave a slow wink as she danced.

She nodded slightly toward the rear of the building, as if she knew what Harald was here for: to take down Deltrassol. It confirmed what Stone had already said, and Harald tipped his forehead to give a fingertip salute before continuing along the red-lit hallway.

22

Reversed words crawled across the far wall, with Harald's shadow blotting out the center. The light came from the shining sign that floated behind him. Moving to one side so his silhouette would not show, Harald advanced with crosswise steps along the hallway.

At the entrance to the rear lounge, Harald checked inside, in case his target was not where Stone thought or there was other trouble. The Tiplog brothers were here, their backs to Harald, and he made a mental note to find out later what they were up to. No one else of interest.

So he went back into the hallway and crossed to the staircase, where two burning wraiths drew aside. One of them opened her mouth to reveal teeth of yellow flames.

Harald ignored them as he began his ascent. The carpet on the treads was sticky and blackened with dirt. Having got this far, the club's patrons no longer needed the illusory glamour that decorated the bar and lounges: a haze of lust obscured the tacky reality, the faded scents of despair and old semen.

The top corridor was floored with bare boards. Paint peeled from flimsy doors; rhythmic groans came from behind two of them. Harald drew his gun. He would kick in each door in turn, regardless of who might be inside.

But one of the wraiths rose up through the floor,

anticipating the damage Harald was likely to cause, and pointed at the end door. She hung in the air until Harald nodded. Then she floated downward and out of sight.

Harald moved fast.

Floorboards creaked beneath his weight, but not in time to warn Deltrassol, as Harald's heel slammed into the door beside the lock. There was plenty of hip thrust, and splinters flew as the door sprang back. Harald swiveled, aiming from the hip—the Fighting Sevens used instinctual shooting, because traditional targeting takes time—then stopped.

"Hey, Ixil." Harald used Deltrassol's first name because that was basic intimidation. "Is everything coming along nicely?"

On the bed, a pale-faced man in a dark suit lay still, eyes widened. The half-manifest wraith sitting astride him pumped her hips several more times before stopping.

The wraith turned to regard Harald, and opened her mouth—it looked like darkness pricked with stars—in what might have been a grin.

Then she grew insubstantial, and Harald tried not to look at the tumescence revealed inside Ixil Deltrassol's trousers. The wraith faded almost to invisibility.

Harald laughed and took three paces into the room, stopping close to the bed.

"Ain't that always the way, Ixil? Here one second, fading away the next." And, to the wraith: "Right, darling?"

The wraith was already sinking downward through the floor. She nodded to Harald and gave a tiny wave in the direction of the bed. In a second, she was gone.

Deltrassol's mouth opened and closed. Then he swallowed and said, "What—"

"I'm arresting you for murder," said Harald.

"No—"

"Yes. Unless you can convince me there's a reason I should let you go. Then you'd fly straight back to Illurium, wouldn't you?"

"I . . . No, I'd stay here. Honest, Officer. I'd—"

"Wrong answer." Harald's hand seemed to flicker into motion. "Try again."

Drops of blood sprang out across Deltrassol's forehead.

Harald raised the weapon again, ready to inflict deeper damage.

"Uh . . . Officer. What—What do you want me to do?"

But Harald's gun was now pointed at Deltrassol's crotch.

"I like tiny targets. It's the challenge, y'know?"

"Look, Officer, I didn't know the dwarves were going to . . . do what they did. I swear, I only heard on the radio afterward what happened. Thanatos . . . I'd never get involved in . . . stuff like that."

Harald lowered his aim slightly, to appear less threatening. He could still shoot Deltrassol's thigh and destroy the femoral artery with minimal movement.

"I'd like to believe you." Harald stepped closer to the bed and leaned forward, wrapping the fingers of his left hand around Deltrassol's throat. "But I'm afraid I can't."

If Deltrassol had had an active hand in what happened to Sushana, then Harald's thumb and finger were going to close, collapsing the laryngeal cartilage. It would take a while for Deltrassol to choke to death.

"No, man . . . Please. Don't."

"One chance." Harald tapped Deltrassol on the forehead. "Relax."

"Please—"

"I don't know whether you know this yet as it's easy to . . . lose control and . . . let go of the body and drift . . . just drift . . ." The tone of Harald's voice deepened and slowed as he looked into Deltrassol's eyes. "...and you can close your eyes...that's right...as the threat fades..."

Deltrassol's eyelids drooped, then closed.

The marines had taught Harald to kill with guns and blades, with hands and feet, and they had drilled him in the use of subtler weapons.

Ixil Deltrassol slid deeper into a trance. Disconcerted by fear, he was totally vulnerable to the unexpected mesmeric tone of Harald's trained voice.

Deeper still.

"...so much pain to sit on...the fence as...defense is unnecessary so...you let it go..."

As an embassy driver, Deltrassol had received trance training, but it was superficial. After Harald penetrated the initial defense, Deltrassol's training made him *more* vulnerable: he had been in trances so often it was easy to return.

"Policeman," Deltrassol murmured.

Harald modulated his voice to match Deltrassol's neurophysiology. "...because I'm the one who can... save you from pain...like a windowpane into memory of...things you have to...tell me...as your unconscious knows what it needs...to help you as it... always has to...tell me..."

"Police. Our contact. He...Setup."

Harald leaned closer.

"...tell me everything..."

Laura walked out into the main office area. Donal had been gone ages getting the coffee—he'd offered to bring back a cup for her—and she wondered what was keeping him. The caffeine meant nothing to her black zombie blood, but it was unusual for Donal to take so long.

On the few occasions Donal had drunk alcohol since coming here, he'd drunk raw, cheap whiskey that Laura wouldn't dream of putting in her car—the Vixen was more fussy than that. To a zombie, alcohol tasted like sour vinegar laced with something worse: rats' piss, or the lymph fluid of crushed beetles.

Drunk as a zombie was an oxymoron that had somehow passed into the language as a simile. Laura used to consider it one of life's ironies, back when she'd been alive.

"Hey, Laura." Alexa was on the phone, cupping her hand around the mouthpiece. "I've got Harald on the—"

Her expression changed to a frown, then she looked up at Laura and shrugged. "Sorry. He just hung up on me."

"Is everything all right?"

"He told me to cancel an EPB. The one on the Illurian driver. Er"—Alexa glanced down at her notebook—"Ixil Deltrassol."

Laura glanced at the door, where Donal was backing in with three cups of coffee clutched between his hands. No wonder he was taking so long.

"What happened? Don't tell me he's..." Laura let her voice trail off. "Never mind."

Alexa stared at her for a moment.

"I don't think Harald's offed the guy, if that's what you mean."

"No," said Laura. "I don't think one of my officers would do such a thing."

"Me neither." Donal approached with the coffees, wincing as he tried—and failed—to put all three down on Alexa's desktop without spilling anything. "Sorry. What bad thing wouldn't we dream of doing?"

"Taking the law into your hands," said Alexa.

"Well, Thanatos forbid."

"In a lethal manner," said Laura. "Causing a suspect to disappear."

"Oh." Donal looked at Alexa. "Who are we talking about, exactly?"

"Deltrassol, Ixil. Wanted for—"

"The embassy driver, right?"

"That's the man." Laura perched herself on the edge of the desk. "And did Harald give any indication why we should kill an Extended Points Bulletin? Doesn't he know how hard I have to work to get one published in the first place?"

"Yeah," said Alexa.

"But he doesn't care." Donal half-smiled.

"I think"—Alexa checked her notepad once more—"he's got the guy and turned him as a witness."

Laura bit her lip. "All right."

Donal saw her expression and decided that Harald was in trouble but would probably talk his way out of it. Donal himself had had such arguments with various bosses. You interrogated a witness, an opportunity to lever something out of them came up, and you took it, offering them a lighter sentence or whatever.

The thing was, however spur of the moment the offer might be, the officer had to follow through on it. On the streets, someone who fails to keep their promises isn't "stand-up," and that is the worst crime of all.

"All right," said Laura again. "That's fine. If I'm not around when Harald turns up, get him to hang around until I am."

"I'll try." Alexa sipped her coffee and nodded toward Donal. "Thanks."

Laura took a sip of hers, then put the cup back down on Alexa's desk and appeared to forget about it. "Donal, have you got the remaining travel details worked out?"

"Yeah, hang on a sec." Carrying his coffee, Donal went to his desk and retrieved a pale-green pad. "Here you are. Are you sure we can afford this?"

"I can."

"Well ... all right."

He was an orphan from the wrong side of the tracks, traveling abroad.

Shit. I'm flying to Illurium.

Sister Mary-Anne would have been proud of him.

Harald leaned closer to Deltrassol.

"... deeper," he said, "and then tell me ... whether ... any commands lurk in there."

He was talking about Deltrassol's subconscious, and there was a reason: if the Black Circle had laid hex traps or guards in place, even ordinary mesmeric digging should expose their existence.

A buried wipeout trap would cause Deltrassol to scream, as inlaid hex scoured his memories all the way back to childhood. Harald was willing to risk that. Part of him wanted it to happen.

"... cashing in on memory where the ... bosses cached their commands ..."

"No." Eyelids fluttering, Deltrassol shook his head.

His personality was still intact. No mages had buried hex traps in his mind.

"... and you want to tell me ... what shipment the dwarves were stealing ..."

"Yes. Champagne. The expensive stuff. Crates of it, worth thousands. We had the plans, police-response plans. How they knew to land the pterabat on top of the skull."

Champagne?

All this for fuckin' champagne?

"... and when you saw that the dwarves had a body aboard, when you saw the van ..."

"I pulled out, man. Aborted. Don't want that kind of trouble."

"...is what we want to avoid as you decide you'll do everything to help me..."

"Yes."

"...and I need to know, your boss, Sir Alvan..."

"That's right."

"...is he your friend?"

"No."

"...while you spend time in his office..."

"The club."

"...because of this place? The See-Through? Tell me..."

"Sir Alvan comes here. By chance, I saw him. Recognized him."

"...though he was in disguise..."

"Yes, a mask. Ensorcelled. But the way he walked. I knew."

"...that this was Sir Alvan, and you blackmailed him..."

"For small amounts, for a man like him."

"...who would do you a special favor if you asked..."

"His secret. Would destroy him. If I told."

"...and he could arrange to fly you back to Illurium..."

"Yes."

So Deltrassol was a blackmailer within his own embassy. He was a lowlife, and Harald wanted badly to take him down. But if there were resources available in Illurium, in Silvex City where Donal Riordan was headed...

Got you, zombiefucker.

The bastards who'd gotten away with Cortindo's body and the—for Death's sake—expensive champagne had a police contact, someone who'd given them the response plans. By itself the evidence meant little, but it closed the chain of cause and effect that stretched all the way back to Commissioner Vilnar's office.

But first things first.

Riordan. You're dead.

Harald told Deltrassol to sleep for a minute. It allowed Harald time to think.

Then, link by link, he put his plan together.

"...and when you return to the embassy, you'll ask him..." Harald drew the sentence out, hearing a raucous shout from the hallway outside. It was a drunkard's roar, somewhere on this floor: one of the club's clients had teetered out of control.

This could be a problem if it pulled Deltrassol out of the trance.

Then a liquid crunch sounded from outside, along with a sudden cessation in the drunkard's torrent of curses, followed by Stone's voice: "That'll cool him off nicely, boys. Be gentle with him."

The sounds of heels scraping along bare floor followed.

Harald shifted into deep command mode, instructing Deltrassol.

"There is a house...in Upper Kiltrin North..."

This was a district containing some of the richer sections of Silvex City, where Harald had spent time in Illurium. The military camp had been twenty miles outside the city. During his assignment with the military police, Harald had spent time in the city proper, liaising with local civilians.

He helped investigate cases and assisted on the Octemday bar runs, where trios of MPs would have to extract carousing marines from the detritus of smashed tables and unconscious civilians. And do it without inflicting lethal damage on drunken men who were trained to kill.

"Kiltrin," murmured Deltrassol. "Pulkwill's Hill."

"...That's right, and from Pulkwill's Hill you descend...where it zigs and zags..." Harald waited for the tiny nod from Deltrassol before continuing. "To the silver-and-white mansion with the three steel...gargoyles...outside, the ones with spread-out wings..."

"Move."

"...that move, that's right. The gargoyles move"—Harald's voice lowered further—"and in that house...that mansion...lives a man called Don Falvin Mentrassore..."

"Don Mentrassore."

"...that's right, and the don has a daughter...called Rasha...and servants, and the chief butler might be called...Adamnol..."

It had been over two years since Harald's last visit. Adamnol was probably still there, but life was uncertain.

"...You will say the code word...that you will remember to forget until...you remember in that moment...that Darksong Lightning is the code...and you won't mind it vanishing from...your mind...inside Don Mentrassore's house."

The don was a thin, elegant man with a silver-gray goatee, usually with a pearl attached at each earlobe, who conducted his affairs with the same kind of diligent yet easy grace that he bore in social situations.

That was why he had been so disappointed in his daughter Rasha when she fell in love with a young student of dubious character and family. It had been that student—part of the local underworld with links into crooked quartermasters among the military bases—who had been one of Harald's targets. Harald and four other MPs, all in plain clothes, broke into a camp arsenal just in time to apprehend the men who were making off with firearms and other matériel.

Two of the criminals had reached for their own weapons, and in seconds a firefight blasted the air

apart—inside an arsenal filled with explosives. It was
good luck that the arsenal remained intact instead of
disappearing in a fireball. It would have taken out the
entire camp, including two thousand men and women.

Rasha Mentrassore's fiancé had been too stupid to
surrender.

He'd also been too stupid to leave Rasha at home. In
trying to show off to her, boasting of his importance
among important businessmen, he'd smuggled Rasha
into the place in the back of his stolen army jeeplet.
She'd crawled out of the vehicle when the gunfire
started.

It might have been a stray round of Harald's that
took Rasha in the right shoulder; it might have been
someone else's. Regardless, Rasha had pitched over with
her mouth working but her throat paralyzed. Her shoulder was smashed meat, splintered with bones.

After Harald and his team had killed the men who refused to stop, they went to work on Rasha and two as-
sociates of the gang, who had been caught in the
crossfire. Using straps from the ammunition cases—nice
ironic serendipity—they tied off the major arteries of the
wounded trio.

By rights they should have handed Rasha over to the
civilian police. But Harald had judged her to be largely
innocent, manipulated by the boyfriend whose body
now came in three parts.

And Rasha's father, the don, had a sense of honor. He
always repaid debts.

"...You will explain...to Don Mentrassore...that a
man called...Donal Riordan...will visit him soon...
and will say he is a friend...of Harald Hammersen...
and the don should act as if this were true...tell him
that...*as if it were true*...but it will be...a lie..."

Harald led Deltrassol even deeper into the trance, inscribing postmesmeric commands: Deltrassol would never consciously remember these words.

"...because Riordan is not to be trusted... *not* to be trusted...and the don must lead Riordan...into a trap...and spring it shut...to the death..."

Deltrassol began to frown, then relaxed, too deep into the trance to argue.

"...and this is how..."—Harald slowed his voice, checking the details within himself—"the don...will kill...Riordan..."

It was an hour later, when Donal was returning to the task-force office with two more mugs of coffee, plus a dark-blue folder tucked under his arm, that he saw Harald walking toward him along the corridor, swigging from a silver hip flask.

Harald saw Donal at the same time. He screwed the top back on the flask and tucked it inside his jacket.

"Hey, Donal. How's it going?"

"Good. I think people were worried about y—"

"Can I give you a hand? Here." Harald took a coffee mug. "What's in the folder?"

Donal waved the folder at Harald.

"The rest of my travel documents. I really am going to Illurium."

They continued walking toward the office. Harald went first, opening the door and holding it for Donal.

"Good news," Harald said. "I thought it was going to happen."

"Yeah...Is there any news on Sushana? We thought you might have gone back to the hospital."

"Nah. Viktor's there."

They went inside the office with Donal frowning, unable to read the change in Harald's mood.

"Hey, Donal," called Alexa. "You went out for more coffee and came back with the marines."

"Good to see you too," said Harald.

"Yeah, well."

Harald just nodded. Then he gave a too-wide smile as Laura came out of her private office. "Hey, boss."

"Hey, yourself. You okay?"

"Sure." Serious now, Harald said, "I hear Donal-boy's going to Illurium."

"That's right," said Laura. "So tell me about Deltrassol."

"Deltrassol."

"Uh-huh."

"I just dropped him off in Pallas Heptagon. Had to get him past the R-H boys. Robbery-Haunting must owe you a big favor, keeping their team in place this long."

"Not anymore."

"Well . . ." Harald glanced at Alexa. "Seems our boy Deltrassol's been blackmailing Sir Alvan in the embassy."

"How?" said Donal. "What's the ambassador been up to?"

"Oh, let's say he likes to step out every now and then for a night on the town. Nothing majorly criminal."

"So why," said Laura, "did you let him go?"

"Because he was scared shitless, too scared to lie, and he knew nothing about Sushana being set up." Harald looked at her. "You don't think I'd have let him go otherwise."

Laura thought about that.

"No. Of course not."

"And now," said Donal, "we've got a source inside the Illurian embassy. Neat work, Harald."

Harald nodded, mouth tightening, saying nothing.

23

The airport was busy. Travelers were dazed by the facade, by the glamour, or by weariness. Security wraiths hovered inside walls, occasionally revealing themselves. Away from the check-in desks, hex-protected entrances led to cargo areas and out onto the runways.

Donal had not seen the place since the day the diva flew in.

Do you feel the song?

For Death's sake, you know I do.

Outside, seen through a full-length window, the opaque skies were near indigo. The wind that blew steadily cut through heavy overcoats, chilling passengers walking to aircraft. The baggage handlers worked fast.

Some of the security men recognized Donal as he stood at check-in. Two plainclothes officers came over.

"Flying to Illurium?" one of them said, as Donal held his ticket ready. "Not bad, Lieutenant."

"Can't discuss it," said Donal. "What you might call family business."

Two of the officers looked at each other. Maybe they knew that Donal had no family, unless you counted the department.

"You want to look around?"

"Sure," said Donal. "Not much changed from before, I hope."

"Maybe a bit more secure." Again the two officers looked at each other. "Wish they'd tried for the diva here, sir, if you don't mind me saying so."

"What do you mean?"

"We've got trance shielding up the wazoo, is what he means, Lieutenant. And we're not supposed to say so, but there're undercover mages on board at all times, in among the passengers."

"I didn't know that," said Donal.

"Well, not many people do."

But maybe some senior officers and politicians know. Interesting to find out exactly who.

Because they would have known that the best place to try for the diva was in the city.

"You want me to check the bags through for you, sir?"

"Um . . . all right."

"Aisle or window?"

"Huh?"

"D'you prefer sitting next to the window or on the aisle?"

Donal blinked.

"Beats me. I'm a poor boy from the orphanage. This is all new to me."

"I think the choice is between having a good view or not having to trample on someone's feet to get to the bathroom."

"Huh." Donal thought about it. "Gimme the window, then."

They checked through Donal's two bags. The older bag was a battered rat-leather suitcase that Sister Mary-Anne Styx had given Donal on the day he left the orphanage. He normally used it to store books, the ones too precious to trade in.

The other case was new and shiny, a present from Laura. Donal tried not to feel uncomfortable about using a piece of luggage whose price could have fed the entire orphanage.

"You want to see the animals, Lieutenant? My name's Piersen, by the way."

"Animals?"

"The ones that're flying. They have to go in the hold, along with the bags."

"Isn't that dangerous?"

"The holds are pressurized, some of them. Come on, I'll show you."

Donal followed Piersen through a door marked *Airport Staff Only* and felt the cold touch of wispy fingers trail across his skin. Donal subvocalized a thank-you, not because he enjoyed the sensation but because he made no assumption that the security wraith enjoyed searching him.

"Did everyone hear about what happened?" Donal asked Piersen as they walked along a bleak corridor. "About the diva?"

"Some of us knew people who were on duty that night, Lieutenant. At the theater, I mean. One of the uniforms told us the place went crazy. He's been seeing a police mage for trancework, trying to get over it."

Piersen stopped at a set of doors made from some heavy, oily-looking material.

"Looks like the audience got ensorcelled, and a couple of dozen or more dropped into complete parazombie mode. Am I right?"

"That's about it," said Donal. "What's through here?"

"Cargo." Piersen pushed open the doors. "Waiting to be shipped."

"Thanatos. So many?"

There were trolleys with baggage piled high, stone-faced handlers maneuvering them into position near the big outer doors. And there were gray hexagonal cases with animals inside, scarcely visible through the small barred openings.

Donal caught a glimpse of sliding metallic-blue scales inside one case, pale-pink membranous wings in another. He heard pitiful mewls and psychotic growls of despair.

"Can't they be tranquilized or something?"

"Yeah," said Piersen, "but it doesn't work too well. Some of them probably *have* been drugged by their owners, but the stress wakes them right up."

It had taken Donal an hour in trance last night to replace his fear of flying with excitement at visiting a foreign city for the first time. This was a reminder that he didn't need.

"Those cages look pretty tough." Donal heard the doubt in his own voice. "The airlines wouldn't place their own aircraft at risk."

Piersen laid a hand against one gray case, ignoring the hiss that sounded inside. "They'll be asleep soon enough."

"I thought you said—"

"Right." Piersen grinned, baring his teeth. "Every flight's got a mage or witch on board, didn't you know? You sure won't get attacked by parazombies on the plane."

Donal blinked.

"And is it right you had to waste a bunch of 'em," Piersen continued, "at the Energy Authority?"

"Uh . . . Kind of."

"Damn." Piersen looked at the crates, then hammered one with the side of his fist. "I wish I'd been there. Zombies of any kind give me the creeps, you know?"

Donal let out an extended breath. "Really?"

"What, you never wanted to draw a bead on one and—"

"Go fuck yourself, Piersen."

Donal turned away and walked out, back to the check-in area and the regular passengers.

At the portal for boarding—meaning, exiting onto the tarmac and walking several hundred yards through the cold, biting wind—a uniformed woman was checking tickets and replacing them with boarding passes. Donal waited in line with everyone else. Finally it was his turn.

"Traveling alone, sir?"

"Yes. First time too."

Donal stopped. The clerk's skin was very white, and the faint tracery of gray veins implied that her blood ran black and cold.

Do you feel the bones?

Yeah.

The clerk's nostrils widened. She stared at Donal for a long, silent moment.

Then she looked down, scrawled something in purple ink on a silver ledger, and annotated a white card that she handed over to Donal.

"The flight's a little underbooked, sir . . ."

"Um, what does—"

". . . and I've upgraded you to first class."

Donal looked at her, not knowing what to say.

"Have a nice flight, sir."

"Er, and you. I mean, have a good day."

The clerk smiled her icy zombie smile.

"I will now. *Thank you.*"

It was Harald's turn to watch over Sushana at the hospital, so Viktor—after two hours' sleep—had forced himself back to work. When the front desk called to say that a Bone Listener wanted to talk to Lieutenant Riordan—

to talk in person—it was Viktor who picked up the call. He went down to meet the Bone Listener.

There he found her staring in silent communication with two deathwolves, their eyes glowing darkly amber. Unnerved, Viktor subconsciously allowed his hands to move to a crossed-wrists position, ready to draw his twin Grausers, before realizing what he was doing.

He cleared his throat and said, "I'm Viktor Harman. I work with Donal Riordan."

"Is the lieutenant unavailable?" The Bone Listener, Feoragh, looked up at Viktor with odd, gentle eyes, dark against her pale skin. "What is the matter?"

"He's flying out." Viktor checked his watch. "Probably just getting on the plane."

"That's a pity." Feoragh stood up. "I'd like to share some information with him."

"What about?" Viktor realized how his tone sounded. "I mean, can't I help? Or one of the others?"

"Who else works with him?"

"We both report to Commander Steele. She's—"

"Laura Steele?" A glistening look slid across Feoragh's big eyes.

"Yes."

Feoragh held a hand out to each of the deathwolves and murmured something in an archaic tongue that Viktor could not have named, much less understood. The deathwolves opened their mouths wide, large tongues lolling as they revealed their fangs in a shared lupine grin. They nodded once as they rose and wheeled away in one motion, padding toward the outer doors.

From the solid desk that he was part of, Eduardo watched with widened eyes as the deathwolves left. Meanwhile, Feoragh was already striding toward the nearest bank of cylindrical brass elevator tubes.

Viktor blinked three times before regaining his composure and following her.

"You know Commander Steele?" he asked, catching up.

"We know who she is." Feoragh gave a smile that shared no warmth with Viktor. "And we have an interest in your case. Your ongoing operation."

They rode in the tube together. When the wraith enclosed Feoragh, it shone with a soft blue glow that Viktor had never seen before. Its grasp on him was the usual cold ethereal grip, but when the wraith ascended, it was smoother and faster than normal.

Feoragh turned to Viktor as they rose. When she spoke, her words echoed with disconcerting overlays in the airflow.

"The people you're hunting," she said, "killed more than a colleague. Mina d'Alkarny was headed toward becoming one of the greatest Bone Listeners in history. Don't think you can understand what I mean by that."

"We're trying to—"

"I know what you're trying to do." Feoragh looked upward as their ascent rate slowed, then back at Viktor. "And we're on your side, otherwise I wouldn't be here."

"All right."

But a strange softening passed across Feoragh's face then, and she waved her fingertips in front of Viktor's forehead, as the wraith came to a halt and held them in place, suspended in the shaft. Viktor felt waves of alternating warm and cool pulses passing through him.

Feoragh nodded, and the wraith pushed her and Viktor through the opening into the gray-carpeted corridor.

"You have old wounds of your own to deal with, Viktor Harman," she said. "And I hope that you heal properly and soon."

Viktor started to open his mouth, before realizing he had no idea what to say to her.

"Come," Feoragh added. "Introduce me to your

commander. I'm looking forward to meeting the famous Laura Steele."

Viktor led the way, yet it felt as though he was following her. It was an unusual feeling, and he blinked his gritty eyes, checking for ensorcellment as he did so—a tendency to blink rapidly and yawn was a symptom of having been recently mesmerized.

There was nothing, and he went through the internal visualizations that he'd been provided with in trance training. Again, nothing.

Laura came out of her office to greet the Bone Listener.

"Hello, I'm Laura Steele." She held out her hand. "I'm sorry about Dr. d'Alkarny."

"Yes." Feoragh bowed, then touched the back of Laura's hand. "It seems that you are."

"How can I help you?"

"Are you able to contact Lieutenant Riordan," asked Feoragh, "before he departs for Illurium?"

"I'm not sure." Laura turned to Alexa. "Get the commissioner's office and ask Eyes to call the—"

Laura broke off as Harald shook his head.

"Scrub that," Laura continued. "Do it yourself, via the ordinary switchboard. Call the control tower or security, whoever you can get in touch with. Keep them on hold."

"I'm on it." Alexa tugged the receiver from the hook and spun the wheels to all zeroes. "Switchboard? I need to—"

But Laura was already leading Feoragh through the doorway to her office and pulling it shut behind them.

Alone with Feoragh, Laura asked, "You have information from the Archives?"

"From deep in the Lattice," answered Feoragh, "having searched far. Lieutenant Riordan was working on a conspiracy case, or the possibility of one. That was what brought him to your attention, I'm guessing."

"That's right. And you know about the diva."

"Yes, and of the precedents. The famous performers who died prematurely so that others might enjoy their bones."

There was a silky tone in those words that made even Laura shudder.

"Am I missing something?" Laura said. "Those performers weren't even in Tristopolis, they were—Oh, shit."

"The Illurian connection is strong, otherwise Lieutenant Riordan would not be going there. But there is more. Have you heard of the Tringulian Triplets?"

"No." Laura thought back to visits to the theater with her parents, when she was young and the world was warm and bright and simple. Her mother had followed the newspaper columns about theatrical stars. "Wait—they're opera singers also, is that right?"

"Yes. And the thaumaturgical geniuses of Svaltirno recently operated on the triplets, not to separate them but to ensure their continued health. The triplets' condition had been worsening, but after the operation"—Feoragh sounded as though she were reciting a newspaper article verbatim—"a hospital spokesman said the prognosis was more than excellent, and the chief thaumaturgical registrar declared the operation a resounding advance in modern operating techniques."

From the outer office, visible through the glass walls of Laura's office, Alexa waved and pointed at the handset, indicating that she had the airport on the line. Laura raised a hand, signifying *Wait a moment*.

"Look, Bone Listener, if you want to tell me something of importance to Lieutenant Riordan, you need to—"

"I can tell that you and he are intimate," said Feoragh. "Perhaps the airport control tower can send a message to the flight deck before they are out of range. Even if the aircraft has taken off, I mean."

"We don't do this kind of thing every day," answered Laura. "What do you need to tell Donal?"

"I'm ninety-seven percent certain that the conspiracy I suspect you code-name the Black Circle is going to target the Tringulian Triplets. The triplets match the profile of famous performers whose bones make a tempting target for those . . . people."

This time there was manifest hatred in Feoragh's voice.

"And the announcement," she continued, "that the triplets are going to live for several decades longer than anyone anticipated is going to annoy the conspirators intensely. The fact that the triplets are performing soon in Silvex City is going to present an opportunity they won't be able to—"

"There's going to be another hit? In Silvex City?"

"Yes, and that's the message you need to get to Donal Riordan. That, and that I've narrowed down the list of possible contacts. With the layers of indirection they've put in place, I cannot tell with an accuracy of more than fifty-three percent, but my intuition says I'm right."

Laura looked at Feoragh steadily. A Bone Listener's intuition was worth more than facts, or at least that was what Laura's mentor, Captain Felthorn, had often told her.

"You think you know who the Black Circle member is? The one who organized the hit on the diva?"

"I'm not sure if that operation was his, but Councillor Gelbthorne has banking and energy interests that have to coincide with the Black Circle's long-term strategy. He's the person that Donal Riordan has to apprehend. I take it he has cross-border warrants?"

"Yes, three blanks hex-entangled to Judge Prior's office." If the judge filled in a name and signed any of the local copies, the corresponding warrant in Donal's possession would display the same information. "If you're really sure about this, we can go over there right now."

"And the airport?"

Laura looked out at Alexa. "You still got them on the line? The airport cops?"

"Just hung up," Alexa called back. "Some guy called Piersen, said Donal's already gone through. I'll have to see if we can call the aircraft, but Piersen said it's impossible."

At his desk, Harald gave a tiny smile, his face hidden at an angle where no one should notice.

The evening was falling outside, purple gloom enveloping the city, and Alexa had already switched on her bright desk lamp. Earlier, wraiths had cleaned the windows inside and out, so that the lamp now shined to produce a reflected interior. And in that reflection, Alexa had seen Harald smile.

Seen him smile when she said Donal was unreachable.

Alexa picked up the phone again and tried a different tack, asking the operator to put her through to the airline's reservation desk. If that didn't work, she would think of something else.

Harald stood up quickly and muttered something about going down to the range. He looked like a man who needed to let off steam, but a gun range wasn't always the best place for that. The range master would soon spot an officer whose emotional state meant he shouldn't be shooting.

Alexa watched him go.

24

Laura slid open a desk drawer and stared at the Magnus lying inside. It was Donal's gun, the one he had not been able to take because no airline allowed anyone, besides on-duty sky marshals, to fly armed.

She wished he'd been able to carry it with him.

"You can wait," said Feoragh. "The judge can wait. It will be three hours at least before the plane lands in Silvex City, maybe a lot longer—you know what the storms are like at the Illurian border. And the warrants amend themselves instantaneously."

"I know." Laura looked back through the glass wall at Alexa on the phone, who was gesturing as she argued. "But we're not getting anywhere here. I need some kind of *progress*."

Feoragh blinked her liquid eyes.

"I intuit the movement of powerful enemies against you, Commander Steele."

"Uh...Right," said Laura. "Who in particular?"

"Unknown so far, or I would tell you. But the thing is, they have made a mistake. Because they never should have killed Mina d'Alkarny."

"How—What do you mean?"

"There are ripples of causation spreading through the Lattice, patterns that will reveal themselves among the information vectors. And..."

"What?"

". . . and we are only human, or"—with a humorless smile—"at least as human as you, Commander. Bone Listeners are supposed to be impartial, and we are, but there is the matter of motivation."

Outside, Alexa slammed the handset down again and swore.

"You want to get her killers, too, huh?" said Laura.

Feoragh gave the minutest of nods.

"Judge Prior takes a while to get motivated," said Laura, watching Alexa cursing outside. "But I think he'll be impressed by your affidavit. At least he'd better be."

"Yes."

If Laura had still been alive, she would have shivered at the Bone Listener's tone.

Donal thanked the scanwraith as he passed through the final gate to the outside. A cold wind held steady across the tarmac, and in front of Donal a thin woman clutched at her wide white hat with one hand, her dress and coat with the other. She walked with tight paces, trying to keep her balance on her stiletto heels.

They headed for the steps that attendants had already wheeled up to the plane. The aircraft's propeller blades were still, pregnant with the possibility of whirling motion, waiting to drag the metal craft aloft.

The thin woman's husband, portly and dressed in a double-breasted suit, kept his head down as he walked, making no attempt to help his wife. Donal shook his head and checked out the other passengers walking with him. All of them looked more richly dressed than he, though they couldn't all be flying first class.

And he wondered, as he continued across the tarmac, whether the scanwraith would have allowed him to carry his most precious accessory aboard after all. But that was spilled milk: the Magnus was safely locked in Laura's desk drawer back at HQ.

The first of the passengers was already climbing the steps, while at the top two stewardesses in black capes smiled their welcoming smiles.

Traveling first class still meant having to climb the steps by yourself, though Donal could imagine some future service whereby wraiths would lift the passengers up into the aircraft. The wind tugged at Donal as he ascended. When he gripped the rail he felt how cold it was: almost enough to make the skin stick.

He waited a moment for the woman ahead to reach the top, then moved up two steps at a time to reach the hatchway and enter the plane.

"Welcome aboard, sir."

"Thanks."

"You'll be seated over here."

In first class, the portly man with the thin wife was already making himself comfortable, sipping the brandy that a stewardess had poured for him. Drawing a fat cigar from a silver case, the man placed it between his lips and sucked hard, igniting it. A near-invisible curtain surrounded his chair, sealing him off from the rest of the cabin.

Donal had always hated cigars. The thought of the essence-of-flamewraith that was used to soak self-igniting tobacco—that was a new wrinkle that made him despise the man further.

"May I fetch you a drink, sir?" The steward who spoke was thin and effeminate. "Perhaps a sherry?"

"Whiskey," said Donal. "Single malt, raw as you like."

"Ah, very good. Thank you, sir."

As the steward went aft, Donal checked the other cabin crew, seeing the limp-wristed men gossiping with the stewardesses and noting the two stewards who looked different: lean rather than thin, with enlarged knuckles and some scarring around the eyes.

If any of the other passengers noticed, they would probably feel worried, but for Donal, the Federal Sky Branch officers represented added security. Still, he regretted now having asked for a window seat: if there was some kind of action, the best place for Donal to be sitting would be next to the aisle.

Yet it had been twelve years since the Goladol Separatist Alliance had hijacked a series of aircraft, seven in all, and forced them to fly to Zurinam. Since the last two loads of passengers had been executed by the Zurinese authorities—the hijackers had deliberately landed the plane during the eighth day of Weeping Week, when nonbelievers were not allowed out of their homes, and the gladiatorial bishops had wept even as they carried out the sentence on the innocent foreigners who'd been forced into Zurinam—people had fought back, and security had been tightened.

The last two attempts had been only partially successful, and the rebels had not even tried for the past nine years.

Still, Goladol Province remained part of Illurium. If the few news reports that made it past the border censors were credible, trouble persisted in the region. No wonder that the Tristopolitan and federal authorities collaborated to keep security tight.

"There you are, sir. One fine whiskey."

Donal hoped it was not too fine, but when he sipped it the liquor seemed to become mist, an intoxicating mist. He closed his eyes to appreciate the overlaid tastes.

Despite himself, Donal laughed.

"Make sure your seat belt is secured, sir."

"Yes, thank you."

There was a central bulkhead up front, some ten feet

back from the entrance to the flight deck. Black curtains screened off the small area, and at first Donal assumed it was a secondary galley, perhaps a wet bar for first-class passengers only.

But then he saw the steward returning the whiskey bottle to the galley that was set aft and noticed the watchfulness of one of the hard-looking stewards as he passed the black drape. This was some kind of secure facility.

Maybe an armory?

It was another eight minutes before the last of the passengers was aboard, still filing down the aisles toward the economy seats in back. The propellers jerked and began to rotate even while eight insubstantial wraiths were hauling the steps out of the way.

The cabin vibrated, and the plane slowly turned on its nose wheels until it was pointing along the runway for takeoff. Overhead, the blank purple sky seemed darker.

The engines rumbled.

Donal took another sip of whiskey.

"Welcome aboard, ladies and gentlemen. I'm Captain Yershwin, and we are ready to take off. Please settle back and enjoy."

The lights outside became a blur as the engines dropped in pitch. Then the lights were dropping away and the aircraft was rising, a pale-green glow emanating from the engine housings as hex-protected turbines drew power from the necroscopic cells embedded in the wings and fuselage.

Going to Illurium.

Donal shook his head again, then tossed back the remainder of the whiskey in one long, beautiful gulp.

Alexa was alone in the task-force office. She had another mug of coffee on her desk, but she wasn't going to drink this one: she'd spend the rest of the evening having to go pee. How Donal drank the amount he did, she didn't know.

Perhaps men's bladders were bigger or something. Maybe when Sushana was well enough to chat again, Alexa could ask her. She might know.

Having failed to get a message through to the airport before Donal left, Alexa wasn't sure what to do next. A sensible person would go home.

A sensible person would never have volunteered to be on Laura's task force.

If they scored a spectacular success, then perhaps the task-force members would be slated for recognition and promotion—but no one likes a snitch, let alone a police officer who rats on fellow officers. As long as they investigated corruption *outside* the department, it was manageable.

Even then, the city politicians could damage anyone's career prospects with a whisper or innuendo, or even some discreet (yet unsubtle) blackmail.

But Alexa was determined to make commander herself someday. When she pulled open the left-hand drawer of her old desk, it revealed a stack of books from the collection she mostly kept at home: the dry tomes she needed to memorize and understand in order to pass her sergeant's exam next month.

Some of the books were slim volumes with cheap covers, and she'd hardly looked at the one on top: *Surveillance II—Reading Lips*. Alexa had all seven volumes of the Surveillance series, plus the "unofficial" eighth volume that no officer could afford to be seen reading: the one subtitled *Running Away*.

Everyone knew that the books were intensely practical, but to be seen reading a book on running away was to invite weeks or even months of ongoing taunts and

insults. It wasn't just this department: surely every police
force in every city of the world was the same.

Alexa pulled out the volume on lip-reading and
opened it atop her desk. She skimmed through the chap-
ters, looking for interesting passages to reread. The author was good at telling personal anecdotes, humorous
and possibly exaggerated, in order to highlight the
points she was making. Then Alexa put the book down
and closed it.

There were other esoteric skills of use to plainclothes
officers, and one of them consisted of deep trancework.
Harald had given her some pointers, taking her through
basic mesmeric inductions and suggestions, showing her
how to manipulate other people's minds, and her own.

Since beginning the work, Alexa had not yet put a
suspect into a trance, but she had used visualization to
improve her scores on the gun range, and she had
Harald to thank for it.

Harald. I don't like the way you smiled tonight.

Beneath his gentle ways, there was a dangerous side
to Harald: the product of his years in the marines, where
he had learned skills that were unknown and unthink-
able to the civilian populace—and to most police officers.

Something's wrong.

Part of trancework, deriving from its original uses in
medicine, entailed developing the ability to revisit memories, to relive past events in such detail that a person
could explore stimuli they had not consciously perceived
when the events happened.

In therapy, such work allowed the patient to make
happy memories more vivid, more intense, and to an-
chor them in a world of confident thinking. The reverse
procedure allowed them to make a traumatic memory
lose its painful hooks.

For police officers—for surveillance officers in particular—such skills had additional uses.

Alexa's eyelids fluttered as she thought back to the sight of Donal and Laura, visible through the glass sides of Laura's office, after Donal returned from the Archives. It was the day he met the Bone Listener Feoragh, who came here today—

No. Wrong time. Alexa shifted her memory to when Donal came from the interrogation that he kept silent about, working with Dr. Kyushen Jyu. After that, black-suited medics took one of the dwarf twins away to a secure ward.

Yes . . .

Alexa sank a little deeper.

This memory.

There was something here, something going on. She thought that Harald might know what it was, because of the way he'd looked at Donal.

Alexa had the time pinned. Now she had to slip back in memory and revisit that time. She closed her eyes and began to count backward from seven hundred, her eyelids fluttering as she leaned back in her chair and smiled.

Her awareness slid deep inside.

In the past, she saw Laura's lips move, saw Donal turn so his back was to Alexa, but the tension in his shoulders was a kind of eloquence. Then he turned, and in her memory this time—unlike her first experience of these events—Alexa could lip-read every word that Donal said.

"*Seven-seven-seven.*" Donal paused, then: "*Two-nine, three-five-one, seven-two-zero.*"

"*That was in the dwarf's—*" Laura stepped to one side, so that Donal's shoulder obscured Alexa's view of her face.

But it was enough.

I don't believe it.

Shuddering, Alexa began taking deeper breaths, feeling like a diver beginning to ascend. Donal had said that the commissioner was implicated. That Commissioner Vilnar's involvement was confirmed, from a second source of evidence. Alexa was sure of it.

Donal had *told* Laura that Vilnar was a suspect.

Yet Harald's attitude toward Donal had changed for the worse.

Not him.

It was hard to believe. Especially with Sushana in the hospital.

Harald, a spy for Vilnar? Impossible.

Eyelids fluttering, Alexa slipped back into her memories.

Five minutes later, her eyes snapped open.

"Harald, you fuckin' cretin."

An hour into the flight, there was a soft moan from beneath the deck. Startled, Donal looked outside, in case part of the wing had dropped off. There was nothing save the strong green glow of turbines against the indigo night.

Another moan sounded, followed by a drawn-out growling. The hard-faced stewards were already moving toward the rear of the aircraft. Donal realized they were heading for whatever part of the plane connected with the cargo holds.

Was one of the animals down there emitting the sounds? Donal remembered his glimpses of the caged creatures. Some of them could be dangerous if they got out.

Outside, in the far distance, a sheet of white lightning flared. This was a sign of the Transition Tempest, of the turbulence and concentrated hex that forever roiled in the skies above the Illurian border.

Yet the flight time, according to Captain Yershwin's announcement shortly after takeoff, included two more hours before they reached the perpetual storms. This was too soon for hex-induced phenomena to manifest themselves.

But down in the hold, an awful screech was followed by a chorus of yowling. Whatever the disturbance was, it was affecting more than one of the beasts. In fact, it sounded like all of them, as they gave howling vent to fear and rage.

One of the stewardesses hurried forward, complexion pale, then stopped as she reached the black drapes beyond the forward bulkhead. Donal had wondered what was hidden there.

"Excuse me." He raised himself up and stepped over the feet of the white-haired woman in the next seat. "I beg your pardon."

"You be careful, young man."

"I'm really sorry, ma'am."

"No, I mean, if you're going to help with those dangerous animals, you be very careful."

"I'll try."

But without a weapon, Donal wasn't sure what he would do if the beasts got free.

"Please don't worry." It wasn't Captain Yershwin's voice over the speaker but that of a younger man. *"This is First Officer Smeltil. Please be assured that we have everything under control. Remain in your seats with your seat belts fastened."*

Another stewardess, not the woman who'd hurried forward, reached out and touched Donal's arm. "Sir, please return to your—"

Donal leaned close to her ear. "I'm a police officer. Let me help."

"Oh, Lieutenant, yes."

So Donal's rank as well as name had been noted on the passenger list.

"Excuse me."

It was the first stewardess, followed by a dark-complexioned woman Donal had not seen before. This woman was dressed in black and purple robes, and the eleven-sided amulet between her small breasts shone silver and jet.

Moving heptagrams rolled across the exposed areas of her skin: her taut, lined face and her bony hands. Her age was impossible to determine. She looked like some sand-weathered sculpture left out in the desert for decades.

Donal was about to hold up his hand and suggest that the woman remain where she was, but her eyes held a strange glint, like oily pools in whose strange depths creatures swam.

A witch?

That's right.

The thought seemed to be Donal's own.

After a few moments, Donal blinked back to full awareness. The two stewardesses yawned, eyelids fluttering, then came awake.

"What—"

The witch had already reached the rear of the aircraft.

"I'm glad she's on our side," muttered Donal. "Er, she *is* on . . ."

"Oh, yes."

"Thank Hades."

At that moment the plane lurched sideways. A dozen people yelled or screamed.

"Shit." Donal caught hold of the nearest seat as a tray crashed on the deck.

"Hurry." A stewardess was pushing him.

"All right."

Donal moved toward the rear galley, where the witch had disappeared from sight. A grim-faced steward was holding open an internal hatch. Metal steps led down into a shadowy space. Donal leaned inside, catching a glimpse of the witch's robe.

"Thanatos. Here goes." Donal grabbed hold of the steel rails and jumped. He slid down the rails on his palms, just like the stairwell in the orphanage. Then his feet hit the lower deck.

"Hush."

The witch was sitting cross-legged before the row of cages, her arms outstretched, her eyes closed as she bent her head forward and sent waves of energy—whatever that might mean: Donal could almost hear Sister Mary-Anne Styx's skeptical voice debunking mysticism whenever it was mentioned—toward the fearful animals. Silver scales and purple skin and gray talons flashed inside the cages.

A thump sounded behind Donal, then a curse. Donal turned to see one of the hard-faced stewards—an undercover marshal, had to be—lying on his side. One knee was pulled up against his chest.

The plane had bumped again just as he was descending the steps. Donal could see right away that the man's leg was broken.

"I'm Riordan," said Donal. "Have you got a weapon?"

"Yeah . . ." Through clenched teeth, the injured man forced out: "Ankle . . . holster. Other leg."

"I've got it."

Donal moved fast, whipping the black short-barreled revolver from the holster. The injured leg needed to be immobilized, but if the animals got free—or the turbulence got worse—first aid would be irrelevant.

Crouching, Donal took aim at the nearest cage, then swiveled the weapon from one cage to the next. A translucent streamer of pale light washed through the cargo hold.

It was only in that moment that Donal finally acknowledged the obvious. This was no ordinary storm, and these were not ordinary animals. And it would take more than bullets to resolve the situation.

A dark glow surrounded the witch.

The plane pitched. Screams and tinkling glass sounded overhead, attenuated by the deck in between and by something more: a thickening quality to the air, a new vibration just below the limit of human hearing.

Around the witch, the air darkened further. Inside the cages, animals quieted as their eyes brightened. Then they, too, began to hum and warble, reptilian throats joining the witch's near-subliminal chant. Donal lowered his weapon.

Go forward.

For a moment, Donal could not figure out who had spoken. The witch continued to hum and chant, but somehow it was her words that he was thinking.

Touch the animals, came the thought. *One by one.*

"I don't—"

Now.

Donal looked back at the officer with the broken leg. The man's eyes were shining and damp with suffering, but he was determined to remain conscious. Donal handed him back his weapon.

"I won't be needing it," Donal said.

"What are you . . . doing?"

"I wish to Hades I knew."

The plane tipped sideways again. Donal rolled along the smooth deck, coming up on one knee. Somehow the witch remained fastened in place, seated cross-legged on the tilted deck, her attention focused inward.

Donal could never appreciate what battle she was fighting or how much energy it required. He could only do as she had asked. He crawled to the first cage.

"Don't." It was the wounded sky marshal. "Don't do it."

"Have to," muttered Donal, grabbing hold of the bars and hauling himself half upright. "I know it makes no—"

A cold black tongue rasped across Donal's hand and was gone.

Do you feel the bones?

"Thanatos," he whispered. "That was a Basili—"

Hurry. It was the witch again, inside his mind. *There's little time.*

Another thought, of a different flavor, followed.

And do you taste the song?

25

The plane was straightening up. There was a series of bumps, and once more a scream sounded from the passenger deck overhead. Loud, it pierced the sound of ongoing panic. Donal pulled himself forward to the next cage and thrust his hand inside.

"Ah..."

Teeth fastened on his wrist. Sharp teeth. An acid burning pierced his skin. Donal forced himself to hold still and not jerk back: those sharp curved fangs could rip his tendons apart.

Do you feel—
Hush. Let me work.

It took all of Donal's trance-trained willpower to override his reflexes and hold in position until the pressure released. Burning still swept through him as he crawled forward. There were four more cages.

There was more danger here than in the hex-laden storm outside. Somehow Donal's presence was part of it.

Do you hear the music?
It's here because of me.

One of the beasts was ethereal, akin to a wraith yet not remotely human. The bars of its cage acted as conductors for the necromagnetic field that held it in place.

When Donal put his hand inside the field, the burning

across his skin was followed by an icy blast as the strange form melded with him, just for a moment. The geometries of space rotated through impossible angles and directions. Donal saw the world like some cuboid painting, from perspectives no normal person could maintain.

Then a massive migraine seemed to cleave his head asunder like an ax. Falling backward, he cried out—and felt fine.

"What the Thanatos?"

The witch shuddered. There were no words in Donal's head, but he got the message: the witch couldn't hang on for much longer. He had to make peace and create some kind of rapport with the remaining animals fast, or the aircraft was going to fall out of the sky.

It's my fault. They need to understand I'm no threat.

There were three cages left. Donal grabbed the next with both hands, steadying himself as the aircraft tilted again. He forced his face between the bars.

Foolish risk...

This time he got what should have been a clear view of the beast, but purple scales swirled in helices too fast for Donal's eyes to follow. It spat something acidic into his face and he jerked back, releasing the bars, and rolling across the hard metal.

He bumped up against a cage.

Not... The witch, bent over, looked close to collapse. *Not an attack.*

"It forgives me," Donal said. "I understand."

No...

For a moment Donal thought the witch was disagreeing with him. Then the plane bucked and she fell, and Donal realized that it was over: the plane was going down with everyone aboard, and it was his fault.

The fuselage screamed as metal twisted. Donal slammed his fist into the nearest cage and something slid across his skin. It corkscrewed and twisted inside, some quicksilver insertion sliding into Donal's bones, delivering pain.

Donal yelled as a percussive wave of air hammered across the hold, slamming him against a bulkhead.

Collapsed on the deck, the witch looked unconscious. The wounded man was curled up, shivering.

One cage left.

The plane was dying, but there was a chance. Donal leaped from the deck toward the final cage as the cargo hold spun upside down and everything went...

NO!

...away.

When Donal came to, several people were taking care of the wounded man. One of the stewards plus a well-dressed passenger were tying emergency splints in place with linen napkins. There was no sign of the witch.

Someone had left a water bottle next to Donal. He picked it up, unscrewed the top, and drank.

The plane was flying steadily.

"Ugh." Donal dragged himself upright. "There's a medical chest... upstairs. I saw it earlier."

"Yeah, we know." The steward looked up at him. "Problem is, there're a dozen injured people upstairs. One of them's had a heart attack."

"He'll be all right," murmured the well-dressed man, continuing to work on the splint.

"There'll be an ambulance waiting when we land," said the steward.

"Assuming we don't hit more storms. Wouldn't it have been better to turn around?"

The steward said nothing for a moment, then: "Keep this to yourselves, but the weather's worse behind us than it is up ahead. Nothing like this was predicted by the Met Bureau."

The medical man chuckled. "Never trust a seer, is what I say."

"What happened"—Donal gestured toward the deck—"to the . . . lady?"

"You mean the witch?" asked the steward. "She's fine. Why?"

"Nothing." Donal had last seen her collapsed, but there was nothing normal about witches. "What about the animals?"

The cages were silent.

"They're quiet. Don't know what spooked them earlier. Well . . . the storm, right? I mean, I don't know how they knew it was going to happen."

"Me neither," said Donal.

But he had a bad feeling that somehow he did know, that the witch had been right and his presence here had triggered everything. He remembered being back in the theater when the front rows of the audience, ensorcelled, had risen in parazombie trance and stepped forward in exact unison, advancing upon the diva—and upon Donal.

Do you hear the bones?

No.

"Where is she now?" Donal added. "The witch."

"Working on one of the passengers"—bitterness surfaced in the medic's voice—"that I couldn't do anything for. I'm making myself useful down here."

Can you feel the music?

It was not my fault.

The injured steward moaned with pain, then slipped out of consciousness once more.

Donal grinned and glanced back at the cages.

"What's funny?"

"Nothing," Donal answered. "Sorry. I had a bang on the head. I'm having a strange reaction to it."

I feel wonderful.

The medic looked concerned. "Just sit down and I'll look at you in a—"

"No, no. I'm not concussed. See?" Donal raised his right hand, using the thumb to keep the little finger bent. "Three fingers, right? No, the weird thing is...how wonderful I feel."

Really wonderful.

"Euphoria," said the medic. "Perhaps the oxygen in here is—Never mind. If you're able to move okay, perhaps you should get back upstairs to the passenger deck. See if there's anything you can do to help. You look capable enough."

"All right." Donal climbed, chuckling to himself. "All right."

When Donal reached the top of the steel ladder, a thin hand took hold of his wrist, then grasped with steel strength and hauled him up. It was the old witch, clothed in black and purple. When she released her grip, Donal's wrist throbbed.

"Er...Thank you," he said.

No one had taught him how to address a witch. Nuns, yes: the steel ruler across his leg taught him to respectfully say Sister (or Mother in the case of the Reverend Mother who ruled the orphanage, cold bitch that she was). But the witch was different, and Donal knew that a lack of ceremony would not bother her.

"The touch of black blood," she said, "is upon you. The tempest field is unusually widespread tonight to have picked up the resonance this far from the—Could there be intelligent direction behind it?"

"I may have enemies in Silvex City, though I've never been there." Donal shrugged. "Part of the job."

"That does not make it a good thing, young man."

"No, ma'am."

A smile cracked the witch's old skin. "But you will face the dangers anyway? Good for you, Donal Riordan."

"How did you know my name?"

The witch nodded toward the rear bulkhead of the galley, where a small typed list stood in a transparent glass pocket. "They call it a passenger manifest."

"Oh."

"Be observant of the world. That's the way to thrive, don't you think?"

Donal inclined his head in a kind of bow.

"Here." The witch reached inside her robes, tugged, and brought out the silver-and-jet amulet that Donal had seen earlier. "This is for you."

"I can't—"

"Take it. *Now.*"

The amulet was already in Donal's hand. "Thanatos. How did you do that?"

"I didn't do anything. Are you saying I can control your hands?"

"Well, I don't suppose it's possible to—"

"Put the amulet around your neck right this moment."

"—command me to"—Donal finished fastening the cord at the back of his neck and let the amulet drop against his sternum—"um, do anything I didn't want to do already."

"Exactly." The witch smiled again, and this time Donal could see the warmth of her spirit: young and dancing, despite the age of her physical body. "Aren't you so glad you wanted to do the right thing?"

"Right."

"You'll excuse me." The witch touched Donal's arm. "There are still a few people who need my help."

"Yes. I'll just—"

"Go back to your seat."

Donal let the witch slip past him in the galley, then he

headed back toward first class. People were snoring softly, despite the earlier panic.

Back in his seat, Donal allowed his eyelids to droop, enjoying the soft orange glow of light seen through closed eyes. Somehow the witch had given him permission to enjoy this. He slipped slowly down into warmth.

Do you...

Smiling, Donal fell asleep.

The Transition Tempest's core was formed of huge billowing sheets of silver and purple fluorescence, the aurora heart of a centuries-old (maybe millennia-old) storm that raged in place above the Illurian border. Silver lightning could strike at any time.

Suddenly, it did.

White light flared inside the cockpit and ripped back along the aisles and concave walls, and then was gone. The plane's systems continued to function, and nobody panicked.

Only the witch was capable of panicking at that moment, but she was too busy to worry about anything. She poured her strength into maintaining the calming spell that enveloped all the passengers, particularly Donal Riordan, as he smiled, deep inside some happy dream, and murmured one word: *Laura*.

Hearing it—or sensing it somehow—the witch also smiled. She had been in love and had remained married to the mage of her dreams for thirty-five years, until his confrontation with a group of parazombies controlled by some unknown power. That had been in a "secure" hospital wing.

The medics had tried to retain control of the ensorcelled parazombies, refusing to let police officers inside the ward to help them, while her husband, Valkton, attempted the group exorcism single-handed, unwilling to wait for help to arrive. The concentration of hex increased by the minute: the parazombies' controller was traveling physically toward the place, increasing the strength of his broadcast (by the straightforward geometry of an inverse-square law) the nearer he drew.

The witch had tasted the resonance of the Black Circle upon the emanations remaining around her husband's corpse. She had not known the conspiracy's name at that time, but she read the same traces upon Donal Riordan.

And you realize, don't you?

All of this she obtained from Donal's subconscious during the twenty-minute interrogation that she had conducted in the galley when he ascended from the plane's cargo hold. In Donal's memory, the conversation had lasted only seconds.

You begin to realize what they did to you, Donal Riordan.

When Donal came awake, the plane had begun its descent. He pulled back the small white curtains inside the window—or were you supposed to call it a porthole?— and noticed two things at once: the black—not purple!— sky above, and the glistening reflections on the perfectly flat ground beyond Silvex City.

He'd missed the beginning of the Glass Planes, the hundred-mile-square glass sheets that were supported like some god's three-dimensional chessboard, stacked one above the other, separated by fifty or a hundred feet of air—the spacing alternated. The supporting pillars were of marble; each was as wide as an ordinary city.

There were legends, plenty of them, about the eons-past origins of the planes. Each legend had thousands or hundreds of thousands of believers. Yet many of the legends contradicted the others. No one knew the truth; many people claimed to.

Donal had slept through the aircraft passing inside the Transition Tempest and emerging on this side, over Illurian territory. What was strange was that, in his mind's eye, Donal could see every detail of that vast, long-lived storm guarding the border.

The engines' pitch changed. Their emerald luminescence shifted hue, glowing a deeper green as the plane banked left and downward, beginning its miles-long arcing trajectory to the waiting runway.

Silvex City shone scarlet and emerald, gold and cobalt blue, with glass spires picked out in violet light. In them, yellow patterns like nebulae swam.

Another country.

A huge grin stretched Donal's face as he watched the nighttime cityscape grow larger and more amazingly detailed while the plane came in to land. Soon there was touchdown. Donal's head rocked back as the tires spun across the roughened opaque glass that formed the runway. Then the aircraft was braking, a controlled deceleration down to taxiing speed.

Only the final ground maneuvers remained before Donal could walk inside Silvex City itself.

Finally the plane rolled to a halt parallel to a terminal building, one of seven spread out in a star-shaped configuration. An oval detached itself from the wall and moved toward the aircraft, dragging behind it an elongating tunnel formed of overlapping metal leaves.

"We would like to thank you all for choosing Air Illurium for your journey, and we look forward to..."

While the first officer's announcement sounded over the speaker, even the most jaded first-class passengers were murmuring their appreciation. One heavyset woman pulling on a fur stole said to her husband, "Wonderful time, dear. Shall we do it again soon?"

"*...seeing you next time. Thanks again, everyone.*"

"I think we absolutely should."

None of the stewardesses blinked at this, not even the young lady with the bandaged hand. How would she explain the wound to herself? Handling a broken glass?

The steward with the broken leg was out of sight. And the black drapes were pulled across the witch's cubicle, though Donal was sure she was inside.

Everyone's happy.

Donal waited until the last, pretending to take time getting his belongings from the under-seat storage, though it consisted only of his overcoat and the battered paperback of *Human: the Heretics,* the next volume he'd intended to read.

The black drapes concealing the witch did not even twitch.

Donal waited. He was the last passenger on board.

"It was a great flight," he told the effeminate steward. "Apart from the interesting stuff."

"I know just what you mean, sir."

Donal stopped by the drapes, considering whether to pull them back. If the witch were in some kind of trance, an interruption might be dangerous.

The amulet, now inside his shirt, felt cold and hard.

Do you—

Shhh.

Three black-robed men were coming aboard the aircraft. The tallest of the trio stared at Donal with eyes that seemed to expand as they focused.

"Who are you?"

"I'm Donal Riordan."

One of the other mages pointed at Donal's chest, straight toward the amulet concealed beneath Donal's shirt and tie. "It was passed on, not stolen."

"Truth," said the third mage.

And all three mages bowed at once.

"You are blessed," their leader said. "Go with our blessings added to hers."

"Er... Right," said Donal. "Thanks. Especially..."

Donal glanced back at the drapes.

"I'd better let you go."

None of the mages moved until Donal had left the aircraft.

There was a five-sided bronze clock powered by water-wraiths. It was ornate, hanging from the ceiling via a braided cluster of bronze chains, encrusted with faceted glass drops, like jewels. The floor was tiled in some lustrous dark-green mineral, through which dark spirals swirled.

And this was merely the baggage claim.

Donal's fellow passengers were waiting for their cases to come down the glass chute set high in the wall. As Donal reached the chute, it was his case that came sliding down. Some of the other passengers stared at Donal as if he had arranged it.

Obviously that was nonsense, but Donal smiled as if it was his due anyway, picked the bag up, and looked around. He could not see a sign, but from the way some of the people were standing around the hall, he intuitively deduced which archway to use.

He walked through, saw the floating flamewraith pointing the way to Customs, and followed that corridor.

It was decorated in something like the Gothic-deco style that Donal was used to, but heavier in its use of glass and bronze. The air smelled clean, almost antiseptic. At the final gates leading to the open concourse, Customs officials were checking documents and nervous people were standing in queues, waiting to be called.

But a white-gloved officer beckoned Donal forward and nodded as Donal began to raise his passport, waving him through.

"Welcome to Illurium, Lieutenant."

"Um . . . Thanks."

Everything was easy.

In an office off to one side, almost hidden, a figure in a dark robe that might have been black or deep-purple made a tiny hand gesture. A good feeling swept down Donal's body at the sight of that benediction. Whether it was a mage or a witch that had cast the hex, he could not tell.

Do you—

Soon. Soon enough.

Donal walked through the barrier and into the vast domed edifice of the concourse. He found an exchange bureau, since he hadn't had time to buy Illurian currency back in Tristopolis, and winced at the smallness of the pile he received for his florins.

There was a bank of red pay phones, and he used the nearest, pushing two fourteen-sided coins into the slot before dialing. The line hummed and hissed, then a switchboard wraith answered, and Donal told it the extension he needed.

Five seconds later, Laura came on the line.

"Guess what, sweetheart? You're off to the opera again."

26

Overhead, crystal shone amid steel spars, among which amber shapes encapsulating flame-wraiths floated. Shops and eateries, glistening and clean, were arranged across a bewildering array of stacked tiers, the floors mostly of glass. The sound of two thousand chattering voices washed over Donal, echoing back and forth in the great space.

A coffee bar caught Donal's attention. According to the hand-painted sign, they offered twenty-three varieties of coffee and seventeen of tea. Donal smiled at the sight and the dark aroma.

He carried his bag across and sat down at a table against the wall. A small translucent sprite rose up from the table and hovered there, beating her almost-invisible wings to stay in place. Donal pointed at the Choco Zurinese and said, "I'll have a medium—no, make it large."

The sprite smiled, or gave what passed for a smile on those tiny, delicate near-human features, then she slipped back inside the tabletop for a second. She reappeared and glided toward the counter, where three ordinary humans worked.

It was the prettiest of the waitresses who brought Donal's coffee, and he gave a brilliant smile and said, "That looks fantastic."

Responding to his cheerfulness, she beamed back. "You'll enjoy it."

Everything was peaceful.

When the waitress returned to the counter, she smiled at one of her colleagues, who was cutting a piece of cake from a dish.

The colleague was serving a portly middle-aged man, who responded to the little joke she made—Donal couldn't quite catch the words—with a gentle remark of his own, then sat down at a corner with his cake and tea. Cutting a piece of cake with the side of his fork, the man raised it to his mouth and closed his eyes in pleasure.

Somehow it seemed to Donal that his simple pleasure in receiving the coffee had communicated itself, spreading among three more people in the space of seconds. And wouldn't it be wonderful if life could always be like this?

So why can't it be?

The only thing Donal knew about the future was that it hadn't happened yet.

And the one thing about the recent past he was sure of was that he hadn't felt this good when he got on the plane in Tristopolis, but he'd been feeling fantastic since he woke up high above Silvex City. Could it be something to do with the altitude? Or even the makeup of the atmosphere here?

After he'd finished the coffee, Donal took the cup and saucer to the counter himself and thanked the waitresses. Their eyes crinkled up as they smiled in genuine happiness, and they voiced cheerful farewells as Donal left.

This was not seduction. They were far too young for Donal.

And if there was one thing about the present he was sure of, one melancholic fact marring the perfection of this moment, it was that he would have loved to share this adventure with Laura. Provided it could be safe.

Craning his head back, Donal looked up at the glass dome and the perpetual blackness pressing against it. Unused to sky that was anything but purple of varying hues, he wanted to see what things were like here. Was the black sky featureless, or was there some kind of visible topology? Visible to the naked eye?

He looked around at the exit signs. *Ground Transportation,* one of them read, which Donal assumed meant taxis and buses. A separate sign for trains pointed down a flight of stairs.

What Donal wanted was a place where he could— There. A sign for *Observation Lounge* directed him to a moving strip that began horizontally and then rose to form an escalator. It carried him up past two levels of restaurants and clothing stores.

At the top he got off and passed a glass bar, ignoring the inviting drinks, and walked to the exit that led outside. Most of the people were content to sit beside the glass walls and look out, but there was a door to the exterior patio, so Donal opened it and stepped out into cold darkness.

There were tiny points of yellow in the black sky. Here and there, pale-blue orbs were scattered.

It's true night.

This was what you could not see from Tristopolis or any part of federal airspace. This was humanity's glimpse of the greater universe, of starlight that had crossed the void over epochs.

As Donal watched, a crimson meteor streaked across the sky, followed by another, and then a third.

He spent a long time drinking in the vastness.

When Donal returned to the concourse, his two bags in hand, it was past twenty-five o'clock. He'd been outside longer than intended.

Alexa had arranged a hotel room for him by phone, not relying on the department's travel office: it had been painful enough getting them to authorize the foreign travel, even though Laura had paid for the air ticket. Whether the Nova DeLuxe would let Donal check in during the early hours of the morning, he had no idea.

Descending a helical escalator, Donal passed through seven stories of concourse until he came to the ground-transportation level. There, among families waiting for relatives or cheap unofficially booked taxis to arrive, stood a disconsolate group of drivers. Some wore dark uniforms and held up placards on which visitors' names had been written.

E. Aalsighsen; Councillor Livko read one; a scrawled legend that might have been *The Family Labrusvhjo*—however that was pronounced—was another; a sign that just read *LexCo Inc Reprezentativ*, which was either a foreign language or bad spelling; and *D. Riordan*—

Donal went up to the man with the peaked cap and the *D. Riordan* sign.

"Who sent you?"

No one is expecting me.

"Ah, Mr. Riordan. Can I take your bag?"

Concentrating on his breathing, allowing his vision to become very sensitive to motion on the periphery of his awareness, Donal said, "But who is your employer?"

"Sorry. I was supposed to say—Don Falvin Mentrassore, sir, is a friend of Harald Hammersen."

"Ah. Right. Lead the way." So this was one of Harald's contacts. "And I'll carry my own bag, thanks."

"Yes, sir. We're headed that way."

"Were you here when the flight landed?" Donal checked his watch. "That was nearly an hour ago."

"Um, yes, sir."

"Sorry I kept you waiting. D'you need to take a break or anything before we travel?"

Donal knew what it was like when you were on stakeout, which was why every car or nondescript room needed at least one large empty bottle, if not several, in case it became an observation point.

The driver hesitated, then said, "I'll just be a minute."

Donal grinned at him. The driver headed off toward the restroom. Donal put his bags down on the polished tiles and looked around the concourse.

There were shops selling trinkets and ordinary food-stuffs and even pharmaceuticals. Perhaps, if this place was easily reached from the city's lower levels, it served as a shopping center for local people. And for airport staff.

A shabbily dressed young man with a lute hanging from one shoulder by a leather strap was heading toward Donal.

"Excuse me, sir." The man's complexion was ivory, his eyes bore epicanthic folds, and his accent was Shorinese. "D'you know how to get to Dalishville Range?"

Donal's knowledge of Illurian geography was shaky, but he knew the place was hundreds of miles away at least. "Not really. The railroad station's that way." He pointed back toward a ramp. "That's the cheapest way to travel, I think."

"Yes, no buses here."

He meant long-distance buses.

"Good luck," Donal told him.

"Thank you, sir."

The youth headed in the direction of the ramp.

"Who was that, sir?" It was the car driver, returning. "Someone bothering you?"

Everyone was calling Donal "sir."

"Not really. He was just looking for directions."

"Oh. And he came to you first."

Donal shrugged. If you looked calm and watchful,

people assumed you were at home. But this was a city like any other, however polished and gleaming it—

Do you feel the bones?

No, but there's something nearby.

Donal stared at the sign for the train station.

"Sir? We really—"

"What's your name?" Donal asked. "And you can call me Donal."

"I'm Rix."

"Well, Rix, how about if you take my luggage, after all?" Donal picked the bags up and offered them. "And take them to Don Mentrassore's house."

"Er . . ."

"Right, just the bags. I'll be along later. What's the address?"

"Of Don Mentrassore's home?" asked Rix, as if unable to believe someone could not know where the don lived.

"Uh-huh."

"It's in Upper Kiltrin North," said Rix. "The road spirals down from Pulkwill's Hill, and the don's mansion is—"

"What's the name of the road?"

"Pulkwill's Hill is the main public road. The house is on a private street with no name."

Donal wondered how the mail was delivered, but for now all he had to know was how to get there. "A taxi will know the way, I presume. What do I ask for, Mentrassore Mansion?"

"Sure, and it's easy to find," said Rix. "Drive slowly down the road until you see the place with the three steel gargoyles out front, usually with their wings spread out like this." Rix gestured wide with both hands. "Or maybe you'll see two gargoyles and an empty whatchamacallit. Plinth."

"The don's renovating?"

"No, it's just . . . things move around, you know? Just never while you're looking."

Rix held Donal's bags with no more effort than Donal had.

"Sir—er, Donal, what do you need to do? The don's got every facility."

Donal glanced back at the storefronts. "Just a few supplies I forgot to bring. Might poke around for a little bit and see some sights."

Do you—

Get a move on.

Rix looked at his watch. He wore it inside his wrist, like Donal. Ex-military.

"Don't worry about me," Donal added. "I won't be sleeping on the streets."

"Okay then." Rix tipped his cap. "Good luck, sir."

Donal watched Rix go, then headed toward the storefronts. When he reached them, he glanced at his watch as though remembering something, then turned back and followed the path that Rix had taken. Looking down to a paved area where limousines and dark-green taxis waited, he saw Rix climbing into a low black limo.

The limo pulled out smoothly and followed the roadway, disappearing from sight beneath a ceiling of opaque glass.

Do—

Yeah.

Donal headed for the ramp that took him down to the rail station. In Tristopolis, it was the bus depot that attracted lowlife predators. Here, subtle indications of geometry and cleanliness told him to make a different choice.

Down in the subterranean station were seventeen long dark platforms. The air was cold; everything was bathed in the silvery strangeness of fluorescent lights.

Three of the platforms, at the far ends, had ramps that led up to the roadway level.

A taxi was ascending one of those ramps as Donal watched, leaving behind a platform on which only bales of sacking-wrapped goods were left standing. A couple of railway workers walked past the train, whose car lights winked out one by one.

Few passengers waited at this hour. As Donal descended to the nearest platform, he noticed a police cruiser pulled up behind a large pillar close to the nearest ramp. Two uniformed officers came from behind him and walked slowly past. The larger man, his shoulders huge and his neck thick with muscle, slowed further as he looked at Donal.

Pretending he had not noticed the officer's regard, Donal slid his ticket wallet out of his inside pocket and opened it, then glanced up at the platform sign—a moving wraith hand was repainting the next train's destination in a cursive purple script—and nodded to himself, as though confirming his travel arrangements. The officers walked on.

Examining the small knots of passengers and the individuals standing with hands in pockets or huddled alone on cold benches, Donal began to think he had this wrong.

Still, he noted the young woman—girl—on one of the benches. Had the officers questioned her on their patrol? She looked to be about fourteen years old and alone, therefore vulnerable.

The officers were getting into their cruiser and pulling the doors shut. Donal watched as they reversed, made a screeching U-turn, then accelerated too fast up the ramp, heading for the roadways above.

Seconds after they were out of sight, a lean, unshaven man came out from behind a pillar and began to walk along the platform, his too-big eyes staring at everyone in turn. Donal subtly bent over as he looked away, feigning the body language of uneasy fear.

Most ordinary citizens *would* feel fear at this hour, in this place.

The man uttered a low growl as he passed Donal, and Donal hunched up tighter inside his overcoat. Then the man was past, heading for the lone girl sitting on the bench.

I thought so.

A swagger entered the man's walk as he reached the girl's bench, produced a smile, and said, "Hi, can I sit here?"

The girl, shivering slightly, gave a shrug. She glanced up at him, then away.

"Don't worry about me, girl," the man added. "I'm a preacher. Nothing to worry about."

Preacher. Perhaps Donal had it wrong.

Do you feel the bones?

Well, now that you mention it ...

Head down, Donal drifted closer. Analyzing the man's stance, he thought there might be an iron rod or truncheon in the right coat pocket. The gun was on the man's left hip, presumably butt-forward; he'd left his long coat open despite the cold.

That was a shame. A stupid or overconfident man might have buttoned the coat up, hindering access to the weapon.

Closer now.

"Looks to me like you need a friend." The man's tone was sympathetic. "And a hot meal. I know a house where—"

That was when he noticed Donal.

"You." His lips pulled back from his teeth, and the chill that entered his deepening voice told Donal everything he needed to know. "Back off. Now."

"Huh?" Donal blinked.

The man was rising from the bench, uncoiling, hand reaching inside his coat, spitting as he said, "You. Fucking. Want. *This?*"

Lapsing into single-word sentences meant he was about to attack, and the time had collapsed to zero.

Now.

As the man's hand tightened and began to pull the gun out, Donal's mental state flipped. He was pure reptile as his left hand smacked palm-first into the man's face, then he grabbed for the gun hand as he hook-punched his right fist to the side of the man's neck, using every ounce of torque from the hips. The man dropped, already out.

But Donal followed him down knees-first. There was a sickening crunch.

Finally, Donal stripped the gun from the man's hand. You don't take the weapon away until they're no longer capable of using it.

Then he searched the unconscious man's clothes, finding an extending steel truncheon—that might prove handy—and a handful of loose shells. Unprofessional.

But the man's real profession was befriending young girls before introducing them to the wonderful world of turning tricks. Then he could take the larger cut of everything they earned, while they sank deeper and deeper into that life.

Not this time.

The man had a wallet, and Donal pulled out all the notes and eight-sided Illurian coins. He handed them over to the girl.

"Here," he said. "I believe he wanted you to have this."

"Mister . . . I'm sorry."

"For what?" said Donal. "He was going to turn you into a victim, but you're not that, you're a person, and you *will stand up* for yourself, all right?"

The prone man groaned.

"All right?" Donal continued. "And you'll buy yourself food and make a phone call. Do they have the Sisters of Death in this city?"

The order was used to dealing with runaways. And they did not do brainwashing: it was literally against their religion.

"I guess . . ."

"Then go back up to the main shops," said Donal, "and do that now. Get something to eat. Make that call."

"Yes, sir." The girl got off the seat. "Okay."

She began to move toward the pedestrian ramp. Then she looked back at the prone man. "What will you—"

"Just get going."

Ducking her head, she turned and left, climbing toward the concourse levels, which at least were bright and safe for the immediate moment. Donal had a feeling she would follow his suggestions. He could do no more.

There was a twitch from the man's hand.

Donal hauled the man up to a sitting position, legs still outstretched on the cold platform. He glanced along the platform: no one was watching; every waiting passenger had blanked out their perceptions of what was happening here.

Working the pressure points at the back of the neck, Donal brought the man back to painful half awareness.

"If I'd left you here unconscious," Donal whispered into the guy's ear as his eyelids fluttered, "you would have died. You think anyone would worry about trash?"

"Uh . . ."

"If you come back here, you die."

The man groaned, swallowed, opened his mouth, and gave a kind of shortened gasp. Donal's hands squeezed tighter.

"If you go back to running the girls, you die."

Only a croak sounded now. Donal released his grip a little.

"Did you run them from a house? The girls?"

"Yes..."

"Which road?"

"Gruytliwik Avenue."

"Number?"

"Huh..."

"House number. What was it?"

"Seven... teen."

"Go back there," said Donal, "and you die. Do you understand?"

The man gave a painful nod.

"Then get up." Donal hauled him to his feet. "And go."

"Where..."

"Out of here. Out of your life."

"Yes..."

Instead of heading toward the ramp, the man stumbled to a yellow-painted metal door and—with difficulty—hauled it open and half-fell through. His footsteps dully clanged down metal steps. Donal followed.

It was an emergency exit down to a grubby road tunnel, where stinking garbage was piled at the sides, next to the dank walls. This was the rottenness that Donal had known must live even at the core of Silvex City.

Donal watched as the injured man tottered out of sight. Perhaps another shadow moved within the darkness, some predator hunting another of his own kind, sensing injury and weakness. Donal looked at the gun in his hand, back down into the darkness, then shrugged.

He pushed the heavy door shut.

Then Donal walked back onto the platform, just as a cheerful rumble sounded along the silvery tracks. A train slid into the station. Passengers began disembarking, some with suitcases, for they had flights to catch.

Donal walked up into the concourse as part of a large

extended family who were chatting among themselves about their upcoming vacation, lively despite the late hour, accepting Donal's presence as sheer chance. They ascended from the station.

Then Donal was back among the glittering facades that promised a civilized world where two-legged rats did not survive, or so people innocently hoped.

And, illegally for a civilian here, he was now armed.

27

Alexa caught up with Laura in the steamy, overheated canteen. New notices proclaimed that this was VOLKOWAN'S RESTAURANT, but it was the same old canteen with the same old food, now cooked by an outside company instead of civilian employees of the department.

Laura had no need to eat, but she did have to keep her contacts happy, to befriend and manipulate those who were useful to the task force—and to her ongoing career. When you got to the level of Commander, there was no other way to play the game.

Understanding that much, Alexa did not care. Her goal was to reach the level of Commander herself, and to be younger when it happened than Laura was now. Oh, and she wanted to be alive when the promotion occurred.

Snitching on a fellow officer who was guilty of poor judgment—now that was rarely the best way to advance one's career. Harald had endangered Donal, Alexa was sure of it. What she ought to do was confront Harald first, without telling anybody else, however dangerous a course of action that might be.

But there was another worry. Xalia.

Laura was saying good-bye to a precinct captain

whom Alexa didn't recognize. Alexa waited until the captain was leaving before walking up to Laura.

"Hi there."

"Oh, Alexa. Is everything all right?"

"Kind of. . . . I haven't heard from Xalia at all. No one's seen her and she hasn't checked in."

"Don't worry," said Laura. "I know what she's—No. Wait."

"What is it?"

Laura was looking at her watch. "She hasn't reappeared?"

"No." Alexa, remembering her trance and the lip-reading, made an intuitive leap. "Does it have something to do with the commissioner? What you've got her doing?"

"Why do you say that?"

Both of them were glancing around, checking that no one could overhear their conversation. But they were far enough away from any wall or pillar that a wraith might be lurking inside. The floor in this portion of the restaurant was covered in a kind of hemp matting that played havoc with stiletto heels but was good insulation.

"I guessed."

"All right." Laura looked around, spotted a black internal phone affixed to a blue-tiled wall. "I need to call and check on Xalia. Come with me."

"Thanks." Alexa walked alongside Laura. "Does Donal feel the same about Vilnar as you do?"

There was a crinkling of Laura's eyebrow and the beginnings of a smile before she caught herself. "What do you mean?"

Alexa let out a breath.

"I mean, either Donal's a spy for Vilnar, or Donal's your spy in Vilnar's camp. Am I right?"

Laura shook her head. Reaching the phone, she picked up the handset and asked the switchboard operator to put her through to Wraith Resonance. She waited, then said, "Commander Steele here. Can you locate Xalia for..."

Her voice trailed off.

"What do you mean?" she said then. "How long? What happened to her?"

Laura listened for a moment longer, then thanked the operator and replaced the handset.

"Shit."

"What happened?" asked Alexa.

"Xalia's hurt. Can't speak, and won't be able to until she's spent time in a healing field of some kind. Could be days, or longer."

Alexa and Laura looked at each other, both thinking of Sushana lying in her hospital bed. The team wasn't doing well.

"I'm going to try to see her now," added Laura. "You'll get back on duty?"

"Yes, of course. And Donal's on our side, right?"

"Bank on it." There was no hesitation in Laura's voice. "If at some time in the future I'm not around and Donal is, treat him the same way as me, all right?"

"Um... Right."

"I'll see you later." Laura strode quickly out of the restaurant, her pace quickening until she was out of Alexa's sight.

Alexa remained staring in the direction that Laura had gone. Then she picked up the internal phone that Laura had used and asked for Viktor's extension. There was a single ring, then Viktor's voice: *"Hello?"*

"Hey, it's me. Alexa. Are you going to be on duty for another hour or so?"

"I'm right here, me," answered Viktor. *"Why do you ask?"*

"I'm going out for a late supper." Alexa didn't want to lie to Viktor. Perhaps she would grab something while she was out. "Can I bring you back anything?"

"*No. Wait—maybe a bagel. Anything.*"

"Sure thing. You all right?"

"*Kind of.*"

Alexa could hear the pain in Viktor's voice. She dared not say anything about Xalia being hurt. The poor guy was suffering enough already, and Viktor had always liked Xalia, however provocative the wraith got.

"Take it easy, big guy."

"*Yeah.*"

A click sounded and the line was dead. Alexa rehooked the handset. Then she followed the route that Laura had taken.

There was a group of people waiting near the first elevator shaft. Alexa hurried on along the corridor to Elevator 7. Alexa stepped inside the lift field.

Where ya going?

"Ground floor, Gertie. Thanks."

Alexa closed her eyes as she fell through the shaft. Gertie was a sensitive wraith who had read the stress in Alexa's voice and knew she was in a hurry.

There you are.

Gertie pushed Alexa out into the foyer.

"Thanks again."

Then Alexa went out past the desk sergeant, through the huge doors, and past the deathwolves. She descended the big steps to the street, where two people were climbing out of a purple taxi. Alexa leaned inside and called to the driver, "You okay to pick up another fare?"

"Sure thing, doll. Where ya headed?"

"The hospital, please."

The two people waited while the driver wrote out their receipt, then they paid the exact fare, no tip. The driver scowled but said nothing until the plainclothes officers were climbing the steps up to HQ and Alexa was sliding into the backseat.

"Skinflints," he muttered.

Internal Security, Alexa nearly answered, but kept her tongue. The problem with being a cop who investigated other cops was that you could never step out of line yourself. You had too many enemies who would love to get their own back.

"Visiting somebody?" the driver asked, pulling the taxi out into the traffic.

"Kind of," answered Alexa.

Perhaps she should buy flowers from the hospital shop on the way up. But Harald was the one she needed to talk to, not Sushana, and what Alexa had to say would not be softened by a cheap gift.

Harald, I think you're in deep, deep shit.

But what mattered to Alexa was the danger threatening Donal.

Donal's cab halted before the wide gateway. The last two hundred yards had been a slow zigzag down a sloping ice-smooth switchback, with the driver growing nervous. There were few streetlights: a discouragement for idle pedestrians.

"They call it Billionaire's Row," the driver said. "Ain't too comfortable around here myself."

"Not your biggest customers, huh?"

"Nah. They got their own limos and such, right?"

"Gotcha," said Donal. "Look, you can let me out here. No need to drive inside."

The driver's shoulders slumped in relief, and Donal wondered what kind of reputation these mansions had. He counted out coins while the driver wrote the receipt.

"Keep the change."

"Hey, thanks. You want I should bump up the amount on the receipt?"

"Nah, that's all right." Donal slid out of the seat.

"Take it easy," said the driver. "Have a good night."

"And you." Donal stepped out onto the strangely smooth road and closed the taxi door. He looked up.

A strange glimmering hung suspended across the night sky, that startling black curtain pricked with yellow and pale-blue stars. When another scarlet meteor slipped across the night's vault, accompanied by a paler counterpart of identical velocity, Donal realized there was a vast layer of glass overhead, insulating the street and the city from the true sky above.

The taxi's engine changed note as the driver maneuvered through a five-point turn so that he was facing back up the snaking hillside street. Then he stopped, watching Donal: checking that Donal was all right.

Donal raised a hand and walked into the open gateway between the big pillars. Immediately, the hairs rose on his head and across his entire body as he passed through some powerful hex scan.

He stopped, then walked on, his shoes crunching on gravel.

Pale shapes slipped across the gravel in silence and sat down, panting. Their eyes glowed crimson rather than the amber of their Tristopolitan counterparts.

Deathwolves, privately owned.

After a few moments, Donal decided they weren't going to attack. He took one pace toward the house, then another. The wolves rose and walked alongside him.

The bronze front doors swung open as Donal reached the silver-chased marble steps. A tall uniformed man stood smiling.

"I'm Hix, sir. Welcome, and please come inside."

"Hix."

"That's right, sir."

Donal walked into the vast hallway, which was richly appointed, as he had imagined.

"Any relation to Rix, the driver?"

"My cousin, sir, I'm afraid to say."

"But he spoke highly of you." Donal smiled.

"Ahem . . . Very good."

There were statues and paintings—nice to look at, but it was after one o'clock in the morning and Donal was tired. Hix led the way to spiraling stairs and gestured for Donal to go first.

The stairs came to life as Donal stepped on the first tread. They flowed upward, carrying him to the upstairs landing. There, he waited for Hix.

"Just along here, sir."

"Shouldn't we keep our voices down?"

"Sir? Oh, no. There's no else here. Not in this wing of the house."

"Ah. Of course."

Hix stepped inside a room and held the door open. Donal followed.

The bed was huge, with soft pillows and a gold frame, over which a pale-blue canopy gently stirred, though there was no draft in here.

"The bathroom is through there." Hix gestured toward an inner door. "And have you eaten? Would you care for a drink?"

Donal nodded toward a cabinet. "Is that a wet bar?"

"Absolutely, sir. And if you check at the bottom of that wardrobe, you'll find your garments have already been hung up for you."

"Well, Thanatos. I could get used to this."

"Very good, sir."

"What does that mean?"

"Excuse me, sir?"

"What does 'very good, sir' mean? Does it mean I've made a witty remark? Does it mean you're having a nice night?"

"I couldn't say, sir."

"Don't worry, Hix. I apologize."

"Sir, there's no need·to do that."

"Nevertheless, I'm sorry. And I'm grateful that you're putting me up for the night." Donal checked his watch. "What's left of it. Don't let me keep you from your own bed."

"Sir."

Hix gave a practiced bow, then backed out of the room, closing the doors shut behind him. They clicked into place, then clicked again: additional locks sliding into place.

Trapped.

But Donal was in the place he was supposed to be, and he was very tired. He looked around for light switches, seeing nothing appropriate.

Shit. How did he work the damned lights?

Is it always like this in a foreign country?

Tiny flames flickered in the bedside lamp, but there were no knobs, switches, or buttons. After a moment, Donal took a guess and snapped his fingers, feeling foolish.

Every light in the room switched off.

Donal stripped and got into bed. He lay down, and slid into . . .

Do you feel the—

Yes, they're everywhere.

. . . sleep.

Soft beeping and moans and twittering sounded from monitor sprites hovering above the patients. Harald held Sushana's hand while she slept. The IV tube into her arm delivered the narcotic coma she needed to kill the pain and allow her body to heal—of external wounds, at least.

A pool of light surrounded the bed; beyond it, curtained-off beds remained in darkness while their occupants slept and, for the most part, crept their way toward death.

Then Alexa came walking down the aisle between the beds, repocketing her golden detective shield that she'd had to flash to be allowed inside. Visiting hours were long over, and Sushana was a colleague rather than a relative.

But it was Harald that Alexa had come to see.

"What is it?" Harald appeared surprised, then stone-faced, clamping down on his expression. "Has something happened?"

"Is that what you're expecting?" Alexa remained standing, having few other psychological advantages over an ex-marine with so many years' experience. "That something bad might have happened?"

"What do you mean?"

"Maybe something bad in Illurium? To Donal Riordan?"

Harald spread his hands. "Hush...I don't know what you're talking about, but this is a Serious Cases Ward, where—"

"Donal Riordan is spying on Commissioner Vilnar for us. For *Laura*. I wonder if you're aware of that."

"No."

"And Xalia's hurt too. Someone's doing the Black Circle's work for them. Perhaps there's something you're not telling us, Harald. Something you've never told Sushana as *you* betrayed us all."

Even deep in a narcotic coma, Sushana groaned and moved her head from side to side before lapsing into stillness. There was a frown on her battered, swollen features. Her eyes remained closed.

"You can't think"—Harald was on his feet now, as though there had been no act of standing up but an instantaneous change in position—"that I'm a traitor.

Look at what they've done to..." He gestured toward Sushana in her bed.

"Just as I can't think Donal's a traitor," said Alexa, her voice low but fierce, "when he's risked so much and suffered so much for us. Who the fuck d'you think got us Vilnar's phone number in the first place?"

"What?"

"If Donal hadn't brought in Kyushen Jyu, the person Donal met when he was in the hospital thanks to the Black Circle... And Donal was the one who talked to Feoragh Carryn, remember? Both evidence trails come from Donal's work."

"I don't—" Harald was frowning now. He turned to stare at Sushana's battered face. "No. I can't have made that mistake."

"Perhaps you need to think more deeply."

Harald's jaw muscles clenched. "Thanatos."

"I saw a chapel to the Sacred Thanatos downstairs. You want to go and pray for a minute, Harald? And think about what you're doing?"

Alexa knew she was taking a risk. This was an accusation of criminal activity, and if she made it official and Harald was convicted—interesting things happened to cops who went to jail.

And it had to be obvious from the way Alexa was speaking that she'd told no one else what she suspected. "Harald?"

Perhaps she should have been more open with Laura.

"Yes," Harald said, surprising Alexa. "I think I'll do that."

"You'll—"

"Go into the chapel to pray."

Then he slipped past Alexa with silent footsteps and padded out of the ward like a ghost. She stood there, confused, not knowing what to do.

* * *

Barefoot on the deep soft carpet, Donal used the luxurious bathroom first, then made his way to the nearest
window and peeked out. The sky was still black, with
scarlet meteors streaking past.

So beautiful.

Gardeners were working down on the lawn. A
handyman was raking the gravel of the huge drive.

According to an ornate clock sitting on a baroque
table, the time was after eleven o'clock. Late morning,
and Donal had felt no need to rise earlier.

He wondered if Don Mentrassore worked from home
or whether he would be elsewhere by now, doing whatever it was he did for a living. Or perhaps all he needed
to do was count his money and spend it.

Donal realized that he had little idea how really
wealthy folk lived their lives.

He went back to the bathroom, filled a glass from the
faucet, and drank. Then he limbered up and worked his
calisthenics and shadowboxing, feeling the exercise
come easier and with a new sense of fiery joy.

Everything was falling into place. He'd felt that way
since the . . .

Can you feel the bones?

It doesn't matter.

. . . witch on the plane had given him the amulet, the
one he wore even now.

Donal stopped halfway through a five-punch combination. An amulet for luck? A charm that let him move
through life taking serendipity for granted?

At the orphanage he'd learned to make his own luck.
Yet Sister Mary-Anne used to say that a boy with the
right frame of mind would create luckiness purely by being aware of opportunities, by having the fearlessness to
follow them.

So . . . He was in a mansion owned by a rich ally, all

set to help. He had a name to hunt down: Councillor
Gelbthorne. That was the name Feoragh had retrieved
from the Lattice.

Perhaps it was time Donal Riordan allowed good
luck to enter his life.

Laura. I wish you were here.

28

Dressed in a clean shirt and the same suit, Donal went looking for breakfast. He'd tried wearing the amulet outside his shirt, but it made him look like a lower-southside pimp, so he tucked the thing out of sight.

"Mr. Riordan." It was a familiar snooty voice.

"Hix. Good morning."

"If you'd care to dine, perhaps the kitchen could help. They're preparing the don's luncheon."

"Which way is the kitchen?"

"Along that corridor." Hix pointed downstairs. "Then turn left and it's the second door on the right."

"Got it. Hang loose, Hix."

Donal gave a sunny smile. He felt good and, whether you were stone-faced or smiling, you never let other people break your composure.

Hix sniffed and turned to polish an antique shield that hung on the wall. A short sword was slung diagonally across it. Donal had seen cheap imitations, but this one probably would have been at home in a museum.

Whistling an old dance tune, Donal followed Hix's directions and poked his head inside the kitchen. It was red-tiled and copper-faced and looked like a chef's dream.

"Hey, guys," Donal said to the four cooks. "Any chance of some breakfast?"

"No problem. Sit down." One of the men pointed to a wooden table off to one side. "What d'you want? Sausage, omelet? What?"

"An omelet sounds great," said Donal. "Any kind you like yourself."

It felt good to let someone else do the cooking, like being in a restaurant that magically expected no payment. For a short while Donal could imagine this was a vacation, which up until recently he would have been happy to experience alone. Now he was missing Laura.

There was strong dark coffee already made, and Donal sipped it until the omelet arrived, replete with blue peppers and strange orange mushrooms and melted blue-green cheese on top, served with two fat slices of buttered toast. Donal dug in, while the cooks continued preparing lunch.

"That was absolutely fantastic," Donal said shortly.

"You haven't cleared the plate."

"I'm full, but that was the best I've ever tasted."

"Thank you." The cook was mollified. "Our pleasure."

Donal waved a hand at the cooking pots, from which enticing smells rose. "How many guests does the don have for lunch?"

"Just three," said another. "Bigwigs from the north."

Refilling his coffee cup from the pot, Donal said, "I wonder when the don will be able to see me."

As if someone had been listening in, a figure entered the kitchen, a shaved-headed man in a butler's suit. One of Hix's juniors, Donal supposed.

"The don invites you to see him now," the butler said, "in the Red Library. If you'd like to follow me . . ."

"I'm right with you."

Donal was still in a good mood.

He wondered what would happen if he took off the amulet.

At the same time, Alexa and Viktor were in the underground parking garage of the hospital, interviewing one of the nurses coming back on shift. They'd already talked to the family of a terminally ill patient who'd spent the whole night conducting a vigil in the hospital chapel.

The family agreed that a man answering Harald's description had spent some time in there, in trance if not in prayer. Then the man had stood up and muttered, "Fuck it," before looking at the sacred relics and adding, "Sorry."

He'd rushed out of the chapel, and the one place Alexa was certain that Harald hadn't gone was back to Sushana's bedside in the ward. Alexa knew that because she'd waited there for over an hour, until it was obvious that Harald had disappeared.

"That's right," said the nurse now, talking to Viktor. "A bone motorcycle, a Phantasm IV. I had a boyfriend who was into motorcycles, and he said—Well, they're powerful beasts, and I noticed that one, all right?"

"And that's the thing this guy"—Viktor held up a snapshot of Harald—"was riding?"

"Yeah, he came running down the stairs." The nurse pointed at a door in the concrete wall. "From there. He leaped on the Phantasm, which I swear started up before he touched it, and it sped out of here faster than you can imagine."

"You're positive?" said Alexa.

"Oh, yes. It was him. Did he do something?"

"No." Alexa's reply was automatic.

"At least not yet," muttered Viktor.

* * *

If you were going to call yourself a don, you had to dress the part, or so Donal supposed. The man who rose from the chair was dressed in a pearl-gray suit and white lace-edged shirt, with a silver cravat pinned in place. The pin sported a large blue diamond.

As for the man, he was thin and his complexion was tanned, and his gray goatee was elegant. In overall impression, in visual shorthand, he resembled the dead Malfax Cortindo, but his aura was very different.

"You're Don Mentrassore." Donal held out his hand.

"And you're Lieutenant Riordan." They shook hands. "If you don't mind sitting in hard chairs like this, take a seat."

"Thanks."

"Can I get you a coffee?"

"I just drank a pot of the stuff in the kitchen, with the cooks."

"Ah." The don smiled. "You know they eat better than I or my official visitors do. I think they deserve it."

"Harald sends his regards."

"And how is he doing, Lieutenant?"

"Marvelous. As for you, I don't need to ask." Donal gestured at the reddish shelves filled with books that were predominantly bound in scarlet leather. "This place is magnificent."

"When you say that, you sound as if you mean it."

"Ha." Donal peered at some of the book titles. There were philosophical texts he'd vaguely heard of and never attempted to read. "You could say that."

Don Mentrassore looked at his wristwatch. Donal had half-expected a watch on a chain, but this looked up to date and superlatively expensive. "I'll get rid of my lunch guests as fast as possible, and I'll clear the evening to do whatever I can to help."

"Thanks. There's an opera being performed soon, with these famous triplets, whatever they're called..."

"The Tringulians. You can't mean anybody else."

"Right. Them. Any chance of us getting tickets?"

"To which performance?" The don leaned back and crossed his legs. "I expect you're thinking of the premiere."

"And the following nights, too, if possible."

"*Every* night? Whatever for?"

Donal looked at him.

"To repay your debt, I guess you'd say."

"Ah, Lieutenant. You haven't met my daughter, Rasha. She's overseas and a brilliant scholar now, but a few short years back...I would pay what you're asking a hundred times over, and it would be little recompense for what Harald gave me. He gave me back my daughter."

"I see."

"And I have a box at the theater, a season-by-season arrangement, though I don't attend often enough myself. We will do this, Lieutenant."

"Thank you, Don Mentrassore."

"As for my business meeting, which we pretend to call a lunch, though I suspect my fellow diners will have little appetite, since they have so much money at stake in our dealings..."

"I'll leave you to it."

"If you like, Lieutenant. But I was going to add that they're in the energy business, and so am I, and a little bird told me that there's a connection between the Tristopolitan Energy Authority and the people you're after. At least I think I understood that correctly."

"It's a possibility," said Donal, unwilling to give up information.

"And I'm wondering if there could be a connection with our own Power Centers. Not that I've spotted anything certain, and I am a major stakeholder. Well, eight percent, but that's the second-largest individual holding in the corporation."

"I don't understand."

"If I could get you a visitor's pass into the main Power Center, with authority to access Records... would that be a help to you? And I'll see about the opera, of course. If my assistants have rented out my box to someone else, I'll override the agreements."

"Thank you."

There was a name that Donal wanted to ask about: Councillor Gelbthorne. But everything that Don Mentrassore had said so far could be flimflam, and giving out the name of a suspect was not the best way to conduct an investigation. Donal would try roundabout means to investigate the councillor first, before asking for specific help.

"My driver will take you there," said the don. "Let me make some calls, and Rix will fetch you when it's arranged. I'll make sure you're back in time for the opera. And you have something suitable to wear?"

"Um..." Donal plucked at his suit jacket.

"Never mind. I'll get one of the housewraiths to take your measurements." The don picked a small bell from a table and shook it. If there was a ring, it was inaudible to human ears, but a bluish wraith appeared fast, rising up through the floor. "Flisswell, measure up this gentleman for a suit of clothes."

There was a blur like smoke, the momentary sensation of damp fingertips across skin, and then the wraith was gone.

"Was that it?" Donal asked.

"Oh, yes. All done. The tailors will already be getting to work."

"Then I'll go and wait. I don't suppose I could borrow a book to read?"

"My dear man." The don stood up. "My lunch will

be ready soon, and I need to greet my guests. You can stay in here for as long as you like and read anything you like. Use that other bell there, the black one"—he pointed—"to summon one of the butlers. Or if you want to leave to go back to your bedroom or whatever, you can just go. Things are perfectly secure. No need to lock doors or anything."

"Okay. Thanks."

The don nodded and walked out of the library. But Donal was already at the shelves, running his fingers across the spines of the grand old books, spellbound by the choice available to him.

It was three hours later when a knock on the library door dragged Donal out of his reading. He looked up, realized someone was waiting for permission to enter, and called, "Come on in."

The man who opened the door was dressed in a dark suit like last night but without the cap. "Afternoon, sir."

"I told you to call me—"

"Donal, all right. I'm Rix, you might remember."

"I do remember, and I've met your cousin Hix."

"Yeah, sorry about that." Rix gave a wry grin. "He's a real old charmer, isn't he? If only we could extract the poker running parallel to his spine."

"I'm sure he's a wonderful human being."

"Ha." Rix clapped his hands together. "So, ready for another adventure? The don's got your scenic drive all mapped out, with a ride to the Power Center, right?"

"That was the arrangement."

"Your pass will be waiting for you," said Rix. "All officially arranged. Shall I bring the car 'round front in ten minutes?"

Donal closed the volume of the Encyclopedia Yelbinica that he'd been reading, with its discussion of

nonlinear hexodynamics that seemed to contradict what
Sister Mary-Anne Styx had taught in the orphanage. His
head was whirling.

"Ten minutes, right," Donal said. "That would be
perfect."

It would give him time to grab a coffee from the
kitchen, pop into the bathroom, and check his stolen
handgun once again: a reasonable precaution with a
weapon that he had never fired for real.

The Power Center was near the docks, or at least that
was what Rix told Donal. What that meant was, they
were headed for the edge of Silvex City, where tethered
airships floated impatiently at the docking pillars. They
waited to be gone, to hitch on to laminar flow currents,
the steady winds that blew horizontally between the
stacked Glass Planes.

Rix stopped the car for a while so that Donal could
watch.

"How do they get back?" he said.

Rix pointed to an airship rising from a great circular
gap in the glass surface. "The wind flows in different directions between the various layers. It's a weird system, I
suppose, but everyone is used to it."

"Amazing."

After a while Rix started the engine again and drove
on for maybe five miles before taking a glass-surfaced
six-lane helical ramp that led downward through the
layers of the city. He exited five layers deeper and immediately passed through a steel archway and along an
echoing tunnel, until he reached a gateway, where he
stopped.

Wraiths passed through the car, flitting back and
forth until they were satisfied. Then a human guard

approached and checked the documents that Rix held out through the driver's window.

"Hey, Rix," said the guard. "Usual drill."

"And my usual 'no problem.'"

"Right." The guard handed back the documents. He had not looked in the back at Donal. "In you go."

The great gates parted and Rix drove inside. And as he parked the car and the gates slid shut and internal doors opened, leading deeper into the Power Center, a strange mixture of hot and cold passed through Donal's sternum. When he glanced down, his shirt was glowing.

Thanatos . . .

Not the shirt but the amulet underneath was fluorescing in resonance with whatever energies they utilized in this place.

Inside, Donal adjusted his jacket so it concealed the glow.

Guards and maintenance personnel alike wore dark-green uniforms, so dark they appeared black, except where the lights shone brightest. Several men and women nodded to Rix and Donal as they walked through the complex proper, traversing a series of corridors that Donal would have a hard time navigating by himself.

Finally they reached an elevator platform that reminded Donal far too much of the Energy Authority's installation back in Tristopolis—and the day both the diva and Malfax Cortindo died.

"Don't tell me," said Donal as they began to descend through the shaft. "The Records section is down with the necroflux reactors."

A crop-haired woman was riding down with them. She looked up from her clipboard, surprised.

"Not exactly." Rix smiled at the woman (and Donal

noticed how she smiled back automatically, reacting to Rix's charm). "I did think you'd appreciate seeing the power generation before we start, because in fact"—Rix checked his watch—"we're a little early. But we don't use reactor piles."

The woman was still looking at him.

"My friend," Rix said, "is from Tristopolis."

"Oh." The woman nodded and smiled at Donal. "Welcome to the Power Center."

"Thanks."

The elevator platform stopped, and when the doors slid open, the woman stepped out.

"What's your name?" Rix called out.

"Debbie Shantol, in the Tuning Department." She held up a hand as the doors shut once more.

Rix frowned as the platform resumed its descent. Then he looked at Donal and shrugged. "Sorry. I have a hard time with names."

"Oh. No problem."

After a minute, the platform settled and doors opened. Rix went through first, and Donal followed. There were no other staff here as they passed along a stone-walled corridor with a plain-carpeted floor, then another utilitarian corridor.

They came out onto a square-edged stone balcony overlooking a rectangular hall in which hundreds of seated statues were arranged in rows.

Not moving.

They were static, but the figures were not statues.

Instead, row upon row of children with shaved heads, dressed in pale-blue tunics, sat cross-legged. Their eyes were directed straight in front, focused on infinity.

"What..." Donal could not understand what he was seeing.

From the center of each child's chest, a flexible glass

conduit led down into the floor. Part of Donal sensed waves of—something—passing along those conduits, glowing bright in a color that had no name. The amulet burned against his chest.

Every one of the two thousand children blinked, at exactly the same time.

Dread squeezed Donal's heart. He saw how the children's pale chests rose and fell in synchrony. He knew that if he could hear their heartbeats, they, too, would beat in time. The atmosphere was heavy with cold energies.

Rix's gun hand came up very fast.

Now.

Donal swept his left forearm across as he pivoted away from the line of fire, trapping the sleeve.

The weapon banged, loud in the great echoing space.

There might have been a collective gasp from the imprisoned children, but Donal was deep into the movement, flowing with the necessity of the situation as he fired a knee shot into Rix's spleen, drove the top of his head against Rix's face, and stripped the gun from Rix's weakened grasp.

He clubbed Rix above the eye with the butt of his own gun.

The gun he'd acquired last night was more familiar, so he drew that now, transferring Rix's gun to his left hand. There was dark movement at the edge of Donal's vision, and he dropped to one knee as he spun and fired once, twice, then twice more as armed guards scattered for cover.

Do you—

Not now, for fuck's sake.

Rix moved behind Donal, so Donal kicked him in the throat.

Then Donal was rolling to one side as a fusillade sounded from the guards. The corridor was a temporary shield and a long-term trap, but he needed the immediate advantage, so he leaped across the balcony and out of sight from the guards.

Now what?

He checked the weapon he'd taken from Rix: a Gladius Armaments .39 Barracuda. Good. One gun in each hand, he aimed out at the hall and back along the corridor simultaneously, while his mind whirled, trying to plan his next action.

A low moan sounded from Rix, failing to disguise the faint running footsteps of rubberized combat boots. Guards ran to new tactical positions.

How many of the bastards are there?

They would use a leapfrog system, one group providing cover as another ran forward. Soon they would be at the balcony and then the corridor entrance. Meanwhile, reinforcements would be coming from deeper in the—

"ALL ARMED PERSONNEL, STAND DOWN! DO NOT FIRE UNLESS IMMEDIATELY THREATENED. STAND DOWN NOW!"

The voice blared from overhead speakers and echoed around the hall where the imprisoned children sat.

"WE RECEIVED A FALSE REPORT; REPEAT, FALSE REPORT. LIEUTENANT RIORDAN IS NOT, REPEAT, *NOT* A THREAT TO THIS FACILITY. LIEUTENANT RIORDAN, YOU NEED NOT LOWER YOUR WEAPONS, BUT KNOW THAT YOU ARE SAFE NOW."

It was a persuasive voice. That was exactly the reason why Donal dared not trust it.

After a time, a cough sounded inside the corridor. Donal took aim around a pillar, but the man who advanced was dressed only in dark-green boxer shorts. He looked thin but soft, no kind of fighter. He bore a pale-blue sheet of paper in one hand.

"Um . . . Sir? Can I give you this?"

Donal kept his gaze flicking back and forth, both ways along the corridor. "Put it on the floor, then go."

"Sir!" The man placed the paper at his feet and backed away, trembling. Then he was around the corner and running on his bare feet, panting as though expecting a bullet in the spine.

Donal placed one gun on the carpet, unbuttoned his shirt, drew the amulet from over his head, and wrapped the chain around his left hand before picking up the gun once more. Then he duckwalked over to the paper note and dangled the amulet above it, waiting for the slightest tingle of reaction, watching for the smallest spark or glimmer from the amulet.

There was nothing from the amulet. These were ordinary words on everyday paper.

Message received from Don F. Mentrassore:
Visitor called Lieutenant D. Riordan is an ally on police business. Earlier information that he was engaged in criminal activity was untrue. Cooperate with this man in every endeavor.

Donal backed away from the paper without touching it and pulled the amulet back over his head. It dangled against his shirt.

"You expect me to believe this?" he shouted to the empty air.

He settled back down, weapons at the ready.

29

Laura sat back on her heels on a padded blue mat. The stone cell around her was dry. It was also too cold for a human to kneel in while wearing only a skirt suit: too cold for a *living* human.

Beside Laura, the ethereal form of Gertie drifted. She had abandoned her elevator-shaft duties again. She floated above the silver bars concealed in the floor, bars that extended through the walls and ceiling.

This was designed as a holding cell for temporarily psychotic mages who might damage others by intention or by accident as their hex forces underwent hysteresis and slipped beyond control. But the silver caging had other uses, and with Gertie's help Laura would be able to see sights most humans, including the no-longer-living, could not dream of experiencing.

Gertie's insubstantial fingertips touched Laura's zombie-cold skin, hesitated, then slipped inside. She reached into Laura's brain, inside the visual cortex. Neurochemical pathways swirled with spillover energies from Gertie's wraith parametabolism.

In a few moments blue shapes swam across Laura's vision and she gasped.

"What is it?"

Can you make out images?

"No."

Wait. Things will settle.

"Oh. There."

An ovoid shimmering field of blueness became sharper in Laura's vision, or perhaps in her mind's eye. There was no longer much distinction to be made between the two. And inside the blue—

Can you see her?

"Xalia, yes. I see Xalia."

There.

Laura understood little of wraith forms, of the incredible complexity that remained invisible to humans, because so little of the wraiths existed in the three spatial dimensions that humans are used to.

But in vision there was somehow understanding. Laura realized that the bright bands of whiteness running the length of Xalia's floating body were a healing phenomenon. Strange hex waves resonated back and forth along her body, mending the rips and tears that force fields around Vilnar's offices had caused.

"Xalia . . ." The whisper was involuntary, and Laura winced as a wave of pale color passed across Xalia's form.

Don't try to communicate.

"No. I'm sorry."

That had been one of the conditions of this viewing, but Laura's reaction was natural. She could tell how much pain Xalia was in.

How much pain Commissioner Vilnar had caused her.

It's best you withdraw now. Leave her to heal.

"Can I—"

Right now, Commander.

"Yes. Take me out."

Then the visions were rippling, growing inchoate and strange, and there was an odd feeling of sadness as Gertie's insubstantial fingers slowly slid out of Laura's brain, leaving her alone once more, trapped in her usual almost-human perceptions.

"Thanatos."

Some time after Laura withdrew from the trance, a faint knock sounded on the heavy metal cell door. Through the view window, face half hidden by the thick bars, she could make out the silhouette of Alexa's head.

"Yeah," said Laura. "Come in. I'm done."

Yes.

Gertie was sinking down through the floor, elongating her form to avoid the hidden silver cage bars.

"Thank you—"

Then Alexa came in, followed by Viktor. Gertie was already gone.

"What's up?" Alexa was staring around the cell. "I wasn't sure what you were up to, only that you were in here."

"Seeing Xalia, with a bit of help." Laura gestured vaguely around the cell. "Tapping into wraith frequencies."

"How is she?" asked Viktor.

He was clutching a sheet of paper that bore an official-looking insignia.

"Healing," said Laura, "but unable to speak. What's that you've got, Viktor?"

"It's a telegram," answered Alexa, unable to remain silent. "A military 'gram."

Few people knew that the military maintained its own network of shielded cables, along which ultra-high-speed protected sprites could flit with encoded messages. Laura had only seen such a telegram once before.

"Who's it addressed to?"

"Us. You and the rest of us." Viktor meant the task force. "It's from Harald, the silly bastard."

Laura ignored the paper and looked at Viktor's face. "What's he saying? And why military?"

"He's called in favors with his marine buddies," said Viktor. "The guys he keeps in contact with—you know how he is."

Alexa and Laura both gave tiny smiles. Harald's networking skills were legendary.

"And?" prompted Laura.

"He says, SORRY I FUCKED UP STOP MAKING AMENDS STOP H." Viktor put down the telegram. "I can't believe him."

"What do you think he means? What's going on?" Laura looked from Viktor to Alexa. "What is it?"

"Harald thought Donal was a snitch," said Alexa. "Working for Vilnar to spy on us."

"*What?*"

"Well, it was a reasonable..." began Viktor, then: "No, it wasn't. Why didn't he say anything to me?"

Alexa touched his arm, then turned to Laura. "It's all right. I straightened Harald out on that score. He knows Donal is on our side."

Laura processed sudden doubt in Viktor's gaze.

"Oh, for Thanatos's sake, of course he's on our side." Viktor swallowed.

"Alexa thinks...Harald set some kind of trap for Donal in Illurium."

"Oh, shit."

"Yeah. Harald took off from the hospital at high speed after Alexa confronted him. Took the Phantasm."

"So where's he headed?"

"My guess?" Viktor gestured with the telegram. "On a military flight to Illurium. We've got bases there, they've got bases here.... Must be flights back and forth all the time."

"But you can't just hitch a lift on a military pteracopter."

"No, *you* couldn't." Viktor gave a tight smile. "But Harald?"

When the Silvex PD uniformed officers arrived, Donal knew it was time to stand down. A plainclothes detective came with them, wearing an expensive bluemole coat that would have sparked an Internal Security review back in Tristopolis.

The detective said his name was Temesin and that the man who had assaulted Donal would be arrested at the hospital, if Donal would allow an ambulance crew to take the man away.

"You're talking about Rix?" said Donal.

"That's right."

Donal lowered his weapons to the ground and stood up, arms raised high. Four officers brushed past him, heading toward the balcony.

"He might need a tracheotomy," Donal said. "But he is still breathing, so maybe not. He had two guns on him."

A tiny smile twitched across Temesin's face. "Shame he's not good on color coordination, not to mention having two guns of different caliber so they can't share ammo."

"Yeah, I thought that was sloppy."

One of the uniforms called back, "He's hit in the trapezius. Artery, but minor."

Temesin looked at Donal.

"Wasn't me." Donal shrugged, still with his hands raised. "There was a lot of firing and I was the target. Would someone care to explain why?"

"What I know is—Look, put the hands down, all right?" Temesin made a lowering gesture. "Someone thought you were a saboteur. Then they decided you weren't. If that's confusing to you, then I can only agree. You want to help me out here?"

Donal relaxed, then pointed at the note on the ground. "I was staying at Don Mentrassore's house." When Temesin's eyebrows raised, Donal added, "Friend of a friend. At least he got me out of this bind."

"Hmm." Temesin watched officers and a paramedic mage carry out a stretcher bearing Rix, whose eyes were flickering as the morphoid spell took hold. "Too bad his driver was of the opposite opinion."

"Yeah. That's what I call a conundrum."

"You think it was the don who claimed you were trouble in the first place?"

"Maybe. Tell me, Temesin. How important is Mentrassore in this town?"

"Huh." Temesin rubbed his long chin. "Very rich, and very connected. You think I know every well-to-do businessman's name? This is a major city."

"You don't like me calling it a town, huh?"

"I'm sensitive." Temesin grinned, then picked up the weapon that Donal had appropriated from the rail-station predator. He gestured, and one of the uniforms picked up the other gun, the one that belonged to Rix. "All right, I've got this one."

He slipped the gun into his overcoat pocket.

"And I'll type up the report, Officer Reilly," Temesin continued. "All right?"

"Yes, sir."

" 'Cause I'd make a great secretary." Temesin looked at Donal. "You want a lift back to Mentrassore's place? Or just a quiet hotel? I've got an aunt who runs a little boarding house, very reasonable . . ."

"Perhaps I'll go back and chat with the don."

"How did I know you'd say that?"

"Because," said Donal, "you'd do exactly the same."

*   *   *

In the task-force office, Alexa finally got off the phone to the hospital administration. On her notepad was the phone number that the switchboard wraiths had rematerialized from memory, while their human supervisor read the digits out to Alexa over the phone.

It was the number that Harald had dialed from one of the pay phones in the hospital lobby, unaware that those calls were routed through the hospital switchboard. To subpoena the city switchboard wraiths and get them to find the number dialed at some random time was a lengthy process, but the hospital monitored calls as a matter of course, just like police HQ—even the outgoing ones.

"It's Illurian," said Alexa. "Want me to try to find out who it is? Intelligence might have foreign street directories. I'm not sure."

"Give it to me." Laura took the notepad. "I'll just call and see who answers."

She dialed the number, and the voice that answered was stiff and strangely accented.

"Don Mentrassore's residence."

"Excuse me, I'm trying to locate a Lieutenant Donal Riordan from Tristopolis. He should be—"

"Oh, yes. There's a . . . vehicle . . . in the driveway, and I do believe I spy the lieutenant sitting in the rear. May I get him to call you back?"

"Is he coming or going?"

"I beg your pardon, ma'am?"

"Is Lieutenant Riordan about to enter the house?"

"Well, I believe so."

"Then I'll hang on the line."

"Very good, ma'am."

Two minutes later, Donal came on the line. *"Hello?"*

"Hey, sweetheart."

"Laura! Hey . . ."

"Everything all right?"

"It is now I'm talking to you. And, yeah, I think it's okay here now."

Laura noticed the word *now* and said, "You've had trouble?"

"Minor stuff, little misunderstanding."

With a glance toward Alexa, Laura said, "That might be because of something Harald said to his contact there. That would be this Don Mentrassore, wouldn't it?"

"That's the man. But Harald . . . Why would he—"

"He might have thought you were a snitch."

"But . . ." There was a pause, then that familiar heart-breaking laugh. *"If it weren't for snitches, Harald would be sunk. That's what he specializes in."*

"Recruiting them," said Laura, smiling. "Not being one of them."

"Yeah, there's a difference. . . . Is everything all right there? How is everyone?"

"The same. Sushana's still recovering. Also Xalia."

"Xalia? What happened?"

"Tried to penetrate Commissioner Vilnar's office. Looking for corroboration. I know you came across the phone number, but I wanted more."

There was an oceanic sound of waves sighing down the line.

Then Donal said, *"I take it you found nothing."*

Laura shook her head, though Donal was a thousand miles away and could not see.

"Oh, I got enough. You don't think a wounded wraith is evidence? Even if she can't speak yet?"

"Ah."

Again the liquid washing of random sound took over the line.

"Be careful, will you? I love you."

"Yeah. And I"—Laura looked up at Alexa and Viktor—"likewise, okay?"

"*Okay.*"

The line went silent.

"All right." Laura replaced the phone and looked at Alexa, then Viktor. "You two up for a fight?"

"Not against you, boss," said Viktor, smiling.

"I was thinking of a police commissioner. It's time he was going down."

Donal put down the hallway phone, then shifted his position so he could check the pistol inserted inside his belt at the small of his back. Temesin had slipped the weapon back into Donal's hand, just as Donal was climbing out of the squad car.

Remaining inside, Temesin had given Donal a sardonic wave and said, "I kinda hope I don't see you again too soon, Lieutenant."

"You too," Donal had told Temesin. "And thanks."

"Right." Then Temesin had slapped the back of the driver's seat and said, "Let's go, Reilly."

"Yes, sir."

Donal had stepped back as the tires spun fresh gravel in all directions before getting a good grip and hauling the car down to the gates and out onto the sloping zigzag street. Then, when he went inside the house, Hix was waiting, immediately telling Donal he was wanted on the phone.

Now Donal looked Hix straight in the eye.

"Your cousin," Donal said, "has caused me a great deal of trouble."

"Oh, I'm sorry, sir." Hix briefly closed his eyes. "People think he's a charming rogue. I hope he didn't inconvenience you."

Donal's senses were on full alert. It seemed that Hix was genuine: honest despite his stiff manner, where Rix had been open and friendly and ultimately an enemy.

"I don't suppose," said Donal, "that the don is in?"

"Oh, absolutely, sir. And insistent that he see you as soon as you came back. Can I take you to his study?"

"Why don't you do that."

"Who the fuck," said Donal, standing at the open study door, "do you think you are?"

Beside him, Hix swallowed, looking as wide-eyed as his master. Then the don gestured for Hix to leave.

"Please come in," said Don Mentrassore. "And I deserve that—except that I acted on false information, as you might have gathered by now. And I *did* manage to stop Rix in time."

"Not exactly." Donal entered the study. "*I* managed to stop your fuckin' stooge. If he dies that'll be good riddance."

Don Mentrassore winced, though whether at Donal's tone or the images he conjured up was impossible to tell.

"I apologize. And I've already arranged for what you said, the seats at the theater."

"What?"

"The performance of the premiere. It's tonight. I've spent a great deal to—well, never mind. But you'll be able to attend the performance every night for the next three weeks, if that's what you want."

Donal's teeth remained clenched.

"I don't care what arrangements you've got with Hammersen. Cross me again and I'll take you down, Mentrassore. All the way."

The don swallowed.

"I believe you," he said.

It was three hours later that Donal took his seat in the plush box in the theater, high above the stalls. He adjusted the winged collar of his shirt and ran his fingers down the lapel. It was the first tuxedo he'd ever worn.

Looking like a waiter had never been an ambition in his life.

Beside him, dressed in a plum velvet version of Donal's tuxedo that would have looked ridiculous on most people, the don sat down and adjusted the lace cuffs of his shirt.

This is stupid.

Donal had no weapons, because he'd known in advance there would be scanwraiths at the theater entrance. Although they were invisible—having been chosen for their ability to be discreet amid the theater's rich patrons—the wraiths had triggered a warning tingle in Donal's amulet.

Finally the lights dimmed, the orchestra in the pit began the overture, and Donal settled back. With his opera glasses, he scanned the rest of the theater once more in the gathering darkness. He caught a glimpse of two late entrants in another box, on the opposite side of the theater.

One of them he didn't recognize—a man dressed in a dark velvet suit similar to Don Mentrassore's—but the other's features were vaguely familiar, and in a second Donal had it.

This was Alderman Kinley Finross from Tristopolis.

Scarcely anyone had mentioned him during the entire investigation, and yet...Donal remembered the letter that had set up the meeting with Malfax Cortindo.

Xoram Borough Council
99 Phosphorus Way
Xoram Precinct
Tristopolis TS 66A-298-omega-2

Tristopolis Police Headquarters
1 Avenue of the Basilisks
Tristopolis TS 777-000

Quatrember 42, 6607

Re: Meeting with Malfax Cortindo, Director, City
Energy Authority

Dear Commissioner Vilnar,

It has been absolutely my pleasure to arrange a
meeting between one of your officers and Director
Cortindo of the City Energy Authority. The latter
body is, of course, a credit to our city, and the
director evinced no hesitation in assuring me that
he will be overjoyed to provide any technical
assistance that is germane.

I have communicated with Director Cortindo that
Lieutenant Donal Riordan will be meeting with
him, as per your indicated request of 40th ult., on
the evening of Quintember 37 at nineteen o'clock,
at the Downtown Core Station. All facilities will
be placed at the lieutenant's disposal.

Kindest regards,
K. Finross
Alderman Kinley Finross

P.S. All best to your honored wife. Sally and I
hope to return the favor at the Styxian Ball.

Donal—and Laura—had assumed that Commissioner
Vilnar had called in favors, using Alderman Finross as a

tool: a dummy so that no one would suspect a direct connection between Vilnar and Cortindo.

But here was Finross turning up right at the venue where the Black Circle was expected to strike next. This on the word of a highly motivated Bone Listener who wanted revenge for her colleague's death.

Since the man with Alderman Finross was dressed similarly to Don Mentrassore, he was probably local. Donal leaned across to the don and whispered, "Do you know who owns that box?"

He gestured. The don leaned back to murmur his answer.

"That's Councillor Gelbthorne. I'll introduce you during the intermission, if you'd like."

Then the overture died away as the spotlights brightened upon the stage, and the don leaned back in his seat and crossed his legs.

Gelbthorne.

Bingo.

It was the name that Feoragh had given Donal from the Archives, the local councillor who was—what was it?—ninety-seven percent certain to belong to the conspiracy, according to the stochastic predictive processes utilized by Archivist Bone Listeners such as Feoragh Carryn. Whatever that meant.

Whether he had the right night or not, Donal was sure he had the right place, and the right suspects in view.

"So this is what a judge's house looks like," murmured Alexa as they walked up the drive. Behind them, the Vixen's engine purred softly in agreement.

"I haven't been here since—well, a long time," said Laura.

It was dark, and the sky was a deep opaque purple,

highlighting the incandescence of the external flame-wraiths trapped in their brass cages, illuminating the driveway and the statuary on the grounds.

The luxury estate was formed of great houses like this one, no two identical, and the dark land beyond was Thesselae Park. It was hard to imagine that Tristopolis proper ringed the entire area and that they were not so much beyond the city as enclosed by it.

The doorbell chimed automatically at their approach. After a few moments the judge's live-in assistant, gray-haired Mrs. Fogerty, answered the door. Beside her, reflected highlights shifted across the brass plaque that read *A. Prior, Judge.*

"Can I help you?"

"It's urgent. If you could tell the judge that Commander Steele is here." Laura held up her badge. "Just say it's Laura."

"Well, it's quite late, and the judge needs his—"

"I'm Vladil Steele's daughter. The judge will see me."

"Oh, goodness . . . Yes. Do come in."

Laura and Alexa climbed the steps and went inside. They stopped in the hallway as the door swung shut and Mrs. Fogerty bustled into the interior somewhere. They could hear her talking, then an old man's voice answered.

Mrs. Fogerty reappeared and beckoned them down the polished hallway. "This way, my dears. This way."

Judge Prior was sitting in his small library, wrapped in his dressing gown, a small glass of milk on a table by his chair. He smiled at Laura and pushed himself up from the chair.

"Well, I haven't seen you since . . . since . . ."

His smile faded away.

"Since the day I died," said Laura.

The judge coughed and lowered himself back into the

chair. Alexa moved to his side and handed him the glass of milk.

"Thanks." He sipped. "Thank you."

His hand shook as he gave the glass back to Alexa, who set it down.

"You're welcome, sir," Alexa told him. Then she backed away.

This was Laura's show.

"Your Honor, obviously I need your help." Laura held out a sheet of vellum filled with purple script in the old style. "This is a search-and-arrest warrant."

"My dear, I—" The judge stopped. "Obviously this is something the night-duty bench can't handle."

"Or won't," said Laura.

"So whom," asked the judge, accepting the document, "do you want to arrest?"

Laura took a deep (if unnecessary) breath.

"Commissioner Vilnar. I want to search his office and his home."

"The commissioner?" The judge dropped the document into his lap. "Impossible."

"No," said Laura. "Anything can be done, if you're willing to sacrifice enough."

She reached inside her purse.

30

Halfway through the second act, several entire rows of the audience began to breathe in unison, and the amulet began to burn against Donal's chest.

"Thanatos."

Someone turned around to shush him.

Shit shit shit.

Donal ripped the amulet away from him, and after that events accelerated. Down onstage, the triplets were singing so impressively that memories of the diva threatened to overwhelm Donal.

Do you feel the bones?

Oh, Death, yes.

The amulet lay on the carpet, its light slowly fading. Its protective hex was dying now that it no longer nestled against Donal. It could no longer shield against dark tidal forces.

Stage spotlights brightened to gold, for in the opera's story, a village festival in the enchanted land of Brismangidor was about to begin. Donal noticed white flickering, like indoor lightning. Overhead spotlights were flashing runes into the audience's eyes, a subliminal induction that for some reason Donal was able to detect.

And now that he was exposed, the Black Circle could use him again.

Thanatos, I've played into their hands.

Because the amulet wasn't to guard Donal from external forces—it was to hide his internal darkness from the world. But now that shield was gone.

Do you feel the bones?

"NO!"

Some of the audience looked up at Donal, startled, but most were spellbound by the flashing runes. The mass parazombie spell would already have fallen, except that the Black Circle had not realized that Donal Riordan would be in the audience. Not here, not tonight.

But if they had, the audience would already have been ensorcelled, exactly as they had been in the Théâtre du Loup Mort. Because it was not the diva who had been the focus of that mass binding spell. She had been the target, but someone else had focused the thaumaturgical waves transmitted to the theater, acting as a kind of lens for the Black Circle mages.

Do you taste the music?

"Yes! Yes, I do."

For Donal was the focus.

Donal was the lens.

He was the weapon that had caused the diva's death.

Donal stood rigid, every muscle tensing into catatonia. All the rehab, all the memory reburning, all the suffering. He had tried so hard to become the old Donal, the man he had been before the bones' influence took him.

Strange harmonics swirled all around: moans and wails that had nothing to do with the orchestra below.

Can you hear the bones?

Always.

Do—

Every damned moment.

Across the theater, in a guest box as plush as the one

Donal shared with Don Mentrassore, two men were intent on the audience. No—Alderman Finross was dividing his attention between the increasingly entranced audience and the triplets onstage.

It was Councillor Gelbthorne whose eyes glittered as he channeled thaumaturgical energies down into the theater.

Gelbthorne.

Some part of Donal's mind perceived wave upon wave of blackness beating downward, though this was an illusion, a kind of metaphor: the energies involved had nothing to do with light. The human retina could not perceive necrons.

Laura.

Do it for Laura.

His old boxing coach, Mal O'Brien, had picked Donal up off the ring floor once. It was supposed to be a sparring match, but his heavier opponent was filled with hate for his own reasons. Donal had gone down, with his forearm snapping from the impact on the floor, his ribs already fractured from an angled punch he'd not seen coming.

Mal had said, *"It will heal, boy. And your spirit? That's still whole."*

And Donal had called out to his opponent leaving the ring: *"Hey, you running away?"*

What had happened after that was a moment of dark joy, as Donal ran forward with his one good arm ascending, powering from the hips, and the uppercut he delivered was the best of his life. The heavy bastard fell backward and did not move.

But it was what Mal said later, as they tied the splints on with wormskin bindings, that came back to Donal now.

"Never worry," he told Donal. *"Broken bones heal* stronger *than before, didn't you know?"*

Here in the theater, waves of shadow ebbed and

flowed around Donal. Then the secret mage, the real enemy, Councillor Gelbthorne, looked at Donal from across the auditorium. He recognized the kind of person, the kind of *device,* that Donal was, which a mage could make use of.

Gelbthorne focused.

Can you hear the bones?

Deep inside, Donal fought, holding on to his thoughts, because being human was all it took: to reinforce his real thoughts, not repattern his neural pathways to become a filter for Gelbthorne's transmission.

Broken bones heal stronger than before.

Do you feel the music?

It was an illusion, but from across the auditorium, Gelbthorne's eyes became bright, became huge, like widening spotlights focused now only upon one thing. Upon the vessel that could focus his energies.

Upon Donal.

Broken bones . . .

Do you—

. . . heal . . .

—feel—

. . . stronger . . .

—the—

. . . than before.

—music?

And every moment of hate from his orphanage days, and every second of love he felt in Laura's presence, strengthened Donal now as he fought back, and deep inside him a kind of laughter rose.

No.

I am the music.

The ensorcellment ripped apart.

Donal was free.

* * *

The audience remained partly mesmerized. Stage spotlights still beamed subliminal gestalt runes directly into their eyes. Not everyone would be susceptible enough to obey whatever commands Gelbthorne managed to channel, but there would still be plenty.

Donal was on his own against hundreds. Gazes from across the theater turned toward him.

A group of men in medics' uniforms stood in the shadows near one of the ground-level fire exits. Their attention was fixed on the triplets. When the moment was right, they would seize the dying (or already dead) triplets and take them away, fleeing through the emergency exits.

Would they flense the bones? Or was that a pleasure reserved for Gelbthorne himself, with Finross perhaps assisting?

I am the music.

Exits—Donal remembered a fire-alarm button in the corridor outside. The memory offered itself up to him now. *So flow.*

He vaulted backward over his seat, brushing aside Don Mentrassore's grasp—the don was now under Gelbthorne's influence—took three long steps out into the corridor, and hammered the red triangular button with the bottom of his fist.

A klaxon howled.

Overhead nozzles sprayed water down from the ceiling. Farther down the corridor was a hose cabinet, with a sand bucket and a fire ax. Donal grabbed the ax and went back into the box.

Water was spraying downward in the auditorium, the performers suddenly came to a halt, and the orchestra sound fell apart in discord. Those audience members who'd been mesmerized were jolted out of the trance.

A woman screamed, starting the panic.

"Fire!"

Across the gap, just for a second, Councillor Gelbthorne's gaze locked on Donal's. Gelbthorne concentrated, willing Donal to drop into a trance.

"Fuck off," said Donal.

The don reached for him from behind, but Donal slammed his elbow back into the don's face, blood spattering as his nose broke, and then Donal was spinning out of the box, ax in hand as he ran into the corridor.

He sprinted, pouring on the speed. Gelbthorne was not going to get away.

I am the music.

But people, panicking, were filling the halls and corridors.

Donal reached the door that led to the stage. It was opening slowly from the other side. Donal grabbed the knob and ripped it open fast, then slid past the stumbling man he'd surprised.

Keeping hold of the ax, Donal ran backstage. With pandemonium among the audience, this was the quickest way to Gelbthorne's box.

And Finross. He shouldn't forget Alderman Finross.

Threading his way among performers and stagehands, Donal reached the far side and looked out. A blocky figure in police uniform was there, directing three other officers to keep the frightened audience streaming out through the fire exit. One of the uniformed men looked familiar: it was Reilly, the officer who'd driven the car.

No sign of Gelbthorne.

But there was Temesin in his dark-blue coat, improbably smoking a cigarette, standing calm while water showered down and hundreds of civilians fled past him.

Donal decided to trust him.

He made his way through the pouring water to Temesin, and said, "He was up there. In that box. The mage who kicked off the spell . . . Must have backfired."

"Yeah, right." Temesin stared at the ax in Donal's

hand for a second, then looked up. "That would be Councillor Gelbthorne. Had a visitor with him."

"From Tristopolis. Alderman Kinley Finross."

"Wonderful. Another politician. And what spell was that, by the way?"

The paramedics who'd been waiting were now in handcuffs. Five uniformed officers surrounded them.

"I suggest you—"

"Gelbthorne's disappeared, before you go on."

"Does that mean you've had men outside trying to spot him?"

"Maybe." Temesin took the sodden cigarette out of his mouth. He flicked it onto the wet carpet. "I'm not sure we have enough for a warrant."

"An arrest warrant?" asked Donal. "Or a search warrant?"

"Either one." Temesin squinted at Donal through the artificial torrent, which was not letting up. "Too bad."

"Yeah..."

Donal looked back up at the box he'd been in. There was no sign of the don.

"You ever notice how things happen in twos or threes?" Temesin jammed his hands in his pockets.

"What are you thinking of?"

"Just that if there was an emergency, like a fire or some such, in Councillor Gelbthorne's house, you'd have no hesitation in breaking in with your officers to bravely rescue the good man... wouldn't you say?"

"Maybe." Temesin looked at Reilly, who was still ushering people out through the fire exit. "I take that back. Definitely."

Something like this should take planning, but Donal knew that Alderman Finross was a coward who would be on the first flight back to Tristopolis, now that the attempted murder and bone-stealing had blown up in front of his eyes. Donal had to take him down tonight.

Two thousand children, breathing in time...

Perhaps it was the synchronized respiration of the audience, as they had begun to fall under Gelbthorne's spell, that reminded Donal of the captive children in the Power Center.

Or were they specially grown inside the Power Center from the time they were newborn? Donal wasn't sure he'd seen true awareness in their eyes. He wondered if using living beings was truly worse than using the bones of the dead.

Donal remembered his conversation in the Energy Authority complex, and Cortindo saying: *"The conglomeration does not truly think or feel anything."*

"Not even pain?" Donal had asked.

"No. At least, that's what I'll tell anyone who asks me officially."

Now he let out a breath.

"How is power delivered to the houses? Big houses."

"Like Gelbthorne's? He's even got his own . . . generators, if you can call them that."

"I've seen what your Power Centers are like."

"Yeah. At least we bury them in peace when they die."

"Shit."

"Right. But subgenerators have long shafts linking them to the main centers, in case of power shortage and in case of accidents. Probably, if you knew someone with influence in the corporation, you could even get schematics of the system."

The nozzles' spray was lessening to a light drizzle.

"If only I knew someone like that," said Donal.

"Mmm."

In his study, Judge Prior leaned back in his chair.

"Young lady," he said to Laura. "I knew your father

for many years, and I remember your every birthday party, you and the other toddlers—"

"Other rich folks' kids."

"If you like. But I can't let you ask me to do this."

"Please, Your Honor. This is important."

"As is the order of justice. And propriety." The judge removed his reading glasses and put the warrant aside. He rubbed his nose. "I'm sorry, Laura."

Alexa took a step, thinking Laura was about to leave, then stopped.

"Excuse us a moment, Alexa." Laura hefted a small object from her purse. "Can we talk in private, Your Honor?"

"Is that a privacy cone?" Judge Prior glanced at Alexa. "Well, my dear, if you like. But I'm not changing my—"

Laura activated the talisman's spell, and an inverted cone of silence rippled through the air as it slid into place, enclosing Judge Prior and Laura in a volume from which no sound could escape.

A *transparent* volume.

Watching carefully, Alexa held herself very still, hoping that both Laura and the judge would forget about her presence. She watched for perhaps two minutes.

Finally, the privacy field shriveled out of existence and Laura put the talismanic device back into her purse. She twisted the clasp shut. Then she waited as, hand shaking, Judge Prior undid the cap of his expensive fountain pen and slowly signed his name at the foot of the warrant.

"There," he said. "You're satisfied now."

"I am. Thank you, sir." Laura picked up the warrant. "We'll see ourselves out."

The judge watched Laura and Alexa until they reached the study door. Then: "You've changed, Laura Steele. You didn't use to be like this."

"Yeah," said Laura. "Death has a way of doing that."

Outside, the Vixen's headlights sprang into full brightness as Laura and Alexa came down the steps. Neither woman said anything until they had climbed into the car and it was rolling down the driveway.

When they were on the public road, Alexa sighed.

"I don't believe that."

"We got the document," said Laura. "What else matters? I hope your lip-reading is as good as ever."

"Just about. Did your father really tell you that he'd bribed a judge? And Old Incorruptible Prior, at that?"

"Not exactly. Dad said it all right, just not to me. I was listening at the keyhole."

"Oh."

As the car drove on past the park—it looked dark and dangerous in the night—Alexa added, "What did you mean earlier, about being willing to sacrifice? The judge?"

"No. I'm the one who's made an enemy tonight."

"Shit."

"Do I look like someone who cares?"

Don Mentrassore, his nose covered in a green worm-skin dressing and his manner furious—though not at Donal—did more than furnish the information. With Hix (not Rix) driving, the don accompanied Donal to the Power Center, where they bypassed the generation halls with their enslaved children.

Donal wondered whether he was right to be pursuing one man in the midst of this, before remembering the diva and what had happened to himself.

Uniformed technicians handed over a rolled-up purpleprint and a large flashlight.

"There're bogies," said one of the men, "that can take you most of the way."

Still dressed in his theater finery, the don nodded to

Donal and said, "That's a little too adventurous for a man of my age. But I wish you luck, sir."

"Yes, thanks." Donal nodded, unable to warm to the man any more than that. He waved the purpleprint. "Appreciated."

It was now around five hours since the don's driver had tried to kill Donal in this place. Perhaps later he would be able to blame Harald for that attempt, not the don.

"This way."

Two technicians led him through a hatchway and down a metal ladder, to a narrow maintenance tunnel along which a single rail ran. There was a bogie as promised, a small flatbed atop two wheels side by side. Donal could not see how it stayed upright or how it was powered.

"Necromagnetic induction," one of the techs said. "And, look, see up there?"

Donal looked. There was a glowing number in orange, 327, high up beside the hatchway.

"You keep on going," the tech continued, "until you reach two hundred one, then get off and ascend the ladder, where the domicile tunnels—that's the tunnels to private homes—radiate outward. Ya gotta take number five, and it's the second house."

"All right," said Donal. "Two hundred one, five, second house."

"And you'll want these." The technician handed over heavy goggles. "It goes pretty fast."

Donal pulled the goggles over his head, clambered onto the bogie, then sat cross-legged on the flatbed, thinking again of the cross-legged, mindless children sitting in rows not so far from here.

"What do I—"

A rectangular portion of the bed, next to Donal's right hand, began glowing a soft orange.

"Press that, keep pressing it . . ."

Donal pressed down and the bogie rolled into motion.

"...and keep pressing until you want to stop, then just let go."

No one had to tell Donal that this was called a deadman switch.

Acceleration was building up, but something prevented him from falling off.

Good ride for kids.

If only the orphanage could see him now, ignoring the plight of hundreds, no, thousands of children. If Sister Mary-Anne Styx were here...

But already the tunnel had arced to the left and downward, and if Donal looked back there was no sign of the Power Center, only the plain walls and rows of safety lights streaming past.

I am the music.

With his left hand, he checked the gun at the small of his back once more.

In Tristopolis, Viktor was leading a group of R-H detectives up the short path to Commissioner Vilnar's blackstone residence. It was unfair of Laura, by Viktor's reckoning, to expect Robbery-Haunting to help out in the slightest way—forcing your way into a police commissioner's house didn't seem like the best method of enhancing anyone's career prospects.

At least, Viktor decided, he himself would do all the talking. Warrant in hand, he banged on the door. In maybe five seconds, it swung open. A scowling woman with a lined face stared at Viktor.

"What the bleeding Thanatos do you want at this hour?"

Viktor held up the warrant.

"Is the commissioner in, ma'am?"

"No, he's not. He went to the Death-damned office for something. You married, detective?"

"Uh, no, ma'am. Not exactly."

"Well, do some poor woman a favor and think about whether she wants to be married to the entire damned department. And was that a search warrant I just read?"

"Yes, that's—"

"I don't know what's going on, but Arrhennius is going to be pretty pissed at you guys. You want some coffee?"

"Arrhennius?"

"You're busting into a man's home and you don't even know his first name?"

Viktor rubbed his face.

"Sorry, ma'am."

"No, you're not. But I suspect you will be."

At exactly the same moment, Laura and Alexa were leading another team of R-H officers, six of them, toward the elevator shafts. Gertie's wraith hand beckoned briefly before slipping back inside the entrance to her own.

The eight women and men looked at one another before stepping into the shafts in tandem. No information indicators showed on any of the elevator shafts.

They rose in silence and came out on the 187th floor, into a corridor ringed with alternating bands of icy cold and searing heat. Laura said nothing as they passed through the outer office.

Eyes was at her desk as always, her long black hair glistening with reflected highlights from the silver cables that linked her eye sockets, via the console, to the rooftop mirrors—to what was in effect the commissioner's private communication and surveillance network above the city streets.

Perhaps Eyes somehow knew about the warrant that

Laura carried, because Alexa noticed her reach beneath her desk to press a button. The door to the inner offices slid open.

Then Alexa was following Laura into the commissioner's office, with the R-H officers behind them.

"What's gone wrong?" This was the commissioner himself, gesturing back the metal visitor's chair that was transforming itself into a hooked, talon-bristling monstrosity, ready to attack. "What is this?"

There were other defenses in here, many of them subtle and unexpected, down to the ashtray that could double as a percussion grenade.

"It's the Black Circle," said Laura, holding out the warrant so that the commissioner would be unable to see his own name written there. "They've penetrated higher in the city apparatus than anyone suspected."

"And you've got proof?" said the commissioner.

"Enough, we think."

"Are you sure about that?" The commissioner's fists clenched. "Really sure?"

"Certain enough," said Laura, "to get a judge's signature on this."

The commissioner's squarish face split in a predatory smile.

"Then let's go and get her," he said. "I've waited a long time for this."

Laura froze, still holding out the warrant.

"What did you say?"

"I said—Well, what the Thanatos did you think I said? Are you deaf?"

"No, but—"

A crash reverberated through the office, a vibration that rippled the air—or perhaps just the eyeballs of everyone inside. They toppled to the floor and lay there. The warrant spilled across the floor, right next to the commissioner's blunt-fingered hand. He levered himself up to a seated position on the floor, staring at the paper.

Then he looked up at Laura.

"You bloody fool," he said.

After a long moment, Laura regained her voice.

"Sir?" Her certainty had slipped. "We have evidence from corroborated sources. We know the phone number you used to contact the . . ."

Laura's voice trailed off.

"What number?"

Alexa answered: "It was seven-seven-seven, two-nine, three-five-one, seven-two-zero. There's no doubt."

The commissioner huffed as he struggled to his feet.

"Which'll be the phone on Marnie's desk."

There was no doorway. The R-H officers had already crawled to the wall where the door had been. Two of them slipped deep into trances, trying to determine what hex enchantment had been wrought. One of their colleagues hammered his fist in frustration on the solid stonework.

"Who?" said Laura.

"Marnie, my secretary."

"Oh, you mean Eyes," said Alexa.

The commissioner's lips twitched.

"Yes, I mean Marnie Finross, the alderman's niece, whom I thought I was keeping under adequate surveillance, until you blew the whole thing wide open."

Laura tried to focus on what was happening. Commissioner Vilnar was tough but slippery when it came to confrontations: everyone knew that.

"Nice try, Commissioner. But hasty lies won't cover up the evidence."

"No, but impetuous actions will certainly mean Marnie gets away, don't you think?"

Laura opened her mouth to reply, but one of the R-H officers said, "He's telling the truth, ma'am."

"And you are . . ."

"Petra Halsted. They said I should help out."

"Laura, I've heard of her." Alexa's tone was quiet. "She's a truthsayer. Notified before federal spellbinders."

"Shit."

The commissioner cleared his throat.

"Recrimination is for idiots," he said. "Why don't we see if we can get ourselves out of this Death-damned mess?"

Donal had his gun out now, walking crouched along the narrow access tunnel. Back in the main tunnel, the wraith-enabled bogie had moved away from Donal as soon as he'd stepped off. There was no means of fast escape.

As far as he could tell, all the narrow branching tunnels led to the subterranean levels of the great houses; none led directly to the open ground. That would have been a security risk.

He came to the next door and stopped. Its necromagnetic lock looked huge, and Donal realized that he had not thought the problem through adequately.

Then power coils hummed and heavy bolts slammed back.

The door swung open.

"Shit."

Two huge men with zombie-pale faces raised their submachine guns—Grauser Howlers with disk-shaped magazines—straight at the center of Donal's body. One twitch of a finger and a stuttering burst of fire would rip Donal in two, the bloody halves would fall with a wet thump to the floor, and that would be that.

31

Disaster whirled in upon Donal, tumbling on all sides as he admitted the depths of his stupidity. Without the chaos he'd intended to cause, there would be no reason for Temesin's officers—even assuming they were outside Gelbthorne's mansion—to break inside under the pretext of rescuing the councillor.

Laura. I'm sorry.

Sorry that he'd let her down. That he would never see her again.

Thanatos.

And then the strangest thing happened, the likes of which Donal had never seen during a police operation.

Both zombie guards lowered their weapons, stared at each other, and shook their heads. Then they turned to Donal and one of them said, "You have the touch of black blood. It is upon you."

"Er..."

"This house," said the other, "is a place of turbulence and mischief."

"Say what?" Donal felt he should not be arguing, but what exactly was going on?

The first zombie handed his weapon to his colleague, then pulled open his own shirt and pressed his fingertips against his white chest in an exact sequence. There was a wet, soft ripping sound, and Donal could not turn his gaze away as the man's chest split open.

Inside, black and glistening, was the zombie's rhythmically pumping heart. The zombie placed his fingertips against its pulsing surface and said, "I will not harm you, brother."

The zombie's colleague placed his Grauser Howler on the floor, then straightened up and likewise touched the other's beating black heart.

"I, too, swear that this human shall be my brother."

The zombies looked at Donal.

"Um, thanks. I mean . . . thank you."

"That is good enough."

The zombie pulled his chest together, and the wound—or access orifice, or whatever—sealed up immediately. The zombie buttoned his shirt back up.

"We've just resigned from Councillor Gelbthorne's employ," the other zombie guard told Donal. "By our actions, we've resigned. We have never liked this place."

"Gelbthorne," said the other, "disturbs the darkness."

Donal still could not process what was happening.

"My name is Brial," said the first zombie, "and this is Sinvex."

"I'm . . . pleased to meet you," said Donal.

Then both zombies turned away and walked off along a featureless passageway. Donal stared after them, bemused, wondering what the Thanatos had happened here.

A submachine gun still lay at his feet.

"Hey, you forgot something."

But the zombies were already gone.

"Waste not, want not."

Donal picked up the submachine gun, checked its magazine and action—full and perfect—and grinned, remembering the time he'd come in second in the battalion

JOHN MEANEY

shooting competition in the machine-gun category. He'd
always thought it was an accident: he was hopeless with
this kind of weapon.

Perhaps this time he could come in first.

It was Gertie who rescued them, her wraith form slipping through the walls to check their condition, then ac-
cessing the trip switch contained beneath Eyes's desk.
Beneath Marnie Finross's desk: Laura was still angry
with herself for having missed the obvious.

The big door reappeared.

Wraith-enabled furniture scampered out of the office.
The living metal chair exited first, followed by a cloud of
assorted items surrounding the big lumbering desk on its
stubby legs. Finally the humans, when they were sure it
was clear, hurried out after the furniture.

Behind them, the portal to the commissioner's office
sealed up once more.

Sorry, Arrhennius.

"What for?" said Commissioner Vilnar.

I think your office is lost forever.

The commissioner smiled.

"I can always get another one."

Laura blinked. The commissioner was on first-name
terms with an elevator wraith? Perhaps she had mis-
judged the man.

"Commander Steele," the commissioner said. "What
are you waiting for?"

"Um . . . Sir?"

"I want you to arrest Marnie right now." He gestured
at her empty desk. "Find her and bring her in."

"Yes, sir."

Laura left the room fast, followed by Alexa. The R-H
officers exchanged glances, then nodded to the commissioner and exited.

The commissioner reached inside his jacket and pulled out a big blue-steel handgun, checked the safety, and reholstered. Then he went to the coat stand, got down his heavy overcoat, and pulled it on. As he did so, he noticed a discarded tissue in Marnie's wastepaper bin, stained with lipstick. He picked up the tissue and pushed it into his overcoat pocket.

"Gertie?"

Yes, Arrhennius?

"Can you drop me down to street level the quick way? Just like the old days?"

My pleasure.

"Then let's do it."

A strange presence was prowling the lower corridors of Councillor Gelbthorne's mansion. Pulsing waves of coldness passed through the air.

Maids and other personnel were scurrying along the corridors, hurrying into offices or hidey-holes and locking the doors, as Donal passed amid the chaos. Donal saw two hulking gray-skinned men, with mosaic armor woven into their skin, who were squeezing their bulk into a linen cupboard, glancing down the corridor.

Whatever had been set loose in here, Donal didn't want to see it.

Donal took a short flight of steps up to an open red-brick landing. It was a vast atrium of white walls and red tiles and fifteen or more balconies arranged at odd angles. Donal caught a glimpse of dark scales, and then he was moving again, racing up steps as silently as he could manage.

More staff bolted out of his way as he hurtled toward double glass doors. Then he saw a tiny red button that reminded him of the fire alarm in the theater, so he did the natural thing: he hammered the thing with his fist.

Nothing happened.

"Shit shit shit."

It had to be a fire alarm. What he hadn't figured was that it would be silent, broadcasting by some means to the house staff but not wailing sirens that might bring outsiders to investigate. But that had been the whole point of—

A metal barrier was rising up out of the floor, cutting off access to the suite of rooms ahead.

Move.

Donal reacted by instinct, trusting his intuition—*I am the music*—and sprinted forward—*fast*—feeling a wash of stinking coldness rise up in the atrium behind him—*faster!*—and then he was hurdling the rising steel, foot touching the carpet beyond, catching it, and he stumbled.

Ceiling and walls rotated past him, and he continued the roll to one side, catching one hallucinatory sight of a vast, dark reptilian eye focused on him as the steel barriers slammed shut, cutting off the outside world.

Donal was safe.

It sings . . .

He felt a cold, eerie singing deep in his bones and knew what it meant. A mage was very close.

Commissioner Vilnar came down the outside of the building like a descending bat, his overcoat billowing capelike as he dropped onto all fours. Startled deathwolves could see the glowing bluish form that enveloped him: Gertie, the wraith whose servitude in police HQ had always been associated with a certain . . . latitude.

Gertie billowed and fluttered back into the safety of the vast dark tower. Around the commissioner, the deathwolves growled, their amber eyes glowing.

"FenSeven," said the commissioner. "And FenNineBeth. Are you ready for the hunt?"

"*Grrr...*"

"Come on." The commissioner led the way, moving fast for his bulk. "Let's check—Damn it."

The Avenue of the Basilisks was filled with people spilling out of theaters, heading for the restaurants. Marnie could be anywhere among the thousands of people along the vast canyonlike thoroughfare or in any of the two-hundred-story-high towers that walled it.

"She's got dark hair," muttered Commissioner Vilnar, "and this is her scent."

From his overcoat pocket he drew out the tissue that he'd retrieved from Marnie's trash can.

"Unless she's hexed this with some kind of trick," he added to the deathwolves. "So you be careful, boys."

The deathwolves flitted off into the crowds, lean and dangerous and scarcely visible to rich folk who were unaccustomed to seeing true predators. They would not have cared to realize that there were dangers deadlier and more immediate than wheeling and dealing in boardrooms and clubs.

Laura and Alexa ran out onto the street. Alexa stopped dead, seeing the commissioner, her mouth opening though she was unable to speak.

Then the Vixen came hurtling toward them and spun sideways in a squealing hand-brake turn, its doors popping open as it slewed to a halt. The car was empty inside.

Laura looked at the commissioner.

"Go on." He made a pushing gesture. "Go after her!"

Blinking, Laura jumped inside the car and got moving before Alexa could even react.

"All right," said Commissioner Vilnar to Alexa as the Vixen moved off into the traffic. "You're with me."

Alexa turned to follow the Vixen, then stopped.

"No," said the commissioner. "We're going back in-side."

Donal entered a gallery of bones. Unmoving, they dragged at him.

Petrified skeleton hands, some gold-framed displays (lit by soft spotlights) that were only a single knuckle-bone, then some isolated ribs, and, in a special triptych arrangement, three entire skulls that grinned at Donal as he stumbled past.

They sang.

Unfocused visions swirled around Donal, and he dropped the submachine gun without even noticing as the pains and cramps shifted through him, a warning against fighting the beautiful dreams.

They sang to him.

No. Help ...

All around, the bones were calling, promising their wild, seductive, artistically sublime dreams.

Diva, help me.

Or was she the last person who would want to help, even if she were alive to come to Donal's aid? Perhaps he deserved to fail, to die immersed in a wondrous trance.

There were inner doors with ornate handles, and Donal had already grasped them in his bare hands be-fore he realized his mistake—for the handles were of carved bone, the bones of long-dead artists.

No ...

A maelstrom of visions pulled him down.

There were ruby seas where the song of small-breasted mermaids lured him to—

No.

—the living forest, where flowers breathed scents such as he had never—

I will not ...

—their myriad hands trailing softly down his skin, cupping his—

... *allow this to* ...

—pulling him into—

... *happen.*

—swirling pastels and the feel of—

NO!

He broke the visions apart.

Because ...

And stood there, panting, soaked with sweat, having thrown the doors open to reveal the final chamber within.

I am the song.

By his own will, Donal had thrown off the bones' ensorcellment, but it was far too late as he saw what lay inside the chamber.

He fought back the urge to vomit.

Three men stood around a flat altar: Councillor Gelbthorne and Alderman Finross, and another whose shock of white hair and photogenic features were familiar, as of someone famous seen only in newspapers. Donal thought he might be a politician. But the corpse that was stretched out on the altar was more than familiar, since it was at Donal's hand that the man had died.

It was the corpse of Malfax Cortindo.

While all around ...

Sweet Thanatos, no.

... lay the pale discarded detritus of the components they had used up in their work, the power source that had fueled whatever strange hex they had cast and shaped. It was almost an anticlimax when the corpse's eyelids twitched, because it had to be worth it, even for the perverted mages of the Black Circle: worth it to have used up the resources they had.

The floor was littered with dozens of dead children, their blank eyes open, never to see anything again.

Gelbthorne raised a hand and pointed at Donal. Orange lightning spat across the room...

...and burst apart as it struck Donal's chest. He took a half step back, knowing he had no time to run into the gallery of bones and retrieve the submachine gun he had dropped while the visions had clutched him.

Last chance...

But that was the moment when Malfax Cortindo's corpse jerked into movement, spun on the altar, and sat up, then stepped down onto the floor, his bare feet squashing the dead children on which he stood.

There would be no complaints from those soft corpses.

"Fuck you," said Donal, and ran.

Laughter followed him as he threw himself out through the doorway into the room where the bones' attraction pulled like riptides through his soul. But it was a second's work to snatch up the submachine gun, turn, and squeeze the trigger.

The deafening, stuttering crash of automatic fire banged and reverberated in the enclosed space. Donal's teeth were clenched as round after round poured back through the doorway, clustered on the targets: the corpse and the three men who...

There was a click as the magazine emptied.

...were still on their feet.

A mist of black powder hung before the trio: the remains of the bullets dissipating as they struck whatever shield the mage, Gelbthorne, had gestured into place.

The gesture that now pulled back the lips of Cortindo's dead face was anything but human. The decayed tongue inside the blackened teeth moved. There might have been a glimpse of maggots within, before the corpse closed its mouth once more.

At least this thing could not yet speak. By the time it had regenerated that far, Donal would be dead.

Oh, Laura. I'm . . .

All four mages, Cortindo included, raised their hands to destroy him.

. . . sorry.

An explosion behind Donal blew the steel doors open. The percussive pressure hammered Donal through the opening, back into the chamber where the mages stood.

He fell atop dead children.

In the doorway, a pale figure stood with a heavy hexzooka over one shoulder. Beyond, revealed in the great atrium, a riderless bone motorcycle was harrying prey, darting at a great scaled reptile that was spitting in fear.

"The marines have descended." Donal smiled.

"We always do," said Harald.

Orange lightning gathered around the four dark mages as they prepared to counterstrike—but in that moment more motorcycles, dark-green with flashing lights, growled and screeched into the atrium.

Officers on foot in dark-green uniforms with white helmets, automatic weapons held at port-arms, flooded in after them. And bringing up the rear, looking calm and relaxed, came the narrow figure of Temesin, smoking a cigarette, holding his detective's shield out in front of him.

Donal looked at the four mages.

"Game over," he said.

"Aaah . . ." The sound that came from Cortindo's dead mouth was horrifying.

But then Councillor Gelbthorne and the white-haired man took hold of the reanimated Cortindo, wrapping their arms around him in a kind of bizarre group hug.

The white-haired man spared time for one malevolent glance at Donal before they lowered their heads and concentrated. The air shifted and wavered and began to rotate. Strange geometries were manifesting themselves.

"No. Don't leave—" This was Alderman Finross, terrified.

But the trio of mages had formed a conglomerate whole that was revolving, faster and faster, until it twisted, turned through an angle that was entirely impossible, orthogonal to every axis of Donal's experience . . . and was gone.

All that was left was the broken, weeping alderman, leaning against the abandoned altar, surrounded by two score dead children, maybe more.

Donal got to his feet.

"No! It was Blanz. He . . . he *ensorcelled* me!" Alderman Finross was almost babbling. "Please, please don't kill . . . I'll tell you everything. They left me no choice but to—"

He stopped as he realized how much he was incriminating himself.

"Senator Blanz," said Donal. "That prick."

Alderman Finross toppled to the floor and lay outstretched.

"I think he fainted." Temesin had walked inside, unnoticed by Donal. "Too bad. I was enjoying the sound of his voice."

Donal's nostrils flared, and he gestured around the room. "Doesn't this bother you?"

Temesin considered the small corpses. "I've seen worse."

"Shit . . ."

Then Temesin turned to Harald.

"Impressive entrance," he said.

"Yeah." Harald spat to one side, then grinned. "Want me to bust up any other buildings while I'm here?"

Laura, inside the Vixen, cruised along the Avenue of the Basilisks, scanning the crowds, looking for the dark-haired figure of Eyes—Marnie Finross.

The problem was that Laura could only envision the woman with those silver cables hanging from her eyes, attaching her to the refractive apparatus that led to the rooftop mirror system. Actually recognizing the woman's features would be impossible.

And there were so many hundreds, thousands of people on the street. If she'd fled inside a building...

"I give up," Laura told the Vixen. "I don't see any chance of spotting the bitch."

But then she saw two low shapes flitting among the people's legs and a sudden scuffling, and the deathwolves had pulled a woman's coat off with their fangs. The woman's long white hair swung as she sprinted away from the deathwolves.

"Damn it, that's her. Even her hair color's changed."

The woman kicked off her high heels as she sprang toward the sheer wall of the nearest tower and began to slither upward. Marnie Finross's palms and soles adhered to the surface as she quickly ascended, while all the two deathwolves could do was sit down on their haunches and howl.

The Vixen screeched to a halt, then trembled.

"Come on," said Laura. "I know you can do it."

Laura touched the gear stick—just a touch—and the Vixen turned and rolled forward, heading straight for the building as Marnie Finross had done. Then the car morphed her rear wheels fast like springs and bounded ten feet upward.

The Vixen's wheels quickly spun and re-formed into splayed talons arranged like steel flowers, and the car hit the wall with all four spiked wheels. It began to climb upward, rolling slowly straight up the surface, engine growling with the effort, slowing.... Then the car stopped and hung there, quivering.

Laura bit her lip.

The Vixen backed down to the sidewalk, groaned,

and rolled back onto the roadway, not bothering to re-morph her wheels back to normal configuration.

"It's all right," Laura said, patting the steering wheel. "Really."

Even as a youngster, the Vixen had been scared of heights.

Then the Vixen's engine sighed. Her headlights swiveled upward, becoming impossibly bright, as all power diverted into the bulbs, transforming them into spotlights whose brilliant white beams swung high up the tower. They pinpointed the still-climbing figure that was Marnie Finross.

"Oh, that's good," murmured Laura. "I think that's all we'll need."

The Vixen's spotlights followed Marnie Finross all the way to the top, where she climbed onto the roof and was lost from sight. For a second Laura thought that was it, the end of everything. Then a tiny red glow, then several red glows from high above, told her that it was fine, it was all right, the case had come to a conclusion.

Laura touched the driver's door and it popped open. She stepped onto the sidewalk.

"I won't be long," she said.

The building's doorman used his passkey, accompanying Laura inside the penthouse express elevator. It shot very fast up toward the top level and slowed only in the last few seconds. He walked with her along the hallway and opened the armored glass doors that led outside, then he stopped and gasped.

"Don't worry," said Laura. "They won't hurt you."

But the same could not be said of Marnie Finross.

"They're, they're . . ."

"My friends," said Laura. "Just my friends."

Ranged all around the rooftop were cats.

Hundreds of cats.

And every cat's eyes glowed crimson in the night, entrancing the one who had dared to look upon them.

Marnie Finross's catatonic body lay curled and paralyzed like some hardened fossil of bygone eons, her mind disintegrated into madness, shattered into shards that could never be repaired.

Laura smiled.

"Thank you."

Meanwhile, deep in the hidden basements of police HQ, it took all of Alexa's strength to haul Commissioner Vilnar's senseless body out of the chamber where he had sought answers. He had known the quest would knock him unconscious, had trusted Alexa to remove him from the place that would kill him if he stayed inside for too long.

She strained—he was heavy!—and pulled and eventually dragged him into the stone corridor, clearing the doorway. She glanced back inside the chamber at the roiling, nova-white light . . . and then the door slammed shut of its own accord, hiding the chamber's interior.

On the floor, Commissioner Vilnar moaned.

"Here." Alexa unstoppered the water bottle he'd told her to bring, raised his head, and poured a few drops between his lips. "Good."

In a minute he had come around. Whatever was in the bottle, it was more than water. He took a deep breath, then held out his hand so Alexa could help him heave his bulk upward and regain his feet.

"You'll go far in this department," he told Alexa. "Not every network of allies is as corrupt as the Black Circle."

"Um . . . No." Alexa could not help glancing at the closed door.

"But you won't ever tell anyone what you saw in there." Commissioner Vilnar's eyes seemed very large and round. "Will you?"

Alexa swallowed.

"N-Never."

"That's what I thought. Now you and I are going to brief the others. All right?"

"Yes, sir."

The smile that crossed Commissioner Vilnar's face looked inhuman. After what he'd just been through, Alexa was surprised he could smile at all.

"That Senator Blanz," he said, "thinks he's such a tricky bastard."

"Sir?"

"Hiding right out in the open. But we'll fix him—No."

Alexa stayed silent, not daring to ask questions. Things were moving fast.

"That honor belongs to the team. Laura Steele will lead the arrest. Somewhat appropriate, don't you think?"

Alexa smiled at last.

"Yes," she said. "I think that would be perfect."

32

The state capitol was a great nine-sided, distorted polygon over which permanent dark clouds floated, like streamers of black ink through the indigo sky. Despite the quicksilver rain, journalists were arranged on the steps to photograph the arriving senators. Today was an important day.

It did not matter that the man who had proposed the bill was not here. Voting on the Vital Renewal Bill did not require Senator Blanz's presence. Part of the interest among the journalists, of course, was to inquire about the conflicting rumors surrounding the senator's disappearance. No one among the state legislature was willing to comment—at least not for the record.

Flashbulbs popped as paramedic mages carried a light palanquin from a newly arrived ambulance. Today's vote was likely to be a close thing, so that even councillors who were on their sickbeds—possibly their deathbeds—had answered the summons to the capitol.

This wizened figure belong to Councillor Will Sharping, a grand old liberal who was an icon for the younger generation. Sharping was respected, even among his opponents, as a gentleman of the old school, one who would never stoop to the sharp tactics seen so often nowadays.

There was speculation as to how the councillor might vote, because he could influence others decisively, and not just members of his own party.

Inside the capitol, from the viewing gallery, Laura and Donal stood beside a stone pillar. They watched the councillors take their seats and observed as the mages bore the palanquin inside and somehow collapsed it, so that Councillor Sharping appeared to be sitting like an ordinary councillor on an ordinary chair.

"Let's do it," whispered Laura.

"Yes."

It had been three days since Donal returned from Illurium, and every nerve was taut as he and Laura descended among the politicians. Could it really be over soon?

The Speaker of the House was enunciating the terms of the bill, prior to the voting.

"...that the rights to counsel, to marriage, and to employment be immediately revoked from all nonhuman, in-human, and ex-human beings..."

The man's voice faltered as he caught sight of Laura and Donal coming down the steps. Perhaps the Speaker was more of a mage than he looked, able to detect that Laura was a zombie just by glimpsing her.

"...to, er, take under state ownership all liens and properties currently held in title by such..."

Laura halted first. Behind her, Donal pushed his jacket open, revealing his favorite Magnus in its new shoulder holster, which was a present from Laura.

Then Laura reached inside her bag, pulled out her detective's shield, and cast her voice: "I'm Commander Steele, Tristopolis PD. And"—replacing the shield inside her bag, she withdrew a vellum document inscribed with purple ink—"this is a warrant for the arrest of Senator Blanz—"

Murmurs grew all around the chamber. Didn't this woman know that Senator Blanz was missing?

"In other words, I'm arresting *you*." In her other hand she already held handcuffs, and now she headed toward the wizened figure with the wispy white hair.

Above her, the Speaker of the House coughed.

"Young lady, you're making a risible mistake. That is most manifestly Councillor Sharping, whose—"

But Donal stepped forward then, taking solid hold of the wizened man's wrist. As Donal had expected, the strengthening of his sense of self—which was the witch's and the bones' true gift—held fast now.

He saw through illusion.

I am...

And he dispelled illusion in the eyes of others.

...the song.

To the assembled state government, it appeared that the air shook and broke apart, until the man in Donal's grasp looked strong and vital, and the hair atop his head, though white, was thick and bushy.

"We've got you, Blanz."

Orange lightning cracked through the capitol chamber.

The impact flung Donal back. Protected as he was by a hexlar vest, reinforced by federal spellbinders flown in for the job, Donal was unharmed by the blast itself. For a second he thought that everything remained fine, that the operation was going down as planned.

Then he saw that Senator Blanz had pulled off a trick that was more sleight of hand than true sorcery.

He held Donal's Magnus in his hand, aimed directly at Donal.

No...

Then Blanz swiveled his aim and squeezed. Donal lunged forward, knowing already what had happened.

Laura's head blew apart in a spray of bone splinters and dark blood.

NO!

Donal's fingers clawed for Blanz's eyes as the impact took him in the heart, and the bang that followed seemed far away, and everything went black as Donal died . . .

33

. . . **a**nd woke, while the medic mages were still working on him. He was lying on the stone floor of the capitol chamber, and some of the councillors were staring in horror at the scene taking place below them.

Donal tried to work his mouth.

"Don't talk," murmured one of the mages. "It'll be all right."

No, it won't.

He raised his chin and stared down at his open chest cavity. Two mages were working inside him, their hands and forearms slick with black fluid. And inside his chest . . .

Oh, Thanatos.

. . . was a beating, slick black heart . . .

Oh, Death.

. . . taken from the one who would need it no more.

NO NO NO NO NO!

Three days later, against all medical advice, Donal stood at the graveside on a dark heath in the Dispersed Vale, at the edge of Black Iron Forest. The diggers shoved wet soil into the grave, and quicksilver rain fell and fell, unceasing.

The priestess and the task-force team stood watching. Behind them—against his political advisers' advice—was Commissioner Vilnar. Whatever Laura had been in her original life, this was a zombie being buried now—and Blanz might be discredited, but his movement was not.

Her heart beat steadily.

Laura.

Steadily, inside Donal's chest.

I love you.

But at least Laura was spared the reactor piles. As Donal would be, when his turn came.

Oh, Thanatos . . .

For undead bones are strong, and their song is wild. Too wild to tame.

ABOUT THE AUTHOR

JOHN MEANEY is the author of four previous novels. His novelette *Sharp Things* was short-listed for the British Science Fiction Award, and *To Hold Infinity* and *Paradox* both appeared on the BSFA short lists for Best Novel. Meaney has a degree in physics and computer science and holds a black belt in Shotokan karate. He lives with his wife in Kent, where he is at work on his next novel, *Black Blood,* the sequel to *Bone Song,* which Bantam will publish in hardcover in spring 2009.

Coming in February 2009 from Bantam Spectra,
the thrilling sequel to *Bone Song* . . .

BLACK BLOOD

Secrets within secrets . . .

He had perhaps twenty seconds before the surveillance
bats returned.

The man began to shiver. He undid his tie and unbuttoned his shirt all the way, and pulled it open. He
undid the front of his trousers, pushed them down. His
skin was hairless, his chest devoid of nipples, his crotch
smooth and featureless.

Fifteen seconds.

The next stages proceeded rapidly. First, the man's
face rippled like liquid. Then his face and torso split
open vertically, from crown to crotch, then forked to
open down the front of each bare leg like a seam, the
entire opening forming an upturned Y. There was a
wriggle inside, then a small lithe man in a hooded assassin's bodysuit stepped out of the larger body, accompanied by a soft popping sound.

The assassin's stretchweb bodysuit was saturated
with shadowhex. The cocoon he had exited was of
flesh-pink animaskin, already sealing itself up to con-
ceal its hollow—now empty—interior.

The assassin pulled up the animaskin's trousers,

while the animaskin's own fingers rebuttoned the shirt. A quick tucking-in and tie-knotting, and the animaskin looked like a functional human being once more.

It was already turning to walk away when the assassin, moving with a gymnast's litheness, vaulted into the display case, and pulled the glass doors shut. For a moment, he watched the bulky animaskin heading toward the staircase that led down to the atrium.

Three seconds.

Behind the displayed weapons, the assassin lay down on one side, curled up to fit into the narrow space, and pulled the shroud over himself. Something shifted, and multiple hues rippled across the shroud. Then the colors settled into place, matching the purple velvet beneath the weapons and the dark rear wall of the cabinet.

Zero.

Under the chameleon shroud, the assassin let out a long, silent exhalation, descending deeply into trance. He would remain in this state for most of the next fifty-three hours . . . until it was time.